Ancient History Between Us

ALSO BY KAITLYN HILL

Love from Scratch

Not Here to Stay Friends

Wild About You

KAITLYN HILL

Ancient History Between Us

Delacorte Romance

Delacorte Romance
An imprint of Random House Children's Books
A division of Penguin Random House LLC
1745 Broadway, New York, NY 10019
penguinrandomhouse.com
getunderlined.com

Editor: Hannah Hill
Cover Designer: Katrina Damkoehler
Interior Designer: Cathy Bobak
Production Editor: Jamie Johnson
Managing Editor: Tamar Schwartz
Production Manager: Tracy Heydweiller

Library of Congress Cataloging-in-Publication Data
Names: Hill, Kaitlyn author
Title: Ancient history between us / Kaitlyn Hill.
Description: New York, NY : Delacorte Romance, 2026. | Audience: Ages 12 and up | Audience: Grades 7–9 | Summary: "When exes Cammie and West unwillingly reunite in Italy and embark on a mission to find Cammie's biological father, their messy romantic history threatens to repeat itself"— Provided by publisher.
Identifiers: LCCN 2025025516 (print) | LCCN 2025025517 (ebook) | ISBN 978-0-593-65097-4 (paperback) | ISBN 978-0-593-65098-1 (ebook)
Subjects: CYAC: Love-hate relationships—Fiction | Voyages and travels—Fiction | Birthfathers—Fiction | Romance stories | LCGFT: Romance fiction | Novels
Classification: LCC PZ7.1.H5617 An 2026 (print) | LCC PZ7.1.H5617 (ebook)

The text of this book is set in 11.2-point Warnock Pro.
Interior art used under license from stock.adobe.com.

Manufactured in the United States of America
1st Printing

The authorized representative in the EU for product safety and compliance is Penguin Random House Ireland, Morrison Chambers, 32 Nassau Street, Dublin D02 YH68, Ireland, https://eu-contact.penguin.ie.

Random House Children's Books supports the First Amendment
and celebrates the right to read.

For my own Dr. Mom, Michelle Tudor,
who taught me to love learning and chase big dreams, and
who knew I was a writer long before I did.
Love you, Chelle Chelle.

CHAPTER ONE

Cammie

DESPITE MY EIGHT-MONTH STREAK OF DAILY ITALIAN LESSONS ON LINGO-Legend, I'm nowhere near fluent enough to trauma-dump on this taxi driver.

Luigi doesn't know how lucky he is. When he asked what brought me to Italy, a question I'm sure he's posed to many tourists on many airport pickups before, I doubt he knew the can of worms he was opening. In my effort to meet him half-way, I use my broken version of his native tongue to come up with "la scuola con la mia mamma."

It's a major oversimplification, though I'm not *not* here for school with my mom. In a way. Ish. But the answer satisfies him, or more likely, he senses that we've reached our multi-lingual conversation limits. He gives me a friendly smile and a nod of understanding before turning up the radio.

As we wind through the city of Naples in stops and starts,

I imagine an alternate universe, one in which I've long since passed whichever LingoLegend level covers vocabulary like "daddy issues" and "existential crisis." One where I'm able to answer more truthfully and comprehensively, after taking a long drag off an imaginary cigar.

Luigi, mio amico . . . how much time do you have?

We pick up speed, and outside my window, the scenery transforms from busy city streets to an open highway. Urban architecture gives way to hillsides scattered with terra-cotta rooftops. Air scented with car exhaust and sunbaked pavement is replaced with a salty sea breeze that whips my hair around my face in a frizzy red cloud. As I try to tame it into a braid, my gaze settles on the deep blue waters of the Bay of Naples glistening under the midmorning sun, and in the distance, Mount Vesuvius herself keeping watch over it all.

It all started in AD 79, my Italiana alter ego continues. The thought has a smile pulling at the corner of my lips, while the view sends goose bumps up my arms and legs despite the summer heat. It would be a little dramatic to begin the story of what brought me here with the two-thousand-year-old eruption of the volcano I can barely believe I'm finally setting eyes on. But it wouldn't be inaccurate. That infamous event was the explosive flap of butterfly wings that led, all this time later, to me, Cammie Lovett, crashing onto these Mediterranean shores with an overstuffed backpack and even greater abundance of enthusiasm.

A fluttery feeling starts in my stomach, anticipation with a little nervousness mixed in, when Luigi's cab exits the highway and we begin winding through the narrow streets of a small town. It's a maze of one alley after the next, lined with storefronts and cafes and other businesses. The taller buildings must have apartments on their upper floors, as clotheslines full of drying laundry crisscross between balconies overhead.

I wonder if these are the same views that greeted my mom when she first arrived in this area a little over twenty years ago. If she felt the same fluttery feeling, too. I'm not the first young American woman with my red hair, sense of adventure, and last name to be drawn here by Vesuvius. Dr. Alexandra Lovett came to Italy as part of her PhD studies in archaeology and to get practical experience in her field. On what was anticipated to be a perfectly boring cultural resource management job in the countryside between Naples and Pompeii, Mom claimed her spot in the history books by stumbling upon a particularly impressive remnant of first-century Vesuvian destruction now known as Villa di Bronzo. Archaeologists have been excavating the site ever since, unearthing the structure and all the ancient secrets it holds.

This spring was the twentieth anniversary of Villa di Bronzo's discovery, which makes this summer the twentieth with an active dig site and field school there. It's Mom's first time back at the place that made her career, after spending most of my life working on other digs around the world. She's taking part in a documentary being made about the villa, as well as in a special celebration of the anniversary and some guest lecturing at the field school. And she's brought me along for the ride.

A ride that, currently, is slowing to a crawl. I was almost

too wrapped up in watching the scenery and people to notice, but we must be getting close, even if this doesn't look like the open, rural landscape I expected. Even less expected is Luigi's sudden transformation into a stunt driver, as he steers us up and over a curb with a series of violent jumps and bumps. A "whoa" barely has time to pass my lips before he brakes hard and I lurch forward against my seat belt.

"Siamo qui!" he announces with a cheery finality as he slams the cab into park, and I look around us in confusion.

"Qui" is, from what I can tell, the tiled sidewalk in front of a shop selling . . . vapes and cheese? *Fuma e Formaggio* proclaims the sign above the doors in lit-up LED letters that flash in a rapid, migraine-inducing rotation of orange and green. The front window shows a display of colorful vape pens and cartridges interspersed with wedges of cheese in all different varieties, providing me with more questions than answers.

The most urgent of which is, Why is Luigi taking my suitcase out of the trunk?

I scramble to unbuckle and meet him at the back of the cab.

"Uh, hi—scusi, signor. I think we . . . non siamo qui?" I gesture to the storefront before making an X with my hands. "I'm supposed to go to Villa di Bronzo? Or it might show up as the Villa Russo Research Residency, which I know is kind of confusing but—okay, just, uh, hang on. Un momento, per favore!"

I lean in to the back seat and dig through my backpack to extract my phone. I don't have any cell signal, but I took screenshots of the info packet Mom emailed me about the place we're staying, just in case, and I vaguely remember it saying something about navigation systems not always recognizing the address.

"Aha," I say triumphantly when I locate the page, skimming it to find that my memory was accurate, and underneath the warning is a bulleted list of written directions from the Naples airport to the villa. "Backup directions! Uh . . . directioni?"

That sounds like a fake word, even to me. Luigi's blank expression confirms it.

"Non é qui," I try again, pointing to the shop, then pointing to the screenshot with words he won't be able to read, but at least it includes a picture of our destination, in which there are neither vapes nor cheese. "É qui. Sí?"

"Not . . . here," the older man says back to me, each word punctuated like its own sentence. He follows my pointing till his gaze is on my screen. "Is . . . here?"

"Sí," I say with an emphatic nod. " 'Villa Russo Research Residency.' La scuola con la mia mamma, remember? Non é"—I look at the lit-up sign and immediately regret it, shielding my eyes from the unpleasant strobe-iness—" 'Fuma e Formaggio.' "

Luigi goes back to the driver's side and retrieves his phone to show me his screen, which still shows his navigation app, confidently declaring that we've arrived at the address I gave him.

"So weird, I know." I nod and put my hands out at my sides with palms up, imitating his what-the-hell expression. "But we can try these directions?"

Luigi squints as he leans in to consider my screen again, giving a puzzled hum that does not sound promising. I'm going to be stranded here—left to survive on toxic chemical vapors and cheese that I'm not convinced is any less toxic, given its surroundings.

But I'm pleasantly surprised when he gives me an encouraging smile. "Va bene," he says, and I *think* that's a good thing but don't want to get ahead of myself until he follows it with a "We try, sí?"

"Sí!" I cry, putting my fists in the air in a victory that's not at all sealed yet. "Va bene!"

"Un momento."

My happy fists slowly fall as my maybe-hero steps into Fuma e Formaggio. But I keep my hopes high, telling myself un momento is nothing. I'm only allowed to start panicking if he hasn't come back in, like, five momentos.

My trust in Luigi as a cabdriver grows when he returns after no more than two minutes with something vape-related I can't identify and a shrink-wrapped plate of at least a dozen varieties of cheese cubes for sampling. But he becomes a friend for life when he holds the latter in the air toward me and announces joyfully, "Snack!"

The journey is, at least metaphorically, all downhill from there. Luigi recognizes one of the street names and manages to get us there as a starting point. But these directions, I quickly come to believe, were written as some sort of test, meant to weed out the weakest of minds and/or spirits before they ever make it to the Villa Russo Research Residency.

"'Drive over three potholes. Just past the third, turn east onto Via Pomodori.' Okay, feels like we could've skipped the pothole part. And 'turn east'? Sure, let me whip out my compass real quick," I mutter the last bit under my breath, then watch for the Via Pomodori street sign in order to point it out to Luigi, relieved to see there is only one possible way to turn.

I'm in the passenger seat, so he can easily see all the hand-talking I'm doing to overcome our language barrier. It also gives us both easy access to the cheese plate. With a few more strange landmarks and an unnecessary commitment to describing everything in cardinal directions, it feels like a miracle that we ever make our way out of the town center and into the farmland and rolling hills I was expecting.

"'At the abandoned tractor'—*what?*—'continue south for three kilometers.'" I don't bother to semi-translate that one, giving Luigi a thumbs-up instead, since it conveys the same message: *Keep doing what you're doing, champ.*

Our surroundings start to feel more familiar, though I know I wasn't old enough to form memories of any of it the last time I was here. It's probably just the effect of cobbled-together images I've seen in pictures, stories I've been told my whole life. I'm popping vape shop cheese cubes into my mouth with growing frequency, as the feelings of recognition intensify alongside my nerves.

"Oh, stop! Uh, halt? No, that's still English, ack—" I rush out, but Luigi correctly interprets my panicked hand-waving and the cab rolls to a stop on the blessedly empty country road. "I really was not about to take 'the tree shaped like a head of garlic' seriously, but damn if that isn't one garlicky tree."

Luigi points at it with a laugh. "Sembra aglio."

No idea what that means, but I laugh with him, because

that's what friends do, and because I'm beginning to think we might actually locate this villa. Just past the tree, I direct him to turn down the unmarked gravel road that we would have completely missed if we hadn't known to look for it.

The rumble of Luigi's car as it slowly climbs the hillside is no match for the shiver that travels through my whole body, and when the first tent comes into view, my instinct is confirmed. We're finally approaching the Villa di Bronzo Archaeological Site.

I wonder if this is how everyone born in some notable, newsworthy way feels when they return to the place where they have that unique connection. Like if a baby who's born on an airplane grows up and gets chills every time they fly. Or the kid I read about a few years back whose mom gave birth to him in the middle of taking her bar exam—and still passed. When he inevitably goes to law school, will that first step on campus come with an overwhelming sense of his destiny being fulfilled?

This moment feels too big to be experiencing it alone with my thoughts, but I'm still lacking the right vocab to help Luigi understand my swirling emotions. With all we've been through together, I don't think I'd hesitate to share if I could.

He might even find it interesting that Villa di Bronzo wasn't the only life-altering surprise Dr. Lovett encountered in this very place twenty years ago. The other was me, Cammie Lovett (Fetus Version). Mom was already pregnant when she made the former discovery, though she didn't recognize the signs until she was unusually far along. She continued to lead the first and most significant archaeological dig of her career, right up until she went into early labor and had no choice but to bring me into the world right there on Villa grounds.

For a short while at the beginning of my life—roughly fifteen minutes, metaphorically—I was known as the Bambina di Bronzo in news stories the world over. And though Mom and I left Italy before I could even say the word *archaeologist,* I've always dreamed of coming back here as one.

More white tents appear as we crest the first hill, scattered out toward the horizon. They're the same kind of white canopy over collapsible metal poles that littered Nolan University's campus during football season last fall, when every weekend brought throngs of tailgaters to every parking lot on school property. When I'd walk by those tents on the way to class or the dining hall, I'd daydream about this moment—when all the temporary shelters around me wouldn't be for kegs, grills, and drunk sports fans.

They'd be for shovels and pickaxes. Tables of artifacts. Sweaty, tired, but happy-just-to-be-there students and their fearless leaders, archaeologists like my mom. Someday, I'd hoped, archaeologists like *me*. The view sends a reflexive thrill through my system, one that speaks to a lifetime of memories tagging along on dig sites and the plans I've always had for my future. But the feeling is quickly chased by a sharp pang.

I miss the naïve version of me who thought I'd be welcome at any field school I wanted. The girl who applied to her dream summer program with the International Institute of Archaeological Studies and had no backup plan. She didn't think she'd need one.

The directors of the IIAS thought otherwise. The rejection email came just weeks ago, a few curt sentences that not only derailed my summer plans but also ground my confidence into dust. I'd imagined my biggest hurdle would be proving to others in the program that I'm more than just the Lovett name. Instead, it was having to face the reality that I'm so unworthy, not even nepotism could save me.

It couldn't get me into field school, anyway. But it *could* get me field-school-adjacent. When I'd pulled my sobbing self together enough to call Mom and break the news, she'd spun it into an opportunity—I could join her here, be part of the documentary with her. La Bambina, all grown-up and making her long-awaited return to her birthplace.

As I look out over the wildflower-covered hillside under a cloudless blue sky, I can't help but think there are worse detours to take. My return to Villa di Bronzo isn't under the triumphant terms I'd hoped, but this place feels full of potential. Maybe getting rejected from my dream program was actually fate stepping in, putting me exactly where I need to be, when I need to be here. Not just to tag along at Mom's side or make a cute little cameo in her big-screen debut, either.

Because ancient artifacts aren't the only secrets long buried in Vesuvius's shadow. And I'm ready to start unearthing a few.

Mom has been a ball of energy and excitement since I accepted her invite here, making it clear how much she's missed me since I started college. She arrived a week ago, just as my finals were ending, and has been sending me countless pictures of the gorgeous Italian scenery now spread out before me.

Meanwhile, I've kept pretty quiet in the whirlwind week of moving back from my school outside Chicago to my grandparents' house in Kentucky, the place Mom and I call home when we're in the States, then repacking for Italy. Mom doesn't need to know about my secret summer side quest or the groundwork I've been laying for it, the hours I've spent scouring every inch of her home office like a CIA operative. As it turns out, archaeologists are really into hoarding old shit and taking good care of it. But I still have a lot of digging ahead of me here in the Italian countryside.

And it all starts at the building coming into view straight ahead. A grove of lemon trees seems to pop up out of nowhere and lines both sides of the road, the fresh scent of citrus lingering as we emerge onto a circular driveway, at the crest of which sits a sprawling estate. The original structure has beige stucco walls and a terra-cotta roof, plus two additions built onto either side in a contemporary style, all boxy and angular and filled with windows.

This is the Villa Russo from the picture on my phone, the modern family home that sits on the property where Villa di Bronzo was buried. After its discovery, the Russo family converted their place into a residential facility for researchers—plus said researchers' wayward daughters, as the case may be.

We roll to a stop and Luigi looks to me with a grin. "Siamo qui?" He poses it as a question this time.

"Sí," I confirm with a smile and two thumbs up for emphasis.

As I climb out of the cab, I'm hit with a delightfully lemony breeze. It's the sensory experience of entering a Bath & Body

Works, but this Italian Lemon Grove scent is *real*. I meet Luigi by the trunk and reclaim my suitcase, almost sad to say goodbye. We may not have been able to communicate much with words, but his actions were above and beyond airport pickup driver duties. We shared a cheese tray—that shit is personal.

"Grazie mille, Luigi," I say sincerely, maybe the most useful of the few things LingoLegend *has* taught me. *I'll never forget you*, I add mentally.

The man gives me a warm smile and a little bow with his "prego, signorina" before retaking his seat and starting back down the lane, clouds of dust swirling in his car's wake. Exhaustion from twenty-plus hours of transatlantic travel, including an especially action-packed last hour, suddenly slams into me now that I've reached the finish line. I start toward the villa slowly, scanning the vicinity and listening closely for any signs of life as I go.

It's eerily silent when I stop, facing the imposing wooden double doors. Not the move-in-day hive of activity or the chaos of a documentary set that I imagined might greet me. This *is* the place from the picture, isn't it? We didn't take a wrong turn, maybe after the second pothole instead of the third, and land me at a different gorgeous villa, this one belonging to a murderer with a preference for frizzy-haired American girls who smell of eau de air travel?

I'm digging through the recesses of my backpack for my phone again, hoping for enough service to send an SOS out to Mom, when the echoing creak of hinges stops me. My head jerks up, one hand gripping my backpack handle tightly while the other clutches the first makeshift weapon I can reach—which is, unfortunately, my e-reader. At the very least, it'll confuse my potential attacker.

The huge doors swing open, and when the person on the other side is revealed, my breath catches. Maybe it wouldn't have been so bad, starting a new life back at Fuma e Formaggio. I think I might've even preferred a murderer. Instead, I get a ghost.

One who looks a lot like the first boy I kissed.

CHAPTER TWO

West

CAMMIE LOVETT LOOKS LIKE SHIT.

I probably shouldn't acknowledge it out loud, definitely not before some kind of greeting, a how-you-doing, or long-time-no-see, and yet—

"You look like shit."

Her mouth, which has been gaping with obvious shock since we first locked eyes, immediately twists into a pout. The berry red of her lips matches the flushed spots on each cheek, the only color on her otherwise ghostly white face. She's an angry spirit, my Ghost of Best Friends Past. One who could clearly use a nap, judging by the dark circles under her eyes, and a long sit in the villa's AC. A hairbrush wouldn't hurt, either.

"You," Cammie practically spits at me, "look like a real nightmare I've had. Am I asleep right now?"

The barb doesn't totally bounce off, but I roll my eyes to

hide it. "No, but good to see you, too." I take a step back into the foyer. "You coming in?"

Cammie's sneakers don't budge, but her arms cross over her chest and one hip cocks to the side. "Seriously, Weston. What the hell are you doing here?"

So that's how she wants to play this. Full-naming me and everything. I cross my arms to match hers and widen my stance, tip my chin up, and let my lips pull into a smirk. She already thinks I'm a dick; might as well look the part. "Really, *Camilla*? What do you think I'm doing here?"

Her blue eyes dart wildly around my face, then lower, over my faded green T-shirt, dark jeans, sock-covered feet. I resist the instinct to straighten my spine. I do not need to impress this girl, and it doesn't even seem like she's really seeing me. Her gaze is distant, as if she's putting together the puzzle pieces in her mind, working out the same conclusion that I did when Dad and I arrived at Villa Russo yesterday and I found out Dr. Alex was here, too.

"Dr. Danny is *not* part of the documentary," she declares, like she can speak it into reality.

"Afraid so," I answer with a coolness that belies how extremely not cool all of this feels. "In case you forgot, he was also part of the dig twenty years ago."

"Okay, but . . . but why are *you* here?" One of her hands goes into the red tumbleweed of her hair. It might never get back out. "You're an adult who should, like, have your own life by now. You don't have to let your dads drag you back and forth across the world."

I refrain from flinching, but only barely. "I could say the same for you," I say, tossing a tired hand in her direction. "Yet here we both are."

"This is . . . Why didn't she—" With a growl that raises the hair on my arms, Cammie charges forward, shoulder-checking me so hard on her way past that I stumble backward. The rest of whatever sentence she was trying to form becomes unintelligible as she mutters under her breath, but just before she turns the corner, I can pick out a clear "no, nope, not happening."

I shouldn't have opened the door. I'd been walking to the communal kitchen to scrounge up a snack when I heard a car pulling away. I thought it might be a field school student arriving, figured I'd try to be helpful.

See if I ever try that again.

I turn from where I just watched the ginger tornado disappear down the hall, ready to close the door, but notice that her backpack and suitcase are still lying there, abandoned and baking in the Italian summer sun.

It would serve her right if I just left them. Let her computer fry or her toiletries melt all over her clothes. She'd sure as shit do that if the roles were reversed. But something in me—probably that pesky voice of reason—tells me not to give the girl any legitimate grounds to be in a permanent bad mood. At least for as long as we're trapped under the same tiled roof. So I drag the bags up the last stair and inside the foyer, leaving them in a heap beside a decorative vase.

When I finally make it to the kitchen, I'm disappointed to

find that my hunger is gone. In its place is a growing lump of anxiety. Seeing Cammie again brings back to mind the stuff she said that day three years ago. Harsh words that still run through my head some nights when I can't sleep.

As I turn on a heel and set off in the same direction she went, I wonder how—despite all my efforts to get a good handle on my mental health, to live a steady, predictable life—I've found myself back here, speed-walking toward chaos in human form.

I should have known better than to voluntarily return to my father's world for the summer, especially to the site that made him famous. Of course no one would make a documentary about Villa di Bronzo without Dr. Alex Lovett, the archaeologist credited with the villa's initial discovery and Dad's close friend and former colleague. And the Cammie I used to know—better than I've ever known another person—wouldn't have passed up the chance to spend this summer in this place for anything.

Judging by the trowel that protrudes from her backpack's outer pocket, at least some parts of my former friend remain unchanged since we went no-contact. She still wants this world as much as she ever has, the one where her mom and my dad have built long and successful careers, learning all they can about people of the past by digging up the pieces they left behind. The world where they raised two wild kids, giving us the run of a different dig site with each new excavation they worked on, a different temporary home, but always the same best friend to explore it with.

Up until three summers ago, when one reckless kiss ruined everything.

Trying to push the memory from my mind, I stop at a side door. I could either turn and continue down an interior hallway that leads to the villa's library, or I could exit to a covered walkway that borders a terrazzo, then winds through some gardens, and eventually connects to one of the guesthouses. Muffled voices through the glass—ones that sound a lot like Cammie and Dr. Alex—make the decision for me, and I step out into the midday heat.

I make a file folder in my head, typing the label *Present Cammie*. If I dig deep into the recesses of my mental recycling bin, I could pull out the *Past Cammie* folder, shake the dust and cobwebs off it. Click and drag the relevant info from the old to the new:

1. Cammie still wants to be an archaeologist, a.k.a. Dr. Lovett 2.0.
2. Cammie also wants nothing to do with me.

While I've had no way to keep up since we blocked each other on all social media three years ago, I assume that by now, a year into college and seemingly about to start her first field school as a student, she's right on track to make number one happen; number two could be more difficult to pull off, but I'm willing to help her try. My mental state would certainly be better for it.

Dad promised a low-stress summer. It's only our second in

this post-custody-agreement stage, when I've aged out of the court-mandated schedule, but I still have to live with *someone* during every school break. Adulthood means the decision of when to spend time with each of my fathers is up to me. A decision that is not at all emotionally fraught and hasn't been the topic of at least a dozen therapy sessions since their divorce.

Neither Dad nor Pops gave a formal pitch; there were no slide decks prepared or formal speeches outlining their most compelling arguments for why I should spend the break with each of them. But I sensed the seeds being planted, less-than-subtle hints dropped over the entire spring semester any time I spoke to one of them. With every phone call, every casual inquiry about "where my head was" on the subject, every allusion to something we could do together "if I was around" after the school year, it was clear what they wanted.

What wasn't clear to me was what *I* wanted. I dragged my feet for months, weighing the pros and cons of being home with Pops versus traveling with Dad. In the end, it felt like fate stepped in when Pops learned he had to teach summer school, majorly limiting the time he'd have to spend with me. Now I'm wondering if what I thought was a gift from the universe was actually a prank. Perhaps a curse. It's clear I upset a higher power somewhere, and in return, they've summoned the only person in the world who sincerely hates me and delivered her to my literal doorstep.

Dad insisted last night that he didn't know Cammie would be here any earlier than I did, that he also only found out when we met up with Dr. Alex yesterday. But those two are so in each other's business, I find it hard to believe they didn't discuss plans to both bring their kids to this summer-long walk down memory lane. I happen to know that back in the day, they coordinated when to give the sex talk to Cammie and me—separately, thank god—and workshopped it with each other to prepare. This feels similarly coordinated, an intentional withholding of key information that could've kept one or both of their offspring from getting on a flight to Italy.

Would I have backed out, had I known about the Lovett of it all? I don't know, but I probably would have packed more anxiety meds.

As it stands, I'm determined to keep my focus on people who do want me here. I haven't spent more than a weekend at a time with Dad since he and Pops split up my senior year of high school. Once he was free of his ex's disdain for his career's demands, his work travels picked back up and kept him bouncing around the world most of the time. Living with Pops was more practical while I finished school, and he became the default afterward. But I know Dad struggles with the distance between us, as much as he tries to make up for it with frequent calls and texts and visits when we can. Even through shitty video call quality, I could see tears fill his eyes when I told him I would join him in Italy. It's safe to say we're both looking forward to this chance to reconnect.

I can't let some tired drama from my past get in my head, or worse, my heart. Cammie Lovett won't ruin anything else for me. I shake my head as the voices I've been hearing grow louder, whether because I'm getting close to my targets or they're working up to a shouting match—either seems possible. Whatever agenda Dad and Dr. Alex have, I hope they're already rethinking it.

Squinting against the sunlight, I finally spot them between a couple of lemon trees, two matching heads of auburn hair—one much messier than the other—and my dad's dark brown hair with an ever-growing bald spot on top.

"Cam, let's talk about it later, just you and me, okay? Dr. Danny and I are finishing up our meeting . . ." Dr. Alex sounds almost too calm, like if she can give off an excess of soothing energy, her daughter will absorb a little. Or maybe that's just the effect of the nearly empty glass of red wine she holds in one hand. Dad takes a sip from his own glass, the bottle on the bistro table between them. Not their best Serious Meeting act.

"No, really—I'm not about to endure two months of Weston Jacobs. He's just, like, visiting for the weekend before he backpacks across the rest of Europe or something. Right?" Cammie's voice shakes on the last word. She has always been easily riled. Quick to spout off, gesture wildly, her freckle-covered face showing every thought in her head. It's one of the things I used to think made her exciting. Addicting. Attractive.

I mentally smack myself for the ridiculous thought, then push aside a branch more aggressively than necessary as I step into the small clearing where the one-sided standoff is taking place. Cammie is braced with her back to me and hands on hips, and I can only imagine the kind of glower she's giving our unfazed parents. Then I don't have to imagine, as both adults' gazes turn my way. Cammie whirls around, too, her fierce scowl getting fiercer and scowlier when it lands on me.

"If I'm ever found 'backpacking' anywhere, call the authorities, because the rest of my luggage must've been stolen," I offer matter-of-factly. "You know I'm an overpacker."

This earns a heavy sigh from my dad as he removes his glasses and rubs at the bridge of his nose. I also catch Dr. Alex pressing her lips together as if to smother a grin before I look back to Cammie. The color of her flushed face is creeping ever closer to matching her hair.

"I don't know a thing about your life, except that it has no business overlapping with mine," she snaps.

"Cam*illa*," Dr. Alex chides, just as Dad clears his throat and both set their glasses on the table with a loud clatter.

"Oookay, let's all just take a breath," Dad says in his most professorial tone. "Cammie, West, I know you two have a . . . complicated history and that this might not be the most joyful reunion for either of you." *Understatement*, I think as I see Cammie's fists clench in my periphery. "But we're all here now, and we get to spend the summer in this beautiful place, reminiscing on the amazing events that brought us all into each other's lives twenty years ago. Alex and I would love to get to relive some of the good old days, when life was a never-ending adventure around the world with our two favorite kids. It might be the last chance we get, before those kids are off living their own lives and adventures without us."

"No one expects you to snap your fingers and become the best of friends again," Dr. Alex chimes in, "but surely you can keep things civil. Act like the mature adults you've become."

They're not exactly easing my suspicions that they've been scheming.

Twenty-four hours ago, I would've agreed that I'm a mature adult. But Camilla Lovett reenters my orbit for ten minutes, and suddenly I'm seventeen again. All these feelings I thought were long buried are back at the surface, nearly as intense as they were the day of our first and last fight. The one that sent a lifelong friendship—and the fragile beginnings of something more—up in flames.

At least I do a better job of hiding it than the girl beside me, who might as well have cartoonish clouds of smoke billowing from her ears as she looks from her mother to me and back. Even though my chest is tight with anxiety, I'm surprised to feel a smile trying to break free as Cammie visibly strains to mellow out her expression and relax her posture.

"Right, well." She finally ends the heavy silence, blowing out an irritated breath before continuing. "For the sake of civility, I'll plan to avoid West as much as possible, and he can just pretend I don't exist. He's perfected that skill the last few years."

The confusion I feel from the biting remark outweighs the hurt. *I've* perfected the skill? She's the one who didn't want me in her life anymore, who cut all ties at the first rough patch in our relationship. But I don't get the chance to strike back, even if I could find the words, before Dad decides to shut down this oh-so-pleasant gathering.

"All right, well, why don't West and I let you ladies catch up awhile?" he says like it's a perfectly natural pivot in the conversation, not a hasty retreat from a battlefront. He even smiles as he gets to his feet, proving that we're living two different realities. The loud scrape of his wrought iron chair across the pavers is a sound I never thought I'd prefer to Cammie's voice, but the chair can't insult me, so. Here we are.

I almost miss the conspiratorial look he and Dr. Alex exchange, too brief to read much into. "Sure, that sounds good," Dr. Alex agrees with a nod. "We'll see you at dinner later on."

Offering the Lovetts a final wave that's downright jaunty, Dad walks out the same way I've come in. He gives my arm a quick squeeze as he passes me, and the message in the gesture is clear: *Save yourself while you still can, kid.*

I should definitely take the unsubtle hint. But I hesitate, even as the soft thuds of his steps fade behind me.

Maybe it's all the literal olive branches in our vicinity, one of several tree species growing on the villa grounds that feel too Stereotypically Italian to be real. Or maybe it's something less benevolent, some petty part of me that just wants to show I'm a bigger person than Cammie. Whatever the case, my feet stay rooted before her and her mom, and my big mouth opens.

"It's good to see you, Dr. Alex . . ." I reach up and scratch the back of my neck, beginning to lose my nerve as quickly as it came. I gulp before adding, "And, uh, Cammie."

Dr. Alex gives me a small smile and a gentle nod of acknowledgment. "You too, West."

When my eyes flick to Cammie, it's an effort not to cower.

Her sharp gaze pierces through me like a knife, and then her sharper words give it a twist.

"Go to hell, Jacobs."

As I walk back to the villa, the sun beating down from above and the hot stone path burning the soles of my feet through my socks, I think I might already be there.

CHAPTER THREE

Cammie

THE POWER OF A MOM HUG IS FRIGHTENING.

I want to hold on to my anger. As soon as West is out of earshot, I'm ready to turn it on the deceptive little sneak who gave me life, to rage at her for luring me into this trap. But when she stands and wraps her arms around me, I'm enveloped in the comforting scent of her lavender soap, the familiar feel of her body, both softness and strength, and everything else fades away. It doesn't matter where in the world we find ourselves; when my mom hugs me, I'm home.

"Welcome back, kid," she whispers, breath rustling the hair atop my head.

I murmur my response into her T-shirt, feeling like I can't lift my head from its resting spot on her shoulder. "It's pretty annoying how I can't stay mad at you."

A soft chuckle vibrates through her, her voice taking on a

breathy, feigned innocence. "Why ever would you be mad at your dear mother?"

"I can't remember anymore," I grumble. "Did you spritz yourself with a sedative perfume or something?"

"I think that's just your post-travel, post-Weston adrenaline crash hitting," she says, rubbing a soothing circle on my back. "Why don't we find you someplace more comfortable to take a load off?"

She gives me one last, tight squeeze before pulling back. I don't even have time to process her suggestion before she's turned on a heel and started toward the villa. It's a comforting normal for the two of us, Mom blazing a path with her blinders on, five steps ahead mentally and physically while I do my best to keep up.

As we walk, she peppers me with questions about the almost-twenty-four hours since I began the journey here. I do my best to comb through my sluggish brain for details, from lucking out with a row to myself on my flight across the ocean, to grabbing a pretzel on my short layover in Munich, then the saga of my taxi ride.

"After all that, I was so flustered to see *him* answering the door, I just dumped all my stuff on the front stoop before trying to find you," I say when we've nearly retraced my steps back to the villa entrance. "It seems like a lot of effort for a luggage thief to get here, but if they did, they hit the jack—"

I come up short on the foyer's tile floor when I spot my bags safely tucked against the wall beside a vase.

". . . pot. Or not?"

Mom bends to sling my backpack over one shoulder.

"Someone must have brought them in for you," she says, shooting an *isn't that lucky* grin my way.

I nod distractedly, feeling this itch start up at the back of my brain. I don't scratch the itch, don't let myself speculate who was responsible for the safekeeping of my worldly possessions, lest I get any wacky ideas about West Jacobs giving a shit about me.

When Mom picks up everything but my small cross-body purse and starts down another corridor like a red-haired pack mule, I have to wonder if she's trying to compensate for the unpleasant Jacobs-shaped surprise. My tired body isn't mad about it, though. We make our way down the long, white-walled hallway lined with windows that overlook a sprawling courtyard on one side and numbered doors on the other. Mom explains more about the space along the way.

"The first floor is where I am, along with Dr. Danny, most of the documentary crew, and the field school directors. The biggest difference between our floor and the students' is that ours has private bathrooms, while yours are communal." She shoots me a grimace over her shoulder with that news. "I figured you'd rather be with folks your age than room with your mom, but you let me know if I'm wrong about that, okay? And you can always come use my shower if the shared ones aren't great, or my toilet if you need some privacy, or—"

"Cool, thanks," I interrupt, because I cringe to think how many of my peers can hear through the walls as my mother loudly muses about my hypothetical bathroom needs. Fortunately, she stops a moment later in front of one of the bright Mediterranean-blue doors.

"This is you," she announces with a smile. Letting go of my suitcase, she digs in her jeans pocket for a minute before producing an antiquated metal key. The lock releases with a much gentler click than the sturdy dead bolt on the apocalypse-proof door to my dorm room at school, and Mom pushes the door wide, gesturing me in first.

The room is what a Realtor would describe as "cozy." Bright, too, with a glass door to a tiny balcony on the far wall that lets sunlight stream in. The walls are the same bright white of the hallway outside with a single piece of artwork hanging on one, a picture of the Bay of Naples. Underneath that is a twin bed, tidily made up with a white duvet over a blue fitted sheet and pillow. A dark wooden writing desk, chair, and chest of drawers fill the rest of the space.

"Ooh, looks like you've got a bigger closet than I do," Mom gushes, and I turn to see her standing by an open narrow door, revealing a modest space with a rod and hangers for my clothes.

"You've got a shower you can use without shoes on," I reply with a shrug. Her answer is a musical laugh that never fails to make me smile. I cross the small room toward the balcony, and it takes me a moment to figure out the handle on the door. It can be turned up to open the top only, letting in some airflow, but when I turn it down, the whole thing pushes open and I step out into the balmy afternoon air.

The balcony isn't getting direct sunlight at this time of day, but the metal railing is still warm under my palms when I rest them there. It grounds me as the view nearly takes my breath away—Villa di Bronzo, right before my eyes. I've seen so many pictures of the ancient structure over the years, I wasn't sure if the real deal would be a letdown. But pictures don't do it justice.

Stretched out before me is the palatial home of a seriously wealthy ancient Roman citizen. What remains of that home, anyway, after two thousand years buried under volcanic matter. From this vantage point, it's almost like a dollhouse with the roof lifted off—a maze of rooms and walkways and courtyards. Half-crumbled stone walls enclose long-ago living spaces. Columns stand sentry in long, straight lines, still majestic even if the loads they once supported have caved in. Pops of blurry color where I know that frescoes have been carefully revealed and restored, and intricate mosaics in the floors form patterns I can't make out from afar but will soon reach out and touch.

I've always thought the word *ruins* feels unfair. It emphasizes what was lost, whether to catastrophic events or the more gradual effects of time, rather than the incredible things that remain. Sites like Villa di Bronzo aren't just scraps of once-great structures, or symbols of devastation and destruction. They represent a persistence that's hard to wrap our heads around, this combination of strong engineering and all-natural preservation that offers us an invaluable connection to the past, if we're lucky enough to find them.

Villa di Bronzo is less ruin, more treasure. And I can't believe it's practically under my feet.

"Bring back any memories?"

Mom's voice startles me out of my spell, the two of us only barely fitting side by side as she joins me on the balcony. I blink, then shake my head quickly to try to clear it before giving the site another sweeping perusal. Then another, like maybe I'm just not focusing hard enough to make a memory surface.

"Not one," I finally admit, even though it's not my fault the toddler brain doesn't store anything long-term. "Does it for you?"

I turn to see Mom's lips purse, her stare going distant. "Oh, absolutely. Too many, maybe." She mumbles this last bit, like she doesn't really mean to say it out loud, and seems to snap out of whatever path her mind started wandering down. "More to come this summer, huh?"

Her excitement shows on every inch of her face. It's in the crow's-feet at the corners of her eyes that deepen with the smile she's almost holding back, the knowing twitch of her lips that says, *This is gonna be a good one, Cam, I can feel it,* just like she has said countless times before.

Guilt squeezes my heart. It's always been her and me against the world. And most of the time, that's felt like enough. It certainly has to her; she always tells me she loves me enough for *three* parents, let alone the standard two.

It makes me feel greedy, or maybe ungrateful, for what I'm trying to do now. Because unbeknownst to my mother, I'm on the hunt for that second parent I've never known.

A shiver rolls down my spine as I realize that at this very moment, I could be closer to my biological father than I've ever been. I don't know that he's still in Italy, of course, but twenty years ago, he was. He met a young archaeologist named Alex, they had a short-term fling, and he opted out of the very long-term commitment of raising the tiny human they accidentally created.

That accidental tiny human grew up to be less tiny, with a relentless need to know everything and a lot of free time on her—my—hands for summer break, time that's happened to coincide with her first chance to come back to the place her parents met.

It's a complicated feeling, this urge to find a dad who, as far as I know, didn't want me. I worry that I'm betraying the parent who stayed, telling her she hasn't been everything I've needed and more. I couldn't stand to hurt Mom that way.

But I want to find out more about myself, and right now, it feels like that starts with this—with him.

So I really need to get better at lying.

"Definitely," I belatedly answer Mom's question, and then in the hopes of sounding more convincing, tack on, "Can't wait!"

Thoughts of my secret dad-finding mission have almost made me forget the unexpected blast from my past. But Mom must misread my emotions as some kind of positive attitude adjustment, as she decides it's safe to steer us back West-ward.

"The Welcome Dinner is at eight this evening, and I'm planning to meet Danny and West in the first-floor common room at 7:50 to walk over. I know you'll be even more wiped by then, but I'd love for you to join us, at least for a little while. It's outside on the terrazzo. You'll have to eat something for dinner anyway, right? And I've heard *such* good things about the chef they have at Villa Russo now, so—"

"Alexandra," I cut her off before she can somehow ramble her way back to my toilet options.

Her lips press together, twitching up on one side even as she tries to give me stern, narrow eyes. "Camilla."

"I will be delighted to have dinner with *you.* I will grudgingly accept the presence of anyone else, and then I will get my long-awaited sleep and hope that when I wake up, West Jacobs being in Italy was only a bad dream."

Mom's sigh creates a pleasant breeze in this stifling heat, an unintentional reward for my petulance.

"Honestly, Cam, I didn't think there was still this much . . . animosity between you. Isn't three years enough time to let bygones be bygones?"

It's clear the woman doesn't realize she raised the reigning world champion in Grudge Holding. I bite my tongue so hard, I'm surprised I don't draw blood. I rarely let myself think about West and what happened between us, so it's easy to forget that Mom doesn't know the whole story. She had enough to worry about, what with her partner in crime Dr. Danny deciding to hang up his adventure hat and get a steady stateside job. I didn't want to pile on with the full extent of my own best friend drama.

"It was plenty of time to let him *be* gone. From my life. For good." Her flat expression says she's not impressed with my wordplay. I cross my arms over my chest. "I don't see why that has to change."

"Maybe because you've both grown from the people you

were back then," she challenges. "You know I'm always on your team. But he's been through a lot these past few years, and it might not hurt to give him some grace. That's the last I'll say about it."

She raises her palms, but neither the words nor the gesture convinces me she's really done with this little reconciliation campaign. I can't concern myself with whatever West has "been through." It's not like our time apart has been a picnic for me. I wasn't just heartbroken when he abruptly left my life; I was suddenly lonelier and more isolated than I'd ever been.

Our nomadic upbringing had made it so that, besides our parents, West and I were each other's only constant companion. We'd been a homeschool-virtual-hybrid classroom of two, since his parents had him start kindergarten a year late to give him more time to come out of his shell and allow us to do all our schooling concurrently. We spent all our free time together, too, with countless rounds of hide-and-seek on countless dig sites where we probably shouldn't have been playing, and as we got older, more freedom to go out and explore our new cities, just us two.

When the Jacobses left, West went to spend his last two years at a "normal" public high school in the Indiana hometown he hadn't called home since he was a baby. I've imagined he was surrounded by dozens of new friends, kept busy with all the extracurriculars that had never been options for us before.

All the while, I was on my own. No one but my mom and a revolving door of her colleagues and students as we moved on to a couple more projects on different continents, until I went off to college last year. It had been an exciting kind of culture shock, living and learning alongside some fifteen thousand of my peers, and between my classes in huge lecture halls and my dorm with a random, social-butterfly roommate, I was never really alone at Nolan. But I hadn't managed to make any close friends, to form connections that went much deeper than study buddies or regular dinner tablemates. I still feel the ache of loneliness.

Time has allowed me to move on from those more-than-friendly feelings for West. It just hasn't let any friendly ones linger, either. Nor has it given me any faith that, if I was to allow him back into my life, he wouldn't drop me again in an instant, any time he felt like it. So if I'm forced to be around him this summer—and it seems I will, if Mom gets her way—I need to stay guarded. Not let him get under my skin, and certainly nowhere deeper.

At least for now, Mom picks up on how little I want to talk about him. At her suggestion, we make our way back into the precious air-conditioning of my room. She offers to stay and help me unpack, which I decline on the grounds that I plan to take a shower before I do much else. It's a convenient excuse, and conveniently true, but I have bigger reasons to avoid her sorting through my overstuffed luggage. Things inside that I don't want her to find.

After I send her on her way, I kneel on the hardwood floor beside my new bed and begin pulling all the contents out of my backpack. I wish I was hiding something as simple as a drug stash I smuggled across the border, or a fake ID. Either of those would probably cause less of an issue than the real contraband. I set everything in a disorganized pile until I can reach the most tucked-away inner pocket, then carefully extract my treasure, which had been collecting dust in the back of Mom's office closet for years. The better part of two decades, if I had to guess.

Until now.

I run a hand across the cover, clearing it of now-nonexistent dust after its long journey—one that's brought it back to its original home. It's a journal, but not just any old travel diary of a twentysomething woman abroad. This book, bound by an elastic band that's barely hanging on, is stuffed full of Polaroid pictures, ticket stubs, clippings from maps, and most intriguing—and perhaps cringey—of all, *love letters*. On the cover, in Mom's familiar, loopy cursive, is *Italia field notes (unofficial)*, and on the first page's *This book belongs to:* line, she's written only *Alex*.

It's still hard for me to fathom that this gold mine of a primary source has been under my nose all along. I almost passed over it in my office closet search, where it'd been tucked away in a box under a somewhat unsettling quantity of my old baby shoes. Seriously, did she think I might want to wear them again someday?

If there's one thing to know about my mother, it's that she loves to document *everything*. It's literally her job, to an extent, but she also keeps careful records in her personal life, including her daily journaling habit she's had for as long as I can remember. I suspect she imagines some archaeologist of the future, centuries from now or maybe even millennia, using her notes to try piecing together how we lived in the early twenty-first century.

Judging by the bizarre hiding spot of this particular volume, I strongly suspect she didn't want anyone in this lifetime to find it. Which, in turn, makes me all the more certain it's my key to understanding the parts of my past she doesn't want me to know.

I normally prefer to read a book no more than once, no matter how much I love it; there are already too many to get through in this one life. But I've torn through Alex's *Italia field notes (unofficial)* from cover to cover, and have done countless additional rereads of specific pages or sections I marked with adhesive tabs that I may or may not have also borrowed from Mom's office.

I flip through a few of the tabs, feeling this illogical need to check that all the two-dimensional people smiling in Polaroids or described in my mom's stories made it overseas safely. One slight challenge when it comes to connecting these characters to the real humans who were once involved in my mother's life is that Young Alex decided to call everyone by their initials. I don't know if she was trying to protect their privacy or trying to save time, or if it was simply an artistic choice. But the result is that all the Potential Father Candidates (PFCs) I've made note of so far are only known to me by two letters each.

All save for one guy, who doesn't even get initials. I stop on one of the pages where he's the focus, which are scattered throughout the first two-thirds of the journal before he is abruptly never mentioned or pictured again. Not that he's very identifiable even when he is present—none of the Polaroids with his sandy-blond curls show his face, only a side profile as he kisses Alex's cheek, or the back of his head as he walks away from her. The accompanying journal entries refer to him only as a heart symbol, their sappy notes to each other written and signed back and forth to *my* ❤ and *your* ❤.

My first instinct was that it had to be him. Boom, search over. But the more I read about their intense feelings toward each other, the more I became convinced of the opposite. Unlike some of the shorter flings in these pages that seemed to come and go with minimal damage in their wake, Alex and ❤ seemed to have something bigger. I'd never been in love, but I couldn't imagine theirs was anything but real and powerful. And someone who loved my mom's twenty-five-year-old self that much wouldn't have left her when he learned she was having his child.

Would he?

A noise in the hallway startles me into snapping the book shut and throwing it back into my pack, before I remind myself that no one else has a key to this room, nor any reason to barge in here. But the sound helps yank me away from the journal rabbit hole I could've easily fallen down for the rest of the night. It's not like my dad is going to pop out from between the pages if I look over them enough.

No, it's time for the real investigation to begin. To get down in the proverbial dirt and start digging. There are answers around here—in the halls of Villa Russo, the trenches of Villa di Bronzo, the streets of Naples, and who-knows-where-else across the vast Italian countryside. I'm more determined than ever to find them.

Twenty minutes later, I'm standing in an indoor pool of my own making. Mom might have been on to something with the offer of her private shower.

I don't know what I thought I was proving, forgoing the more luxurious bathing option in favor of the Villa Russo communal shower. Let alone who I was proving it to, since I still haven't laid eyes on any other humans allegedly living on this floor with me. What I do know is that the only two water temperatures here are "North Pole" or "surface of the sun." And that neither option managed to get all the shampoo out of my hair, though I might have second-degree burns on my scalp from the effort. I also have a sneaking suspicion that the drains in the floor are more cosmetic than functional.

I wring out the heavy, still-slightly-sudsy mass of red curls hanging over my shoulder one last time, trying to aim the excess water toward my stall's imposter drain. It's like trying to keep a wet bathing suit off the outdoor furniture during a tsunami—completely pointless.

My rubber flip-flops feel just as pointless as I begin to slosh my way out of the flooded stall and into the equally flooded room, clutching my towel tight to my chest with one hand and my old clothes, travel-size toiletries, and detangling comb with the other. I peer around, wondering if I've missed something—a series of dials by the entrance, perhaps, that allow users to choose a Level of Difficulty for various aspects of their shower, all of them turned to a setting that's simply a middle finger emoji.

But I only see identical shower stalls with orange walls and doors lining three sides of the large square room, sinks and mirrors along the fourth. I splash-step to the middle of Russo Reservoir, where a long shelf sits at my eye level between two columns. The two rows of hooks on its underside are empty except for the one where I left my fresh clothes hanging, limp and lonely. Between the water underfoot and the steam clouding the air, I don't see any way I'll dry off enough to get dressed while I'm in here, so I grab the clean T-shirt, shorts, and underwear and wriggle them into the bundle already in my arms.

It's only when I reach the door to the hallway that I pause, looking down at the white terry cloth covering me from chest to mid-thigh. The risk of a towel-clad run-in feels low in this ghost town of a residence hall, right?

Wrong, as it turns out. So tragically wrong.

I've almost made it back to my room, just a couple doors away, and glance back at the trail of wet flip-flop prints I've left. When I face forward again, I hear a low, slow creak. I register too late that it's a door opening—the door right beside my own, the one that I'm about to pass by. The one from which a tall figure emerges . . . and walks directly into me.

CHAPTER FOUR

West

THIS IS WHAT I GET FOR THINKING MY FIRST RUN-IN WITH CAMMIE couldn't have gone worse—a smack across the face from fate.

Or a full-frontal smack into my former friend, who appears to be fresh from a shower and wears only a small white towel.

The next and hopefully final smack comes in the form of the fuzzy, reddish sea creature that is Cammie's wet hair when she tries to toss it away from her face, but my shoulder blocks its path. I step back, recoiling from the contact a little late. But she's no quicker to react, freezing when she registers that it's me. Her eyes go wide while one hand grips her towel and the other hangs limp at her side, having dropped a bundle of clothes and bottles during our collision. My own hands are held up beside my head, palms out, like I need to make it beyond clear that these mitts aren't going anywhere near an unclothed Cammie Lovett.

I see the moment she snaps herself out of our ridiculous freeze-frame, a frown that brings every one of her facial features out to play.

"What do you think you're doing?"

It's my turn to look at her with shock-widened eyes. I blink slowly, peering exaggeratedly back into my room, then meet her gaze again. Gesturing over my shoulder with a thumb, I answer, "Leaving my room?"

Cammie squeezes her eyes shut, giving her head a brisk shake as if to recalibrate. When she blinks them back open, they're a shade less angry, making room for more confusion. "Your r— The room that's beside . . . Oh god . . . we're *neighbors*?"

Shit. I didn't realize, either. When did this happen? I just came up here to drop my phone off to charge before I head back to the library in the main house, where I planned on reading and doing some coding exercises until dinner. Still plan on it, I mean. The plan won't be derailed by the angry, undressed redhead who apparently lives next door to me now.

"Looks like it," I offer dryly. "I haven't been here much longer than you, but just a heads-up, I get the sense this isn't the clothing-optional kind of communal living."

The hand holding her towel twitches. My lizard brain sends my attention there before we both remember ourselves, and I see her grip tighten just before I turn my face toward the ceiling. I hear unintelligible grumbling as Cammie steps around me to get to her door, then hear her fumbling to get the iron key in the lock.

Deciding maybe I could earn some points by being helpful, I bend and start to gather the things she abandoned on the floor.

And immediately regret it when my hand connects with a bra.

"Don't touch that!" Cammie snaps, shoving the door to her room wide open before snatching the item from my hand, flinging it and the rest of the clothes and bottles behind her one handful at a time. "Don't look at me. Just . . . don't."

With a final huff, she slams the blue door, leaving me speechless and solitary in the hall. A long sigh gusts out of me, and I wish it came with the unwavering feeling that she's the one acting out of line here. That she's totally unjustified in treating me like I'm the villainous side character she thought she'd long since written out of her life story. But I was there three years ago, and I hurt her first, even if she turned around and hurt me back. Time and distance have only made me less sure of who bears more blame for the way it all went down.

I also wish, as I force my feet to continue down the hall, that I could force my mind to move on from the image of Camilla Lovett's bare, freckled skin.

A few hours later, I find myself, once again, outdoors against my will. At least this time, the sun isn't personally attacking me with its direct, relentless UV rays, mostly hidden behind trees and buildings as it sinks lower in the sky. The heat of the day is slow to leave the terrazzo, where all the summer residents have gathered for dinner. String lights crisscross through the air over parallel rows of long, rectangular tables, each of them filled with elaborate place settings that some event planner is really proud of, from the lemon-yellow napkins folded into complicated shapes to the—fittingly—bronze flatware. Servers dressed in all black mill around offering trays of hors d'oeuvres to the guests filtering in, while the kitchen staff prepares a buffet spread behind the French doors leading to the villa's vast dining room. And everywhere in between, clusters of well-dressed, happy people stand talking, mingling, laughing, and holding sweating glasses of beer or prosecco.

Meanwhile, I hug the side wall of the villa and try to draw as little notice as possible, taking only small sips of the limonata in my grasp so I don't have to navigate through the crowd for a refill. I'm not exactly antisocial, but it's been a long time since I've been to a gathering like this. I'm out of practice with small talk, working a room full of strangers, forming a bunch of surface-level, temporary connections with people I may or may not encounter again. I'm not sure if I was ever good at those things, really, but the bar was lower when I was younger. Now I look just old enough that people expect me to be capable of intelligent, adult conversation, and I can't coast on endearing teenage awkwardness and mumbled half answers. I fear that trying to meet this expectation would inevitably lead me to ramble about my experience taking SSRIs, or my parents' divorce, or another absolute vibe-killer.

It's best for everyone that I stick to this wall. I tuck my plastic cup between my elbow and my side so I can free both hands to once again mess with the cuffs of my shirtsleeves. I thought a 100 percent cotton button-down would be more breathable than this. But with every drop of sweat I feel coursing down my neck, I roll them up another time. At this point, I'd probably be better off just removing the sleeves entirely, going full gym rat with massive cut-off armholes that proudly display my pale, less-than-sculpted body. The idea almost makes me laugh as I take another mini sip of fizzy lemonade.

Then proceed to choke on it when a certain redhead walks through the double doors. Cammie timed her entrance for this moment, didn't she? She doesn't look smug about it, though, or even notice me having a coughing fit from where she stands. No, she just looks . . . dazzled. Her blue eyes are wide and bright as they take in the scene. The freckles across her face still have their wintry faintness, and I remember delighting in that slow transformation under the summer sun, how they multiplied and intensified. There's a slight upturn at the corner of her parted lips, like they're stuck between a gasp and a grin.

Until they flatten, then turn down. I watch in confusion as Cammie's gaze flits across the crowd with more focus, whatever she sees causing the light in her to dim. Her arms wrap around her middle and her shoulders hunch, and it's only then that I register everything happening from her neck down.

Short denim overalls. A faded green tank top underneath. Hair twisted into two braids, one falling over each shoulder. It's like she just walked in from a long day on the farm—all that's missing are cowgirl boots. I do a double take at what's actually on her feet, which are almost certainly the same rubber flip-flops she showered in.

In the sea of classy cocktail attire, she's an underdressed iceberg.

It's the highlight of my day.

"Cam," Dr. Alex says by way of overly bright greeting as she emerges from the fray in a simple blue dress, silky shawl tucked elegantly around both her elbows while she lays a hand on her daughter's arm. She leans in so her next words are inaudible to me.

I sidle closer almost without thought, narrowing the few yards of distance between us. "You only said it was 'outside.' I'm the one who assumed 'casual picnic,'" Cammie mutters in response to whatever her mom said. "Let me just go change, okay? Maybe we can pretend the first girl who showed up was my tacky twin sister."

She begins to pull away when the deliberate clink of metal on glass fills the air, gradually halting conversations and pulling everyone's attention toward the other side of the terrazzo, where a distinguished gray-haired man stands waiting to make an announcement.

"No time now," Dr. Alex says quickly, reeling Cammie back in. "You look great! We'll be seated for dinner anyway."

At which point it'll still be clear that Cammie's wearing overalls, but at least she can hide . . . My gaze lowers, and she wiggles her toes in her shower shoes.

A half-stifled laugh escapes me, not unlike the sound I

made when my drink went down the wrong pipe, but this time it does catch Cammie's notice. Her head whips my way and I fix my gaze straight ahead as quickly as I can manage. But her quiet grumble says she sees right through me.

She extracts herself from her mom's hold and inches the tiniest bit closer. I catch a whiff of the fresh apple scent that filled the hallway during our earlier run-in and tell myself I don't like it.

"I don't want to hear it from you," she whispers fiercely. "Not one word."

I shouldn't engage, but today has proven that I can only listen to the devil on my shoulder when this girl's around.

"Does 'yeehaw' count?" I ask under my breath. "It's more sound effect than word."

She's practically vibrating with irritation at my side. I'm not proud of this compulsion to keep poking at her, but that doesn't stop me from doing it.

"No, really, it's an honor to meet you, Wendy."

Cammie frowns. "Wendy?"

Her subsequent grimace says the question slipped out before she could think better of it.

"Of the fast-food chain Wendy's? I'm a huge fan of your work on the Frosty. Best Frosty since the snowman."

It's a wonder that she's not attempting to choke me with her braids.

"It's like you've already forgotten that I know where you sleep," she grits out between clenched teeth.

The next words that come to mind are something along

the lines of how I couldn't possibly forget that she's just on the other side of my bedroom wall, so it's fortunate that I don't get the chance to voice them. The gentleman now standing in the center of the crowd clears his throat and begins speaking.

"Buona sera, everyone, and thank you for joining me this evening. I am Dr. Gianmarco Russo, executive director of the Villa Russo Research Residency Program." His voice carries a hint of an accent and effortless confidence.

I jump when I suddenly hear my dad's whisper at my side. "He's actually John Mark Russo, born in Ohio," Dad says from behind his glass. "Used to go by 'Johnny,' up until he took over the director job."

I'm nearly as startled by the soft huff of amusement that follows from my opposite side. But when I look Cammie's way, she's already schooled her expression back to blankness.

"But Villa Russo is more than just my workplace," Johnny/Gianmarco continues, a slow smile starting to spread across his face as his eyes sweep over the group gathered on the terrazzo. "It is my ancestral home, passed down in my family for over two hundred years. Since the incredible discovery of Villa di Bronzo on our grounds—two decades ago, as of this summer—it has been the greatest honor and pleasure for the Russo family to open our home to brilliant scholars such as yourselves, to help further the study of the ancient world. Now that you're here, you are all part of la famiglia."

He pauses for the applause, whistles, and hoots that ensue. I tap my free hand soundlessly against the hand holding my glass while I take a sip of lemonade and graciously refrain from pointing out that the man just plagiarized the Olive Garden slogan.

"What is this, Olive Garden?" Cammie mutters so quietly I know it wasn't meant for anyone to hear, but I nearly spit out my drink anyway. I hunch over, trying to get the sip down without any disruptive sounds. When I can breathe non-lemon-soaked air again, I find two sets of furrowed brows directed at me, one dark brown and concerned, the other light auburn and still annoyed that I exist.

I wave off the former and pretend to ignore the latter, refocusing on the man speaking.

". . . so if you'll please join me in finding the seat with your place card and gathering around these beautifully set tables, our staff will invite one row at a time to the buffet line. Then we can settle in for a night of fantastic food and even better company. Buon appetito!"

Dr. Russo raises his glass, and all around him, others share their buon appetitos and salutés. I raise my own glass to my mouth and swallow down the rest of my drink without incident this time. I don't know what I expect when I turn toward Cammie again, but she's vanished.

For the best, most likely. Dad leads the way to a long table he must've already scoped out as ours, stopping when he gets a few seats from one end.

"Here we are," he declares, gesturing to our place cards. The paper they're printed on, our names in metallic gold ink, looks more expensive than my shirt. Just as I pull out my chair, a low groan sounds from across the table. I don't need to look up to know who it comes from, but it's not like I can keep my eyes on my lap the rest of the night.

Actually, can I?

No, I decide. I tip my chin up and meet Cammie's displeased gaze with cool—if completely fake—indifference.

"You keep making that gross noise from your throat. Are you coming down with a cold?"

Cammie rolls her eyes from where she stands behind her chair, arms crossed, acting awfully superior for someone in a denim onesie. "I feel a little sicker every time I see you."

Dr. Alex appears beside Cammie, opposite my dad, but she's immediately swept into the conversation Dad is having with the woman on his other side. I pick up the napkin art on my plate and pretend to be totally preoccupied with studying it while Cammie takes her seat. Then I don't really have to pretend, because what the hell is this supposed to be? It's like a bizarre cross between an origami boat and one of those paper fortune tellers every kid gets obsessed with at some point.

"You're supposed to clean your hands with it," my personal heckler interrupts my musings. "I know learning new skills is scary, but you're probably overdue to give this one a shot."

Before I can counterattack, I feel someone approach the empty seat to my left.

"Ah, here I am," says a refreshingly cheerful voice. I turn my face toward the newcomer, taken aback by the pretty girl with a pristine white smile aimed my way. A halo of light frames her face, like she's an actual angel who's come to save me from feeling highly unwelcome at this Welcome Dinner.

Then she pulls out her chair and sits, revealing that the halo was in fact the combined efforts of a well-placed string light behind her and my astigmatism.

Hey, Girl, Did It Hurt When You Fell from Heaven, or Did I Leave My Glasses at Home Again? The West Jacobs Story.

"Hi, I'm Lila," she says, offering her hand for me to shake.

I take it and give her a smile. "West. Nice to meet you."

"Likewise," she replies, angling toward Cammie and giving her a wave over the candle-and-flower centerpiece.

"I'm Cammie," says the redhead who looks like Camilla Lovett, but this version can produce a pleasant smile. It stays in place—maybe even grows wider—when a server appears and informs us that it's our turn to visit the buffet.

We get separated on the journey there, ending up in different buffet lines, and I'm grateful for the reprieve. The strangeness of being around Cammie again is already taking its toll. I don't know how I'm supposed to survive this tense non-friendship while also catching glimpses of the girl I used to know. The smile I thought was pretty on her sixteen-year-old face is absolutely devastating at nineteen. My defenses will only get weaker, I can feel it, and it's hard to imagine hers ever doing the same.

The only way to protect myself is by keeping my distance. A tall order when at the end of each day, the only thing separating us is one thin bedroom wall.

I can also eat my feelings in pasta and pizza and pastries. So I prepare to do just that, piling my plate high with something from every serving bowl and chafing dish I can reach. Half of the stuff I can't even identify, but it's all making my mouth water with anticipation. I have to walk slowly back to the table to keep my feast secure, and by the time I make it there, I'm ready to stuff my face until it's time to say "buona notte."

But as soon as my ass hits the chair, my dad's hand lands on my shoulder. "Well, there's my son—I was starting to think you'd gotten turned around, wound up down in Villa di Bronzo or something."

I laugh and shake my head, then bite off a giant hunk of bread to tide me over for as long as it takes him to make an introduction, or whatever else he needs from me.

"Ilaria, allow me to introduce the bambin*o* of that first summer at Villa di Bronzo, though he's grown a bit since then—my son, West. West, this is Ilaria de Matteo, the executive producer of HistoReality's documentary on Villa di Bronzo."

Dad gestures toward the woman he and Dr. Alex have been chatting with since we took our seats, but it's the first time I've really looked at her. I'd guess she's a few years younger than my parents, her light tan skin creased only around her smiling mouth and eyes, rosy spots on her cheeks and the tip of her nose. Inky black curls are piled atop her head in some sort of twist. The long sleeves and layered skirt of her dress look loose and breezy, in contrast to the dozens of metal bracelets and necklaces layered around her wrists and neck. They all clink together when she lifts her wineglass toward me in greeting.

"West, a pleasure," Ilaria says in a slightly raspy voice and the thick accent of an Italian who's not from Ohio.

My mouth is still full of bread, so all I can offer is a nod and muffled "Mm-hmm!"

She's unfazed, her gleeful attention bouncing between Dad, Dr. Alex, Cammie, and me. "Wow, *due* 'bambini di Bronzo,'" she says with wonder, pointing two fingers toward Cammie and me before throwing her hands up, like she can't believe two unrelated colleagues had babies in the same year. "I cannot believe I did not know about the boy. Why did the world not hear about West?"

Dad and Dr. Alex share a look and laugh as Dad clarifies, "Well, this guy was born the previous winter, for starters—came into the world in a blessedly boring way at a hospital in the States. He was a couple months old by the time his pops and I brought him over here, nearly eight months by the time Ms. Camilla made her dramatic entrance."

"*Wooow*," Ilaria repeats, drawing the word out with amazement I'm not sure my origin story deserves. "How special for these two, to be in each other's lives from the very beginning."

She clearly has no idea of the minefield she's tiptoeing toward, and I'm not planning to tell her, lest our screwed-up relationship become some subplot of this film I want no part in. But Cammie was always too comfortable playing with fire.

"Those first few months of his life were dreadfully dull," she taunts, not even sparing me a glance. Our parents' quiet laughter is forced and nervous, though I doubt Ilaria hears it over her own real chuckle. Then it's like Cam can't help herself—she has to see if she's earned a reaction from me.

But when our eyes lock, and I see the challenge behind those icy blues, I can't physically keep my mouth shut.

"They were nice and peaceful, actually," I say calmly, not dropping Cammie's stare. "Then she arrived, and I wouldn't know peace again for sixteen years."

While the adults laugh again—two of them as fake as a sitcom laugh track, the other enjoying herself too much to do the math behind my words—the only sign that Cammie even heard me is in the slight narrowing of her gaze.

Somewhere in the distance, I hear the conversation move on, Ilaria asking Dad and Dr. Alex about the transformation of Villa Russo into researcher housing. But Cammie and I are locked in a silent stare-off, neither willing to blink first. It's juvenile, and pointless, and damn if I couldn't do this the rest of the night.

Until the soft clearing of a throat, followed by an even softer voice, puts an end to our deadlock.

"Um, I don't want to interrupt, but . . ." my forgotten seat neighbor Lila begins, her doe eyes darting a wary look between Cammie and me.

"Oh, you're not at all," I say, probably overselling it with the aggressive head shake. "What's up?"

She still sounds a little hesitant as she continues, gesturing to the guy around our age I hadn't noticed until now, who occupies the seat beside Cammie. "We were just wondering if you two are also here for field school."

"Oh, uh, actually no," I hedge, reaching up to scratch the back of my neck. I don't know why the explanation of our presence here suddenly feels so complicated, like I can't explain it without starting at the day of my blessedly boring birth and continuing through all the relevant moments in my life story.

Is this the Cammie effect? Her proximity making absolutely everything seem more confusing and tangled and messy? Or do I just need to shut up, eat my now-cold mountain of carbs, and get a full night of sleep, then everything will be easy-breezy in the morning?

Cammie picks up the conversational baton instead of letting the awkward silence I've left drag on for eternity.

"We're here with our parents. Well, my mom and his dad. We're not siblings. Or even step-siblings. Our parents aren't a couple—never have been! Because he's gay, but it's not like that's the only reason they aren't together. She's also . . . emotionally unavailable?"

On second thought, the silence wasn't so awkward. And I thought *my* social skills were rusty.

Cammie pauses to lift her full water glass to her lips and drain it, then slams it back down with a gasping breath. This is quickly followed by a few seconds where her face pinches up in discomfort and she presses a hand to her chest, squeaking out the words "that was carbonated" by way of explanation.

Lila, Anonymous Guy, and I all seem incapable of anything but gaping at the one-woman show. When her face finally relaxes and her hand falls to her lap, Cammie finishes with: "Anyway, our parents are archaeologists."

Lila is polite enough to ask a follow-up question. "So, your parents are leading the field school?"

I decide to take this one, bolstered by the fact that I can't make things much weirder. "No, they're here for the twentieth anniversary celebration and the documentary about Villa di Bronzo. Her mom was the first to discover it, and she and my dad co-led the first excavations." Belatedly, I add, "Cammie was also born at the dig site, and it was a big news story and everything, so she'll be part of filming, too."

Just when I thought we'd lost these potential summer friends, Lila's face brightens and she lets out a gasp. "Wait, oh my god, what?" Her excitement is entirely directed toward Cammie. "I've heard that story! That was you?"

Cammie nods, and her new biggest fan fires questions at her about her brush with worldwide celebrity, which she spent as a barely sentient baby blob. Cammie's a seasoned pro at this routine, and while the two are occupied with each other, I'm able to eat a few bites of food and almost convince myself it tastes better cold than it would have fresh.

"So, West," Lila says after a few minutes, snapping my attention back to her. "You won't get to be part of the documentary? What are you going to do with all your free time?"

The questions come with a cute faux pout, like she's sympathetic to the plight of the unfamous. But her eyes are smiling and her lashes flutter, and for the first time, I wonder—is this unreasonably pretty girl . . . flirting with me?

I feel my cheeks heat as my ability to form complete sentences crumbles. "I . . . I brought some stuff I'm hoping to work on. Programs, like, coding. On my computer."

Cammie's laugh is like a singular thunderclap, brief but

foreboding. I turn my head to find her looking at Lila with a knowing smile, her tone breezy as she says, "You've gotta watch out if this one starts getting bored." She leans in and lowers her voice, but not so low I can't hear her confide, "He might try to make you his friend with benefits."

I'm vaguely aware of Lila letting out an uncomfortable semi-laugh, and Whatever His Name Is might be choking on a piece of cannoli. Our parents continue to joke and chat and drink, oblivious to the psychological warfare being waged so casually at the same table.

But I'm too consumed by a shock-horror-mortification cocktail to do anything but sit there, perfectly still and laser-focused on this stranger who looks a lot like my old friend. My insides tremble with something like adrenaline. Maybe it's my fight-or-flight instincts battling it out with the lesser known third option: cry.

I don't know if it's to her credit or not, but Cammie doesn't walk the words back. Nor does she drop my gaze as she leans back in her chair and carelessly twirls one braid around her fingers. I finally manage to swallow even though my mouth has gone dry. Several slow, deep breaths later, the emotional five-alarm fire that filled my brain has burned down to something more manageable, and I can start to form actual thoughts.

So I know exactly what I'm doing when I tap into the most spiteful side of myself, crafting the first reply I can think of with a chance of wounding her back in kind.

"Nah, I have too many interests to get truly bored. I guess

that's a perk of starting life in an ordinary way to ordinary parents—it forces you to develop a personality."

She flinches, the rest of her body going rigid while her jaw goes slack.

I know I've struck true. But it sure doesn't feel like a victory.

CHAPTER FIVE

Cammie

EVEN IN MY SLEEP, I CAN'T ESCAPE WESTON JACOBS.

The first night after a long travel day, no matter the change in distance or time zones, I am reliably dead to the world. Thoroughly zonked, from the moment my head hits the pillow until a persistent alarm or brave human revives me the next day.

By the time I fled the Welcome (to Hell) Dinner, I was craving that sweet hibernation. I almost wished West's verbal knockout punch had been literal—that I could've taken the L and skipped straight to being unconscious. But no, I had to spend another half hour actually thinking thoughts and feeling feelings and hiding it all under a polite, composed mask before I was finally alone in my room, regrettable outfit off, pajamas on, lights out.

I told myself I didn't care that West looked so betrayed by

what I told that Lila girl. I'd only said it because of all his little jabs at me and my overalls, each snarky comment like a tug on one of my braids, making me want to swat back. If our words were our weapons, I'd thought mine were a Swiss Army knife, but West had answered with explosives.

Then, instead of enjoying a peaceful, restorative slumber, I proceeded to relive the awful night for nine hours straight. That's how long it felt, anyway, with the weird time distortion that happens in dreamland. I woke up with splayed limbs tangled in my duvet, and similarly tangled memories of the real versus dream versions of last night.

It didn't help that Dream Cammie made some disturbing creative choices. Like devoting a lot of attention to Dream West's effortlessly shiny hair, which fell in a kind of tidy mess I didn't know could be so appealing. And his strong jawline, shaded with a light stubble that hadn't been there earlier in the day, and definitely wasn't a thing the one time my lips had touched his. And his forearms, revealed by the rolled up sleeves of his dress shirt.

I rub my eyes aggressively, like that'll wipe those all-too-real images from where they're printed on my brain in what I fear is permanent ink. I, for one, could have gone my whole life without seeing West Jacobs in a button-down with the sleeves rolled up. I didn't need to know that he's acquired objectively hot forearms in our years apart. It would've been my preference for him to spend the whole summer inside a hazmat suit with a *kick me* sign taped to the back. Something that wouldn't allow me any glimpse of his present-day body, so I could imagine he's become completely unappealing. Like he no longer bathes, because he thinks hygiene is a myth created by Big Soap. Or he got a giant chest tattoo of the word *FREEDOM* and only dresses in revealing muscle tanks that show it off.

But no. He's grown into the kind of handsome where a neon sign could hang over his head, flashing the words *this guy will ruin your life*, and it wouldn't stop most people from letting him.

As the fog of jet-lagged sleep begins to clear, I find that despite Dream Cammie's weakness for the enemy's pretty face, my resolve to steer clear of him is strengthened. I will not let West sap an ounce more of the energy I can put to better use, won't even give him the time of day. Maybe in return, he won't haunt me at night.

I commence what I'm considering the real first day of this summer adventure with a pep in my step and, even better, a clear-cut plan. It's time to hit the ground running on my Dad Quest.

Somewhere in the info Mom dumped on me yesterday, there was mention of a daily breakfast spread available in the dining room, so that becomes my first stop. A few of my fellow late risers mill about by the food stations or sit alfresco enjoying tiny cups of espresso, but I don't grab a plate to join them. I have a train to catch and a story to spin before I get there, so I make a beeline for the pastry tray and wrap up a few options in a paper napkin. I stuff the bundle into the small day pack on my back while an additional cornetto goes to my mouth, my teeth clamping it in place while my hands are busy resituating my bag and pushing open one of the doors to outside.

I step into the sunshine at the same time that I take my first bite into featherlight layers of buttery goodness, and the combination might be the strongest hit of serotonin I've had all year. This has to bode well for the journey ahead of me. Double-checking my phone, I don't find any updates from Mom since the one she sent before I woke, describing her plans to take Ilaria and her crew on a walk-through of Villa di Bronzo. She wasn't sure if they'd be filming today or just generating ideas, but she invited me to join them if and when I wanted.

There's a lot I'm keeping from her, and likely more to come in the weeks ahead. I'm lucky she'll be so busy with the documentary, plus doing some guest lectures for the field school, but even the most hectic workday would not keep Dr. Alexandra Lovett from going into full mom-panic mode if she lost track of me in a foreign country. To keep us all off a first-name basis with the polizia, I'll have to deploy some strategic white lies.

I don't feel great about this, don't love taking advantage of the trust she's always given me. But when compared with the huge secret she's been keeping from me for nineteen years and counting, well, I tell myself I'm allowed a little withholding of my own.

I'm so focused on finalizing a cover story that can satisfy Mom with as few lies as possible that I don't really register where I'm going until my boots hit the first stair. The switch to metal rather than dirt under my sneakers stops me in my tracks, and I look down at the cloud of dust settling around my feet.

This is my first time setting foot in Villa di Bronzo when I'm actually old enough to understand the significance. Memories flash before my eyes, younger versions of me on other dig sites or lying in my bed at night, dreaming of the day I'd make it here. I always thought it would feel like coming home—like as the Bambina di Bronzo, I'm a part of this place and it's a part of me, that my return might be akin to a long-lost puzzle piece completing the picture.

The reality is more complicated. At the bottom of this staircase, installed by the first crews to work on excavations here twenty years ago, is the main entrance to the sprawling site. The closest section is the most thoroughly excavated, rooms and hallways and courtyards all aboveground and open to viewing by select visitors. Not much active excavation takes place on this end nowadays, Mom has said when showing me pictures, but conservators are always working on better preserving these areas from exposure to the elements.

The farther back I look, the less there is to see at the surface, the trenches and tunnels and pits forming a haphazard grid where excavations are active. A part of me wants to head straight there, take the trowel I packed out of habit, and get down in the dirt to see what discoveries are still hidden within.

But a bigger part of me says I need to wake up and smell the espresso. The part that could recite the IIAS rejection email from memory and still feels the slash it made through my self-worth. West's words last night were only salt to that wound, driving home the reality that without my mom's achievements and badass career, I'm no one special. That I happened to be born at Villa di Bronzo, through random chance and a dash of Mom's stubbornness, doesn't make me anything but a quirky blip in the site's long history.

It's time to figure out what more my life can be.

As I resume my descent of the stairs, I can just barely spot the familiar reddish hair of my target amid a small group gathered in one of the rooms farthest from the villa's entrance. I don't let myself look around too much as I wind through the maze of rooms in that direction. I can't let a cool fresco or mosaic floor distract me from my mission.

I'm close enough to hear Mom's voice when a distraction I didn't anticipate cuts off my path.

"Ah, Camilla, fantastico," Ilaria cries as she pulls me in for a hug and one of the double-cheek kiss greetings that folks here are fond of. Mom explained this last night, after I was visibly startled by the one-two punch of air smooches from a colleague she'd just introduced. The couple of instances that followed, I tried to reciprocate in kind, but I always seem to kiss the air too late after the other person's pulled away. This time is no different, but the friendly woman doesn't seem to notice or care as she looks to the crew member at her side, a camera perched on his shoulder. My smile drops. "La Bambina di Bronzo returning home for the first time—oh, we must take some shots of her taking it all in, sì? The light in the portico is stunning at this time of day, or maybe the room with the Athena fresco . . ."

I'm about to attempt an inconspicuous escape, pressing myself against the wall and slide-stepping out of sight, when my mother appears on Ilaria's other side. The words *Bambina di Bronzo* have a way of summoning her.

"There you are," she says with a smile and a quick side hug for me. "I'm glad you got to catch up on some sleep. Were you still able to find food?"

I nod. "I made it before the buffet closed. Good cornettos."

So good that I nabbed two more for the road.

"Oh, perfect. And it sounds like you're here right on time for your film debut—did I hear that correctly?"

She directs the last words toward Ilaria, who finishes up a rapid exchange in Italian with her camera guy before facing Mom and me with her wide smile.

"Sì, it is perfect timing for us, if it is also for Cammie," she says, at least acknowledging that I might have other stuff to do, even if no one expects me to.

I pull a disappointed face that I hope looks more sincere than it feels. "Ooh, I wish I could, but I actually have somewhere to be." To Mom, I add, "I thought I'd kick things off by going to tour Pompeii today. My ticket has a reserved time frame for entry, so I need to catch the train soon if I'm going to make it."

I expected her to be excited about this (fake) plan; Pompeii isn't far, and I'll still be soaking up some archaeology goodness, even if I'm not in field school. At least, I would if that were actually where I was headed. But her lips turn down and worry wrinkles her brow.

"By yourself?" she asks.

"Yep!" I give her a calm, easy smile, pretending I'm not picking up on any of the concern in her question. Just a self-sufficient girl, excited for her day exploring the ancient world.

Mom shifts her weight to her other hip, and I glance at Ilaria, who appears to share the motherly worry for my safety. "Cam, I don't think that's a good idea, honey. I don't want you making the trip alone. Sundays are off days for the film crew and field school—why don't you wait and I'll go with you then?"

I forcefully hold my smile in place. "I'll be fine, Mom—I've gone plenty of places on my own when I'm at school and you haven't even known about it. I haven't been kidnapped yet."

Maybe I shouldn't have started off with that argument, especially the "yet" part. She's always been all for my independence, and female empowerment, and girls can do anything they put their minds to. But she's also seen every movie in the *Taken* franchise and reads too many thrillers. Should anything happen to me, we both know I don't have a Liam Neeson–type dad to run around the world doing vigilante shit to find me. That's kind of the whole reason I'm in this situation, isn't it?

"Yes, I know that," she says. "And I know you're a grown woman." It looks like it pains her to say those last two words. I'm not sure she believes them. "But this is another country and you don't speak the language."

I'm about to jump in with some stats about my LingoLegend streak, maybe a little anecdotal evidence of me communicating just fine with Luigi on my way here from the airport, when I'm saved from myself. Dr. Danny appears at Mom's side, wiping some sweat from his forehead underneath one of his many nerd-tastic bucket hats.

“What’s going on here?” he asks.

Ilaria answers, like she isn’t the C to this A-B conversation. “Camilla wants to go to Pompeii by herself. Alex is unsure if she will permit it to happen.”

Is this how it feels to be a reality TV star? Strangers with cameras, perpetually all up in your business?

“I’m not trying to helicopter you,” Mom says. “There are just safety risks to a young woman traveling alone. I think it’s a valid concern.”

“Of course,” Dr. Danny agrees. Did I say he was saving me? I spoke too soon. “But West could go with her.”

Just when I thought this couldn’t get more needlessly difficult.

“That’s really not necessary,” I say, emphasis on the *really*. “I’m sure he’s very busy doing . . . whatever West does nowadays.”

As if to prove me wrong, West appears. What happened to all those interests that keep him from ever knowing boredom?

“What am I too busy to do?” West asks. Or grumbles, more like.

I don’t know what his problem is; he’s not the one facing down the Three Musketeers of Wrecking Plans. But I also don’t know what he’s doing in Villa di Bronzo, assuming I didn’t summon him like some kind of demon. West never had much interest in archaeology, no matter how hard I tried to convince him that it was endlessly fascinating and exciting. He would retort that he had enough excitement in his life just trying to keep up with me.

West was the stereotypical “old soul” of young children,

always more thoughtful and measured in his words and actions than anyone else our age. He could still be adventurous and playful, but with a caution I never really had. He also over-thought everything to a point that sometimes saved us from harm, but more often just kept him from having a good time.

"Nothing," West's dad answers his question gleefully. A little too gleefully, if you ask me, or West, judging by his face. Dr. Danny isn't even hiding his hope for some forced former bestie bonding. "I was just telling Alex and Cammie that you don't have any plans for the day and can absolutely accompany Cammie on her trip to Pompeii. You've never been either—not that you can remember, anyway. Sounds fun, doesn't it?"

"Again, completely unnecessary," I try, my panic growing. "I like to do these things by myself. I can go at my own pace, get sidetracked, see all the things that I really want to see but no one else cares about. And it's hot out today, and we know West doesn't do well in extreme temperatures, so—"

"Yeah, I'll go," West says, his face clear of any displeasure. Whatever was bothering him before, it's been made better by the opportunity to rain on my parade.

"Oh, that would be wonderful, Weston. Thank you so much," says my traitorous mother.

I really wonder what she thinks West Jacobs would do if a hypothetical human trafficker tried to snatch me while we were walking down the Via dell'Abbondanza. Sure, West has put on some muscle mass in the last three years. But unless he's changed every other thing about his personality, he's not about to step in and throw hands, like some kind of bodyguard.

He's more likely to immediately run in the opposite direction, calling on the relevant authorities for help while ducking and covering, saving his own ass. He'd be the most hated side character in *Taken 12: The Bad Guys Win in This One*.

But at least this puts an end to Mom's protests, and I don't have to do the awkward dance of reminding her that I am nineteen, technically an adult, and don't actually need her permission to do anything at any time. I'd rather not play that card when I'm trying to avoid raising any red flags over my head.

Besides, it shouldn't be hard, once we're out of the helicopter parent fleet's sight line, to send West on his less-than-merry way and relieve him of travel companion duties. As we both know, it's a role he doesn't want to fill.

Or so I believe, until he sticks by my side all the way to the train station.

"Wait, I think this is the wrong one," he says as he follows me on board the exact train I want to be on, looking from his phone to the digital sign on the train platform behind us to me and back. "Don't we need to go the other direction to get to Pompeii? This goes toward Naples."

I ignore him and continue walking deeper into the car. I find one empty seat in a set of four—the other three thankfully occupied—and slide into it. I hear him grumble something about me having lost my manners in the last few years when, unfortunately, the person in the seat behind mine stands and moves toward the door. West claims the spot and turns to speak through the narrow gap between our seats and the windows.

"Did you hear me? I think this train is going the wrong way. We'll have to get off at the next stop and switch."

I wait until the doors have all shut and the train is moving again—in the direction I planned to go all along—before I finally answer.

"No, this is the right train."

I swear I can hear the scrunched expression on his face. "What? I thought you said we were going to Pompeii. Here, look, this sign shows the route."

Instead of looking at anything, I close my eyes and let my head fall back against the seat. West's voice has risen with his alarm, and I can't bear to see whatever reactions he's getting from the Italians or other tourists in my little quad.

I deliberately lower my own volume when I answer. "We're not going to Pompeii. I was never going to Pompeii. *We* were never supposed to be going anywhere. If you don't want to join me, you can get off at the next station and take the train back to Villa Russo. Or to Pompeii—hell, I don't care."

West huffs out an exasperated breath. "Join you *where*, Cammie? I don't even know where we're going."

I am just as exasperated when I answer, "You said it yourself—this train is going to Naples. We go where it goes."

"Is it worth even trying to get more information out of you?" he asks.

He's learning—this isn't like old times, when I'd fill him in on all my plans and scheming, even when I knew he'd be less than thrilled or try to talk me out of things. We're not in this together.

I don't offer a response, which is a response on its own. I should be satisfied when he turns around and stops trying to speak to me. I should feel content. I'm getting to go where I want, so I shouldn't care what West does with his day. But his anxiety is palpable, even through the barrier of sturdy-fabric-upholstered public transit furniture. It almost makes me feel anxious for the first time about today's mission, which in turn makes me resent West's presence even more.

Why couldn't he let me bluster on into this possibly absurd, somewhat half-baked plan without thinking it through any further? One thing is clear—I can't let him in on the truth of what I'm up to. Not unless I want him to bring it all crashing down before it even really begins.

Hopefully he'll turn around and take the train back once he sees me safely to Naples. I pretend that's already a reality as the train rumbles on and I watch the scenery pass by out my window, through a few more stops and different groups of people getting on and off at each station. It seems like a mix of commuters and tourists, lots of different languages filling the air around me, and I enjoy both people-watching and listening. Before I know it, we are pulling into a busy station in the heart of the city.

"This is my stop," I tell West, emphasis on the *my*. But he doesn't take the hint, getting to his feet and following me out the sliding doors. To my dismay, he continues following in silence as I continue toward my destination.

The Museo Archeologico is supposed to be less than a ten-minute walk from here. West waits approximately three of these minutes before his questions begin anew.

"Do you know where we're heading now?" he asks. "Like, beyond where you're trying to go, have you actually looked up a route and are we on it?"

I roll my eyes. "No, West, I've never been to an unfamiliar city before. I figure we just navigate them by vibes, right? It'd be nice if there was some kind of app that could give me directions when I have a place I want to go, or even, like, a book that shows a whole city on paper. Or printed onto a sphere, like the shape of the Earth!"

" 'Yes' would have been a complete answer," West mutters back.

"So is 'no,' which is what I would have answered had you asked if I even want you here. Feel free to take it into consideration now."

He sighs heavily. "Unfortunately for both of us, I'm stuck with you now. I can't just remove myself."

"Oh, you're so noble," I tease in an exaggerated swooning voice. "My hero."

"More like a reluctant accomplice," he corrects me. "Though it might surprise you, I'd really hate myself if anything was to happen to you after I left. Not to mention Dr. Alex and my dad hating me, but the self-loathing would be the worst. So selfishly, I'll stay, just in case the presence of an extra human at your side causes any shady characters to think twice before taking you as a hostage or something. Although they probably wouldn't make it five minutes before deciding they'd rather pay someone else to take you off their hands."

"Gosh, why did we ever stop being friends?" I act like I'm

really baffled by the thought. "You're just so kind to me. Super supportive. I feel much safer having you at my side."

"Real friends are honest with you even when it's not what you want to hear," West says, and when my head jerks his way, he winces, immediately realizing the three-year-old grenade he's clumsily stepped on.

"Riiight," I say, drawing out the word. "Good point. So in hindsight, we were never real friends anyway, were we?"

"Cam," he starts, but I hold up a hand. Now is not the time. I need to focus on today's goal. Not unbury my history with this guy, like it's going to do anything but upset both of us.

"Don't, West," I say. "Let's leave it."

West stuffs his hands in his pockets, and I see his shoulders hunch out of the corner of my eye.

"Right," he says, so it's clear he doesn't actually agree. "Just as we've been doing for the past three years and counting. It's gone so well so far."

The last part is quieter, like he doesn't care if I hear it, or he's talking more to himself. It almost convinces me to break this awful standoff. Put all our issues on the table instead of keeping us in passive-aggressive purgatory forever. Once and for all.

But this is not the time or place. *Focus, Cammie,* I remind myself as I march onward, letting the bustling city be our soundtrack while we wind through its streets. I check my phone occasionally to ensure we're still on the right path, still on track to get to the museum right when it opens. I don't have an appointment with the person I'm hoping to find, figuring the element of surprise works well in this case. It seems like an early arrival should increase my odds of catching him at a free moment.

Finally, the beautiful old structure comes into view ahead of us, one of the most popular destinations for tourists visiting Naples—which is itself not the most touristy of Italian cities, from what I've read. But what it might lack in flashy tourist hot spots, the guidebooks say it makes up for in authentic Southern Italian culture. I've still barely glimpsed that from my brief commute from the airport and our walk today. But I hope to see much more, should my plans play out as intended. I want to try real Neapolitan pizza, see the castles that sit on the waterfront, and, maybe most of all, explore the country's largest collection of ancient Roman art and artifacts at the National Archaeological Museum.

West and I ascend the stone steps in front of the imposing facade. We haven't spoken in so long, I'm startled when he says, "Well, this isn't as bad as I feared."

"Wow. Glowing review. Be sure to put that on Tripadvisor," I deadpan.

"Okay, as cagey as you were being, I expected much worse," West shoots back. "Some kind of underground fight club, or other illegal activity. As you keep gently reminding me, I don't know your life."

He doesn't and he won't, I think. Still, I have to bite my tongue to keep from spilling the whole plan right here and now, just to clear my good name of his nefarious suspicions.

Though we've come to the museum on one of its free entry

days, it isn't too crowded. I do genuinely want to see the exhibits, but there will be time for that later. I pick up a map at the front desk and study it, locating my probable target. Since it looks like I have no chance of losing West now, I wave him along with me as I start through the first grand exhibit hall featuring some of the museum's standing collection.

I wasn't lying earlier when I said I love to go to places like this alone. To take all the time I want reading every single sign, make extra-long stops at whatever sparks my interest or curiosity. My feet are desperately trying to veer off path and take me to every other statue or painting or vase in a glass display case that we pass. But I can't get sidetracked yet. As we reach an intersection of wide, marble-floored hallways between galleries, I stop to refer back to the map.

"Whoa, Cam, check this out," West says from a few feet away. My first instinct is to bite back something snarky. But a softer side of me, one I'm not ready to examine, decides to let it lie, and instead, I turn to see what he's so excited about.

"I read something about this project once," he says, more enthusiasm in his voice than I've heard at any point in the last twenty-four hours. He's standing in front of a display case featuring what look like little charcoal bricks, along with a large mahogany-framed box on a stand with glass on four sides of it, and one of the same charcoal-like lumps inside.

"These are the Herculaneum scrolls," West explains. "Found at this villa in a big library that was buried by Vesuvius. The scrolls were carbonized, so you can still see some of the text on their outer layers, but they can't be physically unwrapped without crumbling. So this computer science research team has been taking CT scans of the scrolls—these little charcoal-like bricks—and developing methods to virtually unwrap them, then pick out the hidden text inside. It's pretty mind-blowing."

I would love to disagree. But, well, it *is* mind-blowing.

And completely unrelated to my mission.

"Very interesting," I say flatly, not revealing how interesting I actually think it is. But West seems to have forgotten I'm here as he continues to nerd out, talking mostly to himself about the power of technology and computer scientists to alter our understanding of human history and blah blah whatever. Maybe this is for the best. He can stay here and drool over carbonized papyrus while I go solve an actual problem.

I turn and start down the hall toward the administrative offices where I hope to find Dr. Constantini. But I don't make it far before I hear footsteps fast-walking behind me and West reappears at my side.

"Okay, I feel like you didn't really recognize what we were seeing there, and we should circle back to it before we go."

"Sure, yeah," I agree half-heartedly. He is *not* the one driving this bus.

When we get to a door marked with something in Italian that I think means "offices," I open it with an air of authority that I do not possess, in my sneaker-clad feet and backpack that suddenly feels very first-day-of-kindergarten. But I hold my head high and approach the desk where a pretty young woman sits behind a computer.

"Buongiorno," she says, followed by several more quickly uttered Italian words that I absolutely do not catch.

"Buongiorno . . ." I reply, then, dredging up what little LingoLegend has given me, "Tu parli inglese?"

"Ah, okay," the woman says with an understanding smile. "Yes, what can I help you with?"

"I'm here to speak with Dr. Constantini," I answer, not dropping the attitude of "I belong here and definitely know what I'm doing," false as it may be.

The woman looks to her computer and clicks around, her head tilting daintily to the side. "You have an appointment?" she asks.

Presumably, she's looking at a schedule and confirming for herself that no, I certainly do not. So I don't try to bluff through this one.

"I don't, but I believe he'll want to see me. He's an old colleague of my mother, Dr. Alexandra Lovett. Would you mind telling him that her daughter, Camilla, is here? I promise I won't take too much of his time."

She looks hesitant, if apologetic, about it, and I can already see the rejection coming. But before she can say the words, another voice, deeper, louder, and more heavily accented, bellows from behind her, "It cannot be . . . the Bambina di Bronzo? I do not believe my eyes!"

The man steps out from behind the front desk and walks all the way up to West and me with his arms spread wide. He's what I would expect Santa Claus to look like, if Santa was a museum curator. A carefully groomed white beard, rosy cheeks peeking out over the top of it, smiling brown eyes, and a broad chest and broader middle under his sweater vest and tweed blazer. I'm prepared for it when he comes in for an air hug and double-cheek kiss, first with me, then with a still visibly-unused-to-this West.

"Camilla, sì?" Dr. Constantini says, to which I nod and open my mouth to say "sì," but he goes on. "And you are . . ."

He looks to West, who clearly wasn't expecting to need to speak at this meeting.

"West Jacobs," he answers with a crack in his voice. It shouldn't be a tiny bit endearing; I should want to make fun of him. But this day is full of unexpected turns, apparently.

"Ah, Jacobs and Lovett, fantastico! This takes me back . . ." Dr. Constantini says with a gleam in his eyes as he smiles at the two of us. "Shall we speak in my office?"

West and I follow him down the hall, taking seats in two leather wingback chairs in front of his desk. He offers us coffee, which West declines but I gratefully accept. While Dr. Constantini makes espressos for himself and me, he hums a tune I don't recognize. I only pretend not to recognize the wide-eyed look of *what the hell is going on here?* plastered across the face of my unwanted travel companion.

When Dr. Constantini finally sits down, I hold the tiny espresso mug up to my lips and blow the steam away from it. I wait until he's swallowed his first sip before I begin. "Thank you so much for allowing us to drop in like this. I've heard a lot about you from my mother over the years and it's amazing to finally put a face to the name."

In truth, I haven't heard much about him from my mother over the years, but I've heard a lot from Alex and her journal in the last few weeks. Dr. Constantini was my mom's advisor when she was here studying and teaching at the university while getting her PhD. He remained a close mentor figure for the duration of her time in Italy, and she always spoke highly of him in her writing. Though never so highly that I worried he was a potential dad candidate, and we'd have some weird professor-student mess to reckon with, thank the ancient Roman gods. I'm extra certain of ruling out that chance, now that I've seen the man in person and can't imagine him ever being anything but a nonthreatening, grandfatherly figure.

"I cannot tell you what a joyful surprise this is to see you both," he replies, again involving West when it seems obvious to anyone with eyesight that West would not like to be perceived. He sinks lower and lower in his fancy chair. "You are here for the twentieth anniversary?"

I'm grateful for the easy segue. "We are," I answer. "Our parents came back to Villa di Bronzo as part of a documentary in the works, and West and I have the chance to see the villa and the surrounding area for the first time that we can remember. It's only my second day here, but I'm very excited to explore more."

"Of course, yes," the older man says. "It is a beautiful summer we're having and the perfect time to explore Campania. I cannot believe it has been two decades since that summer—and since you entered the world. I was there the day you were born, you know."

I almost answer that I was, too, before catching the ridiculous words. Instead, I smile and nod, like, *Yes, I did know, because my mother told me that, and told me plenty of other things about the villa excavations and that time in our lives, and not because I stole her old diary and memorized every detail like the biggest mystery of my life hangs in the balance.*

"It is amazing," I agree. "Which is actually why I've come to speak with you today. They're throwing a little celebration at Villa Russo a few weeks from now to honor the twentieth anniversary with everyone here for the summer. Mom knows it's happening"—she's the one who mentioned it to me while helping create my packing list, unknowingly inspiring the perfect cover story and starting place for my secret search—"but I've been thinking about something extra I could do to surprise her and make the occasion even more special. I want to invite some additional colleagues and friends from her time here, starting with you, of course, and since you worked so closely with her back then, I was hoping you could help add to the list. Any names of people I could look into, to see if they're still in the area and interested in attending."

Dr. Constantini leans back, the chair squeaking under his shift in weight, and laces his fingers together over his middle. The pose is very *and what would you like for Christmas, young Cammie?* Whenever he's done with this curator gig, he *needs* to take his talents to the Mall Santa industry.

He hums to himself, gaze veering toward the ceiling as he raises one hand to stroke his beard. "That is a wonderful idea, this party, and I hope I can be of help with your guest list. Let me see. That was, hmm, my third summer as the program director for the . . . Sì, sì . . ." He trails off—then rolls off, whirling around in his office chair to approach a massive cabinet in the same deep brown, solid wood as his desk.

He continues mumbling to himself in Italian as he digs a small key out of a trouser pocket and uses it to unlock each heavy door in turn, then open them wide. Scooting to the side, he looks back to West and me with a smile, sweeping a hand over what he's revealed: shelves upon shelves full to bursting with binders, folders, and notebooks.

"My computer before computers!" Dr. Constantini jokes. "For most of my career, the only way to 'save' information was to put it on paper. Then the tough part—do not forget where you have put the paper."

"Wow," I say, for lack of a better response. As Dr. Constantini begins to peruse his archives, my hopes of getting anything useful from this visit dwindle. That cabinet is like one of those old I Spy books come to life, all its contents running together, nothing labeled or organized in any way I can decipher. I can't imagine he—

"Aha! Here we are," he declares, and in my periphery, West's head rears back with the same surprise I feel. Constantini rolls back to his desk and sets his find on the surface with a thud. It's an overstuffed, faded green binder, papers already spilling out on all sides. The only thing even resembling a label that I spot is a scribble of black marker that could be a messily written "dB," but could also be one of those inkblot tests.

I shudder to think what this man's computer files look like.

"This is all from the time I was working on the villa project," he begins, gently pulling back the cover to lay it flat. "Let us see what is relevant to us here . . ."

Dr. Constantini's mumbling resumes as he flips through the pages that are bound by the metal rings, and the many more loose papers tucked in between. Some he sets aside immediately or skips over completely, while others get more study. Every few pages, he pauses, picks up his silver fountain pen from its holder, and writes something on a notepad off to one side of the desk.

I hope his notes are more legible than his binder labels. My palms itch, my legs cross and uncross, the urge to reach out and take every piece of potential evidence so strong that I can't get comfortable. I'm so close to just asking if I can take the whole file when the woman from the front desk calls out the professor's name.

With a staying hand and an unhurried, "Scusi, un momento," Dr. Constantini strolls out of the office. I wait for his footsteps to fade before I jump into action.

"What are you doing?" West snaps in an accusatory whisper as I round the desk and pull my phone from my shorts pocket.

"Shh, it's fine," I whisper back, knowing this is neither an answer to his question nor anything he'll believe. But I need to hurry and do what I set out to before Constantini comes back, instead of standing here explaining myself. I grab a pen from a cup filled with the non-fancy, non-fountain variety and use it to bookmark the page the man left open, then flip back the stack of pages he's already reviewed to the very beginning.

One by one, I take pictures of every single scrap of anything in this file, not even checking to see if it looks useful before going to the next page. This is better than trying to find a not-suspicious way to ask for the whole file, even on the very low chance he'd actually let me have it. Because with all due respect to the generations who got through life without modern technology—and we all know my respect is real—I can't keep a big-ass binder in my shorts pocket. Nor can I review its contents till my eyes dry out, under the guise of watching old episodes of *Wild Adventures*, if my mom asks what I'm up to.

"Cammie, you can't . . . He's going to come back and . . ." West sputters, his agitation clear despite his hushed voice.

"If you want to prevent whatever you think that nice old man would do to me, why don't you act as lookout," I say without looking away from my task.

It's not a real suggestion. I half expect him to walk out there and turn me in himself. So it's a confusing but not unpleasant surprise when I glance up and find West standing by the open doorway, pretending to browse the titles on the bookshelf against the wall while also giving himself a view down the hallway.

I look down again immediately, ensuring he won't see the grin that tugs at my lips. For a second, it's like our friendship never missed a beat. Like we've traveled back ten years and a couple continents away, to the time West kept watch at the door to our families' on-site cabin in Peru, while I short-sheeted all the grown-ups' beds. But then I remember all the ways life has changed since then, and the pang of sadness that lands in my chest is so heavy, it nearly steals my breath. That's all the reason I need to shove memories and nostalgia back into the locked closet where they usually stay and focus on the here and now.

I'll have to send Front Desk Lady a grazie card at a later date, because whatever she needed from Dr. Constantini keeps him busy for *juuust* long enough that I finish photographing everything in the binder. I return all items on the desk to where their owner left them and launch myself back toward my chair right as West shouts, "Cam, heads up!"

I freeze, mid-sit, my gaze darting to his frantic expression.

"I mean, er, check out this book I found." He pulls a random volume off the shelf and holds it up toward me while I plop gracelessly into the chair. At my look of *what the hell was that?*, he shrugs and his eyes widen, all *I'm doing my best, okay?*

"Ach so!" Dr. Constantini bellows on his way back into the office, rosy-cheeked and smiley and oblivious to anything amiss. "Sprechen Sie deutsch, Herr Jacobs?"

He nods to the book West grabbed, which I only then register is a German-language copy of *Manifest der Kommunistischen Partei*. My palm covers my eyes before I can stop it, so I try to play it off like I'm scratching an itch.

"Oh . . . oh, no," West stammers. "Or, uh . . . nyet?"

"Point made, since that's Russian," I say.

"But I'm interested in learning it. German, I mean, not Communism." He's wincing before the abysmal attempt at a lie is even out. Fortunately, Constantini is distracted with moving back to his side of the desk and beginning to tidy it.

"I do not suggest you start with Marx and Engels—maybe instead one of the phone applications? I hear they are quite good, from my young friends who study languages." He tears the top sheet off his notepad and looks up at us once more as he holds it out. "But please, take the book for when you are ready for it—I have many other copies. And for you, Signorina Lovett, the names of some old friends of your mamma. I am sorry to have to cut our time short, but other business has demanded my attention this morning. I hope these are still of some help."

"Oh, you've been a huge help," I assure him as I take the list, mentally adding, *More than you know.* "Thank you so much again for your time, and hopefully we'll see you at the party, right? I'll send you the details, if you want to give me your email address."

After heartfelt goodbyes—full hugs to go with our air kisses—and promises to meet again soon, Dr. Constantini sends West and me on our way. I'm practically skipping with delight as we leave the office corridor and reenter the public side of the museum, with a short list of half a dozen names folded up in one pocket and a whole virtual catalog of potential clues in the other.

Later, when I'm alone with my computer, I plan to scour every picture I took and hopefully assemble a vast collection of possible leads to look deeper into. But I have too much energy and optimism buzzing through my veins to not give myself a sneak peek.

I make a beeline toward the first bench I spot, swinging my backpack onto my lap and extracting the small notebook where I've been keeping all my information. I turn to the page where I've listed every pair of initials that gets a mention in Alex's journal. Pulling my knees up toward my chest in a casual way of hiding my work from West's prying eyes, I unfold the paper Dr. Constantini gave me and flatten it against the notebook page so the two lists are side by side.

Carefully, methodically, I run my finger down each line, my eyes darting back and forth to cross-reference the data sets. I don't look at West when he sits next to me, but I feel his stare burning holes in the side of my face.

"What are you—" he starts, but I cut him off with a *shhh* before my focus can be broken.

"I'm putting the names in my notebook in case I lose this paper," I lie easily.

I'm not sure if he believes that answer, but his only response is a weary sigh as he turns to rest against the wall at our backs. I know I still have his attention, though, so I smother the gasp that wants to escape when I spot a match.

Hands shaking, I circle the initials on Mom's side—P.B.—followed by a name from Dr. Constantini's—Paolo Bianchi.

We've got ourselves a lead.

CHAPTER SIX

West

I KNEW I SHOULD HAVE STAYED IN MY ROOM THIS MORNING. I DIDN'T SLEEP well after the drama at dinner, and I had this feeling when I woke up, like from the moment I got out of bed and agreed to face the day, I was about to walk into a bigger mess.

I should have listened to that feeling. I shouldn't have gone down to breakfast out of some sense of obligation to hang out with Dad before his workday got started. Definitely shouldn't have let that same impulse take me down to the dig site, just because he was excited to show me around. That's where the trouble found me.

The trouble, in this case, being Camilla Lovett. I wasn't lying when I said that if anything happened to her, I wouldn't be able to forgive myself. That's a fun little game my anxious brain has liked to play for as long as I can remember, though it got much worse in my early teens. It pretends that I have some nonexistent power to help friends or family members or—I don't know, whatever Cammie and I are to each other now. To protect them from any and all bad things that could happen. Then once I'm out in the world, getting into some less-than-comfortable situations to try to help, I'm too anxious to do anything but shake and sweat and spiral internally.

The past few years in therapy, I've worked through my tendency to catastrophize. I can recognize the signs and usually talk myself down before I let the fears consume me. And at home or at school, in the quiet, secure corners of the world I've settled into, I don't really get into anxiety-inducing situations. I think I'd convinced myself that my capacity for leaving my comfort zone, for having new, exciting experiences, was like a battery. And that all these years of keeping my life so contained and controlled were charging the battery up for a future when I'd put myself back out there.

Now that I'm taking a few careful steps toward that future, I'm beginning to wonder if my adventure battery just corroded from disuse.

The internal doom spiral started up around the same time we boarded the train, especially once I realized we weren't going to Pompeii. If anything happened to Cammie and me, how long would it take for our parents to find out? The carriage was too hot. There were too many people crowded in around me. It's not like any one of them seemed especially threatening, but being in crowds in big cities and unknown places, my unease is instant and inescapable. I'm constantly waiting for some Big Bad to occur.

A part of me is almost grateful for Cammie's antics, as they've been a good distraction from my own mind. I felt better while we were in the museum, not just because there was cool stuff to see—it was also less crowded than out on the street or on the train. I was able to breathe more easily, felt the security of the familiar, calming environment of the exhibits and galleries. Dr. Constantini had been impossible not to like.

But then she went all Mission Possible But Still Inadvisable, digging through the professor's stuff without permission and giving me no choice but to be her accomplice, when she won't even tell me what she's up to.

Now we're back out in the city and my discomfort is ramping up. I've been very patient, all things considered. I lick around the entirety of my cone of pistachio gelato, doing whatever I can to try to salvage my semiclean hands. It's so hot outside that this gelato-eating experience is much more about drip management than enjoyment. A race against time and the sun itself to try to finish our desserts before they melt entirely.

The sun is usually winning.

So we haven't done a whole lot of talking since Cammie and I got our frozen treats from a vendor in a piazza near the Museo Archeologico. Aside from my unease with our environment, I feel this massive cloud of all those unspoken things looming over us. Cammie doesn't seem bothered, however. In fact, she's giddier than I've seen her so far. An extra bounce in her stride ever since we left Dr. Constantini's office, but especially after that break to—very suspiciously—"write the names down" in her little mystery notebook.

I've seen the wheels turning in her head, can tell she's off somewhere far from here mentally. Far from me and my desire to understand what's going on, to know anything about her life and her secrets in the present day. When I take the last bite of my gelato cone and see her do the same with her strawberry version, I decide to revisit the issue.

"So . . ." I begin cautiously. "Your big secret is that you're, what, planning to surprise your mom with some old friends she isn't expecting at the anniversary party?"

Cammie blinks and turns my way, looking disoriented, as if she's seeing me for the first time—wondering how I got here, sitting across from her at a sun-drenched bistro table in the middle of Naples.

"What?" she asks.

"The reason you snuck off to Naples but told your mom you were going to Pompeii, and pried into Dr. Constantini's old files behind his back—all of it is to create a bonus guest list?"

"Oh," she says, and it sounds like *I didn't think I had to spell this out for you*. She shakes her head. "Right, yeah. That's the plan. So if you could try to keep it to yourself, I'd appreciate it."

Where there used to be the sweet aroma of freshly made waffle cones, I now smell only bullshit. I narrow my eyes at the enigmatic girl across from me while she pretends to be laser-focused on folding her cone's wrapper into a paper football.

"I'm not buying it," I state plainly.

"Hmm?" Cammie asks with faux innocence.

"There's something else going on here. You wouldn't give up the truth so easily if that's all there was to it."

Cammie flicks her tiny projectile and it pings off my chest. She snickers, then folds her arms across her torso and meets my gaze with an unimpressed smirk. "You sound paranoid."

Despite this attempt at bravado, her cheeks get pinker and pinker under her freckles. I'm momentarily sidetracked wondering if she has sunscreen she can reapply, if I should suggest it or if she would snap something at me about thinking I'm her dermatologist. Might be worth it anyway.

"Maybe, but I think I'm right." I shrug, matching her defensive posture even though for me, it's more of an effort to hide the growing pit stains on my shirt. "There's also the whole undercover agent act when Constantini left his office—why did you need copies of everything in that file? Did you not trust he'd give you enough names or something? I haven't figured out what that was about, but I think you're looking for more than just a list of people Dr. Alex hung out with twenty years ago."

Her whole body goes rigid, and I know I've hit on something in the neighborhood of the truth. But then her expression hardens and she leans forward, elbows on the table.

"Why do you act like you know anything about me anymore?" she demands. "Even if I was up to something more, it'd be none of your business, Weston. Why would I tell you any of the alleged secrets I have when we're not even friends?"

Before I can think better of it, I blurt out, "Yeah, so you keep telling me. I know good and well we're not friends—you're the one who decided that, and I've spent three years respecting your choice, even though it's sucked every single day."

For a moment, Cammie appears stunned speechless. Her

strawberry-red lips part, her blue eyes wide and unblinking as they study my face, like there's some hidden meaning behind my words written there.

What do I even have to gain from being this honest with her? Most likely, she's not going to suddenly view everything that happened with us in a different light, so I've just made myself look sad and weak for no reason. But what else is new?

Cammie blinks rapidly and gives her head a shake, as if coming back to herself. Then, just as quickly, she stands and starts walking away. My heart rate picks up, my feet moving before I've consciously decided to follow her. I don't particularly want to go on a wild ex-best-friend chase around the city, but she might not give me a choice.

"I can't do this right now," she mutters, barely loud enough for me to hear over her shoulder. Frustration replaces some of my nerves.

"Can't do what, talk to me?"

"Yeah, West. It's just, like, not the time. I have other things to focus on."

"I know, I know, big party plans," I lob back sarcastically. "Doesn't it feel a little ironic, dredging up all these characters from twenty years ago, while you act like our three years of distance after one stupid fight are too much to ever come back from? Blasts from the past are super fun, as long as they're not your own."

Cammie groans. We've reached an intersection of two busy pedestrian streets and she looks both ways before turning right, seemingly at random.

"It's called boundaries, West," she retorts. "I'm allowed to make them and allowed to enforce them, especially when the last time I let someone in, he"—she stabs a finger in the air to count off my offenses—"kissed me, broke my heart, then disappeared from my life, like I'd never meant anything to him."

My gaze narrows in on her red hair, woven into a braid that hangs over one shoulder and sways with each step she takes. On her eyes, blazing blue fire under a sheen of wetness she's trying to blink away. This is the closest we've come to actually confronting what happened between us a few years ago, and I don't want to waste the chance to address it. But I also feel like my head is spinning as I try to process her take on everything, how it aligns—or doesn't—with my own.

"Cam, you told me not to—"

"Can we just . . . just not, right now?" she cuts me off, rubbing a hand over her furrowed brow in what looks like both anguish and exhaustion. "There's no reason for us to go through all this again. No need to force some beautiful reconciliation, when we can get through one summer, then return to our own lives, which were proceeding just fine without each other."

She picks up her pace, so I can't gauge from her expression how much she believes those words. But they hurt just the same.

All at once, I feel the anxieties of the day boiling over, breath harder to force into and out of my lungs. The sounds of the city press in, cars honking, engines revving, voices and people everywhere, an indistinguishable mass of life and activity and heat and smells, and the sun beating down relentlessly. It's too much. I want to be able to catch up to Cammie, offer a coherent reply, keep pursuing a way to sort all of this out. But I can't do it. All I can manage is a shake of my head that she won't even see with her back to me, half a block ahead. Then, for the first time all day, I turn and walk away from her.

CHAPTER SEVEN

Cammie

I NEVER THOUGHT THERE'D COME A DAY WHEN I WOULD RATHER BE INdoors on my computer than outside in the trenches of a dig site, but life is full of surprises.

"Camilla," Ilaria calls out in her annoyingly lovely accent. "Could you brush a little more dirt on yourself? One cheek, maybe. Like this young woman over here, see?"

My gaze follows where she's pointing and I find the young woman in question looking less than enthused about being my example for "aesthetically pleasing dirty person." But she turns her head and resumes what she was doing—a.k.a. actual field work as a real participant in the field school. Not just walking in circles around the villa, running a hand over a wall here, a doorway there, looking pensive and wistful. Like I've been conscripted to do, with those exact adjectives, for what Ilaria calls "B-roll" of la Bambina immersing herself in the place that made her . . . or something similarly woo-woo and contrived. This other girl is absolutely judging me, and she has every right. I'd be judging me, too.

Everything about my being here feels fake. Every silly direction I follow from Ilaria or others on her crew chafes at me. I didn't expect to feel so unenthused about my small part in this film. It's like I'm in a simulation of the summer I'd wanted—on a dig site that's special to me, surrounded by people doing the work I've always aspired to do, but I'm still just the real Dr. Lovett's kid, playing dress-up in Mom's archaeologist clothes.

It definitely doesn't help matters that I'm dealing with an emotional hangover from yesterday. I didn't make it more than a couple blocks before I noticed that West had abandoned me. Some bodyguard he turned out to be. After retracing my steps for a few minutes with no sign of him, I was more concerned that he'd been the one snatched off the sidewalk, and I'd be the one never forgiving myself. Without his number in my phone—thanks to Past Cammie for wiping everything West Jacobs from my digital archives—or any idea of what else to do, I decided to take the train back to Villa Russo and hope he'd already be there. My stomach was in knots the entire way, my braid all disheveled from my nervously messing with it, and it had hit me—was this how it always felt to be West? The possibility was eye-opening.

I'd sweat through every piece of clothing on me by the time I made it back to my floor and speed-walked straight to West's door. Only, as I lifted my fist to knock, I heard his muffled voice on the other side. I nearly collapsed to the floor with relief, and I told myself it was for my own sake, or our parents', now that we both made it back okay and our guardians didn't have to worry, let alone ever learn the truth of what we were up to.

I also told myself it didn't mean anything that even after I returned to my room, assured of West's safety, I spent a good half hour reclining against our shared wall, listening to the muted sound of his voice. I couldn't pick out specific words, but it had the cadence of a phone conversation, long pauses between each time he spoke. To whom, I'd probably never know. It would've come up by now if West had a girlfriend back home, wouldn't it? Not that I cared.

And it isn't like I spent the rest of my day eavesdropping. I had more important work to do as Detective Cammie Lovett with my partner, Deputy Google. Turns out, Paolo Bianchi is not an uncommon name in Italy. Not quite a John Smith, but might as well be, for the overwhelming amount of results I got upon my first basic search. I was able to narrow the terms until I had only a few Paolo Bianchis left who might be *the* PB—and until my eyes could barely stay open and I had to call it a night.

I'd wanted to get back to it after I enjoyed another breakfast from the Villa Russo buffet. But Ilaria had cornered me, begging for "just half an hour of your time." I should've known that "half an hour" of my time would actually mean more like three hours in stops and starts as the crew tried out different settings and the light changed, like the sun is prone to doing throughout the day. Mom had been pulled into helping with something at the field school, bouncing between some of the different pits where student pairs were assigned to survey, with a secondary camera operator catching it all on film. She seemed happy I was here, even if we weren't together much, her grin brightening every time she caught my eye in passing.

If only things with West were so simple and clear-cut. I'm annoyed that after explaining my boundaries and the reason they exist, I'm somehow left feeling like the bad guy. There'd been a deep, genuine hurt in his eyes when he'd referred to years of struggling without our friendship.

But do I really know what's genuine when it comes to Weston Jacobs? I'd been sure I knew, once upon a time, only to be blindsided and feel like the biggest fool in the end for thinking I understood him so completely. Am I just going to be the fool again if I give him any benefit of the doubt, walk back what I said about us not being friends, and actually open up to the possibility? I don't know if I can take that risk.

"Beautiful, yes." At the sound of Ilaria's voice, my head snaps her way. "That focus is just like your mother's when she's thinking through something complex."

Whatever my face had been doing, it was more of a lack of focus. At least the footage was giving what they wanted.

Finally, she calls cut and releases me from my filming obligations for the rest of the day. The documentary crew and field school crew both break for lunch, with the latter dining alfresco on a premade picnic spread while the former heads inside for salads and sandwiches.

After a large breakfast, I'm not especially hungry yet. In fact, my stomach feels a little unsettled. Completely unrelated, it occurs to me that I haven't seen or heard any evidence of my next-door neighbor since last night. I was sufficiently convinced that he made it back from Naples in one piece, but it wouldn't hurt to lay eyes on him just once, for my own peace of mind.

Back at Villa Russo, I decide the most likely place for West to be is with one of the lunch groups. But when I make a circuit through the dining room, then the terrazzo, I find no sign of him.

I try going back to our hall to check his room. Not willing to let him know he's being hunted if I don't have to, I avoid knocking and instead press my ear to his door. After waiting a couple minutes without the tiniest blip of a sound, I go into my room and try the same thing against our shared wall.

No dice, and I'm beginning to feel like a creep. Not enough to dissuade me from continuing the search, as now it's going to bug me not knowing—where else in this place does West hang out?

With decreasing patience, I return downstairs and start exploring the main house's maze of hallways, peeking into each room with an open door in search of a tall American boy. When I turn one corner, I nearly run straight into someone walking the other way and stumble backward in my hurry to stop myself. Two hands reach out and catch me by the shoulders, their palms cold through the cotton of my shirt, and I look up to find them attached to a face I haven't seen since the Welcome Dinner—Gianmarco Russo, the director of the Villa Russo Research Residency.

I hadn't thought much about the first impression he made,

beyond a generic older white man who seems a little self-important, but that kind of comes with the territory for his demographic. Up close, however, there's something off-putting about him. Dark eyes, maybe a little beady, and sharply fixed on me. His mouth is one of those that naturally turns down at the corners, so he's sort of permanently sneering by default.

As if he's heard my thoughts, a broad smile stretches across his face, splitting his cheeks but not meeting his eyes. I bend my knees a little, which prompts him to remove his icy hands from my shoulders.

"Sorry, sir," I say, because another thing about these types of men is they love to be afforded respect, even if it's not real.

"You seem to be in an awful hurry," he observes, not acknowledging the apology.

"Yes, my mistake. I'm just looking for someone."

"Oh?" He quirks one bushy eyebrow. "Anyone I can help you locate?"

"I don't know if you've met him," I hedge. "His name is Weston Jacobs? He's the son of—"

"Of course I know who Weston Jacobs is," Dr. Russo says a little tightly. "Just like I know you're Camilla Lovett. I was familiar with both your parents when we all first worked here, before I was the director. Didn't Alex and Danny tell you?"

While the smile is still in place, there's something a little peeved in his voice. I try to hide my surprise at this information because no, my mom didn't tell me that she knew anything about this man before he became director of this place.

But I have a hunch he wouldn't want to hear that. I guess

no one wants to hear, "No, actually, you didn't matter enough to be mentioned." So I put on a false smile of my own and nod, ducking my head sheepishly.

"Oh, of course my mom told me. Sorry, still jet-lagged," I answer, all silly-old-me. I can only get away with that excuse for so long; might as well milk it. "But yes, I'm trying to find West. Have you seen him around here?"

Dr. Russo hums and his eyes narrow. It takes a lot for me not to shift my weight from foot to foot or start picking at my cuticles. But I never want people to know when they have me off-balance. Especially not this man.

"I haven't seen him today," he answers, "but you might check the library. I've spotted the young man there once before. Back down this hall and to the left." He gestures the way I came from, down a side hallway I haven't yet checked. I turn as quickly as it feels I can without being rude and start walking away.

"Excellent, thank you!" I call over my shoulder with a jaunty wave. Dr. Russo gives a single nod of acknowledgment, his smile dropping slowly. I feel his eyes on me until I'm around another corner and out of his sight.

When I open the door he described on the left, I almost expect to find myself stumbling into a trap, where I must solve Russo's three riddles before I can find what I seek. But lo and behold, he's actually pointed me to a gorgeous library, at the center of which sits an oblivious West Jacobs. All I see of him is his familiar dark brown bedhead from behind, his face too focused on his computer screen to turn my way.

If all I really wanted was proof of life, I could turn around and waltz back out of here, and West would never even know I'd sought him out. That's what logic tells me to do. Didn't I just declare that trying to repair our friendship is unnecessary?

But some deep-down instinct drives me forward. Plus a little nosiness, as his fingers fly across the keys on his laptop with single-minded focus.

I close the door silently behind me, my steps muffled by the thick-pile rug that covers most of the hardwood floor as I step farther into the room. I'm able to walk all the way up behind him without so much as a flinch from him to indicate he's noticed my presence.

I can see the irony here, that I made up a whole spooky, fictional persona around Gianmarco Russo based on a mildly weird vibe, only to turn around and stalk West like an apex predator in a nature documentary. But I continue tiptoeing closer to my prey, until I'm near enough to see what he's up to.

West's fingers continue their furious typing pace. His screen shows a black background covered in neat, orderly rows of text, numbers and symbols and letters in a rainbow of purple, green, red, yellow, and more. I recognize it as computer code, though I couldn't begin to guess what he's programming. It's clear he's not a novice, as fast as he's cranking out line after line, not stopping to think or hunt and peck for characters like I still occasionally do.

After a couple minutes of this, he finally pauses, one hand moving to the trackpad and navigating to a website already open in a browser window. He slowly scrolls down before stopping at a section under the header "Accepted Student Information." My gaze shifts to the top left corner of the screen, where I find a logo for some university in . . . Germany?

Then my attention is recaptured by West's hands. He lifts them from the laptop while he presumably reads the words on-screen, then laces his fingers together to flex them outward. His joints snap, crackle, and pop like a bowl of Rice Krispies before he lets out a sigh and falls back against the leather club chair.

On an impulse I don't think about too hard, I decide this is my best opportunity to pounce.

"Do you think you might have carpal tunnel?"

West nearly sends his computer tumbling to the floor with his full-body convulsion of surprise.

"Jesus, Cam!" he exclaims, slamming the laptop shut and setting it aside before he turns around to lean over the back of the club chair. He pushes a shaky hand through his disheveled hair, then finger-combs it back down again. "I'm more concerned about having a heart attack. You scared the shit out of me."

I shrug, stepping around to take a seat in the club chair opposite him and tucking my legs up underneath me. "Still, those finger joints did not sound okay."

"My fingers are none of your concern," West blusters on. "What are you doing here?"

"I had the same question for you," I say, nodding toward the device he was glued to a moment earlier. "You were pretty consumed with . . . hacking into a German college's computer network? Don't let me stop you."

"I wasn't hacking anything," he grumbles.

"Right," I say with a slow, disbelieving nod. "If you told me about your mission, you'd have to kill me. I get it."

"I feel like if either of us is more likely to kill the other, it's you. Hands down."

My jaw drops with genuine offense, until I see the smile playing at the corners of his mouth. I make a show of flipping my hair behind my shoulder, then holding my hand out to inspect my nails—which I forgot were still caked with dirt. Keeping up the diva act, I reply, "Well, feel free to put in a good word with your employers. Espionage is probably a good fit for a girl without her own personality."

The words are like an anvil hitting the plush carpet underfoot. We're silent for a few moments, until West blows out a breath.

"I didn't mean that, Cammie," he says, voice thick with regret. "I was just . . . embarrassed, and angry, and trying to hurt you for hurting me. But it was out of line, and not something I've ever thought about you. I'm really sorry."

I wasn't trying to squeeze an apology out of him, not knowingly, anyway. But it feels pretty damn good to hear. I try to let the words sink in, to quiet the part of me that believes the worst about myself. At least West doesn't believe that.

His words also remind me that I'm the one who struck first.

"I appreciate that," I begin. "And I'm sorry, too. What I said at dinner was petty, and didn't need to be thrown in your face in front of people we'd just met, who will likely now avoid us both like the plague."

West gives a sad half smile at my joke, then watches me

another moment, face hopeful, or maybe even expectant. He must not have missed the fact that I didn't address whether I meant what I said. Whether I believe he's a guy looking for a friends-with-benefits arrangement.

But I don't acknowledge it, because I don't know what I believe anymore. Instead, I return to my previous question.

"Okay, so really—what were you up to in here?"

He lets his head recline against the back of the chair and his eyes fall closed before he rubs them wearily. Without opening them, he says, "Well, I don't know exactly how long you were lurking behind me, but first, I was working on a programming problem. Casually, just for fun, not hacking into any systems or otherwise up to shady activities. It's what I'm studying, computer science, but it's also a subject where you can teach yourself a lot, if you're interested in it. Which, uh, I am. Then . . ."

West hesitates, blinking his eyes open but keeping them trained on the ceiling. "I was accepted to this research program for the upcoming school year at a university outside Berlin. My spot is reserved but I . . . I'm still deciding whether I'll actually go. I was just checking on the deadline for withdrawing without losing my deposit."

My brows shoot up, not knowing how to respond. A congratulations on his acceptance? An expression of sympathy or something, since he's maybe turning it down? I decide to keep tiptoeing around the subject, see if I can suss out more information.

"So you *did* need that copy of *The Communist Manifesto*

that's still in my backpack upstairs. You're welcome for hauling it all the way home after you ditched me yesterday, by the way."

He gives me a flat look, one brow twitching up as if to say, *You really want to go there?*

I don't, actually, so I steer us back on topic. "That sounds like it'd be a cool opportunity, though. What's keeping you from going?"

One of his shoulders lifts in a shrug. "In a practical sense, nothing. My parents are supportive, it'd be good for my résumé, won't delay graduation or anything. It's . . . well, it's me holding me back, more than anything. I'm not sure if I can handle a year in a foreign country alone. I worry if I try something that huge and out of my element, jump straight into the deep end, my anxiety will get real bad, real fast, knocking me right back to where I was before we moved home to stay."

There's a tightness pulling at my chest, coupled with that sinking feeling in my gut that comes on when I realize I might've horribly misjudged a situation. Right before he moved home to Indiana was . . . I remember West struggling with some stuff toward the end of our friendship. His parents' marriage was on shaky ground, the decision to stop moving the family around so much part of a plan to salvage things. His normal state of cautious worrywart seemed heightened, bit by bit, as we got older, but I'd mainly chalked it up to his family life stressing him out. It didn't change our dynamic, and I was too wrapped up in my growing feelings for him to pay mind to much else. Did my Crush Goggles put a rosy filter over a time that, for West, was actually pretty dark?

"West," I venture slowly into what feels like stormy seas. "What do you mean, 'where you were' back then?"

His gaze, which had gone unfocused, snaps to mine once more. For a second, his expression is blank before he appears to remember himself, remember *our*selves and the shaky ground on which we stand, and it clouds over.

"Cam, once again, *what* are you doing here?" He sounds tired, dejected maybe, more than angry. "What are we doing here? You can't shut me down when I want to talk about our past, tell me you haven't missed our friendship and don't want it back, then seek me out the next day and expect me to tell you shit only my therapist knows. I can't do this whiplash."

And I can't even argue with that. He's right—I'm the human version of that cursed shower upstairs, with my hot-and-cold routine. I know I'm allowed to have a lot of mixed feelings as I figure out how I want to deal with West and all our history. But it isn't fair to expect him to always be here, ready to accept however I feel like treating him at any given hour of the day.

I get to my feet unsteadily. He leans forward with his elbows resting on his knees, head hanging so his eyes don't track my exit from the room.

Just when I make it to the door, I manage to offer to his back, for what little it might be worth, "I'm sorry."

CHAPTER EIGHT

West

WHILE I'D THOUGHT IT WOULD BE EXTREMELY TOUGH TO AVOID CAMMIE AT the villa, I forgot one important detail—she's an outdoor cat.

In the couple of days since she found me in the library, the only brief flashes of red hair I've seen have been out a window, overlooking the terrazzo outside the dining room, or walking down the path that leads to Villa di Bronzo. Only at night, once the sun's down, have I heard signs of life through the thin wall between our rooms.

Admittedly, I'm not in my room much, either. After a half hour of thorough experimentation my first day here, I discovered the Wi-Fi signal is significantly stronger in the library than anywhere else on the Villa Russo property. As if I need any more reason to spend the bulk of my time there, no one else seems to know and/or care that it exists.

It's been ideal for my purposes. My freshman year at Elora

College, a tiny liberal arts school in middle-of-nowhere Wisconsin, my closest friends became a group of guys who had a lot of classes together, all part of the small but mighty computer science and math majors. They got me into this programming challenge called Project Euclid, a website with a bunch of high-level math problems that require you to write code to solve them.

The problems are numbered, so it's like you're moving through the levels of a game. Our group chat has mostly become each person updating the others as they progress through the problems, this informal contest with one another to see who can solve the most the fastest. Sometimes we'll voice chat if someone's stuck and wants to know how another person wrote their code. Other times we'll just hang out and catch up while playing video games, giving our brains a break.

I didn't anticipate how much I'd crave this tether to home, what a comfort it's been as I try to find my footing in a less familiar place, amid a lot of strangers.

The confidence boost from being at least five problems ahead of the other guys doesn't hurt, either.

So we seem to be finding our routines and haunts, Cammie and me, and successfully keeping the two separate. But an unintended side effect of avoiding her is not seeing much of my dad, either. I try to hide my surprise when he points this out at breakfast one morning. I don't think he'd love to hear that the distance between us just feels like business as usual. Since I did come here in part to make up for all that lost time with Dad, I agree to go out to dinner with him on Saturday night.

It's now Saturday afternoon, quickly approaching the time we agreed to meet downstairs, and I'm overdue for a shower if I'm going to look halfway presentable in public. I grab the same small mesh caddy I used for taking my stuff to the communal showers at school, a change of clothes one step up from library loungewear, and my towel, thrown over one shoulder, before heading down the hall.

Only to stop short at the doorway to the tiled room, my path blocked by a small figure. Cammie Lovett, frozen in place, like she has a severe case of showerphobia.

I could still back away—probably should, if I know what's good for both of us.

But I was really counting on this shower.

"Is everything . . . okay?" I try.

Cammie spins on me. "What? Yeah, I'm fine. Lost in thought. Are you . . . Did you need to use one of the showers?"

It's a prime opportunity for a "Nope, I'm auditioning for an indie film about a man who spends a year living in a communal shower—just trying to get in character." But something weird is going on with her, and I don't have time to provoke a pointless fight.

"Yeah. Were you about to . . . ? Or could I . . . ?" I point over her shoulder, assuming that finishing either question is unnecessary. An assumption I rethink when Cammie's head turns to see where I'm pointing.

"Oh, right. No, yeah, I'm—" Her laugh is breathy as she looks back at me with a shake of her head. "I was about to . . . Well, first I went downstairs to use my mom's shower, but she wasn't in her room when I knocked, so I've been weighing whether I'm desperate enough to try with one of these again."

My confusion is getting harder to conceal. "'Try'? Did you not succeed the last time?"

"Depends on your definition of success," she jokes with a grimace. "Why, have you not had trouble? Or have you just not showered yet?"

She takes a half step back with a judgmental scan of my body, like she's just noticed some nonexistent cloud of dirt cloaking me. "Yes, I've taken a shower, damn. But I haven't noticed anything particularly challenging about it."

"Ugh, seriously?" Cammie looks dismayed by the information, but then her eyes brighten like a brilliant idea just hit her. "Can you show me?"

My eyes bulge as I choke out the words, "What, how to shower?"

She waves this away, turning to enter the stall area but still talking like it's a given I'll follow. "No, no, just how to work these showers. I must have done something wrong, right?"

My hand comes up to my hair before I realize I probably shouldn't mess it up any further, as my odds of actually getting to wash it before dinner are dropping. Cam begins arranging her things on the shelf and hooks in the center of the room. She doesn't go so far as to undress yet—small mercies—but gestures toward herself to indicate I should join her. In the showers. *What is happening?*

"It's not that complicated—just turn the handle to start the water, then the hot and cold knobs for temperature."

"Okay, well, there must be some . . . finesse to it that I was lacking, so if you can just show me real quick, I'll leave you alone."

It's apparent that she's stuck on this plan, and I'm as stuck either following through or never getting to shower in peace. Heaving a sigh, I approach the center shelf, stack and hang my belongings accordingly, and enter one of the stalls, still in my sweats and T-shirt. "Stand behind me, I guess, so it doesn't spray you too much."

I reach up to angle the showerhead away from me and feel Cammie's warmth at my back. Forcing very tame thoughts into my head—about calculus, and software, and other stuff far from where I'm standing in a shower with Camilla Lovett—I go through the steps of turning on the water, adjusting the temperature until, testing the stream with my hand, I find it appropriately warm. Then I turn to find Cammie even closer than I imagined she was, looking at me with wide blue eyes like I just solved a Rubik's Cube in record time.

For my own sanity, I step around her, intending to gather my stuff and wait in the hall until she's done in here.

"Well, what the hell happened when I did that? I was in that corner stall right there, and—"

That makes me pause in my retreat. "Wait. The nonfunctioning one?"

When I turn back to her, Cammie points to the stall in question. "Well, yeah, it was shitty, but it functioned enough to wash everything I needed."

With the answers clicking into place, I shake my head. "I

guess no one told you when you moved in—we're not supposed to use that stall. It's got all kinds of issues, apparently, and isn't even supposed to put out water. So maybe you fixed it?"

Cammie scoffs. "I certainly did not! Thanks for the intel, even if it came several days too late. A huge relief, really—any other stall in here is about to feel like a dream." She points to the one still running water. "Are you using this, or can I?"

I shake my head quickly. "Go for it." I weigh my options while she takes her towel from its hook and steps into the shower stall, closing herself in with the curtain.

Then, one by one, articles of clothing are swung over the top of the curtain rod for safekeeping. No part of the girl who was just wearing them is visible, but it still feels like my whole body flushes red as I turn around on instinct.

There is no option. I'll just have to look and smell a little less than my best, and the people in this small Italian village, who I'll likely never see again, can deal.

"West? You still in here?" Cammie calls out.

"Yeah." My voice cracks, because of course it does.

"I thought you were showering."

It takes me a few seconds that sound like hours of silence before I say, "I'm just gonna wait, I think. How long do you think you'll be?"

"It's already so much better than the last time, I might be in here all night," she says dreamily before adding a flatter, "Or roughly twenty minutes."

My jaw drops. *"Twenty?"*

"I don't know if you've noticed this, but I have a lot of hair."

"Oh my—"

"Weston, just start your own damn shower. It's only weird if we make it weird, and I'm not planning to do that. So if you don't either . . ."

I could retort that I don't think we have *planned* any of the numerous points in our relationship where one or both of us "made it weird." But even without my phone or any other clock available, I feel my time running out.

More than that, maybe, I feel the subtle gauntlet she's thrown. The one that says, *I can be a mature adult—so mature as to shower in the same general vicinity as you without losing my shit. Can* you?

My only option has reversed.

"What is there to make weird? I shower with all my former friends."

Cammie's groan is quiet, but not enough to be drowned out by the water. I chuckle to myself while I take my things into a stall I deem a safe distance from hers and pull the curtain closed.

For a couple minutes, it seems like that's the end of it—that we'll each go on about our business with no more interaction. As I've just reminded her, she doesn't want to interact with me anyway.

So I nearly fumble my shampoo bottle when Cammie calls out, "Listen, West . . ."

I go still under the spray of water as it hits the back of my neck and shoulders. When I don't hear anything else, I give the most hesitant "Yeah?" uttered in human history.

She doesn't sound much more self-assured when she finally continues. "I've wanted to talk to you about something, which I guess begins with saying I . . . I want us to talk again in general. Like, to be on speaking terms, because I get the sense there's some stuff we need to talk about at some point. And I know I've given you mixed messages about what I want from you, or for us, but I've decided—final answer—I'm . . . open. To friendship, or trying it, at least. If you're not opposed."

Did she do this on purpose? Lure me in here with the ol' fear-of-showers ploy, then challenge me to not make a Thing out of the objectively weird activity of simultaneous bathing, then wait until I'm as trapped as possible—shampoo-covered head and all—to force a conversation about our friendship?

More likely she's flying by the seat of her pants right now. The pants dangling over the shower curtain a few yards from where I stand.

I finish rinsing the suds from my head before answering. She can afford to sweat just a little.

"I *should* be opposed, given the circumstances under which you've decided to have this chat—"

"Don't you go making it weird, Weston—"

"I think if we surveyed a hundred people, *Family Feud*–style, ninety-nine would agree that *you* are the one responsible for the present weirdness. And the hundredth just misunderstood the question."

"Okay, fine, but are you opposed or not?" Cammie asks, sounding awfully impatient for someone who plans to be showering for at least another ten minutes. "Because there was a part two to what I wanted to discuss. Pending part one going well."

The snap of a bottle cap punctuates her sentence. I turn my water off, cutting the background noise in half, and wrap my towel around my waist before replying at a less shout-y volume. "I don't know if I'd say it's gone well, but—"

"West!"

A smile curves my lips, part amused at myself but a bigger part happy just to be here, smelling Cammie's apple shampoo as it permeates the increasingly steamy air, feeling a semblance of the comfortable dynamic I've missed so much.

"I would love to try friendship again, Cam. Please proceed to Item Two on your shower confrontation agenda."

"I— Okay, great, yes. That's good to hear." I'm certain her face is bright red right now, and it only makes my smile grow while I continue to dry off and get dressed in my dinner clothes. Cammie's next words come out in a rush, like she's exhaling the confession in one go.

"I've been working on something behind my mom's back. Something more than a few surprise party guests."

I pause in the middle of opening my shower curtain. She can't see the flat look I aim in her direction, but I'm sure she hears it in my voice.

"Yeah, no shit." Despite the surface-level sass, I feel a knot of worry somewhere deep in my gut. I wonder if I'm about to wish this revelation had come before I opted in to potential friendship. Still, I soften my tone when I press, "What is it, Cammie?"

I could have been given a hundred guesses, and I seriously

doubt I would have gotten to the truth, which she offers with barely a space for a single breath.

"I'm trying to find my dad."

This time, my shampoo bottle does escape my grasp. I scramble to catch it, the clatter of hollow plastic across tile absurdly loud, and toss it into my shower caddy with its better-behaved friends. Then I stand in astonished silence, wishing there was a simple response to what Cammie just dropped.

"You're . . . What do you mean by 'trying'?" is the best I come up with.

Amid intermittent splatters of water, bottles opening and closing, and a whole fruit salad's worth of soapy aromas wafting out from her stall, she proceeds to tell me about Dr. Alex's journal from her first year in Italy, with all the friendships, flings, relationships, dramas, adventures, and pictures contained within. How she found it, and her list of all the initials of its characters, which she's cross-referencing with the help of Dr. Constantini's list and some other names she's combed from her bootleg version of his files. I have to lean against the tile wall by the doorway, overwhelmed by the whole tale.

"I know it's possible he's not still in this area—I mean, there are a lot of variables here that could be totally off. But I have more to work with now than I ever have, and in a way, I feel like I *need* to know more than I ever have. So . . ." She pauses, letting what sounds like a bucket full of water crash to the tile floor, and it's an effort not to let myself consider what on earth she's doing in there. In the subsequent quiet, her soft voice concludes, "I have to give it a shot."

I'm gritting my teeth against the impulse to declare the whole thing a terrible idea—to encourage her to have an honest conversation with her mother, grown-up to grown-up, and get the answers.

But on the other hand, I'm not Cammie. She and I have always operated differently, and I can't know what it's like to be in her position. I grew up with double the father figures, after all. Dad and Pops had me a few months before Dr. Alex had Cammie, and I was very much planned for. Even though they're separated now and that's all complicated, I've always known I have two parents who wanted me, who love me and are there for me. I can't imagine how it would feel to know one half of the duo who made me fled the scene before my life had even begun.

Still . . . how does this end in any way except with Cammie's heart getting broken?

"I don't know about this one, Cam," I hedge, once again recognizing the strangeness of discussing this while only one of us has clothes on. I try to block that thought out and refocus on the issue at hand. "It sounds like it could be really hard on you, whether you find him or not. And what happens when your mom finds out? Surely you couldn't keep it from her forever, or even if you tried, he might reach out to her. And then—"

"Yeah, I'm not dumb," she shoots back. "I know it could be hard and he still might not want anything to do with me. But I feel like that's not completely his choice anymore." Her words slow, like she's piecing together her thoughts as she vocalizes them over the ongoing flow of water. "Like, I'm an adult now, and just because he doesn't want to know anything about me doesn't mean I don't get to know anything about him, right? How is that fair? Relationships should be a two-way street. And I guess so far, the street hasn't existed at all. But I don't want it to stay this big empty spot in my history and my biology and everything forever. Maybe I'll find out who he is, and it'll be someone *I* want nothing to do with, but at least I'll know. I'll understand this whole half of my background that has always been a question mark. I feel like that understanding will be worth it."

Something about her words starts an itch in the back of my brain. The Cammie I knew before was not someone who felt incomplete. She always seemed to know herself better than anyone I've met, never let on that she felt anything amiss in her life or family makeup. She was confident, self-assured, and, from my perspective, a complete and completely wonderful person. The prospect that something has shaken that sense of self makes me almost sadder than her absence from my life the last few years.

But I suspect she's nearing her vulnerability limit for one talk. Hell, I should be grateful she's even shared this much. I should take this chance for what it is and support her how I can, even if the possible outcomes make me feel the need to double up on virtual therapy this week. That's precisely *why* I should support her, so she's not alone if or when it all blows up. Still, the words stay trapped in my throat, anxiety choking them out.

Especially when she adds, "So anyway, I could use your

help. Mom clearly isn't cool with me gallivanting across Italy by myself, and having you along on my Dad Quest could get her off my back."

"You sure know how to make a guy feel wanted," I mutter.

Finally, the spray of the shower cuts off, and I know for certain I'm keeping Dad waiting. Time to wrap this up, one way or another. On the other side of the curtain, a huffy breath precedes a series of splatters, several more of those small buckets of water spilling onto the floor. Have alternative energy scholars studied the hydroelectric potential of hair like Cammie's, post-wash?

Annoyance colors Cam's voice when she replies, "Well, it's not like you seemed to enjoy yourself last time we went somewhere. You couldn't run away from me fast enough, the first chance you got."

Maybe if I had a few more minutes, I'd tell her what really made me leave her in Naples—open the window to my mental health situation a little wider, in the interest of this renewed friendship thing we're trying. But my feet are restless in these rubber flip-flops, itching to be on the move.

Already backing toward the door, I say, "I think we should keep talking about this later, but my dad is waiting for me downstairs. So . . ."

I hear the tinny sound of the shower curtain being jerked open, but I'm already around the corner, opening the door to the hall.

"So you're running away again?" Cammie calls, and the ratio of real to fake irritation in her voice is unclear.

"Not running away," I say back with purposeful lightness. "Running toward a pizza with my name on it. Later, neighbor."

Italian pizza is, without a doubt, some of the best food I've had anywhere in the world. So it's beyond a shame that I'm barely able to eat half of my margherita pie at dinner, my stomach too unsettled by Cammie Lovett and all the chaos that comes with her to handle any more.

This girl will not ruin pizza for me.

I try to shut out thoughts of her, to enjoy some "quality time" with my dad, who's used the term enough times in reference to this outing that I'm beginning to worry I'll be graded on quality at the end. So far, I think I'm failing.

"Have you thought any more about the program in Germany?" Dad asks, and what do you know? There *is* something that can sour my appetite even further than my recent roller coaster of a conversation with Cammie.

"Oh, uh, yeah. A little," I answer vaguely. Not a complete lie. It was on my mind a lot the day we went into Naples, as I spiraled about my ability to function in the world outside my comfortable bubble. But my thoughts were more of an incoherent "aaaahhhhhhh" than anything productive.

Besides that, my mental space has been occupied either by math or by Cammie. Two areas that share an ability to boggle my mind.

I wish I could talk to my dad about Cammie, could have a

sounding board somewhere outside my head so it's not just me and myself talking in circles. In theory, I could try one of the guys from school. But our group chat, for all the time we (virtually, for the summer) spend together, has never had the vibe of a place to bring your girl problems. Or guy problems, or any form of interpersonal-relationship-related problems. It only occurred to me in the last couple days that I don't know if any of them have significant others—the topic doesn't come up.

Dad and I just aren't on that level. But could we get there? Maybe my possible study abroad plans could be a starting point.

With that in mind, I break the lingering, uncomfortable silence by adding a very delayed, "I'm still not sure if it's the right time for me to do it. I really liked being on campus at Elora this past year and feel like I've got a good thing going there—why upset that?"

Dad nods thoughtfully as he chews another bite of his funghi pizza, then washes it down with a glass of water from the carafe on our table. "I understand the hesitation. I know the past few years have been challenging, and you have seemed to thrive in college, which has been great for both your pops and me to see. But if you think about it—this time last year, didn't you have some of the same reservations around moving away from home, starting your studies, living on campus, all that?"

I pick at my pizza crust like the answer to his question is baked inside. I might have had those feelings, but had I shared them with him? How much do he and Pops still talk about me behind my back? I thought that was one of the benefits offered in the child-of-divorce package—no more interacting between the two people whose every interaction stressed you out.

"Maybe, yeah," I admit.

"I'm not trying to push you any one way; all I want is for you to do what'll make you happiest. Just offering a reminder that you've made scary leaps before and landed somewhere wonderful. I hope you won't let fear keep you from doing it again." He leans back in his seat, his gaze moving from me out to the quiet, small town street, to the view of rolling hills beyond it. "I almost said no to the Villa di Bronzo job the first time—did I ever tell you that?"

I shake my head, both interested in this story and grateful that we're moving away from West's Life Choices. Dad nods, eyes distant as I assume he does some mental time travel.

"It seemed like terrible timing—I mean, it was, and I'm sure Pops would tell this story without my rose-colored glasses." He chuckles, shooting me a wry look. "We were brand-new parents, had just moved apartments. Pops was going to be starting a new job in the fall, and I got this call from a tenacious young woman named Alex, who I barely knew, asking me to come join her team. I was terrified of uprooting our lives for nothing special and almost backed out a dozen times. I wasn't even sure by the time we stepped off the plane in Naples. But, well, we see how that turned out."

He trails off and clears his throat, looking more bashful suddenly as his eyes dart back to me. He takes another sip of water before adding, "It's hard to believe how much of my life was shaped by doing this one thing that scared the hell out of me. Wherever your path takes you, I hope you can look back at my age and be grateful for the times you just went for it, said yes, and figured out the rest later." Meeting my gaze earnestly, he adds, "And I'm very glad you said yes to this summer, son. It may not have been your initial plan, but being back here with you is a dream I didn't know I had. It . . . it means a lot to me."

"I'm glad I'm here, too," I say before I've really thought through the words, but I'm surprised to find they feel true. My stomach finally feels a little more settled, enough that I take a few bites of pizza. They help fortify me to broach a new subject.

"I have a . . . well, kind of random question," I begin.

Dad looks up with open interest. "Okay, shoot."

"Back in your first summer here, what did you—" I cut myself off, trying to figure out how to word the awkward inquiry. "I mean, I know it's when you and Dr. Alex first became close friends. I'm curious what you know, or knew—what she told you about—well, about Cammie's dad."

His brows shoot up, the question clearly catching him off guard. But he doesn't shut down or deflect, which tells me right away he has nothing to hide on the subject. "Honestly, West, I never knew much. Alex and I were close, yes. Her parents were back in the States, so she was sort of adopted into our little family. But when she told me she was pregnant, she just said the father was not going to be involved. Something along the lines of how it wasn't 'meant to be' between the two of them but that she was okay. So I never pushed it."

I consider this. "And it just . . . never came up again?" *Out of all the wine-drunk heart-to-hearts I've overheard while pretending to be asleep?* I add silently.

Dad shakes his head. "From the day Cammie was born, they were their own unit. It never seemed like anything—or anyone—was missing. And to have questioned her about Cammie's father, well, it always seemed like that would have been . . ." His gaze goes distant again as he thinks through his words. "It would have felt like I was questioning Alex's abilities as a parent. I never would have done that to her." He looks back to me quickly. "Not that I think that's what you're doing. But if you don't mind me asking, what brought this up?"

"Oh, I don't know," I say, tilting my head and looking over Dad's shoulder like someone back there might be holding up cue cards. "I guess I've just been thinking a lot since we've been here about what it was like back then. And obviously there's all this talk of the Bambina di Bronzo story . . . for the documentary, and, well, I don't know. It's made me curious."

I manage to veer us toward the topic of the documentary, asking Dad what he thinks of it so far, getting him to talk some shit about John Mark/Gianmarco again as he recounts an argument between him and Ilaria over areas of Villa Russo approved for filming. We're laughing by the time we head back. Under the dark night sky, I feel the lightest I have in days.

My mind keeps returning to Dad's advice about just saying yes. I may not be ready to apply it to the Germany decision yet, but I know where else it'll work. After we say our good-nights and split off toward our respective rooms, I take the stairs to my floor two at a time, then walk down the quiet hallway and knock on the door beside mine.

A few seconds pass before it swings open, revealing Cammie in a baggy T-shirt and pajama shorts that barely qualify as shorts and make it difficult to keep my eyes on her freckled face. The surprise that paints her features is quickly replaced by skepticism, and her arms cross over her chest.

"Can I help you?" she asks dryly. Her hardened facade shouldn't bring a smile to my face, but for some sick reason, it does.

I'm so screwed.

"I don't know," I say with faux nonchalance, "but I think I can help you."

CHAPTER NINE

Cammie

THE GOOD NEWS IS THAT WEST IS ABLE TO NARROW DOWN MY PAOLO Bianchi list until we find, with roughly 97 percent certainty, *the* Paolo Bianchi.

The bad news is it proceeds to rain for several days straight.

The first day, I don't think much of the steady drizzle. Mom and Dr. Danny accompany the film crew on excursions into Naples, where they do some filming with the bronze statues and other artifacts that are kept in permanent collections at the National Archaeological Museum. West and I are left to our own devices, free to shut ourselves in the library and pore over everything in Mom's journal that has to do with "PB." West scans one of the Polaroids in which PB's face is more clearly visible into his computer. He does some weird age-up program-y thing on it, and then some reverse image search-y thing, and before I can say "Are you sure you don't work for the CIA?"—voilà!—he has located one Paolo Bianchi (Middle-Aged Version).

Potential Papa Paolo, conveniently for our purposes, is a boat captain, leading small group tours from the town of Sorrento to the island of Capri. I immediately book two spots on one for the following day.

That's when the rain gets less cute.

I still try to hang in the library with West. When it's obvious that I'm mostly just annoying him with my loud groans and whines about the weather while he ignores me and does his little computer-y thing, I return to my room. I continue to study the journal, making a sort of profile of PB as I prepare to meet him. It looks like he and my mom only went on a few dates, as he appears in just a few entries. Maybe that makes him a more likely dad candidate? If things between them weren't that deep, and he didn't feel very attached to Mom, it would make more sense he wouldn't want to stick around and raise a kid together.

Other than that, I know she met him at a bar near the university in Naples; that he was also in the social sciences, though on the cultural anthropology side; that one of their dates was a sail on his dad's boat, which Paolo borrowed without his dad's permission; and that he was an "amaaazing" kisser, though I'd rather not think much about that. Past Alex was discreet about the physical aspects of her relationships with these men, at least in writing. While it would be more helpful for my search if she had made a list titled "People I've Slept With," I appreciate, for the sake of ever being able to look at her the same, that she kept it vague.

Each day the rain persists, I get an email from Paolo Bianchi's tour company, apologizing for the postponement of yet another tour and giving us a complimentary rebooking. Each day, I rebook for the following morning. Finally, three mornings later, the clouds part, the sun reemerges, and West and I get on a train to Sorrento.

This time, we don't even have to lie to our parents about where we're going. I tell my mom that I'm excited to see the island of Capri—true enough—and that West has graciously agreed to go with me, easing her concerns over my safety before they can even develop. She does make a raised-brow sort of comment about "all this time I'm spending with Weston," looking at me expectantly. But I feign obliviousness, explaining that I'm not exactly surrounded by potential travel buddies here.

On this train ride, West and I try something new for us—sitting across from each other. As I'm reminding him of the day's itinerary, he makes a shushing noise, and I look up to find him peering around us.

"Do you want us to be followed or something?" he asks in a whispered rush. "You never announce your specific travel plans loudly on public transit when you're clearly a tourist speaking a different language. You might as well be calling out, 'Follow me! Pickpocket me! Kidnap me and hold me for ransom!'"

I groan. "Oh God, you've seen the *Taken* movies, too."

"The what?" West asks.

"Never mind."

"I don't know what movies you're talking about, but I do know basic travel safety," he scolds. "I thought you did, too, growing up the way we did."

"If 'basic travel safety' means engaging with the world like a paranoid weirdo, I think I'll continue living on the edge, thanks."

West rolls his eyes. Still, I end my verbal explanation of our day's itinerary, and we continue on in relative silence until we reach our station in Sorrento. While I'm distracted trying to follow street signs and the map preloaded onto my phone to get to the marina, cross-referencing with the email instructions from Paolo's tour company, West seems to have jumped ahead to the next step.

"Cam, hang on," he says, startling me when he grabs my elbow and pulls me to the edge of the sidewalk.

I look up from my phone in confusion. "What is it? We're gonna be late."

"How are we, like, playing this? What do you want me to do when we get there? I feel like we haven't really talked about the specifics of how we're handling the meeting, what you're trying to ask and get out of it, and I just . . . What am I supposed to do?"

I pull my arm gently away from where he's still grasping my wrist, which, by the look on his face, he hadn't realized he was doing. I put a hand out in reassurance.

"Hey, it's fine. We're just trying to meet Paolo, see what he's like, suss out anything about his past with my mom or in general, if we can. I don't know, just follow my lead."

The truth I haven't told him is that I've thought very little about what I'm going to say to Paolo Bianchi other than "Did you sleep with Alexandra Lovett twenty years ago and then dip out when you learned she was pregnant with your child?" It's probably best that he doesn't even realize who I am, in case he kicks us off the boat before we've gotten a chance to say so much as a "buongiorno." I think the best way to increase my odds of acting natural during this encounter is to not overthink it or overplan it.

I'd somehow forgotten that overthinking and overplanning are beloved pastimes for my partner in subterfuge. West was always the more careful of the two of us, and that's one part of him that intensified sometime around our early teens. He was less open to ideas I had on the fly, and I learned to give him at least a few hours' notice before doing something that wasn't on his mental agenda. Or after a big group dinner with our parents' field school students, he would need me to reassure him over and over that one throwaway comment he'd made was not an extreme embarrassment, nor did it make all the cool college students think he was an annoying, immature kid.

I was going through my own awkward adolescent phase and at the time thought that was just West's version of the same. I'm not so sure of that now, with a few years of hindsight and rediscovering this older, more self-aware West, hearing him allude to how bad his anxiety was "before." The ways he changed back then had felt different, I can see in retrospect. It hadn't just been the stress of his dads' struggling marriage taking a toll; I think he'd been in a whole other spiral of his own.

I feel the desire to pry open that box of things we don't talk about, poking me to ask West about what he was going through back then, make him continue what he started to tell me in the library a few days ago. But this isn't the time, so I set that impulse aside.

"Come on, we've got to get going," I say to West. I reach out without really thinking to give him a pat on the shoulder. He rears back like I punched him. *Oooookay. Physical touch, not a level we're at just yet,* I note with the smallest pang of disappointment, deep down in my heart's hidden compartments.

Most of the town of Sorrento sits high atop steep cliffs that overlook the ocean and marina below. After all the rain, we've been gifted the perfect day for outdoor adventures—sunny, but a little cooler than I've gotten used to here. It's even nicer as I start to feel the sea breeze coming off the crystalline waters, blowing through the couple of rogue curls that have already escaped from the bun atop my head.

The wind has its way with West's hair, too. As he keeps a brisk pace ahead of me, the longer brown waves on top of his head get the Troll doll treatment, swept straight into the air in a gravity-defying pouf. He remains oblivious, but I can't contain my smile.

In fact, as we meander down a steep, sloped walkway, turning back and forth on the many switchbacks where I should probably watch my step, I find it hard to watch anything but the guy before me. Even if the new hairdo is giving *just stuck his finger in a light socket,* and he's wearing swim trunks printed with a bunch of zeroes and ones that I refuse to ask the meaning of, there's something so . . . compelling about West. I don't know if it's his perfectly straight posture that's also somehow totally natural, or his long legs with calves rock-solid enough to crack a walnut, or his hands that, for some bizarre reason, I keep picturing when I'm trying to fall asleep at night, the mesmerizing memory of them fluttering across his keyboard.

Okay, I do know, and it's all of those things and more.

I'm thankfully pulled from the WestFest party my greedy eyes have been throwing when we reach sea level and enter the marina. West steps aside to let me retake the lead, and we bypass row upon row of all sorts of watercraft, from Jet Skis to luxury yachts. Finally, I see the Bianchi Voyages flag hanging from a post at the end of a dock, a boat that looks just like the one on the website tethered there and a few people milling around it.

I'm suddenly extra grateful that West agreed to this, so I don't have to go it alone. Even if he has worries or reservations, he hasn't backed out, and his presence still gives me a confidence boost that I didn't know was missing the last few years. I probably shouldn't let myself get used to it, but I can enjoy it while it's here.

As I start down the dock, his soft footsteps are a comforting echo behind my own. Beside the tour boat, a young woman greets us and confirms which tour we're on before gesturing us into a small, shed-like structure on the opposite side of the dock where we'll soon get more instructions and watch a safety video.

Inside, there are several plastic chairs set up, two already filled by an older couple with a distinctly American vibe about them—matching visors on their heads and matching fanny packs cinched around the waistbands of matching jean shorts. I smile as West and I take the seats behind theirs.

I lean his way, careful not to brush any part of me against any part of him, lest he accidentally bust a hole through the side wall of this seemingly flimsy structure in an attempt to get away from me.

"Safety video," I whisper. "Now they're speaking your language, huh? Should we make some popcorn?"

West is unamused. "You should probably pay close attention to it," he murmurs back, "because if we start sinking or hit an iceberg or whatever, I don't think I'm helping you." I struggle to stifle my laughter until he says, "Also, Camilla Jacobs? Are we a married couple now?"

I'd hoped he hadn't heard me give that name to the check-in lady, but of course I'm not that lucky. My cheeks go pink, and I do an awkward throat-clearing-slash-cough combination. The shoulders of the older woman in front of me tense, probably thinking I'm patient zero with some disease we're all about to catch on this all-day tour.

"No, I just didn't want my name to be, like, a tip-off before we even got here. We can trade last names if you want, and you can be West Lovett. Or for all they know, we're brother and sister."

I hear myself overexplaining but can't seem to stop. West's eyes dart away and I see his face flush a little, too. The words *brother and sister* must sound as wrong to him as they feel coming out of my mouth.

The last two members of our group arrive and spare me from saying anything else to somehow make the vibe even weirder. The woman who checked us in enters and begins giving an introduction about the tour company, which unfortunately includes nothing about the boat captain's sordid past with an abandoned love child. We watch a brief video, full of helpful reminders like "Don't take off your life jacket while the boat is cruising just because you want an even tan" and "Don't lean over the side of the boat to try to touch the water."

Then, with no lead-up or fanfare, a man wearing a white short-sleeve button-down and khaki shorts enters, and my heart starts beating triple time as Clipboard Lady and I say in unison, *"Paolo Bianchi."*

Luckily, her announcement of his name after the word *captain* is loud enough to drown out my awestruck whisper. Neither it nor my gaping mouth or rapid pulse has to do with Paolo Bianchi's attractiveness, though he's not bad for someone who could—in the most literal sense possible—be my dad. No, my shock is because this present-day man is so clearly the same person from those twenty-year-old Polaroids. It's like I wasn't fully convinced until this moment, despite West's clever computer tricks and discovery of a few more recent pictures of the captain online. His in-person smiling face is undoubtedly the same smile that was aimed at a young Alex Lovett against a backdrop of the sparkling Mediterranean.

I'm pulled out of my trance by West's voice unexpectedly piping up beside me. "Uh, yeah, I'm West Jacobs, and this is my . . . cousin, Camilla. Cammie," he says, and hopefully no one else noticed the awkwardly long pause before the word *cousin*.

If they did, their faces show no sign of it, the older couple smiling at us, and the newest arrivals, an old man and much younger woman, looking politely interested.

The first couple introduce themselves next as Graham and Marge, two retirees from Michigan. They're on a trip around Italy to celebrate Marge's recent recovery from a hip replacement. Then the last pair go, and I'm stunned to learn that while I would have guessed they were grandfather and granddaughter, they are in fact honeymooners—Victor and McKinsley from Toronto.

"Close your mouth," West murmurs out of one corner of his lips, and it is literally the only circumstance under which I can imagine being grateful for that reprimand.

Finally, it's time to board. Clipboard Lady and Paolo lead us over to the life jackets hanging along one wall and help us each find the right size; then we follow Paolo out to the boat, which sits a little below the level of the dock. We're instructed to step into the area behind the captain's seat, where there's some padded bench seating for guests and a door that leads down to a galley. The front of the boat is a flat expanse of polished wooden planks that look ideal for lying down and sunbathing.

I couldn't be more excited as we all step aboard and settle into our seats. Victor and McKinsley are on the back bench facing forward, Graham and Marge on the far side chatting with them, which leaves the bench behind Paolo to West and me, just as I hoped would happen. As Paolo takes the helm and starts up the boat's engines, Clipboard Lady—now sans clipboard—swiftly and mesmerizingly unwinds the ropes tying the vessel to the dock. Once it's free, Paolo gives her a jaunty wave and steers us out into the open water. We stay at a low idling speed while we meander out of the marina, and Paolo informs us that there are cold beverages and snacks down in the galley whenever we want them, as well as a small bathroom.

I'm working up to starting a conversation with him, opening with some dazzling subject like, I don't know, what kind of boat this is. But the words on the tip of my tongue die when we leave the no-wake zone. Paolo revs the engine and its rumble gets ten times louder while we pick up speed.

Graham and Victor shout back and forth to be heard while they discuss their own experiences with boats like this one, as coincidentally, they've both spent a lot of time on the Great Lakes. The bits of mind-numbing boat conversation I overhear remind me how few shits I give about boats. I scan my brain for a new entry point.

When I've thought of it, I use my loudest outside voice to begin, "So, Paolo . . ."

His shoulders jump and he turns to look at me over one. "Sì, is everything okay, Ms. Jacobs?"

"Oh yeah, I'm good!" I aim to sound as breezy as one can while yelling at the top of one's lungs. To make conversation even more difficult, he has to keep his gaze mainly on the water ahead of us. Less than ideal, but I guess I appreciate his commitment to keeping us alive.

"I was just wondering," I press on, "are you from around here?"

If Paolo agrees that this is a strange time to have a conversation with one of his passengers, he doesn't show it. His eyes stay fixed ahead with his face turned just enough that his words carry back to me. "Yes, I grew up in Naples, actually. My family has boats there as well—it's where the business started. I opened the Sorrento operations, ohhh, ten or so years ago, but I still commute from the big city."

So far this aligns with what I expected. "Did you always want to be a boat captain?" I ask. "To join the family business?"

His head tips to one side as he considers. "As far back as I can remember, yes. My nonno—my grandfather—was a fisherman before he started the tour business. My father began working there as soon as he was old enough and still does to this day, though we all wish he would retire." I see the edge of his rueful smile. "There was a time when I felt this pressure, seeing all my peers go off to university, and I tried to give that a go myself. But it didn't take long for me to realize I wasn't meant for the classroom. Being on the water—it's in my blood, I think."

I peer around the boat as he speaks, realizing for the first time that it's actually quite beautiful. It has a caramel-colored wooden deck, seats and steering wheel in a soft ivory material that looks a lot like leather but I imagine is something more waterproof, and shiny gold metallic railings and cleats along the perimeter. Then I look farther, to the sea all around us, which has somehow become an even more vibrant aqua since we left the marina.

Could I have all of this in my blood, too? The Bianchis' seafarer DNA in my very makeup? The thought sends a shiver down my spine. Not exactly a feeling of clarity, of *yes, this is right,* but a sense of wonder at the *what if* of it all.

I hurry to slide in my next question before the moment has passed, not letting myself get lost in my own wondering.

"So, what about the next generation of Bianchis?" I begin. "Do you have kids who you expect to join you in this business?"

Paolo doesn't turn his face toward me this time, though his hand comes up to scratch the back of his neck. Is that a nervous response?

"No, I don't," he says, voice a little stilted for the first time. "We'll see what my nieces and nephews choose for themselves when they're older. But none of my own, no."

I try to read his tone, though it's hard with the wind whipping around us, the continued roar of the engines, and the lack of any clue what his face is doing. Is there sadness there? Contentment? Or maybe regret, like he'd had the opportunity to have a family but missed it?

What would he think if he found out that he might not have missed it after all?

"No wife, then, or husband? No . . . romantic partner?"

I promptly feel a pinch on my thigh, causing me to let out a quiet yelp that no one seems to hear except the pincher in question. West leans in until I can feel his breath on my neck, and I will not be examining why that sends a shiver rolling through me.

"Now you sound like you're trying to hit on him," he whispers sharply. "Dial back the twenty questions."

In retaliation for the stinging spot on my leg, I reach up and flick him on the nose. I don't care if he is kind of right.

Oblivious to all of this, Paolo glances my way again, letting out a soft laugh as his brow furrows and he gets what might be his first real look at me since we were on land.

"You're very curious, aren't you?" he says with clear skepticism.

I hold up my hands, leaning back into the seat and rushing to say, "Sorry—my cousin always gets on me about being too nosy with people I've just met. Bad habit."

Some of the tension in Paolo's face eases, his friendly smile taking over. "I understand," he says. "I have a bit of that in me, too. Getting to meet new people all day, every day, from all walks of life—it's sort of an occupational hazard. My father and grandfather are the same." He clears his throat before adding, "But no, no partner. I don't think settling down is in the cards for me."

He turns back around, then seems to think of one more thing. "And hey, stay curious, kid. It's a good quality to have."

Normally, I'd bristle at an older man calling me *kid*; I'm hyperaware of looking young and feel like I always have to defend my (Basically) Real Adult status. But something about it works for Paolo. Or maybe I'm just already projecting my fatherly hopes and dreams onto him.

For a while longer, he drives in silence. I turn to West and keep my voice low even though it's doubtful Paolo could hear me if he tried. "Do you think there's any way the sea is in my blood, too? Like, have there been any signs I've missed?"

West grimaces. "How honest do you want me to be?"

I deflate before he's even shared said honesty. "Well, now you have to say it."

His eyes are preemptively apologetic. "My first thought was about the time our parents took us to Disneyland at the end of the summer before fifth grade, and we went on those *Finding Nemo* submarines, and you cried."

"Okay, first of all," I say, thrusting a finger into the air near his face, "I was, like, nine."

"And it was a fake submarine submerged in a pool at the Happiest Place on Earth. 'The sea' does not get more kid-friendly," West counters. "Besides that, haven't you always called the ocean 'suspicious'?"

"I just find it . . . concerning that there's so much happening down there, more than humans even know about," I say, my voice rising. "What are they hiding?"

West rolls his lips between his teeth, but one chuckle still slips out. "Who are 'they'? Aquaman and the Little Mermaid?"

"Maybe! I'd feel better if someone was running things down in the deep dark unknown," I argue, crossing my arms over my chest. "Also, why does it take up way more of the Earth than land does? Like, *tsunamis*? Hello! They're the ocean reminding us who's got all the power."

West clasps his hands in his lap. "Have you answered your own question yet?"

I roll my eyes. "*Nooo.* I can still enjoy water from somewhere I can see the bottom, or safely floating on the surface in a lovely maritime vessel such as this."

"I have bad news for you about the safety of this lovely maritime vessel in a tsunami."

"They don't get those on the Med," I say confidently. "Or on enclosed theme park waters, which I'm sure I could handle now that I'm older and wiser."

"Yeah, I believe in you," West agrees with a smile that I return reflexively.

Marge's gasp pulls our attention her way, and only then do I notice how close we've come to our island destination.

"Graham, look," she says in wonder, one hand to her floral blouse–covered chest. I turn in the direction she's pointing and see we're nearing a craggy white cliff face with a few boats clustered around it.

"Sì," Paolo says, "we are approaching the white grotto—Grotta Bianca. If everyone will stay seated, I promise I will get us even closer."

The instruction was mostly directed at Marge and McKinsley, who had begun to move around to take pictures, sending the boat listing back and forth. True to his word, Paolo does take us very close to the cliffs, where we join a mix of what look like other tour groups as well as some personal watercraft hanging out around the grotto.

Paolo doesn't drop anchor, just lets us bob there in the gentle waves as he tells us a bit about the grotto, how the color comes from the sunlight reflecting off the bottom of the sea onto the deposits of minerals on something-something—admittedly, he loses me as I join the rest of my fellow passengers in snapping a bunch of pictures of the incredible view.

Everyone except West, that is, who's gripping the railing behind our seats like it's his sole tether to this mortal coil.

"Are you gonna come see it?" I turn to ask him.

"I'm good right here," he says shakily. I almost start to tease him, because who's anti-sea *now*, but something stops me. My conscience, maybe, piping up to suggest that I could try being nice to West. Or at least not poke fun at what looks like legitimate discomfort. I decide to listen to that voice, plus pay a little more attention to how he's doing.

After a few minutes for oohing and aahing and selfie-ing, Paolo announces that it's time to continue on. But when he takes the helm, he quickly whirls back around, like something just occurred to him.

"Do you two want a picture with the white grotto?" he asks, pointing between West and me. "Something to share with your parents? I took them for everyone but you, I apologize."

I have to stop my eyes from bulging at the word *parents*, like the very acknowledgment that I have them is going to expose my whole scheme. When I fail to respond, West steps in.

"We'll get the next one," he says. "Don't want to slow us down."

Paolo accepts this at face value. I'd like to believe we're not the weirdest tourists he's ever taken out on his boat. I doubt we're even the weirdest in today's tour group. As he steers us back out onto open waters, our captain turns up some music that would absolutely be the backing track to a movie montage of riding through the Italian countryside in a vintage convertible. On top of all the other noises and distractions, this fully forestalls any more attempts at conversation while we're in motion.

Not that I even know what else to say. Maybe West was on to something, claiming we could have planned this better. Or *I* could have, I guess—I'm pretty sure he would've done whatever I told him, though I don't know why. I look at the boy in question, realizing I haven't heard a peep from him in a while. While he's still clutching the railing, his grip isn't as white-knuckled as before. Some of the tension in his face has eased.

"Do you get seasick or something?" I ask.

West shakes his head. "No, I'm good." When I raise a skeptical eyebrow, he gives a sheepish smile, then concedes, "I don't exactly love the ocean, either. Or being out on choppy water in a boat, at least. It's better when we're cruising, but when we slow down and the waves rock us around, it can put me on edge."

One of numerous things that put West on edge, I think, continuing to piece together the complicated picture of who he is today. But even the fact that he's aware of what sets him off, and the effect it has on him, is different from the nervous boy I remember from when we were younger. That boy never would've acknowledged these anxieties or their triggers out loud, either. These differences only make me more impressed by the ways he's grown—and more regretful that I didn't understand just how bad things were before. Didn't always support him the ways a best friend should have, while absorbed in my own messy feelings.

I decide maybe I can provide more of that support and

comfort now, even if he seems to have a better handle on everything. He's only out here, dealing with things that make him uneasy, because of me.

So as we come to the next stop on our tour around the island, these three huge rock formations jutting out of the water that Paolo calls the "faraglioni," I stay seated beside West instead of getting up to take pictures. The boat slows and I notice him gulping in a big breath, then appearing to hold it. I watch in my periphery, waiting for him to exhale and growing a little nervous myself when he doesn't.

"Breathe," I whisper out of the corner of my mouth, and without really thinking about it, reach over to put a hand on his knee.

"I'm breathing just fine," he whispers back a little severely. Then he sighs and adds more softly, "But thanks."

His eyes stray down to my hand on his leg, like he's only just noticed it. I feel his muscles tense beneath my palm before he says, barely more than a breath, "*Cousins*."

I yank my hand back. Maybe I spoke too soon about us being the weirdest guests on this boat.

"We're now passing through the Faraglione di Mezzo," Paolo explains as he steers us under a natural arch in the middle rock formation. "Legend has it that when a couple shares a kiss under this archway, it ensures they will stay together forever."

Our boat rocks back and forth as he cuts the engine and lets us float farther under the arch, turning to face the group with a cheeky wink. Through delighted laughter, Victor and McKinsley share a kiss, followed by Marge and Graham.

Then, as if they scripted it, all eyes turn to West and me like they've forgotten that we said we're related, too.

"Well, next time you'll have to bring back your sweethearts," Graham offers in the awkward pause that follows, his grandfatherly way of defusing the tension—or covering up the fact that for a moment there, everyone was anticipating some kissing cousins action.

"Ha ha, yep," West plays along, literally saying "ha ha" like they're words, instead of laughing. This, in turn, makes me laugh for real.

When the engine starts up again, I lean close to him and ask, "Is my cousin a robot or an alien?"

"I don't want to hear it from you, Knee Fondler," he snarks back.

I gasp, trying to sound indignant despite my cheeks glowing red-hot. "I was not *fondling* your knee!"

He shrugs. "Tell it to the jury."

"Oh my god, we should have just said we're friends," I mutter.

"Would that have been more accurate?" West asks. His voice is suddenly earnest. So is his expression, his dark eyes pinned on me with unreadable emotion in them.

"I mean," I say with an awkward laugh, "we're at least in the free-trial stage, right?"

His mouth tips up on one side. "The free trial?"

"Yeah, like, testing it out before we commit to the . . . lifetime membership." *Not bad for a metaphor I completely pulled out of my ass,* I think with surprised satisfaction.

West looks dubious but plays along anyway. "How do you think the trial's going so far?"

I study my hands where they fiddle with the frayed hem of my shorts, contemplating how to answer. "Well, what you're doing right now, going on this outing with me even though you apparently hate boating on the ocean and that's literally the whole plan for the day—it's something only a pretty good friend would do, isn't it?" My eyes flick hesitantly up to his face. "So I'd say it's going well."

The tension on his thoughtful face slowly melts until his eyes crinkle at the corners and a smile, small but genuine, tugs his lips upward. I feel an answering leap in my heart rate, then tell myself there's no way the two are related.

"Glad to hear it, Cam," he says softly.

But as our gazes stay locked, and the moment stretches on, it doesn't feel particularly friendly. It feels like something stronger, and so much scarier.

I look away first, shifting so my back is to West and I'm peering out toward the sea. For all anyone knows, my entire focus is on the stunning scenery as we cruise around the island.

My eyes are taking it in, but my mind is floating farther away in both place and time. Salty mist sprays my face as we bounce across the waves, calling up a sense memory from three years ago that I usually try my best to suppress.

The mist that day hadn't been a cool reprieve from the hot summer sun. It'd been part of the chilly drizzle under gray skies I'd grown used to, in the few months we'd lived in that sleepy English coastal town. Mom and Dr. Danny had been working on some Roman ruins found on nearby farmland, while West and I had been living—at least in my mind—the cute, cozy, falling-for-my-best-friend love story that dreams are made of. We had daily teatime at one of our families' quaint rental cottages and always had a jigsaw puzzle in the works on someone's kitchen table. We became regulars at the coffee-and-bookshop down the lane, where we'd do our online classes together with long breaks to browse for new reads and get caught up in discussing our favorite stories. We'd walk and talk for miles up and down the rocky beach, dressed in layers to account for whatever the moody weather decided to do each hour.

And every day, my feelings for him had grown harder to hide. There'd been signs he'd felt something, too—his gaze that always fell on me when he thought I wasn't looking, a gradual shift in the ways we touched, from accidental or casual to brimming with meaning and significance. Then finally, we'd sat on the beach late into the night, under the guise of waiting for the clouds to clear and reveal some stars. Cuddling for warmth had escalated bit by bit, until I'd tipped my face up to his in question, and his lips met mine in answer.

Not even twelve hours later, I could hardly believe I was back in the same place, tainting the site of our perfect first kiss with what I feared was becoming my first heartbreak.

"Tell me it isn't true, West," I demanded, the shake in my voice barely detectable over the rumble of thunder in the distance. "That it . . . That I misheard, or something, and your dad wasn't just telling my mom about his new job. About plans for your family to move back to Indiana *for good*."

West wouldn't even take his eyes off the dreary horizon to look at me. His throat bobbed on a heavy swallow, and I thought I saw the slightest tremble of his chin but decided I imagined it when he set his jaw in a firm line again. "It's true, Cammie. We're moving home, at least until I finish high school."

A choked sob escaped me. "That's . . . I don't even . . . How long have you known?"

His silence was answer enough.

"So what was last night? That kiss?" I pushed a clump of wet curls back from my forehead, where they'd escaped the confines of my rain jacket hood. There was little point in the garment, in this kind of rain that was almost like standing in the path of a sprinkler. But I was grateful for it anyway, as it helped disguise the tears that were spilling down my cheeks at an alarming rate. "Or, like, everything between us these last few months? I thought we were . . . that we'd . . . I don't know, be a *thing* now?"

It sounded so juvenile and silly when I said it out loud, and what I felt for him was anything but that. It couldn't be anything but love—I was certain of it. Had I been fooling myself, believing he felt the same?

West finally managed to meet my gaze, and his eyes brimmed with so many emotions, I couldn't name them all. But frustration was predominant in his voice when he said, "There's been a lot going on that's bigger than you and me, like my dads"—he shook his head to flick back the brown hair dripping water into his eyes under his own pointless hood—"they need this change. We all do. Some stability and normalcy for once. It's what I want, too."

My hands flew out to my sides. "Then why did you make me think you wanted me?"

His hands went to the top of his head as he started to pace in a slow circle. "I didn't mean to— You're my—" A low growl escaped through his clenched teeth before he collected himself and continued. "Whatever I made you think, I can't do a relationship right now. Anything else that's happened between us or anything more that happens in the future, it's as friends only. That's the only 'thing' I can be with you."

The memory after that grew blurry. I knew that I'd pleaded with him to give us a chance, even willing to try long-distance, but he'd been insistent it had to be this way. I'd grown angrier the longer we stood there—not to mention soggier and colder—and by the end, there was a lot of me yelling and him silently taking it.

Then West had walked away. Days later, we hadn't tried to talk again when he and his dads had left for the States. I'd expected he would snap out of whatever temporary personality transplant he'd undergone, regret being so cold, and try to reach out some number of days or weeks later. But after months of silence, I gave up that hope and deleted his number.

I blink rapidly, tipping my face toward the sunny blue sky above to remind myself where I am now, to keep any new tears from contributing to my saltwater facial this time. But the memories have effectively dampened my spirits.

Paolo announces that we're approaching our next stop, the only place where we'll get a chance to swim, and I join in the cheers from my fellow passengers, even while keeping my face turned toward the sea until I'm sure no sadness lingers there. I tell myself a dip in the cool blue waters is all I'll need to reset and recenter on what's important about today.

While Paolo drops anchor, I put all my energy toward readying to swim, whipping off my T-shirt and shorts, applying another layer of sunscreen to supplement this morning's, and determinedly shutting out anything or anyone else on the boat. Then I turn around and am faced with an image I couldn't shut out if my life depended on it, one that threatens my balance far more than the gently rolling waves below.

West Jacobs—shirtless.

CHAPTER TEN

West

SPLASH.

The loud, startling sound is followed by a few moments when the boat rocks aggressively back and forth, like someone gave it a push. Presumably the same someone who, I'd wager, just cannonballed into the sea.

I turn around from where I've been checking my phone for the first time since this morning, surprised to find a mass of soaked red curls springing back up from under the clear blue water—then bobbing along the surface as she paddles away from the rest of us.

"It's a ten from the Italian judge," Paolo calls out teasingly. I see her bright white smile in profile as she flashes it toward him, still swimming in the other direction. Something in my chest squeezes tighter with a mix of feelings. Worry that she's already attached to this guy, when we have very little evidence that he has anything to do with her life, that she'll be heartbroken if this one isn't *the* one. Or worse, heartbroken if he is and still doesn't want anything to do with her.

But there's something else making the organ behind my ribs do funny things. Probably the fact that even though it's been three years since we've had any sort of relationship, I've never met another girl whose smile affects me like Cammie's does. She's still so unbelievably beautiful.

I tear my gaze away, though it wants to linger on her freckled arms as they propel her forward, the long, tangled tresses floating behind her. Frustration creeps in as I look back at my phone, wishing I hadn't given it a second look when I took it out of my pocket to stow it somewhere waterproof. But I did, and my friend Max's name caught my eye, a text from him outside our group chat.

Max has already confirmed his plans to go to the same program I'm considering in Germany, and if I do go, we'll be roommates. He knows I'm undecided and hasn't pressured me to make the call faster, but he does occasionally send related messages, like a cool tourist experience someone recommended we try in Berlin, or something new he learned about the program that excites him.

Mostly, these just stress me out. He's not saying "make your decision *now*, West! No big deal, it's only your entire future hanging in the balance!" But my mind reacts as though he is. I fire off a single emoji in response to some Top 10 Biergartens listicle I didn't read, just trying to get it off my mental to-do list. I doubt Max especially wants to be my roommate by now, as my responses get increasingly nonsensical in my effort to sound chill.

Case in point—"Dear god, West, why the smiling cowboy hat?" I whisper under my breath, trying to block the sun from my screen with one hand while the other scrambles to find the Unsend option. By the time I do, it's too late to use it.

Read by Max P, it says under the blue text bubble. Maybe I should just "accidentally" drop this device overboard. But Max's laugh reaction keeps me from doing so—for now—and I hurry to stuff it in the compartment under the bench before finishing my sunscreen application.

Once I do, I cross to the back of the boat where everyone but Cannonball Cam has descended into the water using a ladder. Before I start down it, I peer around in search of where Cammie swam off to—only to find her gaze stuck on me.

Even across a good distance, I can tell it's not on my face, either. An uncontrollable smirk pulls at my lips, and if no one else were around, it'd be a great time to yell, "My eyes are up here." But we aren't alone, and we *are* still pretending to be related because of my big, dumb mouth. So I keep my taunts in my head, alongside my absolute delight that I'm not the only one of us still attracted to the other, however unwillingly.

I've never been an athletic guy, but I started working out a couple years ago, after the millionth time it was recommended to help with my anxiety. Unfortunately, it does help. Even more unfortunately, I've come to enjoy it. But I don't think I've ever appreciated the results as much as I do at this moment.

I try to keep my smug grin to myself as I turn and start

down the ladder. The water is cooler than I expected as I ease in but feels incredible under the midday sun. I paddle toward Cammie, who's now floating with eyes closed and face tipped up toward the blue sky. She must hear the small ripples as I draw near, because she speaks before I can without opening her eyes.

"You took your life jacket off."

I look down as if to confirm the accusation.

"Yeah, Paolo said that was okay, since the water is so shallow here."

"I just thought you were Mr. Safety and all," she goes on. "Didn't expect you'd want to risk it."

I frown. She really thinks I'm a paranoid mess, doesn't she?

"Being in shallow water like this is way less dangerous than being on a boat getting tossed around in the open ocean. Worst-case scenario, my feet can reach the bottom and I can bounce myself back up to the surface." *Why are we even talking about this?* I think. I'm still antsy from Max's text, but trying to be present, to focus on what I'm here for, I change the subject. "What do we think about Paolo so far? Any major paternal vibes coming off him, or anything clicking for you?"

Cammie's eyes pop open and her head turns abruptly to check if Paolo is within hearing range. Like I would have said anything if he was. But I still follow without comment when she swims a little farther away from the boat.

"I don't know, he seems cool," she says. "I realize it's kind of silly, but I just have this feeling like when I meet my actual dad, I'll know in my gut, and I don't necessarily have that. But maybe that's not realistic." She tilts her head with a sigh, suddenly looking and sounding a little sadder than she was earlier. "I'm not sure how I'll get any closer to the answer today. Short of asking him, 'Hey, did you sleep with my mom twenty years ago and then ditch her when she told you she was pregnant with your child?' He might have a heart attack, and then who would drive us back to land—Victor? Pass."

I laugh even though I know she's trying to deflect from stuff that's actually kind of heavy and difficult, sensing it's what she needs right now. I also don't exactly have any words of wisdom. We float in silence for a few moments, each of us lost to our own thoughts, before Cammie speaks again.

"This probably all seems pretty half-baked, and unlikely to result in a perfect ending where the biggest mystery of my life is tied up with a nice little bow. But I . . ." She looks away, her teeth clamping down on her lower lip as she struggles for the right words, before finally looking back to me and blurting, "I really appreciate you doing this. I don't know if I've said that enough, or, well . . . at all. But I'm grateful you're here. It would be so much scarier doing it alone."

My heart is pounding so hard I wish I'd left my life jacket on. It has to be visible through my chest right now. I swallow a lump of emotion in my throat before I answer, "What are cousins for?"

Cammie throws her head back and laughs, a sound that does not help my heart-racing situation, nor any of my body's other physical reactions to the only girl I've ever wanted, just a foot away from me and looking like a literal dream in her yellow swimsuit in the sparkling Mediterranean waters.

When her laughter subsides and she meets my eyes, hers seem to be looking for something. Studying me intently enough that I feel like ducking my head underwater to hide.

"Everything okay? You seem . . . distracted," she says softly.

I give her a knowing tilt of my chin. "I could say the same for you."

Cammie smirks. "Mm-hmm, but I said it first. So spill."

With a sigh, I lean back, paddling with my arms to keep afloat as I look up toward the craggy cliffs nearby. "It's nothing, really—I just got a text from the guy I was maybe going to room with in Germany, and it reminded me I have to decide. It's just been this big cloud, like, looming over me. But I'm pretty sure I'm not going, so I need to just call it. Then I can stop stressing." I sound more sure than I am, but I also don't want to keep talking about it. I know it'll only make me agitated and anxious. "Your turn."

When I peek her way, her smile is rueful before it fades and her eyes flit away. "I don't know, I . . . I guess I keep thinking about what you said the day we went into Naples. How it's sucked these last three years, us not being in each other's lives. If it isn't obvious, it's sucked for me, too."

It wasn't obvious at all, actually, I want to tell her, but I hold it in.

Her tone is cautious as she continues. "But if it sucked so much, why didn't you ever reach out and try to fix things? For the longest time after our fight, had you picked up the phone and texted or called even once, I would've been ready to mend fences in a heartbeat."

I feel my brows pull together and my lips turn downward as

I replay her words in my mind. "I . . . What? Cam, I was just doing what you asked."

Water splashes as she throws a hand in the air. "What are you talking about? What do you think I asked?"

"No, no," I say, shaking my head. "First, I want to know what *you* think happened back then—how you remember our fight and what got us there."

"Why do I have to go first?" she squeaks out, but I won't let the cuteness deter me.

"Honestly? Because you've seemed so angry with me—still angry, to this day. If I'm going to explain or defend myself, first I need to hear things from your point of view."

Her lips purse, and her eyes shift away, back toward the boat and beyond it. "Fair enough," she concedes, "but I don't think this is a water-treading talk. Some of us haven't spent our entire time apart getting all fit and toned and six-pack-y."

I can't stop the laugh that bursts out of me. "Did you count my abs, or was that just a lucky guess?"

Cammie's back is to me as she starts toward the rocky coastline. She doesn't turn her head when she calls, "Wouldn't you like to know?"

Then she dives under the surface and swims away, as elegant as a mermaid. And like plenty of suckers before me, I have no choice but to follow where the siren leads.

Even when it involves climbing up rocks of questionable stability.

"I thought your goal was to get us away from physical exertion," I pant out as I use the exact same hand- and footholds she does to traverse the cluster of boulders jutting out from the larger formation.

"Did no one tell you when you got your six-pack certificate? There's an international law forbidding you from complaining ever again. It's called the You Owe This To The Rest Of The World Act."

"Please don't make me laugh when I'm perilously close to falling off a cliff."

"Oh my god," Cammie cackles as I watch her boost herself up onto a ledge and sit, then scoot over to make room for me. "This is to a cliff what I am to Serena Williams. We might have a lot of the same pieces, but hers have combined into a much more impressive whole."

"You— What?" I shake my head as I settle in beside her, taking a moment to breathe before continuing. "Let's circle back to that comparison later. First, let's go—list my misdeeds."

What starts as her humorless chuckle turns into a groan. "I don't know, maybe I should throw myself off this non-cliff instead."

"Camilla."

"Okay! Okay." She takes a deep breath and lets it out slowly, her eyes fixed on our legs dangling over the water below. Then she proceeds to recount one of the most painful conversations of my life, or as much as she remembers of it, three years on. It's bizarre, reliving it from outside my own body and head and heart. Words and images her mind held on to that mine didn't, and vice versa. I have to keep myself from interrupting a couple times, correcting the record about my expression, her particular phrasing of some question, the way it changed my answer. But I just listen. Do my best to absorb, to understand.

"The kiss, the romantic feelings—I think it was easier to get over those things." She leans back, supporting herself with her palms on the rock behind us, and her voice is more strained when she continues. "It's the way you dropped me in an instant, like it wasn't even difficult or I hadn't meant to you what you meant to me—that's what still hurts."

I reach up to massage the bridge of my nose, trying to temper my response. There's one glaring detail she seems to have forgotten entirely, while I let it brand itself on my brain and guide my actions ever since.

"Cam . . . you told me you never wanted to speak to me again," I say as gently as I can, while my whole body vibrates with suppressed emotion.

Her questioning gaze darts to mine. "What are you talking about?"

An incredulous laugh escapes me, though I'm not sure enough time has passed for any of this to be funny. "The part you remember about me being some emotionless brick wall—I was a mess on the inside, so mixed up and confused and sad and scared—"

"You had a weird way of showing it," she interjects, sitting back up and crossing her arms over her chest.

"I didn't show it!" I say, voice rising. "I know that—that's what I'm trying to say. The more upset you got, the more I shut down, just feeling worse and worse about everything."

Cammie scoffs. "Oh, so if I'd just *calmed down*, you would've showed an ounce of emotion? My mistake, Weston 'I want to kiss you as a friend' Jacobs."

My groan comes out through gritted teeth. "Do you want me to explain myself or not?"

"I swear to—" she mutters under her breath, then, in an exaggeratedly patient tone, "The floor is yours, Mr. Jacobs. Consider me silenced until you grant me the privilege of speaking once more."

There should not be a part of me that feels like smiling at her petulant tone, in the middle of this batshit attempt at civil conversation or conflict resolution or whatever we think we're doing here. But here I am fighting for my life to keep a straight face.

"As I was trying to say, I had a lot going on inside that made me say and do the things I did that day. I wish I could take all of it back, that I never caused you that kind of pain. But as for why I seemed to drop you, never reached out in the years since, I—" I scratch my neck, any humor or lightness fading as I recall the painful words and have to swallow the lump that lodges in my throat. "I never stopped thinking about what you said. Stuff like 'I thought I knew who you were, but I could never be friends with someone like you' and 'I never want to speak to you again.' All the countless times I thought about reaching out, I'd replay those words and stop myself. I didn't think you wanted me to—didn't think I deserved to, either."

When I chance a look at Cammie again, her jaw is practically at sea level, lashes fluttering over wide, disbelieving eyes. It's a few moments of staring in silence before she says quietly,

"Oh . . . my . . . god. Weston Jacobs. You . . . you're telling me that three years of radio silence was just you . . . what, taking my dumbass, mid-fit-of-rage ranting *seriously*?"

"I . . . I mean, yes?" I shove a hand through my hair and feel it drying extra curly, the combined effects of saltwater and humidity. I also feel my face reddening, like a rapid-onset sunburn, but my recent application of SPF 70 says that can't be the cause. "I don't know if I'd phrase it that way, but—"

"I said a lot of shit that day, West!" she exclaims. "I didn't mean half of it! You don't let a pissed-off sixteen-year-old girl facing her first romantic rejection tell you how to live your life."

"Weren't you just the one explaining the concept of boundaries to me?" I match her rising pitch and volume, throwing my arms out wide.

"Those weren't real boundaries," Cammie says through a laugh that's more exasperation than humor. Her hands go into her hair like she might tear it out. Or more likely, strangle me with it. "They were probably lines copied and pasted into my head from the script of a teen soap opera. TV boys never let stuff like that stop them from getting the girl back—you weren't supposed to, either!"

"Ohhh, got it, that's my bad—I'll try to be more toxic next time," I deadpan. "Send you love letters spelled out with magazine clippings, maybe, or show up in your bedroom uninvited to watch you sleep at night."

She jabs a threatening finger my way. "Do *not* bring Edward into this."

"Your fault for making me read those shitty books."

Cam gasps like I've finally taken things too far.

I close my eyes, tipping my head back like the sun on my face can infuse me with patience. Or some good sense, maybe, as all mine seems to disappear when I'm with this girl. She should not be able to make my blood boil with frustration while also making it pump faster with the incomprehensible urge to lunge forward and kiss her all over again. Since I do have enough sense not to do that, I look over to her and offer into the silence one quiet concession: "*Eclipse* wasn't so bad."

Cammie drops backward in slow motion, until she's flattened against the rocky ledge, save for her legs, which still dangle by mine. I don't realize that my gaze has trailed down her bikini-clad body and come to rest on her bare, freckled stomach until it starts to quake. My misbehaving eyes dart up to her face, which is now split open with a soundless fit of laughter. Her eyes narrow to slits, mouth wide open, whole body heaving with the kind of breath-stealing hysterics that only come on rare occasions, when she finds something exceptionally funny.

I used to consider it my proudest achievement to earn this kind of laugh from Camilla Lovett.

I also always found it impossible not to fall apart with her, and it seems that hasn't changed. I drop onto my back at Cam's side and give in. I have no idea the last time we shared a laugh like this, but it feels, more than anything, like relief. Like finally coming up for air after years of holding my breath.

Cammie's giggles interspersed with gasping inhales are music—they're art. I want to record them so I can start every day with a listen, a better way to invigorate me than any caffeinated beverage.

"Why are we . . . such a . . . mess?" she laugh-cries.

"Hey," I chuckle with mock offense, swinging my leg sideways to kick playfully at her foot with mine. "Speak for yourself. All I see on my end is a respectful, rule-following guy who was trying to figure his shit out before he got villainized by a girl who forgot her own stated boundaries. A sad tale."

"It honestly is," she says through a hiccup.

I clear my throat and reach up to scratch the back of my neck but find that the action doesn't quite relieve the itchy feeling there. So in a more serious tone, I offer, "But honestly, Cam. I'm sorry I didn't fight even a little bit harder for our friendship. Had I known you wanted that . . . I mean, all this time, we could have . . ." A frustrated breath gusts out of me as I think of all the ways I could finish that sentence.

But Cammie doesn't let me. Bumping her foot back against mine, she says, "I know. But I can't think about the sad side of it—all that could have been, 'if only'—or I'll cry, and I'm so done crying over you. So I think we have to laugh at our own past ridiculousness if we're going to move forward."

A few more hiccups interrupt her before she can get all the words out, which does not help either of our laughter subside. What does, however, is a voice shouting from somewhere nearby, "Jacobs cousins, is that you?"

We both sit up abruptly and find that straight ahead, floating in deeper water where rocks under the surface aren't a threat, is Paolo on his boat, carrying all our fellow passengers, who've already redressed in cover-ups, clothes, and life vests. I scramble to my feet while Cammie waves, calling out, "Oh god, yes, sorry!"

Paolo waves back, "It is all right, just lost track of you—but I've received word that there is no wait at the Blue Grotto, so we must hurry if we are going to see it."

Cam accepts the hand I offer and I help her stand. Eyeing the way we climbed up here, I grimace, saying for her ears only, "I don't love the idea of making that trek with an audience."

"Time to throw ourselves off the cliff, then," she answers cheerfully, not an ounce of sarcasm or anything else in her tone to imply she's joking. When I look at her incredulously, she gestures toward the boat below. "Come on, it isn't that bad. And it'll be much faster."

I peer over the edge of what suddenly feels like a high-dive platform on the moon. "Won't we hit the rocks down there?"

"Nah, it's deeper than it looks," she counters with a confidence I know doesn't come from real knowledge. "We just have to jump out as far as we can, and we'll be fine. Here, let's go together."

Cammie holds a hand out toward me, and I don't know what possesses me to take it. Probably my desperation for any excuse to touch her. So desperate I will actually risk my one and only life for it, because deep down, some part of me thinks it couldn't be the worst way to go, if I'm holding her hand.

"Ready . . ." she says as she steps scary-close to the edge.

"Not in the least," I answer, belied by my slow approach at her side.

“Steady . . .”

“I know you can feel me shaking.”

I meet her blue eyes, glimmering under lashes still wet from her laugh-tears.

“Gooo!”

“OhmygodCamillaohmy—”

My stomach lurches when, as one, we leap. Every part of me is weightless for a beautiful half second while we fall, an adrenaline rush unlike any I’ve experienced in years. It’s terrifying and exhilarating and I can’t decide if one outweighs the other before I’m plunging into the chilly water. I pull my knees to my chest as I sink, my descent slowing until I extend my legs and find I’m just close enough to the bottom to give myself a push back up.

That’s when I realize I’m still clutching Cammie’s hand like my life depends on it, now dragging her back up with me. When we break the surface, I hear the nearby cheers of our boat companions, but I can’t tear my eyes from the girl beside me, catching her breath while giving me the biggest smile I think I’ve ever seen on her face. She’s as bright and radiant as the sun itself, and makes me wonder how I lived for so long in the shade.

“I feel like I should get a souvenir to remember this day,” Cammie muses as we shop in a touristy kiosk by the marina on Capri. “You know, something other than a name to possibly add to my birth certificate.”

I snort out a laugh. "What's that saying? Take only photos, leave only memories."

Cammie sticks out her tongue and blows a raspberry in the air in my direction. "*Booooo*. Anti-souvenir propaganda."

I laugh for what feels like the millionth time today and feel another pound of tension lift from my shoulders. Our conversation earlier unlocked something, like a barrier that'd been blocking us from fully being ourselves in each other's presence. The result has been an afternoon full of joking and talking with refreshing ease, both of us gradually finding our footing in this new-yet-old friendship. We saw a few more grottoes and other gorgeous scenery from the boat before Paolo brought us to the marina for some free time to explore Capri.

Cammie and I had lunch—caprese salads, which neither of us knew were invented here, and a few other small plates shared between us, washed down with glasses of sparkling water that Cammie insisted on drinking to be "like a local," determined to train herself to enjoy it, even though she still makes a disgusted face after every sip. We walked around the narrow cobblestone streets filled with luxury shops and fellow tourists, and took in more views of the island and the sea beyond. And, once again, ate gelato.

We're now killing time until we meet back up with Paolo in a few minutes, and while I don't typically enjoy cheesy souvenir shops, I do enjoy how much Cammie enjoys them.

"What about this?" she asks, holding up a mug from a spinning rack of monogrammed Capri drinkware. Fittingly, all the name options are Italian—Giulias and Fabios instead of Emilys and Johns. The one Cammie holds says "Papa." Her face is trying and failing to hide her amusement with herself. "Darkly funny, or just dark?"

"Is that the title of your memoir?" I ask in return, and Cammie gives in to the giggles again. I'm not really paying any attention to the spinner rack I'm slowly scanning, turning it this way and that, too wrapped up in thoughts of the girl I've spent the day with and how wonderfully normal it's felt. *Finally.*

But suddenly, a woman is at my side, gesturing to a row of necklaces.

"You know the cornicello?" she asks in thickly accented English. All the necklaces in the row she indicates are gold chains, each of them strung with a red pendant in a shape resembling a chili pepper.

"No, I don't," I answer, perpetually wishing that I could meet the multilingual skills Europeans seem to have.

"It is an Italian horn, a token of good luck, found in Naples, Capri, and other parts of Campania."

"Oh, very nice," I say mildly. Cammie approaches with a curious expression, and I try to give her the uncomfortable smile of socially awkward people everywhere that says, *Please save me.* I'm not even sure if this lady works at the store or is just an overly friendly local who's a big fan of the Italian horn.

"We do not buy the cornicello for ourselves," she goes on, shooting a smile at Cammie before looking back to me. "A young man like you may want to give this lovely pendant to a beautiful young lady, as a symbol of your affection. We give the cornicello to someone we love, to fend off evil and offer her protection and good fortune—and so every time she gazes upon it, she'll think of her handsome gentleman friend."

There's a brief pause as we all take in her meaning, and Cammie starts to say, "Oh, he doesn't—"

"I'll take it," I cut her off, before I've thought through what the hell I'm doing.

Then, like the confident, mature, sure-of-his-feelings guy that I definitely am, I don't make any eye contact with Cammie, instead catching the saleswoman's knowing wink as she takes a necklace and goes to the register to ring it up. I follow her and pay without even having checked the price tag, then thank whoever's in charge of my own good fortune that it isn't a solid gold chain with an heirloom ruby cornicello and therefore doesn't require me to max out my credit card.

When I've dragged out the transaction as long as I possibly can, I turn around to find Cammie standing there with her arms crossed and a curious expression on her face.

"You really didn't need to do that," she says, and it occurs to me that maybe I've embarrassed her or put her on the spot somehow.

"Do you not want it?" I ask. "I can hang on to it and, I don't know, give it to—"

"No! I mean, I'll take it. It's not doing anyone any good if you keep it, right? Luck-wise." She freezes. "Unless there's someone else you'd rather . . . like, back home—"

"All yours," I say, barely holding back the grin trying to break free at her nervous babble. "Turn around."

She spins and brings her hands up to hold her saltwater-soaked, wind-dried ponytail out of the way. I reach around her to link both sides of the necklace at her nape, surprised to see goose bumps pebbling the skin there. I don't think either of us is breathing for a moment, and I feel the need to say something, anything, to get back the levity we've had most of the day.

"I just figure you can use the good luck, right, with this whole quest? Or the protection or whatever." I give a short laugh. "Safety first, right?"

My fingers feel clumsy, the clasp too tiny to manage, but I finally get it locked into place and let go of the chain. Cammie turns, lifting the pendant between two fingers to inspect it from close range before looking back up to me with a smile that's soft and sincere.

"Right," she says. "Well, I appreciate it."

Despite my best efforts to end our great day on an unnecessarily awkward note, Cam and I are able to fall back into lighter subjects as we reunite with the rest of our group on the boat. Exhaustion has started to set in for everyone, and by the time we set out for Sorrento, conversation peters out in exchange for a peaceful sunset cruise with the engine and waves as the soundtrack.

Back at the dock where we started, the captain ties up the boat for everyone to disembark, then hands us each one of his business cards with instructions to reach out if we need anything while we're in the area. Cammie tucks it in her pocket carefully, and I imagine she's relieved she didn't need a reason to request his contact information, after all.

One by one, Paolo offers his hand to help each person step up off the boat, McKinsley and Victor first, followed by Marge and Graham. Then he gets to Cammie.

"Is that a new necklace from today?" he asks as her hand

slides into his. I doubt he notices the quiver in hers before their palms connect, but I don't miss it, can assume she's having some sort of internal Moment about the possibility that this is the first physical contact she's ever made with her father. It takes her a beat to respond to his question.

"Oh, uh, yeah. West got it for me at a gift shop."

Paolo gives me a funny look, a little tilt of his head and furrowed brow before he seems to school his expression into blank politeness. "Well, that was kind of him. I bought a necklace just like that once, for the first girl I ever loved." His laugh is soft and self-deprecating. "It didn't work out with us, so maybe I could have used some of that cornicello luck for myself."

He shrugs off the memory, lifting his hand to prompt Cammie to step up onto the dock.

"Anyway, buona fortuna!" He turns and takes my hand to help me up, then follows after, hopping onto the wooden planks with a practiced grace. "May you have good fortune the rest of your time in Italy, and wherever life takes you next."

CHAPTER ELEVEN

Cammie

MY MOTHER ONCE SAID TO ME THAT THE WORST PART OF RAISING A GOOD kid is missing out on the classic parent-of-rebellious-teen experiences she was promised by popular media. She never gets to "young lady" me, or order me to my room for talking back, because I don't. There's never been a potential romantic interest for her to strike fear into when they come to pick me up for a date. I've never had a curfew that I could miss.

So I shouldn't be surprised when she leaps at her first chance to sit in a dark room—the lobby of the residence hall—and dramatically flip on a lamp when West and I enter, arriving home slightly later than the rough estimate I gave her this morning. But it'd catch me off guard to find anyone creepily sitting in what I thought was a dark, empty room, trying to look intimidating, and I stumble backward into West. He lets out a quiet huff when my back hits his chest, and the sunscreen and saltwater scent of his skin envelops me in warm, happy reminders of this warm, happy day.

Until I remember Mom sitting in the corner. I hurry to right myself, West's hands coming to rest on my shoulders for only the moment it takes to ensure I'm steady on my feet.

"Uh, hi, Mom," I say, barely concealing how unserious this spectacle is to me.

"Camilla," she answers in an imperious tone that I don't buy for a second. "Welcome back. Same to you, Weston—we'll see you in the morning, all right?"

For all the time he's spent with Dr. Alex Lovett, he clearly believes this is a real, terrifying matriarch asserting her authority—in other words, he's scared shitless.

"Oh, I . . . sure, yep. Morning. I mean, see you in the morning, but for now, um, good night?"

After a stiff little wave to me, he hauls ass to the stairs, practically leaving a cloud of dust in his wake. When we hear the door slam shut behind him, Mom finally breaks.

"That was *amazing*," she whisper-shrieks, slouching in her armchair and letting her head fall back in silent laughter.

"That was mean, Alexandra," I chide, but I'm struggling not to join her giggle fit as I cross the room to take the chair angled toward hers in her lamplit corner. "He's going to have nightmares about you, I bet."

"Next time, I need to draw it out more. Ask about his intentions with my daughter." She rubs her hands together menacingly.

I roll my eyes and hope there isn't enough light for her to

see the blush on my cheeks. "That's the last thing you need to do, and there are no 'intentions' to question, I assure you."

Mom leans forward to prop her elbow on an armrest, then her chin in her hand. "Mm-hmm . . ."

"I'm serious!"

Her eyes narrow with skepticism before she shoots me a wink. "Okay, okay, I trust you—thus why I've never gotten to do this spooky lamp thing before."

I laugh and hope I'm the only one who hears the strain in it. So much for my reliable "good kid" status.

"So what did you two get up to today?"

In my effort to come up with anything to report that isn't "I met your ex-boyfriend—by the way, is he my dad? Oh, and I think there was a vibe between West and me," I proceed to ramble for the next twenty minutes about grottoes and blue water and the sunburn I think I feel setting in on my back until finally, Mom can't suppress her yawn.

"That sounds amazing, Cam—sorry," she says through another yawn. "Up past my bedtime, I guess. But I'm so happy you've been going out and exploring. I admit, I was a little worried that it would be hard on you, being here at Villa Russo, and around the field school kids day in and day out, after . . . Well, anyway." She smiles and I return it, despite the pinch of sadness I still feel when I think about my rejection from field school. "I'm just very glad you're having fun, even if I selfishly wish I could hoard all your time for myself."

I laugh at the faux-devious grin on her face. "Thanks, Mom. And hey, there's a lot of summer left." *A lot of which I'll continue to spend out of the villa doing things I can't be honest about.*

"Oh! On that note—can I steal you for a couple hours or so tomorrow? Ilaria is eager to get some time with the two of us chatting, walking through Villa di Bronzo together. If you don't have other plans already . . ."

Am I detecting the beginnings of a guilt trip? It's at least a guilt staycation. "Of course, I'll be there," I answer with a smile before we both stand and I step into her arms, letting her soft, lavender essence soothe my troubled conscience.

Mom didn't raise me with any sort of religion. No weekly services or Sunday school, in any of the forms they take in various faiths.

I *was*, however, taught more about Greek and Roman mythology than any other kid I knew. It was always in a scientific or historical way, not a "here are some moral guidelines by which to live your life" way. But every so often, the stories are a bit too on the nose, too relevant to some situation in our lives, to be anything but Mom trying to impart her version of religious guilt.

"Ceres—or Demeter, as the Greeks called her—was the goddess of agriculture, grain crops, fertility, and motherly relationships. 'Mother' was so much of her identity that nowadays, we rarely hear of Demeter without Persephone, her daughter, who the Romans called Proserpina," Mom explains to the camera, Ilaria, and the rest of the crew. She gestures to the fresco we stand beside, a depiction of two women in a garden. "The most famous myth, of course, one many of us know, has to do with Persephone being kidnapped by Hades, the god of the underworld.

"So often, folks focus on that aspect of the story. But to me, it's always been more of a portrayal of a mother's love for her daughter. She searches tirelessly for Persephone for months, and grieves this separation from her daughter so intensely, until eventually, Zeus has to intervene and bring her home. But because Persephone had eaten pomegranate seeds in the underworld, she had to return for half the year annually, leaving a heartbroken Demeter again and again. Ancient Greeks and Romans believed that's why the crops struggled for half the year, through what we know as winter, and it's only when Persephone returns that everything starts to bloom and grow again. Demeter is no longer adrift and grieving—with her girl, she's complete."

Catholic guilt, atheist-academic-mom-style.

She looks to me with an unassuming grin and reaches up to run a hand over my hair, left down today and looking not half bad. At least it was, before I got smacked upside the head with myths about motherly sacrifice and thankless devotion to an absentee daughter.

"How fortuitous," Ilaria says passionately. She is relishing this story and ostensibly not picking up the less-than-hidden messages Mom is putting down. "This was one of the first frescoes uncovered in the villa excavations, while you were still carrying Camilla. Do you remember how you felt as it became clear what was pictured? What kind of connections you made, if any, with Demeter and Persephone?"

Mom looks from Ilaria to me and back to the camera, resting her hand on my shoulder casually. "I don't think I felt like a mother myself yet, not truly. I didn't know what was coming for me in terms of responsibilities, yes, but neither could I have understood the kind of love I would have for this person I'd brought into the world. And even once she was here, I couldn't yet relate to Demeter's experience of loss and learning to let go.

"Cam and I were a package deal, attached at the hip for most of her childhood, and I'm so lucky I had that. But as she's gone to college and become her own adult woman, out in the world chasing her own dreams, I've had to learn to let go. To release some of the control and attachment, the right to know all facets of her life. Every parent has to learn this at some point, get their own sense, I suppose, of Demeter's experiences. It's . . ."

Her gaze goes distant, like she's examining thoughts she hadn't known were there until they poured out of her.

"It's strange timing, being back here this summer and seeing this again with my grown daughter." When she looks my way, there's a sheen in her eyes that causes unexpected emotion to rise in my throat. "Strange, but also very special."

"Beautiful," Ilaria says softly. "And Cammie, what does this make you feel? Do you relate to Persephone in turn?"

I swallow down the feelings lump, unwilling to make a melodramatic spectacle of myself on camera. "Um, yeah, I don't know," I say. "I do really like pomegranate seeds."

That gets a laugh out of Ilaria, but a weary sigh and warning squeeze of my shoulder from Mom. While I struggle to come up with a more intelligent answer, one of the cameramen says something to Ilaria in Italian, earning her hum of dismay.

"Our batteries are dying, and there's an issue with the spares," she says. "So we will take a break for now, okay? But this was perfect. Thank you both for your time."

The documentary crew talk among themselves and make their way back toward Villa Russo. As their voices fade, Mom and I are left looking at each other. I step back and put my hands on my hips while her hand drops from my shoulder.

"So does this mean you think West Jacobs is the devil?"

Mom laughs. "Of course not." She pauses, eyeing me with suspicion. "But what's interesting is you don't seem to think so, either. That's a new development."

My brows come together, as if I have no idea what she's talking about.

"Speaking of devils and other things with horns," she goes on.

I choke out an "Excuse me, what?" but it's like Mom doesn't hear.

"Is that a cornicello necklace I see?"

I glance down at the red pendant hanging from my neck like I'd completely forgotten it was there. It was tucked under my sweatshirt last night, or else I have no doubt it would've been part of her fake-stern, post-curfew interrogation act.

"Oh. Yeah, it is."

Mom smirks. "You buy it for yourself?"

I keep my expression neutral. "No, I didn't."

"Interesting."

"Is it?" I turn to study the wall with Demeter and Persephone.

Mom just hums again, turning to stand at my side. We take in the painting in silence for a few moments before she says, "I got one of those from a guy I dated back in the day."

My breath catches, and I hear Paolo's voice in my head, telling me he bought a cornicello necklace for the first girl he ever loved. Was it Mom? Were they together long enough for that?

It's my turn to hum noncommittally. I consider my words carefully before replying, "Interesting. Whatever happened to him?"

Looking her way, I don't see any outward sign that the question makes her nervous or uncomfortable. She narrows her eyes thoughtfully and her mouth forms a little pout. "I'm not really sure," she says.

I honestly can't tell if that's the whole truth or not. I want to press for more, but she usually shuts down when I ask about her old relationships. And I'm worried about accidentally revealing something I'm not supposed to know if I veer too close to talking about Paolo.

Quickly searching my mind for a subject change, I remember something I wanted to run by her.

"Oh, I keep forgetting. You know that Dr. Russo, who welcomed us to the first night's dinner?" Mom nods, curiosity in her eyes. "I ran into him a few days ago and he mentioned that he used to work with you and Dr. Danny here. Was he living in Villa Russo at that point, or what?"

Mom turns and begins walking toward the next room in the complex maze of Villa di Bronzo, shaking her head. She leaves space for me to fall into step beside her.

"No, John Mark—I mean Gianmarco, but back then, we knew him as Johnny—is the grandson of the Russos, who owned and resided at the family villa at that time. Gianmarco's father married an American woman, so little Johnny was born and raised in Ohio—contrary to what his accent might lead you to believe." She winks, then takes a quick look around as if to ensure no one else is nearby.

"He was visiting his grandparents on a 'gap year' from his grad studies when we discovered Villa di Bronzo, but from the get-go, he was way more difficult to work with than his sweet grandparents, who actually owned the property. He wanted to have a hand in every little thing happening on the dig, none of which he was qualified to do, and tried to buddy up to the archaeologists like he was equally responsible for unearthing Villa di Bronzo. Then, when he asked me out and I turned him down *multiple times*, well"—she grimaces—"it was like he retaliated by making our working relationship miserable."

My nose scrunches with distaste. "He asked you out? He looks so much older than you."

Mom chuckles and kicks a pebble across the dirt with one of her boots. "He's a handful of years older than me, but aging hits us all differently, I guess. It wasn't inappropriate. I just wasn't interested, and he couldn't accept that."

We come to one of a few atriums in the villa, where there's a ledge about knee height that Mom turns to sit on. I sit beside her and when I look straight ahead, I almost choke on my own spit.

"Is that . . . ?" I start hesitantly.

Mom nods as we both peer up at the fresco, which depicts two men smoking out of an indisputably phallic pipe. I clamp a hand over my mouth to stifle my inner twelve-year-old's snickers.

"It sure is." She sighs. "The world's always been obsessed with penises. Ancient Romans were just a little more direct about showing it."

I continue to gape, both at the wall and at my mother, who I don't think I've heard utter the name of that particular organ since I got the sex talk.

She tilts her head. "From the little time I've spent with them, I haven't decided if this field school group can handle seeing this room yet. Only some groups earn Penis Painting Privileges."

I let out an uncomfortable *aaaahhh* and clap my hands over my ears melodramatically. "Did I do something to earn this? It feels more like punishment than privilege."

Mom's belly laugh echoes through every ancient nook and cranny of the villa.

"Speaking of field school," she goes on once she's composed herself, and I'm so relieved she didn't go with "speaking of penises." "I should probably grab some lunch before I give a lecture to the group this afternoon. Thanks for giving me the morning. Or giving it to the film crew and me, I suppose, but it's way more fun doing this with you around."

"Of course," I say with a breeziness I don't exactly feel. "It was fun."

She eyes me speculatively as we stand. "Everything's good with you, yeah?"

I nod, maybe too quickly. "Yep! I'm having a good time here so far."

She reaches out and brushes my hair back behind my shoulder where it's fallen forward on one side. "I'm glad to hear it, Cam. Just don't be a stranger, okay?"

As we start back out of the villa the way we came in, I nod decisively. "You got it. I won't follow Hades to the underworld, either, even if I've heard great things about their pomegranate seeds."

CHAPTER TWELVE

West

GETTING A LIFE SINCE I'VE BEEN IN ITALY HAS REALLY CUT INTO MY TIME sitting on the computer and ignoring the outside world.

The guys back home have noticed, too. They've all reached the hundreds in Project Euclid problems over the past few days. I'm still stuck on seventy-two and have barely touched it since before Cammie told me about the dad search. The jokes at my expense are piling up in the group chat. It's brutal, and makes me feel loved, in a way that can only be understood by those with a close circle of emotionally stunted nerd friends.

Still, I'm past due for a night of my particular brand of self-care. It just happens to work out that I also need a distraction from Cammie, who I've barely seen since we returned from our Capri excursion.

I'm still afraid the cornicello necklace was a bridge too far—the bridge, in this case, being the one with all those "love locks" that started to collapse under the weight of Too Much Love. She gave me an ounce of understanding, forgiveness, friendship—whatever one could call our talk about our past—and what did I do, mere hours later?

Smothered her under the weight of thousands of cheap, heart-shaped padlocks inscribed with "CL + WJ 4EVR." Or under one tiny necklace, that—in terms of romantic symbolism—might as well have weighed the same.

I've considered a multitude of ways to try to talk to her about it but worry I'd only end up making things even weirder. Like if I was all, "You know that was no big deal, right? I wasn't trying to tell you I'm in love with you or something," it kind of just sounds like the opposite.

If there is any hope left of upgrading from free-trial friendship, Cammie cannot see me this unhinged. On the train back that night, she sheepishly admitted that she no longer had my phone number and asked me to give it to her so we could easily talk about any new plans or ideas for our search—and it does feel like ours now, for better or worse.

So far, we've only exchanged a couple texts about dad-hunt-related things—me requesting the list of names she's assembled so I can keep looking into them, and pictures of her notes from the journal so far; her sending all of that back to me, adding that she was still thinking about next steps and would let me know when she came up with anything. I've done my own brainstorming, too.

But I've decided I need to put it aside for a second. It's a Saturday, the night is young, and these math problems aren't going to solve themselves. Laptop in my arms, I head for the library. Dad and Dr. Alex went to a bar in town to see some live jazz or something similarly adult and European and classy. I don't know what Cammie is up to, and I've told myself I don't care. Our hall was loud and lively when I left it, more than I've seen on any other night, voices and music and people around my age coming in and out of each other's rooms, talking about pre-gaming plans and which clubs and bars they're headed to. I doubt any of theirs involve live jazz.

The farther I get from the noise, the more my mind eases and my heart rate slows, and I almost feel like goofily smiling at nothing. I'm so looking forward to a few hours of complete peace and solitude.

I push open the heavy wooden door and my brain plays a record scratch sound, my feet coming to an abrupt halt. Over the edge of the antique fainting couch on the opposite side of the room, I see two sock-covered feet propped against one of the bookshelves. Their toes wiggle beneath a pattern of smiling croissants and baguettes.

Not wanting to startle the person, even though I have a sneaking suspicion I know who they are, I shuffle along the carpet the rest of the way so my feet barely make a sound.

"Um, hi," I say, similarly soft and cautious.

The toes stop their wiggling.

"Oh, hey, West," Cammie says, like she was expecting me any minute now. I guess I should have expected her, too. That's the way of things lately, isn't it? Me, walking along, expecting silence and serenity. Cammie, bursting through the wall like a pint-sized Kool-Aid Man who makes my hands sweat and my chest feel funny.

I cross the room and round the couch to find Cammie lying on the floor, her legs extended up against the shelves and her hair sprawled on the carpet around her like an auburn lion's mane. Her laptop and her mom's journal both lie open a few feet away. She's wearing short pajama shorts and an oversized T-shirt that she's definitely had since we were in middle school, the faded lettering on the front displaying the words *Hey girl, are you a five-meter square of dirt covering up an ancient civilization?*

I don't need to see the back to know that it says *'cause I dig you*. Dr. Alex got it for her at a conference in London where she and my dad gave a talk. I remember Cammie opening it at the hotel where we both stayed with Pops, and she didn't stop laughing over it the rest of the trip.

I am so not doing any math tonight, am I?

"Hey, Cam," I say, sliding a finger under each lens of the glasses I remembered to wear for once, rubbing my eyes. "Whatcha doing here?"

She blinks wide, slightly watery blue eyes at me, a little dent forming between her brows. "Using the good library Wi-Fi," she says matter-of-factly, but there's something off about her voice. "You wear glasses?"

"When I remember to. And I meant more like, what are you doing"—I wave to the L shape that her body forms between the floor and shelves—"here?"

She looks to her toes, uncurls them, and gives another

wiggle. "I don't know, this is supposed to help circulation or something. I kind of just wanted to see if staring at the ceiling instead of the wall would give me any new ideas of who my dad could be."

I can't help but smile at this unfortunately adorable wrench in all my best-laid plans as I take a seat on the rug, next to her head.

"One of the weirder sentences I've heard," I comment.

She giggles and it ends on a hiccup, which is when my suspicions really take root. Even more so when her next words are noticeably slurred.

"Stick with me, kid. There's a lot more where that came from."

I study her face from this closer vantage point, asking carefully, "Cam, are you feeling okay?"

She hiccups again before answering, "Yes and no." My eyes have just clocked a glass bottle that's rolled under the fainting couch when she continues. "See, I was feeling thirsty."

"Uh-oh," I say under my breath, but she still hears it.

"No, no, it's fine, it's fine. It's just, I thought this bottle I picked up in the kitchen said *limonata*. But I was kind of distracted, since I was reading through the journal again, and I uncapped it and took a sip on my way back here before I realized the bottle I'd grabbed was *limoncello*. I nearly spit it onto the floor but ultimately forced myself to swallow this cursed liquid that tastes like if lemonade and cough syrup had a baby and then poisoned that baby, I mean seriously *blech* . . ."

"Oh no," I sigh more than say. I crawl forward and reach for the bottle, rolling it out from under the couch. When I pick it up, I find that while it's not very big, it has alarmingly little left in it.

"*Cam*," I say more emphatically. "This is half empty."

"Or is it half full, my dear Weston?" My unamused expression doesn't keep her from laughing at herself as she insists, "It's fine, West! I'm totally fine."

"Why did you keep drinking it if it tasted so bad?" I ask in bewilderment.

She blows out a breath from her puffed cheeks that sounds like the air spluttering out of a balloon. "I didn't want to put it back when I'd put my whole mouth and all my germs on the bottle. That seemed wasteful. But it also seemed wasteful to only have one sip, and I've never really had more than a few sips of any alcohol, and I thought, what the hell, you know? I'm in Italy, I'm basically in my own secure, contained, homey little space, where there aren't too many ways I can endanger myself or others. Everybody else is out having a wild Saturday night, so why not experiment a little? Like, for science."

The monologue is punctuated by a hiccup. I could name several reasons why not, some of them included in her own explanation for why she did it. But the last thing I want is to make a drunk Cammie into a sad drunk Cammie. She seems pretty happy for now, she's unharmed, and I can make sure she stays that way until she's safely back in her room. I suppose I don't need to be the literal buzzkill.

Plus, she's impossibly cute when tipsy. Because of course

she is. But it could quickly get less cute if she ingests any more of this stuff, so I tuck the bottle discreetly into my open backpack behind me.

"Hey, just out of curiosity," I say, feigning indifference to her answer, "have you eaten anything recently?"

"Okay, the country of Italy should, like, sue the Subway restaurant chain," Cammie declares through a mouthful of bread. The loaf was made by the kitchen staff for breakfast this morning, its leftovers placed in a wooden box for us to pick over during their day off tomorrow. Or, as it so happens, tonight, when all the villa's other residents have left the premises and there's a first-time-drunk in need of something to soak up the limoncello in her stomach.

"They should?" I ask. I dip my own piece of bread into the plate of olive oil and some spice blend that I got from beside the bread box, then put it in my mouth.

"Mm-hmm," she hums. "Because they call their plain white bread 'Italian' and it tastes *nothing* like the bread here. Honestly, it sucks compared to anything I've eaten in this country."

"I'm sure the Italian government will be very glad you've brought this to their attention," I say sincerely.

She nods, just as serious. If I was a meaner person or had any dreams of ruining Cam's potential future in politics, I would absolutely be filming the off-and-on conversation we've been having since I put the rest of her things in my backpack, pulled her up off the library floor, and corralled her into the kitchen for a let's-try-to-keep-you-from-vomiting snack.

I hope she remembers every absurd thing she said when she wakes up tomorrow. I should at least write some down. Cross-stitch them onto a pillow, maybe.

"West," she says abruptly a few minutes later, like there is absolutely anything else occupying my attention right now.

"Cammie," I say back just as urgently.

"Do you think I could have actually, like, scorched my throat drinking that limoncello? Because I swear it still feels like it's burning."

I fight the smile that threatens to tip up my lips with everything I have.

"No, I really don't think you did," I assure her. "That should go away soon, especially if you keep shoveling in bread to chase it."

She seems to accept this as truth, even though it's coming from someone with barely any more drinking experience than she has, from what I can tell. My freshman year experiments with alcohol consisted of forcing myself to drink a majority of one can of beer any time I met up with the guys for studying or gaming and found myself the only one without a drink. I was trying to train myself to like the taste.

So far, it still hasn't worked. If anything, it's only made me believe that anyone who claims they like the flavor is straight-up lying, or they've never tried, like, ice cream, and don't know what it means for something to taste good.

"Did I ruin your plans for tonight?" Cammie asks suddenly.

My brows rise at the complete shift in tone from her other delirious musings. "No, I wasn't doing anything important," I say, because echoing her earlier "yes and no" feels like it again only opens up the potential to make her sad. Somehow, that's quickly become the thing I most want to avoid in this life.

"What were you up to?" she asks, her gaze so focused on tearing a hunk of bread into tiny bits that I'd almost think her question was aimed at the bread pieces. I reach up to scratch at the back of my neck, unsure if this is something I should admit, even with the strong chance she won't remember it by morning.

"I was going to work on some math problems," I say at last.

Cam startles me by blowing a loud raspberry into the otherwise quiet room, followed by a similarly—and still unnecessarily—loud *boooo.*

"Okay, I was gonna be sorry if I threw off your night, but actually, you're welcome. That plan sucked."

"Damn, okay," I say with exaggerated offense, though it's belied by the chuckle in my voice. "Sorry for enjoying the pursuit of knowledge. Sue me along with Subway, I guess."

Cam throws her head back and laughs, her uninhibited joy making me laugh, too. Her eyes sparkle when she meets my own. "Now that I'm not mad at you anymore, I'm just bullying you for fun. It's a loving kind of hating on you, you know?"

My laughter dies out, and all at once it feels like there's not enough air in my lungs, or in this kitchen, or anywhere that I am with her and with those big blue eyes looking at me with nothing even resembling hate in them. They're filled with something more like the opposite, in fact.

I nod and open my mouth to respond, but before I can assure her that, yeah, I do get it, she keeps going.

"I figured you might have one of those long phone calls lined up with whoever you're always talking to—"

My eyes widen. "I might . . . what?"

"Probably a girlfriend, right? I've heard you a couple times through the wall, and I can never tell what you're saying, but your voice just sounds low and rumbly and romantic, so you can just be honest with me, okay?"

I cover my mouth with my fist, pretending to clear my throat into it to disguise the laugh I can't keep in. Fortunately, Cammie is still too interested in her bread to look at my face. Once I can keep it together, I reply solemnly, "You're right—it's time you learned the truth. That low, romantic voice is what comes out when I'm feeling really passionate." I hear a hitch in her breathing, and it's a miracle I can go on without breaking, let alone make my voice even deeper, draw the words out slower. "Like on long calls . . . late into the night . . . discussing linear algebra or number theory. Maybe even combinatorics, if the mood strikes."

Her head jerks up, face twisted in something akin to disgust. "Ew! Is that, like, your version of dirty talk?"

A laugh bursts free and turns into more of a wheeze. "*What?* No, you freak—I don't have a girlfriend, and I'm always on the phone with my friends, who also do math for fun, and sometimes we talk about it. I'm sorry to report that I'm not carrying on a long-distance love affair. Just a boring nerd doing boring nerd things."

"Oh. Well, that's good. But you're not boring. You're the coolest nerd I know, Weston. You always have been . . ." That sentence trails off into a yawn that blurs into more rambled words. "And it's even more absurd now that you're this"—she waves a hand to gesture up and down my body as I lean against the counter opposite the one she's sitting on—"this hot, grown-up man-person."

I feel my face burst into flames right on impact of the word *hot.* The rest of my body, too. Did the temperature just shoot up ten degrees or something? My mouth is still open, but now it's just because it's kind of hanging there, unable to close or to find any appropriate response.

"Like, what the hell, dude? It was so annoying when you opened that door on my first day here, all 'you look like shit,' and I couldn't even say it back to you, because you didn't. You look like the picture an average guy would use to catfish girls on dating apps. It's disgusting!"

"Okay," I say, and I can hear how short of breath I feel in the word, though I don't think Cammie even remembers I'm here, lost in her own musings. It doesn't feel fair to let her wax poetic about how attractive she apparently finds me—though it also feels great, don't get me wrong—when she's inebriated and I'm completely sober. This is a talk we should be having when we both have the same amount of our faculties.

"Think we're ready to call it a night?" I ask, but I'm already putting the bread and olive oil away.

"Nooo," she says, dragging the word out for at least five seconds. "We haven't even found my dad yet!"

"Yeah, I know, but hear me out—I think we'll have better luck if we both sleep on it and try again tomorrow," I propose.

She lets out another huffy breath, but ultimately nods, her eyelids drooping like she's already well on the way to dreamland.

"Come on, let's get you up to your room," I say, slinging my backpack over a shoulder before helping her hop down from the counter with my hands on either side of her waist. I don't let myself linger any longer than necessary, as nice as it would be to pull her close, hold on for a while, maybe— No, I'm not going there. I'm not thinking about going there, either.

Instead, I lead the way back to our side of the building, up to our floor, and even help unlock her door when she struggles with the key.

"Hey," I say before I completely lose her. "Here's your computer and journal back."

I swing my backpack around to unzip it, retrieve Cammie's things, and hold them out to her.

She does a little twirl, in no hurry to take them from me, and singsongs, "Thank you, Weston. West, West End." She laughs to herself. "Does anyone ever call you 'East,' just, like, as a joke? Imagine if that was your name—Easton. Southward. Northington." She dissolves into a fit of giggles at her own weird humor. "Nicknames are so strange. Like, yours doesn't even have to be West. It could be 'Ton.' Should I start calling you that as an inside joke? 'Ton Jacobs.'"

I'm about to roll my eyes when an idea hits me. Something I can't believe I haven't thought of before now. Even more shocking is that Tipsy Cammie inspired it.

But I yank the journal back to my chest, still holding the laptop out toward her and giving it a shake. “Actually, I’m gonna hang on to the journal for the night, if that’s all right. I have something I need to look into.”

Cammie absolutely does not care right now.

“Look your fill, Ton,” she says as she takes the laptop, shooting me a wink that Sober Cammie would *never* and Sober West will never forget.

Then she twirls on one sock-covered heel and saunters into her room, letting the door fall shut behind her. The last thing I see before it closes is the back of her T-shirt: *’cause I dig you.*

CHAPTER THIRTEEN

Cammie

I'M COMING TO LEARN THAT THERE ARE MANY REASONS WEST JACOBS IS A prince among men, but this morning, two stand out above the rest:

1. He is eating breakfast with me on the terrazzo, instead of in the dining room, because any and all light makes my killer headache worse, and it's only socially acceptable to wear sunglasses outdoors.

2. He's tracked down my second potential dad.

"I can't believe I didn't think of *nicknames*," I whisper in between nibbles of a piece of dry toast. "As if I didn't feel dumb enough from limoncellogate. I'd be a shitty detective."

"If you think about it, the limoncello actually led us to

this discovery, so maybe it wasn't the worst decision," he rebuts.

I down another giant sip of water before shaking my head slowly. "I remember way too much of what I said and did to agree with that."

West diverts his gaze to his computer screen and I see a wash of pink crest his cheeks, because he remembers every bit of it, too. Like me demanding he tell me his relationship status, then going on about his hotness. I might as well have invited him to share my tiny twin bed, for all the subtlety I showed.

"Anyway," he says, "I'm pretty sure this is one of our guys. Do you want me to just, like, show you, or . . . ?"

"Yes! Show!" I say, circling a finger for him to flip the screen around.

West does as directed and hits a button to turn the brightness up so I can see it despite my Shame Shades.

"T.C. from your mom's journal, a.k.a. Anthony Campbell from Dr. Constantini's list," West explains, "a.k.a. Neapolitan chef and pizzeria owner Tony Campbell-Costa."

My stomach flips with excitement at what feels like another huge step toward knowing my dad's identity. It could also be some lingering limoncello roiling around in there. But my mind feels suddenly alert, clear, ready to absorb everything I can about the man pictured on his restaurant's website, light brown hair peeking out from under a chef's cap and a friendly, dimpled smile on his face that has aged well from when it was smushed alongside my mother's in Polaroids twenty years ago. It's so clear that it's him, the T.C. from Mom's journal.

"But how did he get from whatever he did with the university archaeological program to becoming a chef and owning a pizzeria? And Costa, is that a married name?"

West shrugs, giving me an encouraging smile. "Those sound like good questions for Tony Campbell-Costa when we meet him. Now, do you want the good news or the bad news?"

"Oh god," I groan. I don't like where this is going. "I don't care. Both. Whatever order. Just quickly."

West says, "The good news is his job is well-suited to tracking Tony down for a chat. The bad news"—he grimaces—"is the pizzeria isn't open again until Tuesday."

I blow out a relieved breath. "Okay, all things considered, I was expecting worse. That's nothing." I take another bite of toast while West eyes me dubiously. "And in bonus good news—I can go back to bed today."

On Tuesday, West and I are both bright-eyed and bushy-tailed and back on a train to Naples.

We arrive at Antonio's in plenty of time for its 11:00 a.m. opening. The pizzeria sits on a lovely street on the waterfront, which is mostly a pedestrian thoroughfare and clearly heavy with tourists. There are historic hotels side by side with their modern glass-and-chrome counterparts, most of the ground floors filled with restaurants that boast huge outdoor patios. Spaces that are already starting to fill with folks hoping to enjoy their midday meal with one of the best views in town.

West follows my lead as we approach the patio filled with

umbrellas bearing the same Antonio's logo from the website. At the hostess stand, a young woman tucks away stacks of menus and shoots an apologetic smile our way when she notices us.

"Sorry, we don't open until eleven," she says before immediately turning back to her work.

"Oh," I say in my best polite-young-lady voice. "That's fine. I just have a question when you have a second."

She turns around again, face expectant, so I clasp my hands together atop the hostess stand and go on. "I'm wondering if Tony is around today. He's an old friend of my family and I wanted to see about speaking with him."

It's unimpressive, as cover stories go. Fortunately, Tony's not some important government official or celebrity with an intense security detail, and his hostess doesn't seem to care about protecting his privacy from strange Americans.

"Sorry, Tony isn't in this morning," she says. "He's teaching the workshop tonight." My ears perk up at that. Even better than a surprise one-on-one ambush in which I have to fabricate some connection he has to my family.

"Oh, a workshop?" I ask, not trying to hide my excitement. The woman riffles around under her stand and pulls out a brochure that she hands to me. *Scuola di Cucina con Antonio*, the cover reads, straight out of Unit 1 on LingoLegend Italian.

"You can go to that website and see if there is still space available."

With a sincere thank-you for her help, West and I turn back toward the boulevard.

"If Tony is my dad," I tell him as I try to simultaneously walk in a straight line and type the tediously long link from the brochure into my phone's browser, "I'm gonna have to help him bring his marketing materials into this decade. QR codes are your friend, bro."

"Nah, I think Tony knows exactly what he's doing," West says. "QR codes have made us lazy. This way, only the students who are serious about learning to cook will make it to his website. They have to be willing to put in the effort."

I roll my eyes. "Well, I guess I'm not a dedicated amateur cook, because in any other case, I would not be taking the time to type all this."

I hit go and wait a moment while my phone thinks about taking me to the website, only for an error message to pop up, informing me that I don't have internet service.

"Ugh," I groan. "No service. It seems we have no choice but to find a gelateria with Wi-Fi."

"And it's rude to use their Wi-Fi without buying something," West reasons.

Fortunately, these lovely little vendors of frozen heaven are on practically every block, and it doesn't take us long to find one proudly touting its free, fast Wi-Fi. I grab a table while West goes to order his gelato. I'm planning to check out the workshop website and hopefully get us signed up before I have my own treat, but to my surprise, West returns with two cups in hand. One holds his favorite, pistachio, and the other is strawberry. I don't even think I've told him this is my favorite, and I'm weirdly touched that he noticed.

"You didn't have to do that," I say a little sheepishly.

West's shrug looks careless, but his self-conscious grin tells the real story. "You can get the next round. I have no doubt there'll be one."

I like that plan almost as much as I like frozen strawberry desserts. Finally, I get the website to load and consequently add its revamp to my mental list of things I'll do if Tony Campbell-Costa is my dad. The main page looks like a basic calendar that someone made in Windows 95. I find today's date and click the link, then have to reassure my phone three different times that this sketchy-ass web page won't give it a virus before it'll finally let me view the class info. The title of the workshop on the calendar said something like "Pizza Making 2," which I assumed might mean that there is a "Pizza Making 1" prerequisite. But the additional info on the class says that it's open to beginners and only requires that participants register as a pair.

"It's forty euros," I tell West, because I do need to check that he's cool with that part. "I think we can swing that."

He nods. "Sure. I'll add it to your tab."

I sign us up and pay successfully. With several hours to kill before the workshop starts, we take our time at the gelateria, each updating our respective parents on our later-than-anticipated return to the villa tonight, followed by some googling of what to do for fun in Naples.

In the end, we decide to get tickets for one of those hop-on, hop-off bus tours, as an easy way to get to different parts of the city with sites to see. We board a double-decker bus by a big piazza in front of the medieval Castel Nuovo, and both immediately head for the open-air second level.

"Wait," West says once we choose two seats in the front row—and in direct, blazing sunlight. He studies my face with concern. "The sun is intense today. Maybe we shouldn't—"

I wave off this concern. "I'll be fine," I say. "That's what sunscreen is for."

For most of the day, this holds true. We don't spend much time on the bus, anyway, never riding for more than one stop before we "hop off," sometimes winding through the city streets on foot when a few places of interest are close together.

We start by checking out a few different churches and cathedrals, each somehow uniquely breathtaking. They're practically galleries, with art covering every surface, from stained-glass windows to marble statues to intricate carvings and painted biblical scenes on every ceiling. At one point, while we sit in a pew in a quiet chapel that predates the oldest buildings in the US by at least a couple centuries, West leans over to say in my ear, "This place is so beautiful, it almost makes me wish I wasn't so sold on evolution."

I make us leave before my snort-laugh can disturb the reverent atmosphere, or before West gets lured into priesthood by the pretty marketing materials.

We arrive at the Teatro di San Carlo just in time to join a tour, where our guide encourages the group to split off and sit in our own private box seats that circle the theater floor while she tells us some of its history.

"I've never been in a theater box before," I whisper as I take in the elegant trappings, all red velvet and gold accents, keeping with the color scheme of the rest of the magnificent building.

"Doesn't it feel like you're a historical romance character, awaiting a night of scandalous handholding with your secret lover, protected from the view of your fellow patrons of the opera?"

In his own damask-upholstered chair beside mine, West grimaces. "In all honesty, I was getting more of an Abe Lincoln vibe."

I gasp, then sputter as quietly as possible, "Oh my god, what is wrong with you?"

He holds his hands out to his sides. "What, like it's too soon? Not every historical figure had positive experiences with theater boxes, Cam."

Shaking my head, I try to turn my attention back to our guide and try harder to push the twitching corners of my lips downward, muttering out of the side of my mouth, "Forget I said anything, please."

"But I guess in both our versions, the night ended with a ba—"

"Weston!"

A quick jog across the street—seriously quick, to avoid the many motorbikers who apparently believe stoplights don't apply to them—takes us to the Galleria Umberto I, a massive Industrial Age structure housing shops and cafes at street level, offices and residences higher up. Sunlight streams through its glass-domed ceilings down to the mosaic floors and countless eye-catching, neoclassical-style details on the walls and windows in between.

It's the most spectacular location I've ever seen for a McDonald's.

West and I have just been to a bakery a few storefronts away, where we bought sfogliatelle, delicious Neapolitan pastries made from thin layers of dough stacked into a clamshell shape, filled with sweet ricotta, and topped with powdered sugar. We agree we aren't going to be Those Americans who get McDonald's in a city with such a rich cuisine . . . but then he sees a menu item called a "Parmesan snack" and can't resist.

"I don't know what I expected," he deadpans a few minutes later, returning to the table where he left me, holding a small, half-unwrapped brick of solid Parmesan cheese.

I pause in brushing off the powdered sugar and flaky pastry crumbs that now cover my shirt, then laugh at the outcome of his investigation. "The name didn't lie."

With some of our energy restored, we decide on a whim to join a Naples Underground tour. Neither of us knows what to expect as we descend over a hundred feet below the city streets, and at nearly every other turn in the long wooden staircase, I check in on West. He insists that he's fine, that he'll tell me if that changes, but a part of me has begun to worry that this day has gone too well, relative to our last time in Naples together. If he decides to make another break for it, I don't want to chase him up hundreds of stairs.

And unlike the last time, I would very much chase him. Just about anywhere, I'm beginning to think. It's like now that we've cleared up the reasons for our distance the last few years, I've fallen hard and fast back into the effortless friendship West and I had, rediscovering how much fun life can be when we're together, and I never want to lose this again. It's hard not to run a dozen steps ahead and imagine all the adventures we could have in the future, when we're back at our respective school homes and get to bring each other into these separate lives we've built. To imagine how much brighter mine will be, with him back in it.

It's beyond exciting—and beyond terrifying, because I'm still not quite convinced I get to keep him.

But all my complicated feelings and fears fade into the background for a while as I'm swept up in the unexpected highlight of my whole day. Our Underground tour guide leads a dozen or so of us through the long and complex history of Naples by way of the rocky earth beneath it all. We walk through cavernous rooms with walls that still bear markings from ancient tools the Greeks used to mine rock to build the city they called Neapolis; narrow tunnels that were part of the ancient Roman aqueduct system, which was still used into the nineteenth century; and finally, the makeshift bathroom stalls and anti-fascist graffiti from the tunnels' time as World War II bomb shelters.

I feel breathless, invigorated by the time we exit to the tour company's gift shop, but instead of hitting the city streets for fresh air, I want to return underground. To spend much more than one brief hour retracing my steps and those of everyone else who used these spaces for all number of purposes over thousands of years. To run my eyes and hands over every scratch in the rock walls, every marking on the floor, learning what I can about their meaning, who made them, what else they tell us about life at the time they came into existence. To hear every story that's been long buried deep under the bustling city.

"Doesn't it just blow your mind?" I say to West, raising my voice to be heard as we navigate a busy shopping street, working our way toward the nearest bus stop. I can feel myself talking his ear off, see his eyes getting glassier, but it's like I can't stop. "That we were occupying spaces carved out of the earth *before Ancient Rome existed*? The way a place like that can endure and evolve as civilizations rise and fall right above it, and humans continue to find ways it can meet their needs, tying them to all the other humans across the centuries, it's— Hey, you good?"

West blinks back to focus on me from where his gaze had gone distant and, if I'm not imagining things, a little panicked. His nod is too quick, his "yep" too squeaky. He can't hide that his head is doing the swivel thing that I noticed last time we were in a crowded part of town, like he's trying to take in the overload of sensory details around him but not really absorbing any of it.

I step from his side to walk ahead of him a little, parting the sea of people in our path so he has more space to breathe. I reach a hand behind me and say over my shoulder, "We're almost out of this alley. Then it's just a block or two to our stop." My worry eases when his clammy palm slides over mine and I clasp it tight, all the way out to the cross street, with its wide sidewalks and way fewer souvenir-hungry tourists.

I give West's hand a final squeeze of reassurance before letting it drop. "That was intense. Sorry if I added to the overstimulation with all my rambling," I say with an awkward laugh.

He rubs both hands over his face and blows out a breath before shaking his head and looking at me, his eyes thankfully focused and clear again. "No, it wasn't you. I just . . . It was getting hard to breathe in that crowd. I'm okay now." With a shy smile, he adds, "Thanks for looking out for me."

"Of course. I only wish I'd noticed sooner, instead of being so caught up listening to my own voice."

"Hey, stop that," he chides. "I don't blame you—I'm a big fan of your voice, too."

I bump my shoulder against his while mentally sending a wish out to the universe or whoever else is listening: *Please, please let me keep him.*

We reach our bus stop just as one of the tour buses is approaching and find seats in our go-to top-front spot. I sink into the hard plastic chair, suddenly feeling the soreness in my feet now that they've stopped moving. I've almost forgotten what we were talking about, when West says, "That tour really brought out your Dr. Lovett Junior, huh?"

He gives me a teasing grin that makes me want to duck my head into my T-shirt like a turtle retreating into its shell, but sadly, I have no such anatomical hiding place. I'm stuck with covering my eyes with my hands.

"Oh god, no," I groan.

West chuckles and bumps his shoulder against mine. "What? I love that you're so passionate about history, ancient civilizations, all of that. It's amazing that you found your thing so early and grew to love it more than ever."

His words send reality crashing into me like a double-decker bus. A reality I haven't fully let him in on, I realize. But we're on a long stretch of the route heading to the outskirts of the city, so it's as good a time as any to open that door.

"Yeah, uh, about that," I begin, fixing my gaze on the road ahead, now following the coastline. "I'm not really sure it's 'my thing' anymore."

West's head rears back so aggressively, I see it in my periphery. "I'm sorry—did body snatchers get to you in the last five minutes? Because the girl who was just reciting verbal love letters about a bunch of holes in the ground is basically a next-generation Indiana J—"

At the sharp look I shoot his way, a smile splits his face wide and he points an accusatory finger at me. "Ha! See? That was a *test*, because the Cammie Lovett I knew was a staunch believer that Indiana Jones, while giving the field a badass reputation, was less of an archaeologist than a glorified looter, and she was quick to correct the record whenever his name came up." He pauses, brow furrowing as his gaze drifts sideways. "She was also weirdly into Harrison Ford, even as older, present-day Indy."

One thing about me that hasn't changed and never will, much like Harry F's hotness.

I sigh and face forward again. "I had somewhat of a wake-up call recently, and it's made me reconsider things. I applied to a field school that I thought would be a dream come true. It's pretty exclusive, so I probably should have known better, but I was so sure I'd get accepted. I mean, I've only been hearing how smart and special and interesting I am since birth." My laugh is mirthless. "But I didn't even make the waitlist."

"Cam . . ." West starts, and the pity in his voice makes me want to "hop off" this bus while it speeds down the highway.

"It's okay. I'm okay, because it's the reason I'm even here now, for one thing. But I also think I needed that—I've coasted long enough on my mom's name, on the Bambina stuff, and I know you said you didn't mean the no-personality thing, but you weren't totally off-base, either. I think I made the love of archaeology so much of who I am that it became this . . . crutch? I haven't really done much for myself before, haven't had to figure out what I could be good at or passionate about. Trying to find my dad, it's partially to understand more about who I am and where I come from, partially in the hope of forming a relationship with my other parent. But it's also, I guess . . . to prove to myself that I can do it."

West is silent, presumably processing everything I've confessed. Maybe struggling to form a response that's not "About time you got hit with the humility stick! Welcome to the real world, Bambina di Nepo!"

But of course, the words he eventually finds are the opposite of harsh. "Cammie, you know that one rejection from one program doesn't have to change the whole course of your life, right? Whatever you've convinced yourself lately, you *are* qualified and capable and brilliant and passionate. So what if you knew what you loved from the jump? Some people just luck out early."

My lips twist and I look out toward the bay as we ride higher up a hillside. A large part of me wants to take his words as truth, but my cynical side still resists, tells me I just want to keep coasting through on credit I didn't earn. More powerful than either of the warring emotions, however, is an exhaustion that's quickly pulling me under, between the busy day behind us and the important night to come. I don't want to talk about my personal crises anymore.

"You might be right," I concede, mostly to bring things to a quicker close. "But if you don't mind, can we just . . . chill for a while?" The question fades into a yawn, and West eyes me with a knowing smile, one that tells me we're hitting pause on this conversation rather than stopping it entirely.

"I wouldn't mind kicking back and enjoying the ride until pizza time," he agrees. "You can take a nap, if you want—I downloaded a podcast I haven't had the chance to listen to yet. It's an interview with one of those researchers working on the Herculaneum scrolls, like we saw at the museum in Na— Okay, covering your yawn with your hand doesn't make it less offensive." West gives me a flat look, and I hold my free hand up with apology as another yawn hits.

"I'm sorry, I can't help it," I say in drawn-out yawn-speak.

"Yeah, yeah. Pretend indifference all you want, but I know you know that project is cool as hell."

I snicker while he leans over to get his headphones out of his backpack and pops one in the ear not facing me. As he queues up his entertainment, I angle myself a little closer to him until my head can rest against his shoulder. I feel him pause for only half a second before he shifts lower in his seat, giving me easier shoulder-resting access.

"Hey, should we move downstairs, or under the shade in the back?" he suggests gently. "Your face is getting a little pink."

With my eyes already closed, my consciousness quickly slipping, I roll my head from side to side. "I'll be fine, Mom."

He lets out a weary sigh and I grin to myself. I assume the issue's been dropped, that he's only getting more comfortable as he does some more adjusting of his position with minimal jostling of my head.

But then the world on the other side of my eyelids gets dark. Opening them doesn't help, either. "What the—" I start to sit up, to pull at whatever kidnapper-style burlap sack has been tugged over my head, when a hand presses me back to West's shoulder.

"My rain jacket. Allegedly the material is SPF 70, but even if that's an overestimation, it's gotta be better than your 'fuck it, that's what aloe is for' method of sun protection."

My laugh echoes under my pseudo-blanket.

"Uh-huh, sure. If you don't want to see my hideous face anymore, Weston, just say so," I tease.

His answering laugh is incredulous. "Believe me," he mutters, "when I say that I can't imagine ever getting tired of your face."

And even though he still manages to make the words sound grumpy, the effect on me is a full-body-on-fire, heart-racing feeling, and it has nothing to do with the sunburn. The fire fades into a less intense, lingering warmth that settles in my chest. This complete comfort in being safe and cared for is something I doubt I'd ever tire of, either.

I tuck my smile against the clean scent of his cotton T-shirt sleeve, drifting off to sleep while sinking deeper into the familiar feeling of falling hard for West Jacobs.

CHAPTER FOURTEEN

West

THE FIRST THING I NOTICE ABOUT TONY CAMPBELL-COSTA IS THAT HE'S very much not Italian. After his welcoming "buona sera," he proceeds to address our workshop with Australian-accented English.

The second thing is that his hair looks much more strawberry blond in person. I see Cammie clocking it, too, from her place a couple feet to my side behind our butcher-block-island cooking station. While her eyes take in the man's unexpectedly reddish locks, her fingers mindlessly fidget with one of her own curls.

I know enough about genetics to realize that one physical feature being sort of similar does not mean Tony is Cammie's biological father. But it's one more physical feature than she and Paolo had in common, as hard as I tried to find anything. Cam still looks sleep-rumpled from her afternoon nap on my shoulder, even though it's been more than an hour since I woke her as gently as possible so we could leave our bus and head to Tony's restaurant.

That time with her warm against my side, the pleasant breeze on my face as we cruised through the city and along the coast, and even the ten minutes of the podcast I listened to before realizing I wasn't paying enough attention to retain anything, well, it's the best afternoon I've had in a long time. Ordinarily, it had the hallmarks of so many similar situations that would make me paralyzed with anxiety—being in an unfamiliar area of a still mostly unknown-to-me city where I don't speak the language, not being totally truthful with my parents about where I am and what I'm up to.

Maybe I was wrong about my adventure battery. Maybe it's not a complete loss, after years of disuse; it just took a minute to boot up again. Somewhere, the one electrical engineering major in my group chat is cringing from how badly I've misused the battery metaphor, but I want to believe it's real. That I could actually be finding my footing again, embracing the unfamiliar, being open to new adventures.

My mind has drifted a few times toward the Germany program, and as much as I've told myself it's not for me, I can't help but reconsider. I still haven't officially enrolled or withdrawn, nor given Max a final answer. Is this why I've held off deciding—because somewhere deep down, I know I'm more capable than I've been telling myself?

Or am I just so caught up in Cammie that I'm ignoring my own needs and wants? Just pretending I'm in the driver's seat when I'm actually riding shotgun, too busy drooling over her freckles to ever operate a motor vehicle? I don't want to let attraction and emotions convince me I'm the type of independent, outgoing guy who can keep up with her, then get out on my own and find that I'm not that guy at all, not without her leading the way, making the plans, grasping my hand when the anxiety presses in.

Regardless of what it means for my future, I'm enjoying the hell out of the present. The feeling I get every minute I spend with this girl, it's like all the best parts of being seventeen again. Of falling in love with my best friend, with no intention of letting her go in a storm of my own confusion and fear. I never expected to find that kind of happiness again, especially not with her.

"West," Cammie prompts, snapping me out of my daze, her tone indicating this is not the first time she's tried. I blink her back into focus, though I'm pretty sure I've been staring blankly in the direction of her face for a while now, and realize she's handing me a flute of prosecco, holding another for herself.

I glance to the side as I take it and see Tony passing them out to each pair at their respective cooking stations, identical to ours, around an industrial kitchen that sits above his restaurant. Out the windows, we can see the sun setting over the bay, blanketing its golden light over peaceful evening waters and the boats that float through them.

I can't decide if this is one of the most romantic scenes I've ever been a part of, or if I've just got it so bad that a landfill would look romantic to me, as long as I was there with Cammie.

Returning to the front of the room, Tony raises his glass and gives the class a "Saluté."

We echo his cheers and take sips from our glasses. The bubbly beverage is somehow both refreshing and burns a little as I swallow it down, and I barely suppress my grimace. Cammie is not as successful at this, but I think I'm the only one who sees the scrunched-up expression she aims toward the counter. I remember her asking me about her throat being scorched by limoncello and bite my cheek to keep from laughing.

"It's a pleasure to have you all in class with me tonight," Tony continues. "I'm Tony, the chef and proprietor here at Antonio's. I suppose to start out, we might as well address the elephant in the room. I realize that very few people, if any, come to Napoli with the intention of taking a pizza-making workshop with an Australian." He's met with light, if slightly uncomfortable, laughter from around the room. "But rest assured that I am well-qualified, having lived in Campania—and in Napoli specifically—longer than I've lived in my home country, making this place feel like my true home.

"My mother is Neapolitan, and I came here straightaway after high school, in the hopes of getting more in touch with my roots and studying at university. But then, like all of us here tonight are familiar with, I fell in love." I raise an eyebrow at the comment, because what does this man know about my romantic experience? "In truth, I fell in love three times." He raises three fingers and is met with a couple *ooh*s and a few more raised brows. “The first time was with a young woman named Luna Costa, now known as Luna Campbell-Costa, my wife and the mother of our three children.”

My gaze darts back to Cam’s face just in time to see it fall from her interested smile to something slightly dimmer. *Shit.* Immediately, my mind runs through the implications of that information, like the fact that, if Tony is her father, this means he has other children who he did want to raise.

But that’s ten steps ahead of anything we know right now, so I try to refocus. Any intel we don’t have to dig for is priceless.

“Second, I fell in love with the city of Napoli, a place unlike anywhere else in the world and the home of my heart. And third, much to the dismay of my parents, I fell in love with pizza.” Laughter rumbles through the kitchen again and Tony smiles, bringing his hands together. “Not just with pizza, but with cooking as an art. I left university to pursue culinary school and never looked back. I run this pizzeria, where we use recipes and inspiration from generations of Neapolitan cuochi, including my mama and nonna, as well as Luna’s and other restaurateurs and chefs in town under whom I apprenticed. Every day, I get to share my true love with people from around the world who visit Napoli—the birthplace of pizza, and don’t let anyone tell you differently.

“Now, I love running these couples workshops. They’re my favorite classes to teach. Because my story with cooking and with pizza is, at its heart, a love story.”

I choke on the sip of prosecco I just tried to swallow. Did he say “couples workshops”?

"Couples workshop?" Cammie murmurs. I look to the other pairs. Two women with their arms wrapped around each other's waists, an older man and woman with their fingers interlaced, and another pair of middle-aged guys, one of whom is gently rubbing the other's shoulders casually but tenderly.

"Couples workshop," I confirm with a nod, sweat beading at the nape of my neck as it suddenly feels ten degrees warmer in this kitchen.

Abruptly, Cam's arm shoots out and smacks a hand to my back as if she's squashing a bug. It knocks me forward with a quiet *oof*. Then she moves the hand in clumsy circles, as if smearing the imaginary bug guts around on my shirt.

I shrug her off and whisper, "Is this your attempt at couple-y affection?"

Her eyes stay fixed ahead when she replies, "Not now, honey, Chef Tony is speaking."

Am I being punished? Did some higher power hear me thinking about Cammie's legs in her cutoff shorts while we were sitting in a church earlier? Now I'm in a sort of relationship purgatory, where we're not really dating, not really just friends, but this strange, in-between, fake-couple bullshit? Can I buy my way out of here, or did Martin Luther kind of ruin that shortcut for everyone?

Tony claps his hands once, yanking my attention back to where it should be—on him. On figuring out whatever we can about this man, and what part he could have played in Cammie's story. Now that I know even more about why she's looking for her dad, it's all the more important to me to be involved. I need to be here for her, protect her heart and her already shaken sense of self-worth, no matter the outcome with any of these men.

When Tony sets us free with our first instructions for starting the dough, I gesture to the aprons we were given when we arrived. Souvenirs, Tony said, that we'll get to take home to remember this workshop forever. They're red with a loopy white script that says *I left a pizza my heart at Antonio's di Napoli.*

"Do you think these come with all the workshops, or just the ones for *couples*?" I emphasize the last word with an accusatory look.

Cam meets my gaze with an apologetic wince. "I swear I didn't know. It was just called Pizza Making Two!"

I nod toward a flyer taped to the wall by the entrance, one I hadn't noticed when we walked in that advertises the recurring weekly workshop in this exact time slot. "Uh-huh—Pizza Making for Two."

Cammie looks at the sign, then back to me with a cute scowl. "Adding this to my list of grievances with that archaic website."

"I'm sure Tony will appreciate that," I tease. I peer around the kitchen to find everyone else too busy chatting with their own partners and starting their pizzas to pay attention to us before I continue. "So, what, now we . . . pretend we're together?"

"Was that not clear from my gentle caress?" she demands in a serious whisper, then breaks into a quiet chuckle at my unimpressed look. "Okay, I panicked and just went for it, but I'll do better from now on. It's probably easiest to be a fake couple for tonight, for the sake of blending in?"

Her voice goes up at the end, making it sound more like she's gauging how I feel than expressing a firm opinion. I'm no more confident when I answer, "It can't be all that different than how we act as friends, right?"

"Right, of course," Cam agrees quickly, nodding a little too vigorously to look natural about it. "Just act natural, act like ourselves, like friends, nice and normal."

It quickly becomes clear that Cam and I have different definitions of nice and normal.

"Hey, babe, do you want a turn with the dough?" she asks in a sugary-sweet voice that isn't even her own, making cartoonishly wide doe eyes that are beginning to scare me.

"Sure . . . darling," I try.

It's all I can do to follow her lead, try to match her lovesick energy so no one thinks there's trouble in paradise or that I'm not as into her as she is into me. The latter possibility is laughable.

"Beautiful, West, yes," Tony enthuses as he passes by our station while I'm kneading the dough. "Now *that* is a man who's good with his hands," he jokes with a pointed look to Cammie.

She giggles, the sound reminiscent of a Tickle Me Elmo I had as a toddler whose sound box started glitching. The resulting demonic laughter it released led me to sleep in Pops and Dad's room for a week.

Between the wood-fired pizza oven and my rising panic

from the pressure of pretending to be hopelessly in love with my friend, while secretly, possibly inching toward those feelings for real, I am sweating profusely by the time we add the finishing touches to our unbaked pizzas. I am holding the tub with shreds of a fresh mozzarella ball that I tore off by hand, weighing where to place another couple pieces on my margherita pie, when Cammie suddenly presses up against me, her front to my side. I flinch so hard, I drop the tub, sending mozzarella spilling out to cover the whole round of dough and sauce.

"Mmm, lots of cheese," she says with a flirtatious lilt that the words do not call for, followed by a casual kiss dropped on my shoulder. "Looks so good, babe."

It's not a good performance. But if they gave out "Tried Way Harder Than the Role Required" Oscars, Cam would be a contender. She's at least got my heart—and every other part of my body, save for my brain—convinced. Every one of my systems is on high alert, blaring SHE KISSED US alarms while the single rational brain cell I have left slams down a bunch of buttons with labels like FAKE and ONLY OUR SHIRTSLEEVE.

"Thanks, sweetheart," I manage to grit out between clenched teeth. "Can never have too much dairy."

It's a lie that my stomach will be refuting later, if I'm able to chill out enough to eat any of this. My unease isn't entirely because of my fake girlfriend's real PDA, either. It's also from what I see happening with Tony, one of my fears about this whole dad hunt endeavor playing out in real time.

Cammie is dazzled by the chef. He's charming, sure, with his dimpled smile and endearing mix of dry Australian wit and ridiculous dad humor. Every time he comes by our station, her smile brightens, her posture straightens, all the deep-down parts of her that so sincerely want to be loved and noticed bursting at her seams.

This is feeling increasingly like the worst idea. Like something I should have protected her from somehow, as if I even have that power. But I see the determination in her eyes, telling me this isn't over until she has her answers—even if they're not the answers she wants.

All I can do now is knead some dough, crush some tomatoes, and wait, ready to stop Tony Campbell-Costa from breaking her heart in whatever way I can.

"All right, all right, all right, Camilla and Weston," Tony says in what I think is meant to be a Matthew McConaughey impression. We're the only Americans in class tonight, with two British couples and one from Switzerland.

Cammie and I carry our pizzas by the edges of the squares of parchment paper on which they sit over to where Tony stands holding a pizza peel. Beyond the brick opening of the oven is what looks like the fires of hell.

"Who's up first?" he asks.

I don't even get the chance to think about it before Cam eagerly steps forward.

"I'll go!"

She trades her pizza for the peel in Tony's hands and holds it up while he helps transfer her creation from the parchment paper to the flat, floured square of metal.

"Now remember," he tells her, reiterating the instructions

he gave us all for pizza oven best practices before we each get our turns. "You have to just go for it. Don't hesitate, but also know your strength. Don't overshoot it or your pizza's going into the flames."

Cam nods eagerly and wastes no time stepping up to the oven that verges on too tall for her to comfortably use, then jabs the pizza peel forward like a fencer on the attack. The pizza slides perfectly into the "sweet spot" Tony described, where it'll get cooked all the way through but not charbroiled.

Unlike the pizza I'm used to in the States, these take less than a minute to bake in the heat of the brick oven. And Tony, I guess realizing that he can't fully teach us his craft in the course of one evening, takes charge of turning the pizzas once they're placed to ensure they cook evenly, then helps extract them with the peel.

When he judges that Cam's is ready, he slides the big paddle into the oven with ease and pulls out the most perfectly brown, bubbly, cheese-covered, garlic-scented pizza perfection that I've ever seen.

"Absolutely brilliant," Tony proclaims, studying the result of Cam's efforts.

She beams like she's never received a kinder compliment. Then it's my turn. Cammie sticks by to watch and offer moral support—or so I think, until she teases, "Don't know how you're supposed to follow that up, but good luck, I guess."

I scoff, pausing with my pizza on the peel, ready to slide in the oven. "Camilla Lovett, are you trash-talking my culinary masterpiece?"

"I would never, dearest," she replies with a devious grin, more of the real Cammie in her voice than Girlfriend Barbie.

When I look to Tony, expecting a reminder of proper pizza peel handling, he seems distracted, his eyes narrowed and unfocused in Cammie's direction. When he feels my gaze on him, he gives me a nod that I realize is the only signal I'll get, so I try not to overthink it as I slide my pizza into the fiery cavern.

Just when I bring the peel back out, Tony gasps. My head jerks his way, and I practically see a light bulb glowing over his head as he points to Cammie.

"Camilla Lovett? I knew there was something familiar about you!" he says, more than a little awestruck. His eyes are wide and shocked as he wipes a hand over his mouth. "You're Alex's daughter."

The three of us remain there, frozen and unsure what to say or do next.

Until a puff of dark smoke curls out of the oven, and then another, and we realize, one by one, that my pizza is up in flames.

CHAPTER FIFTEEN

Cammie

"YOU'RE SURE YOU DON'T WANT ANY CANNOLI? MY MOTHER-IN-LAW makes *outstanding* cannoli, and I'm not just saying that to up-sell you. If anything, I'm costing myself."

Tony gives West and me a cheeky smile as he looks back and forth between us once more, holding his hands out with palms up in offering. I can only shake my head as I swallow another sip of my lemon spritzer—alcohol-free, for the sake of my head and pride—and West leans back with a hand on his stomach.

"I can't do it right now, as much as I wish I could," he says sadly.

"Ah, well. That's what takeaway boxes are for, right?"

Even though we're the ones who were purposefully—and still secretly—deceptive, Tony feels responsible for burning West's pizza. As a result, after he wrapped up the official workshop for everyone else, he brought the two of us down to the patio of Antonio's and began plying us with apology food.

Once he got over the initial shock of seeing his ex's grown kid twenty years after they broke up, Tony seemed genuinely excited to meet us. West had been frozen with clear discomfort, looking to me to see how I reacted before he said anything—whether I'd admit to knowing about Tony and my mom, therefore revealing that West and I are weirdos who'd snuck into this cooking class like undercover agents and inviting at least a few more questions about our motives . . . or if I'd go with the easier out by pretending to be just as shocked as Tony.

Of course, I chose faux shock. We're in pretty deep with the subterfuge already; if we're not going to be honest, we might as well be consistent.

It's sort of a wonder that all my breathy *woooowww*s and *that's sooo wild*s and *what are the odds*es have been convincing enough to keep Tony from seeing right through me. Then again, I suppose "she's trying to ferret out whether I'm her long-lost father" isn't a place most normal people's minds would jump to. Plus, he's been too wrapped up in his own memories and reminiscing to develop any suspicions.

Tony turns his curious expression back on me. "So Alex is good, you said? Still doing her Indiana Jones thing?"

I tap my foot against West's under the table in silent acknowledgment of the irony.

"Still an archaeologist," I say with a nod. Mom is where I got the Indy-is-a-low-key-looter opinion. "She's actually around here this summer—back at Villa di Bronzo for the twentieth anniversary summer, if you remember that whole thing."

I wave a hand, like "that whole thing" doesn't encompass not only the biggest achievement in my mom's career, a massive contribution to world history and cultural heritage, but also, oh yeah, my birth. Like I'm not holding my breath, acutely attuned to his every move, down to a tic of the jaw or blink of the eyes, in case anything gives me a hint of his role in that part of Mom's life.

But the bright smile that takes over his face gives me absolutely nothing to work with. Just pure, selfless happiness for my mom's success.

"Twenty years," he says, scraping a hand down his jaw. "That's incredible. And makes me feel ancient." He laughs. "You know, she was interviewing for that contract job with the developer right around when we stopped seeing each other. I always wished I'd done a better job of keeping in touch afterward."

Now we're getting somewhere, I think. "Was there . . . any reason you didn't?"

His casual shrug is not the gesture of someone revisiting the painful memory of the girlfriend and child he abandoned. Unless I misread Tony somehow, and he actually is that cold and unfeeling. My head is spinning, trying to parse the meaning of everything in real time.

"The breakup was definitely mutual, at least from my memory. Being with Alex made me realize the strong feelings I still had for Luna, who'd broken things off with me a few months earlier because I was being a typical twenty-three-year-old who couldn't commit. But I knew I had to try to win her back, and at the same time, Alex was falling harder for this other bloke—she and I were never exclusive, so it wasn't a surprise. I think she and he really had something for a while there. So we were both too wrapped up in new—or renewed—love to make the effort with each other. The more time that passes, the harder it gets to reconnect, that sort of thing."

I have to press my lips tightly together to keep from blurting out the flurry of questions that arise about this other guy, questions I doubt Tony would have answers to. It's definitely a subject I'd like to pursue.

Before I can figure out how, though, church bells begin to ring from somewhere nearby, signaling the top of the hour. Tony taps his phone screen to check the time before he says mournfully, "When did it get so late? I'm afraid I should be heading home to la famiglia. But you two are welcome to stay as long as you want, order anything you like. It's all on me."

He scoots his chair back and begins to stand before West and I do the same. "Oh, we'll probably head out soon. We have to catch a train back to Villa Russo."

"Of course, of course. I'm so glad that of all the pizza workshops in all of Napoli, you two stumbled into mine," he says with one more of his mischievous grins, and then his face brightens as something else occurs to him. "Hey, if you find yourselves back in town before the end of summer, give me a ring or an email, all right? Here's my card."

He passes over the card with the Antonio's logo, and I return his smile as I tuck it safely into my pocket, grateful for this opening. "Actually, there's something I'd like to invite you to, if you're free . . ."

I recite my now-practiced story about the party, and surprising my mom with old friends. “If you think of anyone else I should invite, people she was close with . . . maybe the name of that other guy you mentioned?” My voice becomes a squeak at the end, thwarting my efforts to subtly slip the suggestion in, but I continue. “That would be awesome. So, uh, here, I’ll give you my email address, too.”

Reaching into my backpack, I tear off a corner of the first blank paper I can find and jot down my info before handing it to Tony.

“Of course,” he says with a nod, tucking the slip into his pocket. “Let’s not be strangers, yeah?”

West and I agree, and then we all say our goodbyes. As we watch Tony walk back into his pizzeria, the melancholy taking root in my chest makes me wonder if I’m still doing the right thing here. If maybe some questions are better left unanswered.

We begin our meandering journey back toward the train station. There are still a couple hours before the last one sets out toward Villa Russo, so our steps are unhurried along the wide waterfront street, the night air filled with the sounds of diners laughing, glasses clinking, conversations from couples and groups walking around us. Lights from the restaurants and hotel lobbies illuminate our way, along with the glow of the moon overhead, perfectly visible in a clear, deep blue sky. I spot a little offshoot with stairs leading down to the water, where a collection of colorful rowboats is tied up along the banks, bobbing in the gentle current. A few other pairs of young people sit on stone benches, or some on the ground, letting their feet dangle over the water.

When we're a comfortable distance from anyone else, we sit and I cross my legs. West copies my position, his body angled toward mine. While I watch the boats and the moonlight glinting off the bay, I feel his eyes on me.

"Euro for your thoughts?" he asks, the first time either of us has really spoken since we left the restaurant.

I laugh softly, turning my head to look at him. "That's a high price to pay."

"I don't know what their one-cent coins are called, and you're worth it anyway."

My pulse jumps and I look down to my lap so he can't see the adoration in my eyes. It feels like it must be so obvious, I might as well have cartoon hearts popping out from my face.

"I don't know, in the case of tonight's thoughts," I answer carefully. "They're kind of all over the place."

"I'll take the gamble," he says.

I take one slow, steadying breath. "Well, it probably won't surprise you to hear that I really like Tony. He's someone who I could easily see myself coming to love, forming that father-daughter bond with. But like, at the end of the day, even if it is him, I'm left with the fact that . . . well, he left. He didn't want me, and went on to have three kids, apparently not too much time later, who he has stuck around for and raised. I don't know how I would deal with that truth. And if it's not Tony"—I let out a laugh with nothing joyful in it—"this could get exhausting."

How does this end? It's the question I've thought about more than any other, and in my daydreams, it's all tied up with a pretty decorative bow. I have a dad who instantly loves me, a relationship that's immediately close and deep, and I feel, all at once, complete and capable and sure of who I am and where I belong in the world. But of course, that's not how these things go outside of movies.

And each of the potential fathers I've met has pulled me further into reality.

West hums thoughtfully. He probably doesn't know how to respond to all that word vomit. But just when I'm about to try for a "Ha ha, anyway, let's catch a train," he answers, his voice soft and serious.

"Those are two-euro thoughts, at least."

My head falls back with a much-needed laugh. It's a relief to feel the weight of the worries lifted off my chest, like he's taken some of them on for me. I think, for maybe the hundredth time, how lucky I am that he's by my side on this bizarre journey.

But his next words bring some of the weight back. "Cam," he says, reaching out to rest a hand on my knee where it nearly touches his. "Are you sure this is the way to get your answers?"

I feel my smile fade. "Of course I'm not sure. But it does feel like we're getting closer . . ." My voice fades into something small and insecure, and I cringe at the sound as I add, "Doesn't it?"

He sighs, and my heart sinks a little further at the weariness in it. "Maybe, but neither of our leads is guaranteed to go anywhere—for all we know, we might never see them again. And even if we do, on a practical level—what's the plan for rounding up all the suspects and getting to the bottom of who the one true father is? Like, say they arrive at the party, to everyone's surprise, and then what? We just hope Dr. Alex greets one of them with 'Hey, Cammie's dad'?"

The steady rise in the volume of his voice conveys the growing sense of worry that he's kept close to his chest. Like now that he's uncapped these bottled-up concerns to let one out, they're all bubbling up and over. The guilt I feel for causing him stress is mixed with a touch of defensiveness at his tone, which veers toward condescending.

Irritation—especially toward West—is a feeling I'm much more comfortable with than self-doubt, so I lean into it, raising my voice to match his. "I'm not stupid. I know that's not going to happen. I know I haven't figured it all out yet. So if you have anything helpful to contribute, feel free. Otherwise"—I swivel my legs around so that I'm kneeling instead of sitting with them crossed, one step closer to making a run for it if he keeps this attitude up—"no one's forcing you to be here. If you think this search is such a terrible idea, then just go back to the villa. Hole up in the library with your math problems and the friends in your phone. If you hate spending time with me so much, you can just stop."

"If I hate spending time with you—" he starts to echo, rubbing a hand over his tired eyes before shifting to bend one leg at the knee, ready to push up to standing and run right after me. We're fighters in a ring, circling each other and seeing who's going to lunge first, or give up and hit the locker room. "Of course I don't hate it—being with you is the only thing I want to do these days, after years of thinking I'd never get the chance again. I'm just struggling with this because I see you struggling, and it's like I'll do anything, even make myself the bad guy who tells you things you don't want to hear, if I think it's going to make you feel even an ounce less pain in the end."

"I'd rather you just be the good guy," I cry. "The one who trusts that I've already thought of all the risks and bad outcomes and has my back when I keep going after what I want anyway. The one who believes in me and helps me believe in myself. I need that guy more than the devil needs another advocate."

"You have me, Cam!" he shouts back, maybe the loudest I've ever heard him. "Don't you see that? I wouldn't be here right now or following you onto every train or bus or boat or off a goddamn cliff if I wasn't determined to be everything you need."

His arms are flung out wide, pulling his T-shirt taut across his chest and emphasizing its rapid rise and fall. Almost as rapid as my own heartbeat. But West isn't done.

"So yeah, I'm worried, but I'm also not going anywhere, not ever going to stop believing in you, supporting you, loving you—"

The words are like a clap of thunder, the silence that follows them all the more profound in comparison. I know there are other people no more than a few yards away, but West and I might as well be the only two left in the world, any other noise on this night drowned out by the echo of *loving you, loving you, loving you* in my ears.

His dark eyes are wide and wild, like he can't believe what he said, either. I don't know how much time passes before his intense stare is ripped away as if by force, and before I can even close my gaping mouth, he's leapt to his feet and turned for the stone staircase leading up to street level. When he hits the first step, my own feet finally move.

"West, wait," I call after him, not caring that we are an absurd American melodrama playing out on a busy city street on a random Tuesday night. West doesn't wait, and the focused, determined strides he takes make me think he could easily ditch me again if I don't get my ass in gear.

"Weston Jacobs!" I emphasize every syllable, like I'm scolding a child. Whatever it might take to stop him before he's crossed the distance from here to Villa Russo on foot, bypassing the half-hour train ride entirely. As the street begins to curve around, back toward the city center and train station, I finally reach his side in a quiet spot by a gently bubbling fountain. Or get close enough to his side, anyway, to make a grab for his T-shirt, clutching tight when my fingers meet cotton, then pulling until he lurches backward and swings around to face me.

His gaze is hard and dark under equally dark, furrowed brows, but it doesn't have quite the unfocused, unsettled quality of the last time he ran away from me, or earlier on the crowded street. It sends a shiver through me, my stomach doing the kind of fluttery acrobatics reserved for rare moments when I've been totally, delightedly surprised. It's a new side to him, so far from chill and controlled, entirely due to his feelings for *me.* Feelings that are messy and complicated and all the things he tries to avoid, but he couldn't stop them—couldn't even keep them to himself. I'm breathing almost embarrassingly hard, and it has little to do with chasing after him.

West loves me.

I'm aware, in the back of my mind, this does not necessarily mean he is *in* love with me. But it does necessitate further conversation, at the very least.

"Did you not . . . just say . . . you weren't . . . going anywhere?" I pant out.

West pushes a hand through his hair, looking up and away as he replies, "Yeah, but I hadn't planned on saying what I did right after, and when you weren't saying anything back—I mean, it was kind of an obvious rejection. It's okay, though, I get it. No hard feelings, I shouldn't have—"

"Um, no," I argue, squeezing my eyes shut and giving my head a brisk shake. "That was a clear 'holy shit you just said you love me and I'm gonna need a second to process.'"

"Okay." He sighs, lifting his hands in acquiescence. "Then take your time. Maybe we should both cool off and, like, leave it for now. We can go back to the train and we don't have to talk about it."

"No, you beautiful dummy. I've taken my second."

West blinks back down at me, confusion and alarm crossing his face. Before he can ruin both our nights by doing something monumentally absurd like retracting his love confession, I take matters into my own hands.

The matters, in this case, being West's face. I reach up, grasp his jaw, and pull, while my feet roll forward until I'm standing on tiptoes. The slight widening of West's eyes is the last thing I see before I close my own. Then finally, I press my lips to his.

He's frozen at first, which in light of my own recent actions, I have to understand. But after a couple moments, he melts into me like gelato under the Italian summer sun. His body curves toward mine, head angling down to make it even easier on me to deepen the kiss. I bring my arms around his neck, thread my fingers up into his hair, and grab on. His hands find my waist, one sliding up my back while the other glides down to my hip, both pulling me in to him until it feels like there's no part of the entire front of our bodies where we aren't connected.

This is not the hesitant, fumbling first kiss of two kids who are still unsure what it means, whether it's right, after spending their whole lives as close as friends could be.

It's the pent-up hungering, missing, loving, caring, hurting, *wanting* of our older selves. It feels inevitable—the slide of his tongue over my bottom lip, the way our mouths fit together, pull back, lock in, again and again.

Until all at once, a loud boom rips through the night air. It startles both of us enough that we break apart and stumble back from each other in shock. We're breathing heavy as our dazed eyes meet. A crackle follows the boom. Then another *boom, crackle, boom, boom.*

Fireworks. I whirl around, West's hands coming to land on both my hips as he steps up behind me, the heat of his front at my back. Pops of red, green, and gold light up the sky over the Castel dell'Ovo, a fitting finale to one of the most surreal days of my life. I turn my head, leaning slightly sideways to see West more clearly. I wait until I have his eyes—half lidded and wholly adoring—on mine before I speak.

"In the interest of only saying what I really mean this time around, I should add that I love you back."

Slowly, his flushed lips lift on one side. "I was starting to suspect that."

"And that you should kiss me again. Many times."

"As you're now aware," he says, his heated gaze dropping to my mouth, "I always follow your instructions."

He closes the distance between us to do exactly as told, while colorful explosions continue overhead. And together, we make our own kind of fireworks.

CHAPTER SIXTEEN

West

THERE ARE MANY DIFFERENCES IN THE DAY AFTER WHAT CAMMIE DUBBED our "first kiss, round two" versus round one. Like:

* Both of us are three years older.
* I manage my anxiety by going to therapy, taking meds, and other ongoing self-care strategies, instead of pretending I'm fine and white-knuckling my way through everyday life.
* I am not on the verge of several major life changes that make me confused about what kind of relationship I want with Cammie and am subsequently way less likely to say or do anything so out of line that we don't speak for three years.

There is also one major similarity:

* I don't know what the fuck I'm doing.

Waking up this morning, I'm half convinced the last twenty-four hours were a dream. There's no way that I, West Jacobs, have been so lucky as to win Cammie Lovett's affections for the second time in this one short life.

The first time, in all the years I've had to analyze it from every possible angle, could have been written off as a product of naïveté or convenience. We were pretty much each other's entire social circle for most of our childhood. Stick us together on one cool international dig site after another, add a healthy share of teenage hormones, and puppy love was nearly guaranteed to result.

This time around, I know the last thing she wanted was to like me, let alone more. And still, in a hostile environment of our own making, feelings took root and grew. So they have to be real, and lasting, and not just because we were forced into close proximity for the summer.

Right?

My confidence in that fact is dropping the longer I go without any sign of Cammie. As is my certainty that we ended last night in a good place. After the fireworks—literal and in my mind—wound down, Cam and I were the kind of disgustingly affectionate couple I usually steer clear of if I see them in public. Holding hands on the train ride and on the subsequent walk from the station to Villa Russo, exchanging giddy smiles over nothing and everything, stealing a kiss every few minutes like we were trying to meet a quota. At the door to her room, I'd slowly leaned in for a good-night peck, and she responded by gripping the fabric of my T-shirt in her fist and pulling me closer until she was pressed between me and the door, and I forgot where we were, what day it was, my own name. Nothing existed anymore but Cammie, her smile, and the way she makes my heart feel like it could beat straight out of my chest.

We finally managed to separate ourselves and retreat to our own rooms, only to meet again at the sinks, where we brushed our teeth side by side, and then I learned that Cammie's toothpaste has a slightly sweeter mint flavor than my own.

When I told her this, she replied teasingly, "Maybe it's just me."

Maybe I'd already been thinking the same.

This morning, I've heard nothing but silence from her side of the wall. She wasn't at breakfast when I went, which gave me plenty of time to sip my coffee and overanalyze every word that left a certain redhead's mouth yesterday. All the ones I remember, at least, from when I wasn't distracted by staring at said mouth or thinking about kissing it.

I'm busy staring at my phone as I start back toward my room, my message thread with Cammie sitting open with a blinking cursor as I try to figure out what to say. It needs to give the appropriate vibe of "just FYI, I'm still into you, twelve hours and a full night of sleep later, but in a chill, low-pressure way."

But without saying exactly those words, thereby sounding like a chatbot's best effort at mimicking human flirtation.

I've just started typing something pathetic like "good morning" when a text pops up.

Cammie: are you wearing those glasses again to seduce me?

I choke out a laugh as I stop in my tracks and look around the corridor from the dining room to the residence hall, my heart doing a backflip when I find Cammie leaning against the doorframe to the kitchen. I probably just missed her when I walked past, ironically preoccupied with finding her.

She smirks up at me as I approach, sliding my hands into the pockets of my sweatpants and forgetting about my phone as I tuck it away.

"I'm actually wearing them because I've forgotten too much lately, and I'm trying to stop my nightly headaches," I answer, feeling my lips pull up uncontrollably at the sight of her with a messy riot of curls wrangled into a ponytail, a T-shirt printed with the poster for the movie *Holes* over cutoff jean shorts, and her dust-covered walking sandals. Dazedly, I ask her freckled legs, "Why, are they working?"

Her chuckle draws my attention up to her knowing grin. "I can't speak for the headaches, but they're very much working for me."

I swallow even though my mouth feels dry. Is the villa's AC malfunctioning, or is it just me? Cammie reaches out and gives my chest a pat, right around where my heart is beating double time. "Okay, guess it's a little early to start objectifying you. I was about to walk down to Villa di Bronzo, make an appearance with Mom, earn myself more time to get up to off-site shenanigans. Want to come with?"

I'm already feeling relief, seeing her and how normally she's acting about us. I know if I go off and do my own thing, I'll only end up spiraling about where we stand. It's an easy invitation to accept.

We agree to meet on the terrazzo, and then I hurry upstairs to change. As I look for something lighter than fleece sweatpants to wear, none of my clothes feel right. Who packed all this shit? Have I always dressed this badly? Was anyone ever gonna tell me?

A quiet voice in my head says that my closet only looks like it was filled by someone who hates me because I'm on edge about other stuff. I'm beginning to spiral about messing things up with Cammie before they can go anywhere again, and I'm fixating on things that don't matter, convincing myself they're more dire than they are.

I try to believe that, finally tugging on a pair of khaki shorts and a plain blue T-shirt and telling myself that neither item will repel Cam as much as making her wait another ten-plus minutes for me to choose a different outfit. I'm finger-combing my hair, about to start toward the terrazzo, when my phone vibrates in my pocket.

On-screen is a new text from Max, reminding me that the deadline to submit our roommate request is coming up. He's been more patient than I deserve, and I owe him an answer. One I still don't have, but I at least text him back with words this time, promising to give him a definite yes or no soon.

The reminder doesn't help my unease as I return to Cammie, now sitting at one of the outdoor bistro tables with an odd expression on her face.

"Hey?" I say it like a question, and in answer, she gives two pointed but subtle nods—first toward the chair beside her, then to indicate something behind her.

I sit in the chair, then try to appear casual as I scan the terrazzo beyond Cammie's shoulder. A few tables away, Johnny/Gianmarco Russo sits with a younger man I don't recognize, both of them alternating between peering at the screen of a tablet and then at the assortment of loose papers and folders around it. Cammie's fingers fly across her phone screen and a moment later, my phone buzzes.

Cammie: they're talking about the anniversary party

Cammie: and I'm nosy

I suppress my smile as I meet her eyes again, mischief sparkling in them. I'm more interested in studying their particular shade of blue and all the little streaks and flecks of other shades within than in details of this party, but I try to listen in anyway.

"No, no, this is not correct," Johnny says, barely concealing some mix of panic and frustration. "Who designed this banner? No, Dr. Lovett's name is not to be included."

Cammie straightens in her seat, widening her eyes at me.

"Ah, va bene," the other guy says hesitantly. "Although we

were under the impression that this was a celebration of the anniversary of Dr. Lovett's discovery and therefore—"

"It's the anniversary of the discovery of Villa di Bronzo," Russo cuts in sharply. "The celebration is not in honor of any singular person, but of the incredible gift that the villa has been to us all. The focus should remain on Villa di Bronzo, and on the Villa Russo Research Residency Program, sì? Allora, about the ice sculpture . . ."

Cammie scoffs as she gets to her feet, chair scraping across the stones. I catch Russo's gaze darting her way and surprise flickers there before it narrows into something more displeased. But she doesn't spare him a glance as she heads toward Villa di Bronzo, and I hurry to follow.

"Is his ego seriously so fragile that he can't get over my mom's rejection *twenty years later*?" Cam rants while we start down the dirt path side by side. "I'm embarrassed for him. I'm tempted to bring some spray paint and graffiti her name on that goofy banner anyway."

I make what I think are the right noises in support, but I'm having trouble staying present. My head is spinning off into Worst-Case Scenarioville, imagining a series of catastrophes in which I decide to go to Germany and my anxiety goes through the roof once I'm there, resulting in me ruining this relationship by being the world's worst long-distance boyfriend and generally an anxious mess, and she'll never take me back because "fool me twice" and all that, and I have to crawl on home to Pops's dingy, unfinished basement, single and unwell, my lesson learned in what happens when I try to have it all.

If I hadn't left them back in my room, I would pop one of

my anxiety pills right now, the ones I take when I feel my panic worsening before it gets to full-on attack phase. The same thing that would have helped that first time Cam and I went to Naples, if I wasn't always forgetting to keep them on me.

Okay, I tell myself, *you don't have to let things go there. You're not the same guy you were three years ago. You can do better this time around. And where does that start? Communication!*

"All right, I give up," Cammie says, abruptly reclaiming my focus as she jumps off the bottom step down into the Villa di Bronzo entrance and spins to face me. I follow cautiously, my chest tightening. Was I too busy worrying about losing her to notice that I already have?

"What do you mean?" My voice shakes and she must hear it, because her determined gaze softens as she studies my face.

"On waiting for you to tell me what's wrong instead of me having to ask. I was trying not to pry, but I forgot nosiness is kind of a core feature of my personality. As is impatience. So what's going on?"

I open my mouth to answer, planning for half a second to deflect or claim all is peachy. But my better instincts prevail, along with my inner voice yelling, *We JUST talked about this, dumbass—take the opening!*

On a sigh, I let out the words, "I think we should talk about our fight again."

"Oof," is Cammie's answer as she rocks back on her heels and scrunches her nose. "That's one way to follow the most romantic night of my life."

"Same." I take a step closer and reach out my hand. Thankfully, she accepts and laces our fingers together. "I mean, it was for me, too, which is why I'm so in my head today. Because that's the kind of high I felt last time, only to absolutely wreck it the next day. I know we worked through why we stopped talking, but I don't think I've totally explained what led to our fight in the first place. And maybe doing that can help me—help us—avoid repeating history."

Cam's blue eyes are wide and wary, but she doesn't break their contact with mine and gives my hand a squeeze. "Okay, then, let's dig into it. Walk and talk?"

We're stopped in a high-traffic spot, a group from the field school approaching to take the stairs up, so I nod and let Cammie lead the way.

"I won't take you to the penis fresco room," she says over her shoulder as we start on a dirt path around the perimeter of the villa. "But remind me to tell you about Mom not giving me that same courtesy."

That earns a bigger laugh than I've had all day. "I don't know if I want to know."

"That's probably not the label they use for it on the villa map. Here, I think if we go this way . . ."

We enter the building through a well-preserved doorway, designed in a style I'm sure most of the people in the vicinity could identify, but I am not one of them. After a couple more turns, we're at one end of an elegant, black-and-white-tiled walkway that runs the length of a long, open courtyard. At least a few dozen columns divide the formerly indoor space from the outdoors, and while I imagine they were once identical, they're now a range of different heights and states of disrepair.

"This is one of my favorite spots, I think," Cam says, voice soft with reverence as her eyes scan the space. "I like to imagine philosophers, or other important people in togas and leather sandals, taking a stroll around the courtyard, discussing . . . I don't know, the meaning of life?"

I can't help but grin, watching her light up from this place that inspires her. I play along: "Or maybe, 'Hey, should we be concerned about the smoke coming out of that big mountain?' "

She tries to shoot me an admonishing look, but I see the laugh she's holding in. "You always have to take it to the darkest place, huh?" She shakes her head and starts walking again, still holding my hand. All we're missing are the togas. "All right, you have the floor. Let's unbury this hatchet so we can get to the reburying and, more importantly, more kissing."

Unable to resist, I brush a quick kiss to her temple before I straighten my spine and, with a deep breath, begin.

"You might remember a little of how I'd been struggling back then. My anxiety was getting worse. I was having panic attacks—I tried to keep it all contained, but I'm sure you weren't totally in the dark. I'd come to hate all the upheaval, moving around to temporary homes for Dad's work and constantly having to adapt to new environments. I was desperate for some calm and stability, especially as we got into high school.

"My parents were struggling in their marriage, and that was hard on me, too. Between my issues and Pops kind of laying down an ultimatum, Dad felt like he had to compromise and let our family be together in one place for a while. So much was changing already, and I felt like I was spiraling out of control. Then there were these big feelings for my best friend."

I chance a look at Cammie to find her eyes already on my face, mixed emotions swirling in their blue depths. She gives me a small, encouraging smile.

"You were the brightest part of an otherwise dark time for me, and my escape from everything stressful, and when it finally slipped out that you were feeling the same for me, it felt necessary to kiss you. I'll never regret that—best first kiss ever, bar none." I let out a soft laugh, knowing even that much is an understatement. "Then reality came crashing in—we were about to move, I'd be far away from you, my parents would still be fighting all the time, I'd still feel an elephant-sized pile of worry and fear weighing me down, and why did I ever think that at a time like this, I could handle the monumental privilege of becoming Cammie Lovett's *boyfriend*?"

"Oh, West," Cammie says, voice soothing and sympathetic. "I wish I could give past you a hug. And that past me hadn't gone raging bitch on him instead."

I shake my head quickly. At the end of the courtyard, there's a stone ledge that may or may not be a real bench, but I decide it'll suffice and pull Cammie to sit alongside me there.

"That's the thing—you couldn't have known. Because when I tried to explain my feelings without the heavier stuff, what came out was some nonsensical garbage about how I'd only kissed you as a friend, and couldn't do a relationship, and other shit that ensured I sounded like an emotionless asshole instead of a dumb kid hanging on by a thread."

Cam lays her head on my shoulder. While I feel a wave of relief at off-loading those years-old burdens, I know they're landing on her for the first time. She might need a moment to process.

"It all makes a lot more sense now," she says after a lingering silence, both of us lost in these shared memories that looked so different until we each let the other see our version. "Of course a part of me wishes you'd told me everything back then. But I don't know how much help I would've been. I wasn't exactly a beacon of maturity. So, while we both probably could've done without years of hurt and hostility toward each other"—she laughs, but her smile fades as she lifts her head to meet my gaze—"maybe everything happened as it was meant to, for us to end up here, together."

I nod, struggling to swallow the lump of emotion in my throat. Once I'm able to, I say, "It feels good, being able to tell you everything. I want to keep being this honest with each other, and I just—I'm in a much better place than I was three years ago, in so many ways. But there's still a lot of stuff in flux, a lot I'm figuring out in my life, and even though I manage it pretty well, anxiety comes out to bite me sometimes. I want to be with you more than anything. And I also feel this fear creeping in, that real life will get to be too much, and I'll handle it terribly once again, and ruin what we have for good."

I'm holding my breath by the time I get all the words out. This is the exact kind of feeling I was trying to express last time, and I did it so badly that we stopped talking for three years.

But maybe this really is the time we get it right. Instead of putting distance between us, Cammie pulls me closer, both her hands cupping my face as she looks directly into my eyes.

"I want to be with you, too. And not because I think you're the perfect guy with your entire life figured out, who will never have a bad day or get upset. Actually, I wouldn't want to be with that guy, because I don't know if you've noticed, but I can be somewhat of a shitshow."

Laughter bubbles up out of me and doesn't subside until a couple tears are trailing down my cheeks. "You're not a shit-show."

"Somewhat," she insists with a chuckle of her own. "But I love that you're imperfect, and a work in progress, because I am, too. And I think you don't want me to be all polished and perfect, either."

I give her an exaggerated grimace. "Oh, uh, now that you mention it . . ."

"Uh-uh." She sits back and wiggles a finger side to side in my face. "You missed your chance to be with someone perfect when you kissed me. No take-backsies."

I bring my finger up and hook it around hers in midair, drawing her hand in to press my lips to her knuckles.

"Good," I declare, brushing the word against her palm like a promise, then closing her fist to keep it safe.

Cammie leans in again and I meet her halfway in another

perfect kiss with my imperfect girl. I wouldn't take it back for anything.

After some time practicing our nonverbal communication skills, we come up for air—and remember why we came down to Villa di Bronzo in the first place.

"So much for giving Mom the impression of 'everything is fine and normal with your daughter, nothing to see here,'" Cammie whispers as we walk through the site and hear the voices of Ilaria and Dr. Alex getting closer. "I'm an hour later than I said I would be and have a *boy* with me. Might as well write *mischief* on my forehead."

"I can go," I offer, gesturing over my shoulder with a thumb. Cammie knows I find the documentary thing to be A Lot. Now that I've had some time with her and feel like things with us are solidified, I'd be fine to head back to the Villa Russo library and see about earning back some of my group chat respectability on Project Euclid.

But Cam shakes her head slowly, saying, "Nuh-uh. You don't get to smooch and scram—you're stuck hanging out with me."

I'm about to give "smooch and scram" the heckling it deserves, but she whirls on me suddenly, finger pressed to her lips and eyes wide. I clamp my mouth shut, though I don't know why. Nor do I know Cammie's reason for tiptoeing the rest of the distance to the opposite wall of the room we're in, then pressing herself flat against it to peer discreetly out the doorway. But I follow suit, making myself as undetectable as possible, despite the height and weight I have on my stealthy companion.

I feel a little ridiculous as I press my cheek to the rough stone wall and follow her gaze. I see Dr. Alex in the next room over, one of the bigger and more famous of the many excavated in the villa due to its sprawling, immaculate mosaic floor that depicts a battle at sea in tiny black-and-white tiles.

Bringing my lips as close to Cam's ear as possible, I whisper, "Why are we—"

Her hand shoots in the air and effectively silences me. I strain to hear what her mom is saying.

". . . that'd kind of run its course, as these things do, so it was time for me to move on."

My brows shoot up. There's no way—she couldn't be speaking directly, in front of a *camera*, about her past relationships, could she?

Ilaria's response pops that balloon of hope. "I'm sure it was hard to move on from Villa di Bronzo, though, when your life had changed so much because of this place."

"It was, absolutely. But it felt right for me, and especially for my daughter. I wanted to have other adventures with her."

"Of course," Ilaria agrees, and though I can't see her, I hear the smile in her voice. "I am interested to know—why did you stay away for so long? This is your first return in eighteen, maybe nineteen years, sí?"

Even from this vantage point, a room apart and only getting one side of her face, I can see the tension that enters Dr. Alex's smile.

"Yeah, closer to eighteen, I think. You know, I haven't been asked that before," she begins carefully. "I suppose it was . . . well, there's this way that places, or people, can be so tied to a particular stage of our lives, we can't untangle one from the other. For me, Villa di Bronzo, this beautiful countryside, Naples—they were all intrinsic to the person I was in my early to midtwenties. And for me to be able to grow up, become the person, the mother, the archaeologist I wanted to be, I needed to close this chapter. Needed to take space and time, find who I was past this one very transformative stage of both my career and personal life.

"I would miss it at times—when I would've killed for a Neapolitan pizza but my only option was Domino's. Or I could've used one of the legendary hugs from my mentor, Dr. Constantini, but had to settle for an email pep talk. Or wished I could stroll one more time down Via Camilla, bring my daughter to see the place she was named for, where I . . . I had some special memories."

Beside me, Cammie lets out a quiet gasp. But she doesn't move from her not-so-hidden hiding place, so I stay, too.

"For quite a long time, I knew returning would cause me to fall right back into who I was then, in ways that would no longer be right for me or for Cammie. Only in the past few years, as she's grown into a self-sufficient, independent young woman, and I've reached a point of feeling like I've achieved more than I thought possible, it's felt like I could come back and actually enjoy all the good it brought me." She gives a self-deprecating laugh. "If that makes any sense outside my own mind. I could've given you the short answer: It's complicated."

We continue to eavesdrop—for reasons that remain unclear to me—as Ilaria asks a few more questions and Dr. Alex answers, though nothing else seems as fraught as the topic of why she hasn't returned to Villa di Bronzo before now. When Ilaria calls "cut" and we hear the crew milling around, packing things up, I expect that Cam will make her presence known and we'll go talk to her mom, as intended.

Instead, she puts another finger to her lips, then waves for me to follow as she slinks back along the path we took here. Once there are enough stone walls between us and the documentary folks that there's no way they'd hear us, I say, "Okaaay, want to tell me what that was all about?"

Cammie continues speeding through rooms and hallways, floors that switch from dirt to tile to dirt-covered tile, and while I hear the occasional murmur under her breath, she doesn't answer my question. We're almost all the way back to the stairs when she stops and turns to me with hands on hips. Her eyes are blue fire again, a particular intensity I've only seen when she was pissed at me or had an idea she couldn't wait to explore. I don't think this is the former.

"Okay, hot nerd," she says in a playful tone, but the words are serious. "You and your glasses need to help me do the math. How many Via Camillas are in this region, and how quickly could we get to all of them?"

CHAPTER SEVENTEEN

Cammie

WEST INSISTS THAT WHAT I CALL HIS "TECH WIZARDRY" IS ACTUALLY "basic computer literacy," but it's a turn-on all the same.

One I didn't know I had, until this guy came back into my life. West and his six-pack and his glasses he misplaces more than he wears them and his laptop with its portable stand and ergonomic keyboard. All of which he uses—okay, maybe not the abs, unless he was flexing under his T-shirt the whole time—to save me from running back and forth across the Italian countryside looking for my street namesake.

I forgot about the "street view" feature of online maps. It's a little alarming that you can type in any address in the world, and in seconds, pull up a virtual image of whatever the place looked like the last time a car with a fancy camera strapped to the roof drove by. Alarming, but useful for the determined sleuth with limited time on her hands.

I hadn't planned on going low-budget 007, covertly listening in on my mom's latest interview. But when she mentioned Via Camilla, the description immediately struck me as odd. The story she's always told me about my name is that she got it from a street sign, yes. But she'd always made it sound like a random place she'd passed once when she had baby names on the brain.

This was the first I'd ever heard of Via Camilla being a place where she had "special memories," a descriptor she noticeably struggled to get out.

I realize I could be making Mount Vesuvius out of a molehill—that she could have deliberately made the story of my name more interesting for the cameras, or stumbled over her words because she was tired from all the talking, or any number of perfectly normal explanations.

But I couldn't shake the feeling. So we'd retreated to the library, our pseudo command center, for further investigation. Upon a quick search, I could count on one hand the number of Via Camillas within a pretty wide radius of Villa Russo. And thanks to West and his handy knack for remembering all that online maps can do, we only had to virtually "walk" down two of the streets before we struck gold.

"Holy shit," I say now, standing on the sidewalk of the One True Via Camilla the day after we found it online, holding up a Polaroid from Mom's old journal in the very spot where it was taken. We're in a nondescript suburb of Naples, in every way a middle ground between the rural village near Villa Russo and the bustling city center.

"Don't you mean 'Mamma Mia!'?" West asks. When I shoot him an unamused look, he smirks, then continues. "No, you're right. This is a 'holy shit' moment. Good instincts, Agent Lovett."

It feels like ten kinds of serendipity, coincidence, or sheer dumb luck that got us here. As West scrolled the little cursor down this street's virtual copy, something stood out to me and made me ask him to pause in front of a particular building. That building—a residential one, condos or apartments or the like—had distinctive-looking balconies, almost Gaudi-esque with their curved railings and spindles, each one slightly different in shape from the others. They hadn't undergone any transformation, natural or man-made, in the last twenty years, nothing to make them look different than they do in the picture a young Alex Lovett snapped and saved in her journal.

A picture in which the young man she calls ❤ is seen in profile, kissing her cheek, though she's clearly tried to fit a lot of the facade behind them in the frame. The caption she wrote in the strip of white at the bottom of the print reads "the ❤ nest."

"I don't know if I ever would've thought to search for the *building*," I tell West as I continue looking from the picture to the structure and back. "I wouldn't assume any of these guys still live at the same address they did twenty years ago, even if I'd been able to track the info down."

Goose bumps pebble my whole body, the hair up the length of my arms raised from the surreal feeling of standing in this spot. Feeling like it *must* mean something—this street, this man, my name. I don't know if it means he's my father. Or whether Mom would do something like make her daughter's name a secret homage to the man who left them both, and keep that hidden close to her heart for all this time.

But it feels like I'm pretty damn close to getting answers.

"You said it was a place his family owned, that he was using temporarily?" West asks. I nod. Alex's journal actually went into surprising detail about this guy's home, though I hadn't thought it was worth anything to me until now. She was obsessed with not only the funky balcony, but also the high ceilings inside, the cozy, broken-in furniture, some floral wallpaper that family lore said his great-great-grandparents, the unit's first residents, put up. "So there's a chance either he or someone from the family still occupies it. Let's see if there are names anywhere on the exterior—like if they have those buzzers assigned to every resident's unit."

I do a little hop-spin to face him, smacking my hands to his chest as I declare, "*Yes*, you're a gorgeous genius, Weston Jacobs!"

He laughs, catching my wrists in his hands to keep mine where they are, then bending to press a kiss to my forehead. "And I think *you're* too easily impressed, Camilla Lovett."

We approach the front door to find that, sure enough, there is a gray-and-black box with a row of buttons down its length, and next to each button is a unit number—one through nine—and what appears to be each resident's first initial and surname. After checking to ensure no one is watching or, most importantly, coming into or out of the building, I pull up my phone camera and snap a few pictures of the names—good to have options, I reason in my head.

Before we head back to Villa Russo, I step out toward the street to take a few pictures of the building, then one to capture the view of Via Camilla in both directions. It isn't especially remarkable—not a hotbed of sightseeing with architectural wonders left and right. But it has wide sidewalks sheltered by pretty trees, an assortment of historic and modern buildings, many with storefronts and restaurants on the ground floor, homes or offices above. It's got some activity but is still quiet, peaceful even.

It makes me happy, envisioning my mom walking through here all blissed out and in love. So enamored with this place—or maybe the man who occupied it—that she made it a permanent part of me.

It makes me sad, too, because whatever it may mean, she's never shared it with me.

But I let my determination to solve this mystery overtake the feelings wrapped up in it. West and I return to the library after enjoying the lunch buffet at the villa, refueled for an afternoon of cyberstalking some strangers.

"Remember when I told you I don't use my computer to do illegal, shady stuff?" West says when I describe our activities that way out loud. "That remains true, for any authorities listening through my webcam right now. None of this is illegal or . . . overly invasive. Only the normal level of invasive that is the wealth of information available on the internet about all of us."

“You’ve gotta be *so* fun at parties,” I say without looking up from my own computer, where I’m sprawled out on the cushy carpet.

“Hey, Pot, I’m Kettle,” he calls back, not missing a beat.

My smile is irrepressible as I think, *This is love.*

I start from the top of the list of names while he goes from the bottom up, each of us using whatever methods we can think of to find more information on the residents, anything that could connect them to our mysterious ❤ man. In my case, this means a lot of searches like:

L Romano Napoli

L Romano Via Camilla

L Romano Alexandra Lovett

L Romano archaeology

Ad infinitum, for all the other combinations of names and words that might be relevant to find what we need. I imagine West, in classic tech wizard fashion, is casting a spell to open a portal that leads to a different internet than the mortal world uses, one where answers come immediately with the right series of keystrokes and a secret handshake with the devil.

Needless to say, zero out of two of us are surprised when he’s the first to say, “I think I found him.”

“What?” I spring to my feet and practically body-slam him as I jump onto the couch where he reclines. I grab for his laptop.

“Whoa, okay, hang on, *ow—*” he mutters as my elbow lands somewhere around his lap where an elbow probably shouldn’t be. “Holy— Give me a second, will you?”

“Sorry,” I say half-heartedly as he holds the device out of reach and, still wincing from my unintentional low blow, gingerly shifts himself so we can sit side by side. “What’d you find? I’m dying here.”

West angles his screen my way, showing a LinkedIn profile for one Luca Goedhart.

“No profile picture—red flag,” I blurt out, already chewing on my thumbnail. I’m not even a nail biter. My nerves are finding whatever outlet they can, I guess.

“Okay, slow your roll—it’s very reasonable to limit the pictures of yourself you put online. Lots of people who work in tech don’t even use social me—”

“Right, right, snap judgment retracted,” I interrupt. “Let’s get to what you know, please, thank you, love you, et cetera.”

West lets out a dramatic sigh. “Anyway, Dr. Goedhart here was going to be my last guess, to be honest, because . . . I mean, it’s the least Italian-looking name of them all. But I gave him a shot, and as soon as the words *professor of archaeology* hit my screen, he had my full attention. From there, I got the following—most of which, for the record, came from his LinkedIn alone, and who knew anyone still used that site these days, right? But I digress—

“He was studying at the same university in Naples as Dr. Alex at the same time she was, but he appears to have transferred to some school in the UK around—you guessed it—twenty years ago. Finished his doctorate, has had a globe-trotting career taking him from digs in Turkey and Greece to a university professorship in Thailand, until just this year, when he returned to his roots as an archaeologist by working on an excavation project"—West's eyes lock on mine, his brows lifting for emphasis—"at the Pompeii Archaeological Park."

I don't think I've taken a breath since "professor of archaeology." Don't know if there's still air in my lungs, actually. All of this information coming together, and so quickly, it's painting a picture that feels entirely too obvious, too in our faces, to be real. This *must* be him.

Though I don't need any more convincing, and I doubt he does, either, West goes on. "A few other bits of supporting evidence, if we need it—he's connected to my dad on LinkedIn, and not to be a broken record, but who knew my dad used LinkedIn? Dr. Goedhart's dad is Dutch, thus the name, but his mom is Italian, thus the family flat, where, yes, according to doorbell labels, he is once again in residence. And finally, this is my own conjecture, but Goed*hart*, *Love*tt, my heart, your heart, wordplay that is both romantic and cheesy as hell. Now, then"—he pauses to exhale a heavy breath, then reaches over to lace his fingers with mine—"thoughts?"

It's all I can do to give him a dazed, awestruck smile. "You really are a wizard."

He scoffs. "Okay, this is truly not that difficult, and if you had been the one to search 'L Goedhart archaeologist,' you'd have laid out these same findings for me, your thoroughly dazzled audience."

“Maybe,” I concede. “But you wouldn’t be dazzled, because you’d be all ‘oh neat, I could’ve found all that, too.’ ”

“Is that really what I sound like to you?”

“Regardless of how much or little effort it took,” I go on, “my mind is pretty blown. So, should we, like . . . send him a message on LinkedIn or something?”

West’s lip curls with distaste. “What are we going to do, make a catfish account for a fictional Gen Xer? Give him a name like ‘Chuck Chapman,’ a vague job title like ‘consultant’?”

“You came up with all of that way too easily for a guy who *isn’t* dying to catfish someone on a professional networking site.”

The compromise we land on, in the end, is West using his real identity to email Luca Goedhart. I write the message, using the connection of Dr. Danny to fabricate a story about a project for school and looking to reach some of his dad’s contacts and blah, blah, blah. I/West request that they/we meet up sometime, promise to cause minimal inconvenience, and even offer to come to him at Pompeii. West gets to edit the message to his satisfaction, then sends it off.

It’s a delicate balance of lies, truths, and things in between, but I can tell it still makes West uneasy, being the one to go out on a limb like this. Especially for the meetup that feels like the most promising yet.

Or the one with the most potential for disaster, but I don’t say that part out loud.

“You know I really appreciate you, right?” I say softly as we lie there on the library couch, all electronics pushed aside. Just my head on his chest, his arms wrapped around me, one hand rubbing gentle circles on my back. "Thank you for all you've done for me already, helping me get this far in my search. I can't imagine doing any of this without you."

His chest shakes with a soft laugh, and in a wry tone, he answers, "The same can definitely be said for me."

It's been five days since our discovery of Luca Goedhart and subsequent attempt to contact him, and still no response. I've tried to remain calm, even cautiously optimistic. West and I have each spent time with our parents while we wait—and heard the passing remarks about what a "refreshing change" it is, and the "long time, no sees" loud and clear. So far, we've refused to give them the satisfaction of confirming or denying whatever they think is going on between the two of us. Things seem to be winding down for the documentary filming, while they ramp up for twentieth anniversary party preparations. Each day, new tables or chairs or random pieces of décor appear in new spots around the villa grounds, like little pop-up reminders of the looming surprise-sorta-reunion I've begun to regret ever planning.

If only Mom could've dropped the Via Camilla tidbit on day one. The trouble that would've saved me . . . but I suppose it also could have kept me from growing closer to West. The hint might not have even led me anywhere, without all I've learned since and without his help.

So I can't dwell on what could've been. Nor does it do me any good to obsess over a response from Luca Goedhart that might never come, no matter how many times I make West check his spam folder.

In an effort to distract us both, and surprise West with something nice, I decide to arrange a chill date night at Villa Russo. It's one way of saying, "Hey, sorry I'm an agent of chaos most of the time and haven't let you have the relaxing summer you were hoping for, but I can sit still sometimes too!"

Unfortunately, I am who I am, and who I am is the girl who's burning her second attempt at stovetop popcorn. If I was getting any wild ideas about my culinary prowess after making one (1) decent pizza at Tony's workshop, all I had to do was spend a few minutes in a kitchen unsupervised to bring myself back down to earth.

"This wouldn't be an issue if this country had Orville Redenbacher Movie Theater Butter," I grumble to myself as I remove the skillet from the cooktop. The ladies who make most of the meals here looked skeptical when I came in with a bag of popcorn kernels and some good old-fashioned American overconfidence just as they were packing up to head home for the day. But I tried to give them my best *I promise not to burn the place down* smile.

I might have been lying.

"*Shitshitshit*," I whisper-hiss in rapid succession when the heat of the skillet handle starts to seep through the dish towel I'm using as a potholder, and I have to drop the pan in the farmhouse sink with a loud clatter. When my ears stop ringing, I realize my phone is chiming with the signal for a new text. Tapping the screen, I see that it's West, wondering where I am.

Guess we won't have popcorn at this movie night.

I asked Dr. Danny if he could keep West busy this afternoon—anything to occupy him somewhere outside the library until dinnertime so I could work on a surprise date night in peace. I didn't even include the date night part, or any information about why I needed this favor. I don't know if it's a sign of Dr. Danny's trust in me or his extremely hands-off parenting style, but he didn't ask any questions.

I got most of the setup done this afternoon so I could show up to dinner in the dining room as normal, then play it cool as West bemoaned the bizarre events of the last few hours, during which his dad kept presenting him with new gadgets that weren't working the way they should, in the hope West could fix them. His phone, his e-reader, even the hair-dryer in his room—"Dad doesn't even blow-dry his hair!"—each with a weirder story of what caused it to break. I feel a little guilty and make all the sympathetic noises and *ugh, that sucks* commiserations, while inside I'm cackling. And a little frightened of Dr. Danny's ability to cause such creative diversions with so little preparation.

West will agree it was worth it, I've convinced myself. And it was admittedly hilarious to see his absolute despair when Dr. Danny came by our table, right as I'd requested, and asked West to swing by his room one more time, just take a "super quick look" at the TV, which had mysteriously started putting

Japanese subtitles over everything. A super quick look that's lasted twenty minutes—just enough time for me to put finishing touches in place, plus burn two batches of popcorn.

I scurry back to the library, looking upon the transformed room with pride. I've made a sort of pillow-and-blanket fort, bordered by the furniture that I've moved into a semicircle. It faces a wall of bookshelves, on which I've hung a white bedsheet I had to beg a nice housekeeper for, and behind my fort is a chair on which a projector sits. I found the little gem right here in the library and hooked it up to my computer so we can have our own private movie theater. All that's missing is the scent of buttery popcorn that I'd hoped to have filling the air and creating some ambiance.

But this is as good as it's going to get, so I answer West's text to let him know I'm in the library, then sit down among the cozy, cushiony fruits of my labor. My nerves grow as the minutes pass, and I'm beginning to wonder if this was a silly idea. Then the heavy wood door swings open and West enters the room, and my worries are squashed by the emotions flickering across his face—confusion to surprise to complete delight.

"Cam," he breathes out, "what is . . . Are we . . . You made a . . . pillow fort? For me?"

"For us, really," I correct. I pat the pillow beside mine in wordless invitation. "I know I've done a lot of dragging you around outside your comfort zone recently. So I want you to know that I'm grateful for you and that I love the comfort zone, too."

West's smile is soft and grateful as he toes off his shoes before stepping into our fort. "This is significantly more comfortable than even the comfort zone I'm used to."

I'm preening from his admiration and from the happiness in every relaxed inch of him as he reclines among the pillows. "Mission accomplished," I say.

For the next couple hours, I almost forget about the big looming questions that have consumed nearly all of my thoughts this summer. I simply enjoy myself in the moment with West. It's like a reset, reminding me that there are more people in the world than the one mystery man who contributed half of my DNA and pretty much nothing else to my life so far. Maybe I've been giving him too much real estate in my mind and heart, and not enough to the ones who *have* shown up for me. Who continue to be here, loving me now, just as I am.

At the very least, it's good to give the search a brief hiatus. Or it is, right up until we're about to fall asleep. West has already mumbled a couple of nonsensical sleep thoughts out loud that I can't wait to tease him for later. My eyelids are getting heavier, too.

But when I hear the quiet vibration of a phone, I check mine, where I tossed it on the floor a few feet away. Seeing nothing on the screen, I poke West's side and whisper, "Hey, can I see if you got an email?"

"Mm-hrmmmph," he replies, a sleep-talker's version of "Yes, dear." Without opening his eyes, he drags the phone from his pocket and holds it out.

What I find when I take it has me bolting upright and shaking West's shoulder.

"What? What is it?" he slurs, drowsy eyes darting around before landing on me. I hold up his phone, barely able to form the words I can't believe I'm saying.

"Luca Goedhart wrote back."

CHAPTER EIGHTEEN

West

"DO YOU THINK MY MOM IS SUSPICIOUS THAT WE CAME TO POMPEII FOR A second time this summer?" Cammie asks, taking a bite of the cornetto she stole from Villa Russo's breakfast buffet and stashed in her backpack for later. It's clearly Stress Snack O'Clock.

"I think Dr. Alex Lovett is one of the only people in the world who wouldn't find anything odd about it, actually."

While enjoying the lovely night in she planned for us, one in which we didn't discuss her dad, or lying to our parents, or anything else that raises my heart rate, I'd started to feel like maybe this project wasn't the only thing that matters to Cammie—that she was getting some perspective about the bigger picture. Then she got her last potential dad's reply, and that perspective zoomed right back into a Luca Goedhart–sized frame. Her hopes are higher for this one than they were for the other two combined, and I understand why.

She's named for his street. If we ignored absolutely every other piece of evidence in our long and winding search, that one truth would be enough to bet on. It's as close to a giveaway as we'll get, without asking Dr. Alex for the answer.

With Paolo and Tony, we could read into those experiences and make connections that may or may not be real to paint them as The One, but both also gave us plenty of reasons not to believe it. Luca is the last candidate we have who's yet to show us any reason he couldn't be Cammie's dad.

She's still able to believe she'll see him and it'll click. That he'll so obviously be this missing piece of her background and he'll see it, too, and they'll have a beautiful moment of shared "Aha! Finally," and ride off into the sunset as a happy father-daughter pair. If that doesn't happen, I'm fearing the fallout.

One way or another, we'll get some answers today. Dr. Goedhart's agreement to meet me—not a very enthusiastic agreement, all told, but maybe that's just his email style—included a plan to connect here at the Pompeii Archaeological Park at the end of his workday.

"Are we a hundred percent sure we're at the right gate? Here, can I read the email again?"

This is the third time Cammie's asked me this, and the third time I confirm, "Yes, it's the Herculaneum gate. No, I'm not letting you read the email again."

Cammie shoots me a narrow-eyed glare, though there's no real heat behind it. I don't point out that I remember a time, not all that long ago, when she read me the riot act for asking if she was certain of where we were going.

Exploring the park has been somewhat effective in distracting her. We got here a few hours before the meeting time, and Cammie, as much as she tried to play it cool, was practically bouncing as soon as we passed through the ticket turnstiles.

This is, one might say, her Roman Empire. We have stopped at every single point of interest in the virtual guidebook along our meandering way to the Herculaneum gate, spending extra time at places that were especially thrilling to her, like the forum, the Temple of Jupiter, or the two theaters. We also spent a while at the Lupinar, or brothel, where frescoes on the walls advertise some of the services offered there and made my face flush so red, a park employee pointed me to the nearest water fountain.

Cam even bought the audio guide at the entrance, because of course she did, and we've huddled close together to share the headphones when there's a particularly interesting bit of information that she decides I should hear. I feel lucky to experience this with her, even if I'm also hot from the unrelenting sun and distinct lack of shade in a city where most of the rooftops and ceilings were destroyed by a volcanic eruption two thousand years ago, and even though my feet are sore from taking more steps than they ever do in a day, on rutted, rocky streets and walkways.

I've also felt my own anxiety grow throughout the day in anticipation of this meetup. Luca Goedhart's email style was the first of the red flags for me, along with the time it took him to respond. But I've also wondered if there's some fraught history with my dad, making Luca unenthused about meeting me.

"Okay," Cammie says, stopping in the middle of pacing back and forth across the stone road that once connected Pompeii to its neighboring city in ancient times. "I don't know how it's possible with as much sweat as I've produced today, but I seriously have to pee."

She looks determinedly at me with her hands on her hips, as if this is a matter that requires my input.

"Then you should seriously go to the bathroom," I say.

She releases a frustrated breath. "Okay, but he could get here at any moment. He's already ten minutes late."

"Yes," I agree patiently, "and he doesn't even know you'll be here. It's going to be fine and you'll feel a lot better if you just go now."

Her groan is the specific kind that emerges when she knows I'm right about something and doesn't want to concede. But before I can put up any more arguments that really shouldn't be necessary in the first place, she's jogging back into the city, calling over her shoulder, "You better not let anything remotely interesting happen before I return!"

I give an exasperated shake of my head that she doesn't even see as she turns a corner and leaves my sight. Then I pick up her pacing habit. I have a bad feeling that we're being stood up, though I haven't voiced it to Cammie. I've been internally strategizing how to manage her disappointment and salvage the great day we were otherwise having. *I bet something came up with his work*, I'll tell her, like there's anything about a place that's been buried for a couple thousand years that's so urgent it couldn't wait until the following business day.

But who knows? Maybe Luca Goedhart is a really important guy with particularly important ancient dirty stuff to deal with. Not just another man in Cammie's life who's let her down without good reason, even if he doesn't know he's doing it.

"Weston Jacobs?" A deep voice interrupts my thoughts suddenly, and I whirl around so quickly I drop the water bottle I've been shuffling back and forth between my hands. It makes a loud clatter as it tumbles across the hard ground.

"Whoa, yeah, hi," I blurt out frantically. I scramble to pick up the stainless-steel bottle-turned-accidental-gong, not even looking at Luca Goedhart head-on until I'm standing again, my cheeks hot with embarrassment.

But then I find myself frozen in my spot, feeling the color drain from my face, and suddenly, I don't know what to say. It's not that the man before me is a dead ringer for Cam, though they share some features. He has gray-blue eyes not unlike Cammie and Dr. Alex's brighter blue—it's more their shape than their color that I recognize, the same wide-set, round, perpetually curious look to them, eerily close to the eyes I've spent a lot of time staring at lately. But his are paired with sandy-brown hair, not a hint of red. Their noses are similar, a little rounded at the end, and the lips—okay, nope, I can't let myself stare at this strange man's mouth, can't think too much about its resemblance to the one I've come to know by the way it feels on mine. Not if I'm going to be able to look him in the eyes—which I do, as I realize I've spent an uncomfortable time clocking every one of his features, and hurry to end the silence.

"You can call me West. Thank you so much for meeting

me, Dr. Goedhart." I'm impressed by how little tremor I hear in my own voice, as much as I'm losing my shit on the inside right now. If this man isn't Cammie's biological father, I'm calling my eye doctor and requesting emergency vision-correcting surgery.

The man gives me a tight but not quite unfriendly smile and a brisk nod. "Just Luca is fine. Apologies for my tardiness—there was a matter that took longer than expected at the end of my workday. I hope you've found your way here okay?"

"Yeah, it was easy for us to find. Good place to meet up."

I realize my slip only a moment after he does, his head turning to scan our immediate area for the mystery companion I'm referring to.

"Us?" he asks. It's not like this was going to be a secret much longer. Had nature not called, Cammie would have been beside me when he walked up. But I hadn't expected to be the one to introduce her solo, and as we already saw from the "cousin" incident, on-the-spot introductions are not my forte.

"Oh, y-yeah," I stammer. "My friend came with me. She's just gone to the bathroom but should be right back."

That was simple enough. There's no reason I should be sweating harder than I did during peak afternoon heat in a nearly shadeless ancient city.

"Should we wait here for your friend, or begin to walk and talk?"

I'm getting a slightly impatient vibe from him, and before I can think better of it, I'm word vomiting out, "No, yeah, she's fine. Walk and talk is good."

Cammie's bladder is on my shit list, bathroom pun not intended.

I decide that if we're going to walk because of my impulsive mouth, I can at least set the pace so there's no way we lose Cam. I start down the street in the direction she went, taking long, slow steps. Luca matches my stride, sliding his hands into the pockets of his khaki work pants.

"So," he says almost immediately once we're moving, "remind me why it is you wanted to meet."

No beating around the bush with this guy. *Another Lovett-like quality,* I start to think before scolding myself for passing too much judgment on him before Cammie's even seen his face. It's not my place to jump to these conclusions.

"Right, yeah," I say carefully, because if there's anything a Jacobs is going to do, it's beat around the bush. "I'm not sure how much you keep up with anything happening at Villa di Bronzo—"

"I don't," he interjects sharply, though I wasn't expecting an answer to that part. It throws off my train of thought and I take a second to get back on track.

"Oh, okay. Well, then you might not have heard that this year is the twentieth anniversary of its discovery, and my dad's back here for a documentary being filmed about it, so I—"

"Oh, there you are. I went back to the gate, and I was worried you—" Cammie's voice cuts off with a gasp.

I turn to face her and Luca follows suit. I'm about to introduce the two of them—or try to, anyway—when I notice that it's Luca's turn to have all the blood drain from his face. He raises a hand in Cammie's direction, not quite pointing, not quite giving a *stop right there* outward palm, but something in between the two. I'm not sure if he looks more like a ghost or a human encountering one for the first time as he stammers, "You . . . you're her . . ."

Cammie, who has been similarly stunned into stillness, looks less haunted than invigorated—like her heart is probably trying to pound out of her chest. Her eyes are shining and eager, her cheeks a rosy pink under her freckles.

"H-hi . . ." She steps forward, extending her hand like she's willing to pretend Luca is going in for a shake, not rudely gawking. "I'm Cammie," she says with a fragile optimism that I hope isn't about to be blown to pieces. Like an afterthought, she adds, "Camilla Lovett."

I wonder if she's picking up on the bits of resemblance I am. If she feels any of that immediate spark of connection or rightness that she'd so hoped for. In a selfish way, I'm already itching for the meeting-Luca part to be over so I can check in with Cam. To assure us both that she's okay, or if she isn't now, that she will be—to see to that myself.

"Yes, I . . . I can see that," Luca responds, giving her hand the briefest shake I think I've ever witnessed. "Alex's daughter," he adds, confirming what we all already know he knows. His head whips my way with a stern set to his jaw. "This is the friend you came with?"

"Uh, yeah, she's—" I begin, but he cuts me off with a decisive shake of his head.

"I'm not sure what's going on here, or what you know about

my history with your parents, but Alex and I did not part on the best of terms, and I know she and Danny are very close. I . . . I don't think I feel comfortable with this."

"With what, exactly?" Cammie prods.

"This covert meetup with their children—I assume you haven't told them, anyway. It doesn't quite seem appropriate, given the circumstances. I'm sorry to do this when you've made the journey already, but I think it's best if I go."

"Wait!" Cam steps forward, but Luca swerves around her, shaking his head again.

"I wish you both a pleasant time in Italy," he says before speed-walking back in the direction we came, exiting through the Herculaneum gate, and turning out of sight.

Cammie and I look at each other at the same time, matching expressions of bewilderment on our faces.

"That was—" I begin as she says simultaneously, "Do you think he—"

We both stop like we're out of breath and words at the same time. Luca Goedhart took both when he ran away from us.

CHAPTER NINETEEN

MYSTERIES ARE MUCH MORE FUN WHEN THEY DON'T HAVE ANYTHING TO DO with your real life.

That's the conclusion I've come to after our short and not especially sweet meeting with Luca Goedhart. After a few moments of standing there, taking in the what-the-fuck of it all, West deferred to me for the decision of what to do next. A large part of me wanted to curl into a ball right then and there, on the bumpy streets of this ancient city as modern tourists surround us, to let out some pent-up stress tears that I think I've needed to release for a while.

But my dignity prevailed, the more sensible part of me deciding, hey, we don't have to let this guy ruin what was previously a really cool day of exploring the world's largest archaeological site. There was still more I wanted to see of Pompeii, and I didn't think I should let anything keep me from taking full advantage while I'm here. So we continued on to the outer reaches of the park to the Villa dei Misteri, a name that I now think might be a little too on the nose for my current circumstances.

Where's the Villa dei Very Clear-Cut Answers and Truths when I need it? It's probably insensitive to make the major tragedy that took place here two thousand years ago about me and my problems. But that's why these are inside thoughts, no matter how hard West tries to get them out of me.

He's doing his best to give me space, I can tell, doesn't want to force me to talk about my confusion and disappointment over what went down with Luca. But I can read Weston Jacobs's face like a book, and those troubled eyes stay pinned on me the rest of the afternoon, wide and worried and desperately wanting to pry into my thoughts.

I choose to focus on my new best friend, the audio guide to the park. She tells me all about the mysterious frescoes that give this villa its name, and all the theories about what they depict—cults and Dionysian rituals and various gods and goddesses. I try to imagine what it would have been like to be the first archaeologist to come across one of these paintings, to begin to realize what a massive treasure you were unearthing, so incredibly preserved for millennia.

My stomach flips. It's how I've always felt when I've thought about Mom first discovering Villa di Bronzo, first putting together the pieces of what a gold mine she'd stumbled upon. Until recently, I thought the fact that I was technically there with her, even as a tiny life-form that barely had a heartbeat, meant we'd shared the experience in a small way. That it was embedded into the very makeup of who I am and no one could take that from me, just as they're unable to take away my mom's greatest professional achievement.

So why did I let that happen in the end—let my confidence, my certainty that I knew what I was meant for, be shaken by a little rejection? I guess the better question now would be, do I think I could get that back?

I allow myself to put off answering, instead enjoying the rest of my self-guided walk through the Villa dei Misteri, back down into the center of the park and around a few more of the fascinating structures that make up this sprawling city. I also determinedly ignore West's sympathetic eyes, sharing the best fun facts I learn from the audio with him, taking pictures of the two of us together as we cross back through the forum with the view of Vesuvius and the crumbling temple columns behind us.

I keep all the other stuff contained until we've left the park and started our unhurried journey back to Villa Russo, which includes a stop at a gelateria near the train station. Normally on a hot day, something fruity sounds most refreshing to me, thirst-quenching while also sweetly delicious. But today is a double-chocolate day, stracciatella and bacio—a chocolate hazelnut mix—one scoop of each stacked in a sweet, crispy cone.

West notices the change when we sit across from each other at a bistro table outside, the sun beginning to set over the bay in the distance.

"This is a departure for you," he says, tone quizzical. He

has, of course, opted for pistachio. I lick around the edges of the cone, where my gelato is just beginning to get drippy.

"Chocolate is for eating your feelings," I say by way of explanation.

West hums as his tongue darts out to lick his own melting scoop. "So we're acknowledging that we are having feelings now."

I give him an affronted look. "You might recall that I have acknowledged my own feelings many times in recent history, West Jacobs, or did my pouring my heart out to you mean nothing?"

His lips flatten into an unimpressed line, a single, dark eyebrow raising as if to say, *Yeah, yeah, now cut the shit.*

"Okay," I concede. "Yes, of course I'm having feelings. But you better be sure you're ready, because once I start letting them out, there's no stopping the flow. She and I are alike that way." I gesture over my shoulder to the hulking presence of Mount Vesuvius in the distance, then at West's grimace, tip my head and mimic his follow-up question to his own dark quips. "What, too soon?"

He takes a couple more licks before responding. "I'm trying to figure out if I'm supposed to push you to keep talking, or if it's one of those occasions where laughing at your jokes is actually the best way to be here for you."

I pause at his observation—such a thorough read of me, the kind no one else has ever been able to do. It really shouldn't be the thing that finally makes me crack, tears filling my eyes to a blurry sheen before I even feel them coming on.

"Oh, Cam," West says, and his hand takes mine across the table, holding it tightly. I hear the scrape of his chair legs across concrete as he moves in closer. "What did I say? I . . . I'm a dumbass. Don't listen to me. Please, just don't cry. Or do . . . whatever works for you right now."

"I think . . ." I say in gasping breaths between sobs, the words disjointed and hiccup-y, "what I need . . . to do . . . is cry."

"Okay," West soothes, "okay, that's good. That's healthy, I think, not that I'd know, but I support it. Do you want me to get you a tissue, or napkins? I don't know if there's a farmacia open, but—"

"Just sit with me," I warble, so he does, pushing his chair closer until it's right beside mine. I can't even summon any embarrassment about being one of those couples who sit on the same side of the table, because I want his nearness. Want his arm that comes around me, strong and warm and the perfect fit over my shoulders as he pulls me in to his side. I want the soothing comfort of his lips as they press a kiss to the top of my head, then just stay there, every so often murmuring words of love and reassurance.

When my tears finally subside enough that I can form a sentence without sounding like I'm in respiratory distress, I turn my face up to look at West.

"I'm just feeling . . . lost, I think," I admit in a small voice. "It isn't only the huge fail that was that interaction with Luca, though it was kind of wild and does raise at least a dozen more questions that I don't know I'll get the answers to. But it's . . . it's everything."

I finish off the last bit of cone that I've been sadly holding on to while I've cried, like it's my emotional support gelato vessel, before I continue.

"I've been so head-down, full-speed-ahead, basically since the moment I stopped crying over my field school rejection. Which only happened when Mom invited me to come with her this summer, and I got this wild idea to find my dad. But from the start, it's . . . it's just been a distraction.

"I've used it to distract me from all the things that rejection made me feel, made me question about my worth, my purpose, my future. I've treated it like this great mystery from someone else's story, like it isn't tangled up in a lifetime's worth of my very personal, very messy feelings about the parent who didn't want me. But I was never going to be able to outrun all of that forever, was I?"

West's smile is sad, the extra tight squeeze he gives me his only answer to the question.

"I just want . . ." I begin, pausing for a sniffle and another beat to think through the end of that sentence. "I want to feel like I'm enough. Like I'm good and capable and . . . and someone worth keeping."

"Cam, you are," West murmurs, rubbing soothing circles on my back with one hand while the other grips me tight, like he's worried I'll slip away. Like he very much intends to keep me. "You're all of that and more. I'll tell you as much as you need to hear it, and help you figure out how to believe it for yourself. But I promise it's not tied to whether some snobby summer program makes a big, huge mistake not accepting you"—that gets a watery snort-laugh out of me—"or if you can track down some guy who might've contributed half your DNA twenty years ago, but hasn't done a thing to deserve you in his sad, Cammie-less life."

I try to let the words sink in, to let them soothe the wounded parts of me, some of which have been here since the very beginning of my life but still feel fresh and painful.

After a few minutes of silence, holding each other while dusk descends and my tears dry up, West offers carefully, "And you know . . . you can still get your dad question answered, if that would help you find some peace."

I give him a small, conciliatory smile as I begin to uncurl from shrimp posture and ready myself to face the world beyond West's chest. "Yeah, I know," I admit. "One of these days, I'll work up the courage to ask her."

He nods slowly. "There's no rush, though. You're allowed to do this on your own timeline. And whatever your parental situation, it doesn't change the fact that you're a complete—and completely wonderful—person."

Emotion bubbles back up in my throat and I have to look away while I blink back the returning mistiness in my eyes.

"I mean, look at my life," West continues. "I have two dads, no mom, and wouldn't you say I'm just as whole and complete and also plenty fucked up as someone with two happily married heteros who raised them and their one-point-five siblings?"

I laugh, loud and surprising to us both, causing a couple straggler tears to slip out and roll down my cheeks. West reaches over and wipes them away with a gentle touch, an equally soft look in his eyes.

"You make a good point, Jacobs," I say. When I meet his gaze, I hope he sees the same depth of affection and love reflected back at him, because I think maybe no one's ever deserved it more. "You're as completely wonderful as it gets."

Slowly, giving me plenty of time to pull back if I'm not here for it, West brings his lips down to mine in a kiss that is sweet, lingering, and absolutely, ridiculously full of love. One that leaves me feeling like I've already found everything I needed this summer.

CHAPTER TWENTY

West

THE DAY OF THE PARTY BEGINS WITH A BEAUTIFUL GIRL KISSING ME.

The same beautiful girl who fell asleep next to me last night in my cramped twin bed during a screening of *The Mummy*. With all that's changed over our years apart, I was comforted to find that she's still the worst person to watch any archaeology-related movie with. She pointed out every place the fictional characters went wrong, according to real-life, twenty-first-century archaeology standards and ethics and best practices, while I reminded her that a film about a reawakened mummy with supernatural powers wasn't exactly aiming for realism.

It's been a week since our meeting with Luca Goedhart ended before it could really begin, and Cammie and I have settled into a comfortable routine, one that doesn't involve running around the Naples metropolitan area on a hunt for Cam's glorified sperm donor, as she's decided she should rebrand the mystery man. Who's much less of a mystery in my mind, since I laid eyes on Cammie's Dutch Doppelgänger (Twenty-Years-Older Man Version). But if she noticed their physical similarities, she hasn't addressed them, so I've kept my opinion to myself.

Instead of the Dad Quest, our days have been filled with a refreshing return to our individual interests—for me, catching back up with my friends in our race to solve as many Project Euclid problems as we can. For Cammie, spending more time down in Villa di Bronzo with Dr. Alex and the field school students, now that the documentary has largely moved into post-production mode and her mom couldn't resist getting her hands back in this familiar dirt. Cam has finally put her trowel to use, after all the time it spent neglected in her backpack. It seems like she's gradually allowing herself to love what she loves again. It's the best feeling, seeing her come back up to Villa Russo every time with more freckles and a smile she can't wipe off her face.

We spend nearly all the rest of our time together, either just the two of us or with our parents, who exchange smug smiles when they think we're not looking, clearly confident in the success of their scheme. But they've yet to stage a joint family meeting on our relationship, for which I couldn't be more grateful.

Cam and I wander the gardens of Villa Russo hand in hand, taking a picnic basket and a quilt out to the sunny hillside on milder afternoons. We talk about everything and nothing we've missed in each other's lives, and what the future could look like once we return to school.

The only topic I find myself avoiding is the Germany program. Cam steers clear, too, and I'm not sure if she assumes I've already declined it, based on what I last told her on our day in Capri. But I'm reluctant to ask and instead keep talking about us both being on our stateside campuses like it's inevitable. It's only a couple hours' drive between Nolan U outside Chicago and Elora in Wisconsin, making weekend visits easy. Even if those weekend visits might not be able to start until next year, when I've returned from a whole different continent.

The fact that it's even a conversation I get to have—how we'll fit into each other's everyday lives—is still surreal. It's all I can do to daydream out loud with her, imagining how amazing it'll be to have her around back home, meeting my school friends, building our routine there. We both acknowledge that a long-distance relationship could be more difficult in reality than in our musings. Neither of us acknowledges that the distance could be a lot longer than we're counting on.

We can handle it, if we have to—we've gotten past much bigger obstacles before. And I'm too stoked about the chance to be together to dwell on the hypothetical hurdles. Very un-West of me, all things considered.

Whatever else the future holds, I hope it comes with many mornings just like this one—a disgustingly blissful hour of sleepy cuddling and kissing and whispering sweet nothings that feel like everything. Cammie reluctantly leaves my room to get ready for the day and do whatever pre-party primping Dr. Alex has planned for the two of them. And leaves me to think about how the hell I got this lucky.

Thoughts that are interrupted by the text I get from Max. He says that he met a guy in the Germany program's chat server who is looking for a roommate. If I don't think I'm going, he adds, he understands—he just has a backup roommate lined up, waiting on my decision before they submit the necessary form.

Sinking into my desk chair, I reread his text a couple times. Then open my computer and pull up the roommate interest form.

I don't know why this message, of all things, finally lights a fire under me—sparks a feeling of decisiveness that I'd yet to find until now. I want to room with Max. Something about the glimpse of the alternative—the world in which I withdraw my commitment, go back to campus as normal, and follow along through social media while Max has what I expect will be the time of his life in Berlin, studying things that excite me and living with some other guy—it feels all wrong.

This summer, being with Cammie, has shown me not only that can I do things that scare me, more than I'd come to think was possible. But also that it doesn't have to be a breeze, that I'm allowed an adjustment period, to feel uncomfortable and anxious at times—and still make it through. I have the tools to navigate the fear, and people who will listen when I need to vent or hold my hand to share their strength.

I've seen how much more I'm capable of if I allow myself to try. If I give myself a chance, I can live a much bigger life than the one I've built while in survival-then-recovery-mode these past few years. I think I'm ready for more adventures.

So before I can change my mind, I open Max's text. And finally, I say yes.

To prepare myself for a night of mandatory socializing, I spend much of the day hiding in my library cave. I put Germany and the future and all the people I'll need to update on both of those subjects out of my mind, telling myself I have time to deal with that later. Cammie and my parents—the only ones who really need to know—will be excited for me, I think. I hope. For now, I enter a sort of hyperfocus zone only brought on by the right combination of caffeine—in this case, three espressos—and competitive shit-talking in the group chat.

Over the course of the afternoon, I complete a new personal record number of Project Euclid problems in one day. I feel the achievement in the aching of my wrists and fingers, which crackle like bubble wrap as I roll and stretch them this way and that, having pushed the limits of my ergonomic keyboard's capabilities. I've made my pre-arthritic bed and I must lie in it.

I'm surprised and a little ashamed to find it's nearly sunset when I emerge, my laptop tucked under one arm and my phone in my opposite hand, which I use to scroll through all the notifications I missed while in a coding fugue state. The only ones I really care about are the text updates from Cammie, photos that only partially display each step of the all-day glam process she's been through.

One focuses on the painted fingernails of her left hand, a glossy shade of pink that reminds me of the flush of her cheeks when she's embarrassed or excited. The next is of a lone, curling tendril of red hair against the lightly freckled skin of her neck, a view that shouldn't make me have to remind myself to breathe, but does nonetheless. Most recently, I got a close-up of gauzy, pale green fabric, presumably some part of the dress or skirt she'll have on tonight. I'm looking forward to seeing the rest, even though I was already gone for her when she showed up to the last fancy gathering in cutoff overalls and half-undone braids.

I've never felt like I'm literally buzzing with anticipation of seeing another person the way I do as I return to my room and begin a much less involved getting-ready ritual. I feel like a scrub, putting in so little effort compared to her, but I think the results will fairly represent the difference.

After I've pulled on my one pair of dress pants in a medium-gray shade and a similarly unexciting white button-down, I knot my blue-and-green-striped tie around my neck. Convenient that one of the two I packed can even attempt to match Cam's outfit. I work a dab of the one hair product I use—and only sparingly—into the dark brown mess on my head, attempting to make it appear halfway tamed for once. Then I slide my feet into a pair of leather loafers and check the clock on my phone.

Ten minutes well enough spent, I guess. Time to hit the terrazzo.

Heading downstairs, I consider not for the first time how glad I am that Cam isn't expecting any of the potential dads to show at this gathering. We—well, she, using my email account—did write to Luca once after the meet-awkward, letting him know about the party, the same spiel about surprising her mom with old friends, but with a little extra emphasis on how much she hoped he could make it. A part of me was tempted to secretly follow that up with my own addendum, giving him a piece of my mind about this deadbeat dad act I'm almost certain he's pulling on an amazing girl he'd be lucky to know . . . but I am, at the end of the day, pathologically nonconfrontational, and therefore refrained. Unsurprisingly, he never responded.

Tony is the one I probably would've found least stressful, but he replied to Cam's initial email with an apologetic note about not thinking he'd be able to make it. Paolo, the seafaring enigma, was also unresponsive to Cam's one effort to reach out. We figure he didn't know what to say, given that she'd never revealed her identity as his ex-girlfriend's grown-up child until she tried for a "Hey, remember me? Well, I just realized the craziest thing . . ." approach in her message. Cammie joked that he probably thought she was a scammer trying to profit off his boat tour empire.

So unless Dr. Constantini somehow finds his way here—Cammie is convinced he isn't the type to check his email more than twice a year, and she'd have been better off sending his invitation via carrier pigeon—there will be no surprises on tonight's guest list after all. This leaves me considerably more relaxed than I'd hoped to be, as I step outside to the same space where we had the Welcome Dinner. The first night I saw Cam again and began to realize, however much I shrouded it in insults and snark, that none of my intense feelings for her had been squashed by time and distance.

I slowly scan the area, groups of students, faculty, and staff mingling and enjoying the first cocktails of the night. A jazz band provides live music from their spot between two sets of open French doors off the dining room. Inside on its own honored table is some large, brown, rectangular object that I'd wager is the scale model of Villa di Bronzo, made entirely out of chocolate. I'm about to make a beeline to check that out when my eyes catch on the only part of this evening more exciting than a giant chocolate sculpture.

Cammie is an almost otherworldly vision in a green dress, doing her own perusal of the terrazzo, not far from the band. Her red hair is pinned up except for a few loose tendrils that I want to twist around my fingers, her wealth of sun-darkened freckles highlighted rather than hidden by the elegant makeup that she said in an earlier text would be impossible to replicate on her own without years of training "and possibly some dark magic." The twinkle lights catch the shimmer on her cheekbones when she turns her face, her eyes looking bigger and bluer than ever under dramatically darkened lashes.

I think I swallow my own tongue, taking her in. But I try to pull my shit together enough to cross the paving stones to her, certainty settling in that it doesn't matter the number of decades or thousands of miles that could separate us—my feelings for Cammie are never going away.

"Cam," I say when I draw near, and only when I hear the gravel in my voice do I realize it's the first word I've said out loud since she left my room this morning. The thought gets an almost guilty laugh out of me, for how much I've enjoyed a successful day of seeing and speaking to no one. No one but the only one who matters, anyway.

She spins on one shiny-sandal-clad heel, and if I thought she looked gorgeous from afar, it's nothing compared to the full-on, close-up radiance of the smile that takes over her face when she realizes it's me.

I rub a hand over my jaw, sparking the less satisfying realization that I forgot to shave. See? Scrub behavior. I don't know what this angelic girl is doing, looking at me like I'm the only guy at this party, this villa, maybe on this earth. If she doesn't realize how much better she can do, I'm certainly not going to tell her.

"You look . . . unbelievable," I manage, still a little gruff despite multiple throat clearings.

A blush blooms on Cammie's cheeks, and I look down to where her fingers fidget around her waist to confirm that, yes, the shade perfectly matches her nail polish.

"You're not too bad yourself," she replies softly, like a secret between us. But lest I think she's shy or self-conscious about being with me in semipublic like this, she reaches up to finger-comb some curls that have evaded my efforts to civilize them. I bend my knees slightly to make it easier for her to reach until, apparently satisfied with her touch-ups, she brings the hand down to my cheek and gives it a quick pat.

"Better," she says with a wink. The word settles over my racing heart like a weighted blanket—heavy, but the comforting kind. I had a good day of being mostly in solitude, yes. But being back with her, this is better. Always better. We lace our fingers together and I follow her to the bar, where we both order limonata for old times' sake.

After the first refreshing sip, I dismiss my fear of smearing her makeup and give in to the impulse to steal a swift kiss. She tastes like lemon, and smiles like she couldn't be happier to share her lipstick with me. But she still reaches up to swipe the smudge of pink from my skin with her thumb.

"I *knew* it," a voice chirps from somewhere nearby. Cammie and I both turn to see Lila, the girl who sat beside me at the Welcome Dinner and witnessed the hostile spectacle I made with the girl I was just kissing. Lila's mouth is open in a laughing smile, and she delivers a playful swat to the guy beside her—the one who'd sat by Cammie, whose name neither of us held on to.

"I knew you two were into each other at that first dinner," Lila continues, looking back to Cammie and me with glee and maybe a little pride. "But he said I was being ridiculous and clearly you were enemies, and I was like, 'yeah, the kind who want to jump across this table and go at it,' and he was all 'and you wonder why you only have messy situationships,' but look. Who's. Right!"

Cam and I are both frozen, unsure how to respond to a stranger who's nearly as thrilled about our relationship as we are.

"That's . . . so nice?" Cammie finally manages, and Lila doesn't even register that it comes out like a question, already pulling us into the group of other field school students she was chatting with. We sip our drinks and half answer endearingly invasive questions about how we fell in love. Eventually, Cammie steers us toward other topics with some of the group who she's gotten to know on the dig. I'm beginning to think I don't dislike parties as much as I thought I did.

That's when a voice with a thick Italian accent that I can't quite place bellows at close range, "Camilla! Weston! Oh, it is a joy to see you both again."

Cam and I whirl around in unison, confusion clearing when we lay eyes on the new arrival.

"Dr. Constantini!" Cammie squeaks, cartoonishly high-pitched with surprise. "Wow, I'm so glad you're here—we weren't sure if it'd work out with your schedule, so what a great surprise." She and the professor exchange a hug and cheek kisses, and then, before I can awkwardly go for a handshake out of habit, he pulls me in for the same hearty greeting.

"It is my pleasure to be here," he bellows, smoothly turning toward the rest of our group, who are immediately swept under his charming spell. While Cammie makes introductions, I smile and sip my fizzy lemonade, trying to examine the itchy feeling starting around the base of my skull.

It's a good surprise, seeing Dr. Constantini again. If anything, he'll make the social experience of this party easier, with his ability to befriend seemingly anyone. I'm sure Dr. Alex will be pleased to see her old mentor whenever she arrives.

But now that I think about it, why hasn't she arrived yet? Is something wrong? Did something tip her off to potential surprises in store for tonight, and now she's going to skip it entirely, then furiously demand answers from Cammie and me?

I give myself a mental shake for essentially base jumping off the rationality cliff. This is still on track to be a perfectly lovely evening. Dr. Alex will get here soon. No one is mad at me. It's all going to be fine.

Even if that itch is still there, making me wonder if we haven't wrapped up the Dad Quest as neatly as we thought.

I see the flash of red in my periphery just before I hear a gasp similar to Cammie's, but a bit more subdued.

"Dr. Constantini!" Dr. Alex cries. The smile that overtakes her face makes my shoulders sag in relief. Okay, good surprise.

"Oh, thank the gods," I hear Cammie mumble through a clenched-teeth semblance of a smile as she relaxes against me a little.

We can work with this. Nothing strange going on, just as long as he doesn't say anything to her about—

"Ah, bellisima," the older man shouts, drawing attention from people across the whole terrazzo, including, I notice for the first time, my dad. He looks as pleased to see the older man as Dr. Alex was. Both parents' gazes follow Dr. Constantini's to see what's so beautiful.

Which is when their smiles drop, and my heart goes along with them.

"Paolo, you made it," Dr. Constantini says to the newest arrival of his former students. Paolo Bianchi moves cautiously through the crowd, which parts like it's been choreographed for maximum drama.

"Paolo?" Dr. Alex echoes her former professor, though she says the name more like a bewildered question.

"Alex," Captain Bianchi greets her, and when they stand before each other, both lean in for the hug and double cheek kiss. They linger a little in the embrace, but in a way I read as old friends who haven't seen each other in too long.

I thought Cammie was fooling herself to think that she'd see Dr. Alex with these men and judge whether they were her father. But sure enough, this perfectly pleasant—if confused on both ends—reunion solidifies what my mind was already inclined to believe. Paolo couldn't possibly be Cammie's dad.

"Gosh, it's been ages," Dr. Alex says, pressing her hands to her flushed cheeks.

"Twenty years," Paolo agrees with a goofy grin, sticking his hands in the pockets of his corduroys, his posture easy and comfortable. He nods to indicate the balloons hanging over the not-yet-filled food table along with a banner proclaiming *20 Anno di Villa di Bronzo*. No mention of Dr. Alex, per Johnny Russo's instructions.

"Congrats, by the way. I can't believe it's been so long, but you wouldn't know it from looking at you."

"Oh, stop it," Dr. Alex says with a girlish giggle I've never heard from her. Cammie and I both look back and forth between the pair like we're watching a Ping-Pong match. "But what on earth are you doing here? Not that it isn't great to see you, just . . . I thought you'd left all this academia stuff behind.

Did Villa Russo's event folks reach out to everyone who was in the classics department at the time, or . . . ?"

Cammie's hand clamps around my wrist as my stomach lurches.

Here we go.

The Italian leather boat shoe is dropping. Paolo looks around quickly, his eyes first passing right over Cammie before they land back on her, and he waves a hand our way.

"It's an interesting story, one I'm not sure I know in full," he starts, "but the short answer is that your daughter invited me."

CHAPTER TWENTY-ONE

Cammie

I MAKE A NEW ADDITION TO MY GROWING MENTAL LIST OF USEFUL PHRASES to translate into Italian: "I'm so fucked."

The lucky part of this whole ex-boyfriend surprise ambush is that Mom hasn't yet had even a second to interrogate me. She's too busy catching up with her ex-boyfriends. Plural, because it wasn't wild enough for Paolo to show after ignoring my attempt to contact him like he was Caspér the Ghost, Casper's rude Italian cousin. Tony Costa-Campbell decided to roll up, too, having escaped from his other obligation with enough time to stop at home and bring his wife, Luna, along.

He at least had the courtesy to arrive at the perfect time, distracting my mother right when she'd turned to ask me how or why or whatever other questions she had about my role in bringing Paolo here tonight.

"Tony?" she'd shrieked, somehow even more stunned than she was with Paolo.

I guess one long-ago ex at your party is a wacky coincidence. Two is a tinfoil-hat-worthy conspiracy.

"Buona sera, darlin'," Tony said in his confounding Italian-Australian-fake-Matthew-McConaughey fashion. "Been a minute, hey? Allow me to introduce my missus."

Before Not My Dad #2 could doubly blow my cover, I'd grabbed West's hand and retreated to the other side of the terrazzo. We're behind one of the potted lemon trees brought in to create a "natural-yet-decorative border," as I heard one of the event planners say earlier in the week, because I guess the many already planted in the ground all around the villa weren't natural or decorative enough. But I'm grateful for the sort-of-hiding-spot it creates without us having to leave entirely for some privacy.

"I know 'RSVP' is a French term, but surely the concept exists in this country," I whisper sharply to West, once I'm confident enough no one can see our faces and I can drop my *everything is bellisima* smile.

"At least the food is buffet-style?" he offers by way of a weak upside.

"I don't care if there's enough food for these party crashers!"

"You mean the guests you specifically invited."

"Weston, I need your commiseration right now, not the old 'well well well, if it isn't the consequences of your own actions' schtick."

We lock eyes, and the laughter in his, even if he's trying

to contain it, is a nice change of pace from the anxiety that's been there since Paolo's appearance. I don't want him to feel stressed over the scheme that was my idea all along, something I dragged him into and he shouldn't suffer for, if anyone's going to.

But I'm still holding out hope that no one will. Now that I've seen both Paolo and Tony reunite with my mom, seen how little tension—romantic or otherwise—exists between either pairing, I get the sense that they ended on perfectly fine terms twenty years ago. No huge, love-child-shaped secret looming over a fraught dynamic. Mom and Luna are hitting it off so well, they'll probably exchange numbers and save each other under the contact name "Bestie."

In other words, I'm over 99 percent certain that neither man is my father.

At least they're nice guys and seem to be enjoying catching up with Mom. From what I can tell, the feeling is mutual, even if she still has questions about their presence here. If she doesn't find a natural way to interrogate me during this party, I'm expecting a long night on the receiving end of her we'll-talk-about-this-later eyes.

While my dad may not be present, I do think I've acquired a new grandpa. Dr. Constantini is the first to eventually spot West and me again, dragging us out from behind the lemon tree, then putting an arm around each of us while wedging himself in the middle. I bet if I asked nicely, he'd turn this into the group hug I feel like I need right now. West does, too, judging by the tight semblance of a smile he's using to mask his nerves.

Instead, the older man brings his hands up from each of our shoulders to land on the tops of our heads and ruffle our hair, as much as mine can be ruffled with the copious amount of hair spray holding it together.

"I Bambini di Bronzo!" he declares with a conspiratorial wink in my direction, probably influenced by the handful of espresso martinis I've seen him go through. "I cannot imagine a more beautiful night for such a special gathering. I am very grateful you thought to include me."

I'm about to say there's no need to thank me, that we're just glad he could make it, when a new voice pipes in from just behind us.

"Yes, that was very generous of both of you." Gianmarco Russo makes the word *generous* sound like it actually means "heinous and unforgivable."

"Johnny!" Dr. Constantini says, smile wavering as he turns the three of us around as a unit. Gianmarco's posture somehow goes even stiffer at the name. I'm not even sure if Dr. Constantini is being petty or just using the only name he knows for the guy.

"Dr. Constantini," he says to the older man. "If you will excuse us, I need to speak to Camilla."

Dr. Constantini's face is still as relaxed as can be, but I feel his grip tighten ever so slightly on my shoulder. I peer quickly at West out of the corner of my eye and, finding him already looking back at me, guess he felt the same thing.

"Oh, speak freely," Dr. Constantini says. "There's no need for either of you to miss out on the party."

Russo's perma-frown deepens before he opens his mouth, an argument on the tip of his tongue. But it snaps shut again, like he realizes he's not going to pull me away from my squad.

"Very well. I simply wanted to inquire as to whether we should expect any more surprise attendees tonight, Ms. Lovett."

His tone is severe, even though I know logically, this guy is in no position to scold me for anything. That right is reserved for my mother. I'm not going to apologize for things I didn't even really intend to do.

Okay, maybe I once intended them. But I changed my mind, and I'm as surprised as anyone else that Mom's exes showed up.

"Well, that's the thing about surprises," I answer, a clearly false innocence in the words. "None of us know when they're coming."

Russo's face darkens and he takes a step closer, leaning forward to emphasize his height advantage over me.

"This is highly disrespectful, not only to the Villa Russo staff who put this event together, but also to me. We have a strict quota for attendees and only enough food for a precise number of plates, so I'm afraid that I will need to ask some of your guests to take their leave. And in the future"—another step closer, and I flinch involuntarily—"I would advise you to refrain from exploiting the generosity of my institution by bringing whatever outsiders you feel like. Your mother's name may have let you get away with everything you want thus far, but it will not keep you from facing consequences here. Is that understood?"

"Absolutely not," says my mom as she suddenly steps in front of me, a ferocity in her tone that I've never heard her use, even when I've been in huge trouble or a student of hers has screwed up big-time. She is a protective lioness as she faces Russo—red dress, red lipstick, copper-colored hair matching the fire in her expression.

"You do not get to speak to my daughter that way—not for any reason, but especially not for something as absurd as insufficient food to feed a few extra guests, when it is literally a buffet and your kitchen always prepares more than we need at meals. You will not take out your power trip bullshit on my girl."

A wiser man would step back, would notice the attention this altercation is drawing from all the other attendees across the terrazzo, and stand down. But Johnny Russo's pride must outsize his common sense, because not only does he hold his ground, he also rolls his eyes. Thirteen-year-old Cammie could have told him how well that one would go over with Dr. Alex Lovett. She wouldn't, though; there are some things people have to learn for themselves.

"Alex, please. If you want to go relive your tawdry past with every ex-lover from your wild years in Italy, you may do so outside a professional social function."

"Johnny," Dr. Constantini starts in as Mom calls the man something much less appropriate for polite company.

As for West and me, both our jaws are on the floor, stunned speechless at the behavior of our alleged elders. Dr. Constantini steps up to my mother's side, abandoning his post between

West and me, and I slide into the gap he left, pressing close to West to reassure myself with the comfort of his presence in what is becoming a highly uncomfortable situation.

"That was uncalled for, mate," Tony Costa-Campbell says, appearing at Mom's other side in our growing semicircle of the People versus Gianmarco Russo.

"Yes," Paolo agrees, "that is not why I came here tonight." Turning to Mom, he starts, "Alex, I hope you don't think—"

"God, of course not, Paolo," she cuts him off. "You don't even have to justify it. I'm glad to see you all. Sorry the hospitality leaves so much to be desired."

She waves a dismissive hand toward Russo.

"Wait a second," Tony says as realization lights up his eyes and he points to Russo. "You're the prick who was always hanging around back in the day, upset that Alex didn't want you. You're not still trying to, what, make her pay for that? Because that would be—"

"Of course not," Gianmarco scoffs. "If I still wanted Alexandra, I would've had her by now."

In the moments that follow, Johnny Russo becomes forever indebted to the Jacobs men. They are the primary reason this doesn't turn into the Agatha Christie kind of party, with one wealthy asshole winding up dead and no question as to whodunnit. It's a blur, really, as exclamations of "I think the fuck not" and "incel-ass bitch" and even "you're from Ohio" are flying, two heads' worth of ginger curls along with them, five feet four inches of pure rage—times two—lunging forward, until West's arm cinches around my waist, Dr. Danny's around

Mom's, and Paolo and Tony physically push Russo in the opposite direction. One unworthy life spared.

When I can catch my breath and see through the irate haze that briefly fell over my field of vision, I meet West's steadying gaze, his hands still braced on my waist, and cry, "This is my fault."

Through the cacophony of multilingual anger, insults, and ranting, I somehow hear his quiet answer of, "No, it's not. You didn't invite any of this."

"It's more drama than a *Real Housewives* episode," I say as I peer around at the chaos. West lets out a small chuckle before a new thought occurs to me, and I add, "We're just lucky Luca Goedhart didn't show up. I can only imagine how that would have . . ."

I trail off as I notice the abrupt silence sweeping over the arguing group, the rest of the bewildered partygoers following their lead. West and I turn to follow the collective stares and find that I spoke too soon.

"Hello," Dr. Luca Goedhart says in his measured, naturally authoritative voice as he steps out from the main house, his eyes scanning the terrazzo until they land on my mother. Even from a distance, I can see the flare of intense emotion in the gray-blue depths. "What have I missed?"

I don't think anyone at the party breathes for the next few moments, even if the majority has no idea who the new guy is. Mom certainly doesn't exhale, just stands there in shock. Luca seems similarly frozen by the sight of her, though he surely knew to expect to see her when he decided to show up tonight.

And holy shit. He showed up.

I get the same gut feeling from our first meeting, though I'd wanted to deny it or tell myself I'd imagined it, after how that ended up. But it's back, this instinctual pull, like even though we barely met once, some part of my soul is connected to some part of his. I know it's illogical to read much into a gut feeling, that I could just be seeing what I want to see, desperate to believe that all this searching wasn't for nothing. But it's still there, this voice whispering, however cautiously, fearfully, hopefully, *"It's him."*

I've tried to keep from thinking about him since Pompeii, or the possibility that the reason he was so weird is because he *is* my dad, and he knows, and he doesn't want to know me.

But now the possibility is here, basically on my doorstep, no longer able to be ignored. And when my eyes drift from his shell-shocked expression back to my mom's, I find that she is no longer frozen, looking at Luca.

No, she is laser-focused on me, striding determinedly in my direction. But it's what I read in her face that makes me feel like my heart has dropped through my stomach, onto the paving stones below my feet. She doesn't appear furious, or like she's coming to me to demand an explanation for why I brought yet another piece of her ancient history here tonight. She doesn't look upset with me at all.

Instead, her wide blue eyes hold something like apology.

"Cam," she says, low and urgent, when she's only a couple feet away. A hand tightens around mine, West's, and I don't even know when I grabbed it or if he grabbed mine, just that I'm holding on for dear life now. Bracing for impact, maybe.

"Honey, we need to talk somewhere alone. Now."

I start to ask what's wrong, even though I'm pretty sure I know, but I'm cut off by the return of Dr. Russo's shouting.

"You need to leave now," he's saying, and when I look past my mom, I see the command is directed at Luca Goedhart.

What does he have against Luca specifically? Or is this just more posturing about his authority over the guest list?

"Excuse me," Luca says in a careful calm that says he's barely keeping his real feelings leashed. "I was invited."

"An invitation from a nineteen-year-old girl with no right to extend it is invalid, I'm afraid."

Luca's face pinches tight, some mix of confusion and anger reminiscent of what he showed upon seeing me for the first time at the archaeological park. "Are you referring to your daughter? Because I don't know if you're aware, but *she* came to see *me*. I had nothing to do with—"

"His *what*?"

The screeched words are so unlike any noise I have ever produced that I don't even realize they came from me at first. Three gazes dart my way, from Mom, Luca Goedhart, and Gianmarco Russo. Certainly plenty of others, given the inhuman sound, but my world has shrunken down to the four of us, like some absurd Renaissance painting, or maybe a still from a soap opera. I don't hear anything but those two words from Luca tossed at Gianmarco Russo, echoing over and over in my head.

Your daughter. Your daughter. Your daughter.

I'm suddenly short of breath, and spots appear at the corners of my vision. *This can't be happening,* is all I can think. *No.* I might even voice it out loud, denial of the horrifying revelation.

There's a hand at my back, West's voice in my ear murmuring, "Cam. It's going to be okay. Breathe."

I do as he says, letting him spin me to face him and locking his gaze with mine as I match his deep inhales and exhales.

It clears the panicked fog enough that other sounds start to filter back in, namely my mom's highly confused, "John Mark has a daughter?"

Wait. What?

That's my first thought as I look to her, feeling as mixed up as she sounds. Because if she doesn't know he has a daughter, then Goedhart couldn't have meant . . .

"What?" Luca asks, like he pulled the incredulous question from my head. "You . . . you . . ." He points to Mom with one hand, Russo with the other. Then one of the accusatory fingers drifts to me, followed by a dazed, barely audible, "She . . . she's his, right? And yours, the two of you—"

"What?" Mom screeches, making it clear where I get the ability from. Her absolute horror at the implication is written in every scrunched-up line of her face, in her arms flung wide, shoulders up near her ears. "Absolutely not. What on earth would make you think that?"

She is a combination of fuming and completely baffled that I've never quite seen on my mother. Luca is matching this energy, though leaning more toward the baffled end of the scale. I'm trying to put together the pieces, maybe more confused than anyone, given that I was, you know, a fetus when everything between these folks first went down.

But the only person who doesn't look totally lost is Gianmarco Russo. No, his expression is carefully blank, though he is nearly vibrating, with tension or anger or whatever else, I don't know.

Before I have time to analyze it further, he calmly turns away.

And then—very not calmly—starts running.

CHAPTER TWENTY-TWO

West

THERE ARE A FEW MOMENTS, AFTER JOHNNY RUSSO SETS OFF LIKE A sprinter from a starting block, in which those of us he's left behind—Dr. Alex, my dad, the exes, Dr. Constantini, and, of course, Cam and me—look back and forth to one another as if needing confirmation that we're not all sharing the same surreal fever dream or drank the same bad batch of limonata. *You're seeing this, right? And you too? And we all . . . ? Even if we don't quite get . . . ? Yeah, this is all really happening?*

Then Dr. Alex is the first to give chase.

That sets the rest of us in motion, and soon the whole crew is running after the mysterious-but-clearly-guilty-of-something villa director. Because it's still highly unclear what's going on, what caused him to run, and who—if anyone here—is Cammie's father. But we all seem to know Russo has answers.

Fortunately for this group of not particularly experienced

runners, Johnny's run is a sprint, not a marathon. One that goes only far enough for him to reach, of all places, Villa di Bronzo.

He makes it to the bottom of the stairs of the dig site before he begins losing steam. Cammie can make fun of me all she wants for being an overly cautious person, but if I was on the run from someone—several someones, in this case—I have enough basic self-defense understanding to know that you can't run into a big hole in the ground and expect you won't get caught. Just like bears can climb trees, your human pursuers can follow you into the ditch and will be there waiting when you realize you've hit a dead end.

Or so it seems, until I watch Johnny charge straight into one of the tunnels in the yet-unexcavated side of the villa. I stop short and fight to catch my breath. What is traveling in a large pack of people good for if not letting others go into the dark scary place to get the bad guy so you don't have to?

But there isn't even enough time for anyone but Cammie to notice I've stopped my pursuit before Paolo, Luca, and Tony reemerge from where they followed Dr. Alex into the scary ancient cave without hesitation, the three of them dragging along Gianmarco. He is sullen and exhausted, and appears to have accepted he's been caught.

Dr. Alex brings up the rear, hands on her hips, her chest rising and falling under her elegant red silk dress. Most remarkably, her high-heeled shoes are still on her feet. I don't know if Russo is scared of this woman, but I sure am.

"Okay," Dr. Alex draws out when she's able to speak, though her breathing is still rapid, "explain yourself, Johnny."

For a moment, it still looks like he's going to try to evade or lie, but finally his chin drops to his chest, his shoulders slump inward, and his own heavy breathing turns to the world-weary sigh of someone whose time is up. He doesn't look at any of us as he begins his story.

"It seems it's no secret that as a young man, I did have feelings for Alex."

"You can call me Dr. Lovett," she interjects, to which Russo presses his lips tightly together and gives a faint nod.

"Dr. Lovett, that is. And my interest was not returned. I do not consider myself a vindictive man—"

I see my dad make a funny *you sure about that?* face and know he has some stories that must prove otherwise.

"But I struggled to accept this. It was a difficult time in my family, you see, as my grandfather had fallen ill, and the future of our family villa was uncertain, and I personally took a leave of absence from my studies to do some soul-searching in my homeland—"

"Is this relevant?" Luca Goedhart cuts in, voicing what I imagine we're all thinking.

"Yes, why don't you get to the point, Johnny?" Constantini agrees.

It's satisfying to see the prideful man flinch every time someone uses his American name.

"I'm getting there, I am. So when Dr. Lovett made the discovery she did, she was immediately hailed as a hero, rightfully so, and that is when my admiration began. But as excavations proceeded, it became difficult for me, accepting that this relative outsider to my family, our home, our country"—there are multiple eye rolls from the ones among us who know the guy's actual background—"had been the one to uncover this incredible find. That while it was on Russo land, I was not able to feel a part of the Villa di Bronzo revelations.

"My pride suffered, as I had lost my sense of purpose in my own career journey while others thrived for finding what felt like my birthright." He waves a hand to encompass the site around us, inadvertently drawing attention to the fact that he's still being gripped on either arm by Paolo and Tony, like a fugitive. "It suffered further when I faced rejection from a romantic interest, then had to watch her gallivant around with other men. I was hurting. I was also, I realize, young and immature, and did not channel my hurt in an effective or healthy manner."

He swallows heavily, and my stomach, empty save for a few glasses of fizzy lemonade, roils in anticipation. "In turn, I caused hurt to others, the extent of which I am ashamed to say I did not begin to confront until this summer."

"What did you do?" Dr. Alex asks through gritted teeth. She is barely tamping down her rising fury. A couple feet from her side, Goedhart looks similarly close to exploding, one fist clenched in front of his mouth, the other tucked against his side as his hard stare remains fixed on Gianmarco.

"I came across a letter that was meant for Dr. Goedhart. Dr. Lovett and he had been involved for a while, which was especially challenging for me, as both worked on the villa team, and therefore I had to see them together daily."

"John Mark, I cannot tell you how much of a fuck I don't give about how hard my dating life was on *you*!" Dr. Alex shouts. “If you don’t fess up in the next thirty seconds, I swear, I know where a lot of sharp objects are located nearby, and—”

“The letter was informing Dr. Goedhart that you were carrying his child,” Gianmarco blurts out in one breath, promptly stealing the rest of ours.

Beside me, Cammie trembles. Her knees buckle, and I instinctively bring my arm around her to keep her upright.

“I found the letter, and in my heartache and wounded pride, I made an impulsive and selfish decision.”

“No,” Dr. Alex whispers, and it reverberates around us like she spoke into a megaphone. Her voice shakes, her hand doing the same as she brings it up to cover her mouth, before lifting it a couple inches to say, words thick with tears, “You . . . you told me he left, that it was because he didn’t want . . . didn’t want us.”

Luca paces a slow circle, his eyes wide and unseeing as he tries to reckon with the information. When he speaks, it’s like he doesn’t even remember the rest of us are here.

“He asked me to meet with him when I got to the villa one morning, then told me,” he says, voice gruff and even deeper than usual, “that you and he were expecting a child together. That . . . that you didn’t want to break my heart, so he’d offered to deliver the news for you. Like he was some kind of hero, for you and your—his—family you were starting.”

“And you believed him?” Dr. Alex cries, turning her anger on Luca.

He shouts back, “You believed I didn’t want you, or my own child! That I read your letter and just left without a word. What gives you the right to . . . I . . . I can't fathom how—" He shoves both hands into his hair. "I was so in love with you, so sure I wanted to spend our lives together. I would have . . . We could have—"

The sobs that rack both of them fill the night air, and all at once, I feel like an intruder on this highly personal situation unfolding for the Lovetts and Luca. I look down at Cammie, now noticing that she, too, is shaking in my grasp, but her face is stoic. No tears, not even a wobble of her chin. I think she must be in actual shock, and justifiably so.

I feel helpless to do anything for her. The longer I stand here, in a space so heavy with the weight of secrets and lies, pain and heartache, my own shock has time to set in, mingled with the familiar creeping sensation of an anxious episode coming at me full force. But I can't fall apart right now. Not when I need to be here for the girl I love on probably the hardest night of her life.

I don't know when her shaking subsided and mine began, but both happened somehow, mine noticeable enough that while Dr. Alex, Russo, and Luca are still in an emotional maelstrom of shouting and furious tears, Cammie has the presence of mind and thoughtfulness to ask if *I'm* okay.

She doesn't deserve this. I don't think I've ever hated my own anxiety more, nor felt less capable of handling it, handling anything. I mumble something about just being stunned, tell her I'm more concerned that she's okay, because it is the truth, or part of it.

Because for the first time since we reconnected, I'm once

again keeping the full extent of my emotions under wraps. Not because my feelings for Cammie have changed, or I don't want to be with her anymore, but because I'm suddenly unable to turn off the voice in my head telling me that what I want and what she needs might not align so well after all.

Dad was the one to eventually suggest that we all give the Lovetts and Luca some space and time to talk, or whatever it is that people needed upon being newly reunited after a twenty-year separation that was due entirely to a supervillain's meddling. It isn't exactly a situation any of us are familiar with.

He and stand-in bouncers Paolo and Tony escorted a miserable Johnny Russo back up to his family villa, which we now know he received along with a massive inferiority complex, like a free gift with inheritance. The guy is a bigger piece of work than I ever would have thought possible.

Exhausted from the emotions and stress the evening brought on, it's all I can do to return to my room and get ready for bed in a fog. I don't anticipate hearing from Cammie again tonight, after she gave me the go-ahead to leave her with her mom and Luca. But I send a text to let her know I love her, and I'm in my room if she needs anything. I only hope, with a little rest, I'll feel more capable of whatever she needs.

A very little rest, as it turns out. Some time later, I wake to a knock at my door. The sky is still as dark as it gets out my window, and I'm groggy enough that it couldn't be anywhere near morning yet. I stumble across my dark room to see who it is.

I'm more than a little surprised to find Cammie on the other side, giving me a small, watery smile. Her eyes are bloodshot, her face cleaned of makeup, her hair transformed from its fancy updo to a simple braid, the pretty dress traded for pajamas. She's still so beautiful, my chest aches from it.

"Hi," she whispers. "I don't need to talk it out or cry on you or whatever. I just . . . I don't want to be alone right now. I mean, not just that, I want to be with you. Sleep next to you. Can I . . . ?"

Realizing I've just been staring at her, in some sleepy state between dumbfounded and lovestruck, I step back to welcome her in. "Of course. That sounds perfect."

And for the rest of the night, it is. I fall back into a deep, dreamless sleep with Cammie tucked up against me, my arms wrapped around her, breathing in the scent of her apple shampoo for blissful hours.

If only I hadn't set an alarm.

"I'll get it," I hear Cammie murmur, still half asleep myself. A few seconds later, the irritating jingle goes silent.

A few seconds after that, enough that I've begun falling back into a deeper sleep, Cammie's voice comes out louder and more alert. "West?"

"Hmm," I sleep-speak.

The mattress depresses beside me and Cammie repeats, not as a question this time, "West."

"What?" I blink a few times, try scooting into a sitting position. When my eyes can focus on anything, I see hurt clear on Cammie's face. "What is it, Cam?"

She holds up my phone, but it still doesn't click for me. "When I turned off your alarm, your email notifications were on the screen. I wasn't trying to snoop, but I saw—there was, uh, something from that Germany program. About your housing assignment. So . . . you're officially going?"

Understanding crashes into me, nearly knocking me horizontal again. I scrub at my face with a hand, hoping this isn't the beginning of the extreme fuck-up I fear it might be. "Oh, yeah, I, uh . . . I did make that decision. Just yesterday, officially."

The hurt in her expression becomes more upset. With me, to be specific. "Were you going to tell me?"

I shake my head, thinking I'd give anything to snap my fingers and have a caffeine source on hand right now. "Of course. I was, sometime soon. I didn't think you'd be so upset—we talked about doing long-distance already, right?"

"Yeah, and you never even casually mentioned there was still a good chance that distance would be a whole ocean's worth. Were you planning to drop the news, then bounce the next day, just like three years ago?" She lets my phone drop to the bed as she stands. Her words are as effective as a gut punch. I know her emotions are high from everything else going on, but it doesn't make her wrong about this—that I should have been more open with her, and that she deserves better.

That I'm already repeating past mistakes, when I'd been so sure I'd get it right this time.

"I wouldn't do that to you, Cammie. I know I should have

told you sooner that I was leaning toward going, but I . . . I think I worried that you wouldn't want to take that chance on me. To be the girlfriend of a guy who's about to live thousands of miles away and might be kind of an anxious mess the whole time, especially with everything else you have going on in your life. I wouldn't blame you if this was too much."

She scoffs, and the hurt in her eyes before she turns and stalks toward the door makes a permanent imprint on my memory. As do the words she hurls my way before she walks out.

"If that's what you really think of me, then maybe you're right. Maybe I shouldn't take the chance."

My divorced parents are talking about me again.

I can immediately tell when my dad finds me in the library, quite literally wallowing on the floor. I didn't know he even knew where the library was, only that Pops had to be the one who sent him looking.

I wonder how long it took Pops to call Dad after hanging up with me. I didn't think I gave off an especially concerning vibe—I didn't cry or even tell him much about my current emotional state or romantic situation. But I guess discussing the logistics of flying back home early—as early as today, perhaps—was enough of a red flag on its own.

"Hey there, Westie," Dad says casually, strolling into the room and settling in on the couch like he hasn't a care in the world. Like everything about the past twenty-four hours and especially the present moment is just business as usual. "Heard you were looking at plane tickets."

I close my eyes, adding to the whole corpse-in-a-library-in-a-period-drama role I'm playing. But I know I won't get away with silence, so I reply, "Might've been."

Dad clears his throat. "Also heard you might've asked your pops for access to his airline miles so you could book one."

Sighing, I open my eyes again and peer over at his relaxed pose. Still just shooting the breeze.

"Can you get to what you really want to ask me?"

To my surprise, Dad smiles. Then he kneels next to me on the floor, finally lying down so we're side by side, both looking up at the ceiling.

"West," he says softly. "If I can take away anything from last night, aside from 'don't trust a Russo as far as you can throw him, and maybe not even that much' "—a hint of teasing colors his voice before he turns serious again—"it's that I don't want to waste any more time missing out on my son's life. Not getting to know what he cares about, what makes him tick and gets him excited to get out of bed in the morning. Not being the first person he comes to—or hell, even on the list of contacts—when he needs help. Believe it or not, I'm not completely obtuse. I know I haven't made myself available to be that person the past few years. But I want to do better, I . . . I do, more than I can tell you."

Emotion thickens the words, and it's the first time all day I feel tears sting behind my own eyes. In the silence that follows, while I hear my father sniff and clear his throat, I'm grateful my parents have never hidden their vulnerability, that I grew up with two examples of strong, capable men who also feel things deeply. Who've always let me fall apart in front of them without shame and been there to pick me up when I've needed it.

It's that thought that finally makes me start talking.

Dad listens patiently as I spill out the story of my last few weeks, all that's happened with Cammie, and looking for her dad, and falling for her again for what felt like the first time. I tell him about Germany, and how long I put off the choice to go, and what made me finally say yes.

Then I get to today, and the future—how I've started to convince myself that I should give Cammie space and time while she processes everything and decides what she needs. How I and my needs don't have to get in her way, or loom on the other side of her bedroom wall, in the midst of all the other chaos she's facing. How I'm not sure if she broke up with me this morning or if we were even officially together or if she was just saying stuff she didn't mean again, but she said she would stick with me when things got tough, so I should probably believe her, right? And maybe sticking with her, for now, means taking away the pressure of my presence—supporting her, while giving her room to breathe.

I don't know how long it takes, how long we lie there on the bizarrely comfortable carpet for a room that seems so underused. But Dad doesn't rush me or admit how exhausted he must be. He just listens, like there's nowhere he'd rather be.

Finally, I let out a puff of air and conclude, "I think that's everything."

In the ensuing silence, I hear Dad rub a hand over his jaw, a gesture I picked up from him, however unwittingly. The realization would make me smile if I didn't feel so miserable right now.

"I'll be honest with you," he finally says. "I think this flight instinct—no pun intended—is not the kind of . . . reprieve, or whatever, that you think you're giving to Cammie. Or to me or anyone else around you. You're not a burden, no matter what your brain might want to tell you. And acting on the belief that you are might just hurt you and Cammie both, not help anyone. Does that make sense?"

My brows pull together as I consider his words. "Maybe. I don't know."

Dad lets out a soft chuckle. "Well, I am very obviously not the expert on relationships and being a good partner. But especially with where you and Cammie are in your lives—don't put it on pause right when things are getting good! The best is yet to come, buddy. I feel fairly certain of that. If she wants to be with you, no matter that you're in Germany, or that your brain tries to screw things up for you sometimes, or that you're a big ol' nerd"—he bumps his elbow against mine—"then I think you should trust her. Trust that you have so much going for you, it's no wonder this girl who you find to be so amazing thinks the same of you. I know I come with some bias, being the parent of the best guy in the world. But Cammie is a smart girl, too—she wouldn't fall for a dud, you know?"

"That should not be as comforting as it is," I admit a little grudgingly.

"It's a gift." Dad laughs again, clearly pleased with himself.

Sincerity returning, he asks, "Can you promise me that if there ever comes another time when you're going through something and need advice, and I'm in the same ten-mile radius . . . you'll consider giving me a shout?"

Emotion clogging my throat again, I nod.

Probably sensing I need the company and the comedic relief, Dad sticks around the library for a while, telling me about some embarrassing but hilarious experience he had trying to order in Italian at a bakery the other day. He asks more about my life, even has me show him Project Euclid. I try to talk him through the current problem I'm working, but don't get very far before there's a glazed look in his eyes.

"The last math class I took was first semester of undergrad, and for good reason," he says.

Even as it does my heart and mind good to have the time together, both parts of me are only half present. The other halves are with Cammie, wondering how she's feeling now. Concerned how things are going with Luca and Dr. Alex. Considering how I fit into the transforming picture of her life.

When Dad decides to turn in, he gives me a long, tight hug, and tells me everything will look brighter after a good night's rest. I go to sleep hoping more than anything that he's right.

I wake up to find he's not.

CHAPTER TWENTY-THREE

Cammie

"YOU KNOW, ONE THING ABOUT BECOMING A SINGLE MOM IN MY EARLY twenties, far from home and completely terrified," Mom muses, lying beside me on her bed a few hours after I left West's room, both of us staring up at the ceiling, "was that I read a shit ton of parenting books."

The unexpected curse earns a surprised snort-laugh from me, though it shouldn't. I heard her yelling at Johnny Russo, after all.

She goes on. "And would you believe that not one of them told me how to discipline your nineteen-year-old, after she pulls off an elaborate scheme to find the father who you never let her know of, because you yourself had been conned into believing he didn't want either of you, when, in fact, he was under the impression that he didn't even have a kid?"

I hum thoughtfully. "Yeah, that is a pretty unique set of circumstances that I can't imagine a lot of moms relating to."

"Well, aren't they lucky?" she scoffs.

I give her a conflicted sort of smile as we turn toward each other, just a few inches between us on the pillows. "Yeah. I think the answer is you just have to have some difficult conversations."

"I think you're right," she agrees, "and I think I probably should have tried that a long time ago."

I feel a pang of sympathy for twenty-years-ago Alex, who I've gotten to know pretty well by now. A young woman not much older than me, who was just trying to figure it all out as she went. Exactly as I am.

"I also could have asked," I say, "but neither of us is that into the hard conversations."

She reaches over and takes my hand in one of hers. "You are handling all of this almost scarily well," she says, a little accusation in her voice. "But I'm so sorry you have to handle it at all. That I got us into this mess twenty years ago and couldn't even manage to sort it out until you grew old enough, and sharp enough, and doggedly persistent enough to sort it out yourself."

"I tried to, anyway," I correct her, "but the truth was beyond the scope of my imagination. Maybe even beyond the imagination of, like, Shonda Rhimes herself."

Mom laughs. "She would totally write a Johnny Russo type of villain."

"Right?" I agree.

Her voice turns serious again. "But now that it's all out in the open, or, you know, at least the essentials are, can I clear up anything else? Other things you want to know but might have been afraid to ask?"

I consider the question for a minute. "Is he like . . . the one that got away?" I try at last, forming the thought carefully. I don't have to say who "he" is. Besides Johnny, who we more often call "that bastard" or "dickhead" or other derogatory names, there's only one man who's monopolized our conversations and thoughts since last night. The man who stayed down in the depths of Villa di Bronzo with us for nearly an hour after the others left, in the aftermath of his entire world shifting irrevocably. He did an admirable job of pretending he wasn't losing his grip on his sanity, but when the silences between the three of us grew longer, conversation more stilted and less meaningful, as it's wont to do when all parties are dealing with everything they thought they knew changing on a dime—and are up far past their bedtimes—we said our good-nights, with the vague agreement to talk again soon. I assume he went back to his place on Via Camilla, while Mom and I returned to Villa Russo, both of us too physically and emotionally exhausted to talk anymore.

I'd rested well in West's arms, safe and warm and loved. But learning he was hiding stuff from me again came as a rude awakening. Now I feel similarly to how I did from my first and only hangover not that long ago. I guess I am emotionally hungover. But the espresso Mom fetched for me from downstairs is gradually reviving me, as is the knowledge that's slowly setting in amid all the chaos from last night and this morning: I know who my father is.

I just didn't expect the information to be brand-new to him as well. And if Mom is offering, I'm certainly going to pump her for all the details I can on my no-longer-a-mystery parent. The next time I see him, I'll go into the meeting armed with intel, if few other defenses.

She takes a while to form her answer, which is a sort of answer in itself, though I don't make fun of her for it.

"'The one that got away' feels so melodramatic," she says with a groan, pinching the bridge of her nose in a familiar gesture. It wasn't my intention to make her cry. But it's probably healthy, in light of all she's reckoning with. "I do believe we were very in love—deeply, authentically. I mean, you read our letters to each other, as absolutely mortifying as that is."

"You think *you're* mortified," I grumble with mock indignation that I don't have the right to even pretend is there.

"Okay, you snoop, watch it." Her laugh turns into a wistful sigh. "But of course that's one of the hardest parts of this whole thing. Wondering what could have been, had he just gotten my letter. Kicking myself for not, I don't know, trying to follow up in person when I thought he'd dumped me by proxy. Though he skipped town so quickly, it would have been tough, but I could have tried harder. I was just heartbroken, thinking he'd left me, and left you, and the one person I thought was really it for me had turned out to be the biggest letdown of them all. That's an awful feeling, and the would've, should've, could'ves will probably haunt me for, oh, forever." She has to pause, her voice wobbling as she gets a hold of her emotions. "But we're all going to have to live with that and figure out how we go forward now, you know?"

She's voiced many of the same thoughts I've had in the last twelve-ish hours. Moving forward feels daunting, terrifying, and, okay, kind of thrilling.

"My turn to ask you a question," Mom begins. "Camilla Lovett . . . you just found your biological father, against all odds and the nefarious machinations of a fake-Italian sociopath. What are you going to do next?"

I scrunch my nose. "Go to Disney World?"

Mom makes a buzzer sound. "Try again. Pretend either of us is capable of dealing with serious, completely life-altering matters without using humor to mask our real feelings. When you first decided you wanted to find your dad, what were you hoping would come next?"

I think about it before answering slowly, carefully, like I'm unsure yet how high I can aim. "I loved to imagine that he would be thrilled to meet me, and we'd have a relationship, as wildly unlikely as that seemed. But as we've already established, the wildest possibilities I thought of don't even touch the reality. So I guess . . ." I take my lower lip between my teeth, biting back the truth for a few last moments before setting it free. "I guess I hope that Luca is game for getting to know each other, and, I don't know, we go from there."

She gives me a soft, encouraging smile, and I see the tears welling up again in her blue eyes that are so like my own. And not *un*like Luca Goedhart's.

"Okay," she says, barely a whisper. "I support you, Cam. Whatever you want, I want to do what I can to give that to you. And Luca . . ." She sighs, the sound of it doing nothing to dispel my suspicion that she still has the hots for my long-lost dad, all this time later. "He has no idea how lucky he is to get the chance to know you. But he will very soon. I'm sure of it."

In a turn of events I absolutely did not see coming this summer, let alone only twenty-four hours after learning my dad's identity, I think he and my mom are on a date.

"It's not a date," she told me while she put on a dress that I had definitely never seen before. I'm shocked she even packed it for her time here, most of which has been spent digging in the dirt, walking through the dirt, covered at any given moment in dirt. But she wasn't tonight, when she set off in her slinky cocktail dress.

"It's not slinky" had been her retort when I referred to it as such in front of her. More denial of reality. She's even wearing perfume; I didn't know she owned perfume.

Now that she's left me behind, I'm wandering Villa Russo like the ghost of a woman scorned here or something. The word around the residence hall is that John Mark has fled the premises, and his resignation from his role as director is anticipated any time now. I didn't realize, until I found out he was gone, that I'm much more comfortable knowing I won't turn a corner to find him looming there, all creepy and angry-eyed.

I'm not sure what to do with myself, since I'm still frustrated with West and how he handled telling me about Germany. He was doing the whole "I don't know if I can be what you deserve" bullshit again, and I hate that. He needs to get it through his beautiful, apparently brainless head that he is exactly who I want, exactly as he is.

But that would probably be a more effective message to deliver when I can do it without sounding so angry. Still, I need to assure myself he's okay. Not having heard any sounds in his room when I stopped by, I head to the library, where I find the door ajar and voices drifting out to the hall.

Dr. Danny and West.

Apparently I haven't quite learned my lesson when it comes to eavesdropping, because I tiptoe closer, nearly pressing my ear to the door. They're discussing . . . is that math terminology?

"Okay, I know what 'linear' means and I know what 'algebra' means—well, sort of—but it's when you put them together that you lose me," Dr. Danny cracks with a laugh.

I tiptoe back the way I came, a reluctant smile spreading across my face. God, does West come by his weirdness naturally. But if they're talking about one of his very favorite things in the world, he can't be doing too badly. The thought settles my mind enough that I return to my room, ready to queue up a comfort show and get some sleep.

I shut off my phone when I crawl into bed, starting up some episodes of *The Great Pottery Throw Down*. What could be more therapeutic than watching Judge Keith be moved to tears by the beauty of a well-made teapot? I certainly can't think of anything.

But when I fall asleep, instead of visions of ceramics dancing in my head, the only thing occupying my mind is West, the need to feel his arms around me like it's been a year and not a day since I felt them.

When I wake up in the morning, it's to drool running down my chin and the mildly passive-aggressive "Are you still watching?" pop-up message on my computer screen. But I feel surprisingly refreshed. Even if West hasn't tried to talk to me again, I'm ready to talk to him.

With a calm, can-do spirit, I set out on another West Quest.

He's not in his room or the library. But more concerningly, all the furniture that he moved for his optimal computer hyperfocus zone comfort has been moved back to the original layout he'd described. It's like his presence, which felt as essential to this room as the shelves lined with books, was erased overnight.

I don't know where else to look, so I return to my strategy of wandering the halls, checking behind all the open doors, jump-scaring a few miscellaneous Villa Russo staff in the process.

"Mi dispiace," I murmur, only half certain it's the actual term for "I'm sorry." I let my LingoLegend streak lapse on day two in Italy and haven't returned to it since.

I give West's room one more try—this time, with *feeling*. "West!" I call out as I knock. "Weston Jacobs, paging Weston Jacobs. This is Camilla Lovett—red hair, freckles, mouth you seem to be fond of kissing . . ."

I press my ear to the door and hear absolutely nothing, not even the quiet movements of someone pretending they're not around when they really are. That's when I decide to text him. Hi, I type out. Wondering where you are?

If ever a situation called for double-texting, it would be this one. So I do.

I think my mom went on a date with my dad last night!

Oh, what the hell, might as well make it a triple. It's not like I can double-lose the shame I've already abandoned.

And I don't know what to feel about it!

I turn toward my room, trying not to stare obsessively at my dark phone screen and willing it to light up with his reply.

Which is how I see a piece of paper I hadn't noticed on the ground, lying in a haphazard way that makes me think it fell from some precarious, wedged-in spot on my door. I lean down to grab it, unfolding and scanning the contents as I step back into my room, then stop in my tracks. I'm unable to focus on any of the words long enough to read the thing in full, jumping frantically to different phrases that stick out in an endearingly messy handwriting that I recognize as West's. Groupings of words that barely make sense to me, like *made a tough decision* and *give you space* and *going home*.

As I piece more together, it only makes less sense. This absolute imbecile thinks that he's . . . what, gracefully bowing out of my life, now that I've found my dad and need to focus on that relationship, figure out what I really want and need next? Apparently so, at least temporarily. But even temporary space is drastic when it involves flying back across an ocean.

This feels like confirmation of some of my fears that I've thrown too much at him this summer, asked too much of him, and made his anxiety worse somehow, with all this forcing him out of his comfort zone. But his belief that he's some kind of extra burden while I have more important stuff going on, or anything other than the partner I both need and want holding my hand while I figure the rest out—it's beyond comprehension to me.

Is this just a letter full of excuses? Anything to try to cover his ass, to give him a pass to drop out of my life again with no real discussion? If he thinks I'll let that happen, he really doesn't know me like I thought he did.

I hurry to throw on a clean T-shirt and shorts, barely getting my feet into the first shoes I see, which happen to be my rubber shower flip-flops, before I'm hop-stepping down the hallway to the first floor. I'm so focused on my target, Dr. Danny's door at the end of the hall, that I jump back in surprise when a different door swings open right as I'm walking past.

I look over to see who's just scared the shit out of me, almost choking on air when I find it's Luca Goedhart. My new-to-me father dearest, emerging from my mom's room.

"Oh" is his very smooth reaction as he freezes, door falling shut behind him. I squeeze my eyes closed, not wanting to even begin to engage with this right now. And because I'm fresh off that whole "I'll support however you want to handle it" conversation with my mom, I simply don't engage, offering a wave and a clipped "Morning!" as I duck my head and march on. When I reach Dr. Danny's door, I don't look back to see if Dr. Walk of Shame is still there, or if he's expired from the awkwardness of it all.

And I thought I had daddy issues before.

Dr. Danny, at least, does not scandalize me by opening the door in last night's clothes or with any unexpected guests. He's just in plaid pajama pants, a book tucked under his arm because, as he tells me right away, he was on the terrazzo reading. The only thing middle-aged-dad types should be doing at this hour, really.

Still, I don't respond to the information, as—with no disrespect—I simply don't care right now. "Do you know where West is?"

I try not to let my worry slip into my voice but I'm not sure I succeed, because I have a very bad feeling I do know where West is. And it requires a passport and boarding pass to get there.

Dr. Danny grimaces. "Oh, Cammie," he says, and the sympathy in his voice makes any hope I have left die. "I thought he was going to tell you . . ."

I pull the letter out of my back pocket where I tucked it, and hold it up.

"Yeah, he did. Well, he wrote to me, because apparently he learned nothing in the last couple days about the dangers of conveying important information in handwritten letter form."

Dr. Danny doesn't bring a palm up to smack his forehead at

his son's antics, but his face says he wants to. "Well, no, that's not how I expected him to go about it. But he left very recently, so he isn't on a plane yet, not that I endorse any dramatic, movie-montage, running-through-the-airport situations, and not that you can even get that far in airports nowadays without a ticket somewhere, and in the same terminal as the object of your affections, and—"

I don't hear the end of that rambling explanation, because in time-honored Villa Russo tradition, I have already started running.

CHAPTER TWENTY-FOUR

West

IT'S ALMOST A FEAT, HOW LITTLE OF THE ITALIAN LANGUAGE I KNOW AFTER all my time here. Not a feat I'm proud of, by any stretch—I wish I had more of a knack for picking up languages of the human, not electronic, variety. It would've come in handy on many different occasions.

But especially times like now, in the back of a taxi with a driver who seems very kind, but with whom I am tragically bad at communicating. I tried to explain, through slowly spoken English—as if the speed makes a difference—and lots of hand gestures, that the first cab I ordered to take me to the airport was a no-show. I'd waited twenty minutes before deciding I should call another, uncertain how these things work. Then it took another twenty minutes of getting redirected, being put on hold, rinse and repeat, until I was finally able to speak to another real-life person who understood enough of my language to help the monolingual American get a much-needed ride to the airport.

Luigi might as well be an angel, as relieved as I was to see him pull up. But if this angel could flap his wings a little faster, I would appreciate it.

"Plane," I say, stretching my arms out by my sides like I'm flying, "taking off"—I make the motion of soaring down a runway and lifting into the air with my hand as the plane—"very soon." I finish by tapping an invisible watch on my wrist.

"Sì, sì," Luigi says with an emphatic nod that doesn't convince me he gets the urgency, especially with how slowly we are still rolling down the gravel drive. We're not even off Villa Russo property yet.

"Grazie," I say, and even my untrained ears know my Italian accent is terrible. Add it to the growing list of my incompetencies.

It's not like I'm especially eager to go back to the US. I'm far from certain that doing so is the right decision, but once I booked the ticket, I was locked in. I've never missed a flight in my life, and as an already nervous traveler with, frankly, a lot of shit going on right now, I'm not inclined to test my fragile mental state by showing up late to the airport.

I let my head rest against the leather seat, trying to trick my sweaty body into believing that the breeze through the open windows is cool, rather than more hot air to go with my hot air. Soon, I'll be back in the USA, land of overly air-conditioned everything, to the point that sometimes we wear layers indoors when it's ninety-five degrees out.

What a beautiful disaster of a society. But it's the one I call home, and I tell myself I am unreservedly happy to be headed there.

It will be good to see Pops, to spend a solid three to five business days in my bedroom, where I have all my familiar comforts and favorite snacks and the sleep setup I've optimized like it's my job. I try to tell myself that all these things can make up for what I'm leaving behind.

It's not quite working yet. I probably should have told Cammie to her face, and I wince at the prospect that I've contributed to some permanent trauma around handwritten correspondence that she might have from now on. But I knew if I saw her, I couldn't go through with this. I would lose my resolve and decide to stay, even if it was a bad idea. If it meant smothering her, adding stress to a time when she has more than enough of it. It's probably just as good for me, this distance—it could help me from getting too attached too soon.

But who am I kidding? I'm already so attached, the mark she's left on me couldn't be removed with industrial-strength cleaner. Maybe not even a magic wand, if those were real. What do I think leaving is going to do to me, other than send me into a lonely, depressive state?

No, I'm not doing this for myself. It's for Cam, to give her a chance to process the roller coaster of her life right now, and decide if she really wants me to ride it out with her. Even if the thought that she might not want that makes me want to throw myself into the darkest underground tunnels of Villa di Bronzo and wait for them to collapse on me.

I already miss the sound of her voice, the mischievous twinkle in her eyes when she pokes fun at me, the way she says my name.

"West!"

I don't know why she's yelling it in my memory, when that's not my favorite way to hear it in reality, but—

"West!"

Wait. That Cammie is not in my head.

"Weston! Jacobs!"

My eyes pop open, and my head whips around to see that not only are we somehow still on the long gravel drive from Villa Russo to the main road, but there is also a slightly unhinged—if still ridiculously beautiful—girl running at full tilt toward the taxi.

"Hey, hold on, stop the car," I say frantically to Luigi, inexplicably making the time-out motion with my hands, like that will mean anything to him. But my panic must be obvious enough to transcend the language barrier, because Luigi brakes, hard and sudden.

Cammie, for her part, does not brake, only stopping her chase when she more or less body-slams the trunk of the taxi, splaying herself across it like a bug on a windshield.

A little more drama than necessary, given that the car had already stopped, but what else would I expect? The thought brings an irrepressible smile to my face, but it falls when I see the anger on hers. She peels herself off the trunk and stomps around to one of the rear passenger doors, then flings it open.

"Just where do you think you're going?"

She looks damn near as angry as she got the other night, when I had to restrain her before she tore Johnny Russo's face off. Oh god, have I just made her hate me more than the guy she called an "incel-ass bitch"? It's a low I didn't think was reachable.

"I told you—the airport," I say weakly, knowing I'm done for before she even starts in on me.

"You didn't *tell* me anything," she says, whipping a folded piece of paper out of the back pocket of her shorts and brandishing it at me like a weapon. "You wrote me this weak-ass explanation of your totally misguided idea about what I need, without, oh, I don't know, consulting me on the matter! So what did I have to do?"

I have just enough sense to recognize a rhetorical question when it's yelled in my face, and keep my mouth shut accordingly.

"*Run*, Weston. And I am not a born runner, even with the right shoes, which"—she lifts a foot in the air to display the rubber flip-flop hanging off her foot by its one unbroken strap—"these are most certainly not. So of course one broke before I made it twenty feet past the front door! You know what happened then, as I hobbled half barefoot down this gravel road?"

A pause for her to turn and show me her upper arm, where a splatter of something white is slowly dripping downward.

"A bird shat on me. A bird. In the big, endless blue sky above, with endless other places from which it could've done its business. Chose the particular patch of real estate over my shoulder. To *take a gigantic dump*. And to think, I thought rock bottom was running into your ex-best-friend-and-first-kiss who broke your heart, for the first time in three years, and having him greet you with 'you look like shit.' But no! There is an even rockier bottom, where I look, quite literally, like shit."

I clench my jaw, unsure whether I'm keeping from defending myself and possibly making this worse, or laughing and definitely making it worse.

"Do you think I'm unintelligent, Weston?" Cammie asks just before using the car door for leverage to swing herself into the back seat beside me, careful to keep the shit-shoulder off the upholstery. My eyes flick to Luigi, who does not seem the least bit fazed. Rather, he gives a happy "buongiorno, signorina," as if he and Cammie are old friends, and her "buongiorno, Luigi, mio amico!" is equally delighted.

Then her gaze goes flat as it falls back on me. I have to remind myself what she last asked. Was that a trick question?

"Of course not," I answer carefully.

"Then why do you think I would start up a relationship—one that's been, as far as I can tell, really damn good so far, at least in our second attempt—with someone who was any of the silly things you've described in here?" She waves the letter. "Have you considered, you handsome, sometimes smart, infuriating man, that I am with you because you are already all the things I want? Including so many that I didn't even realize I needed, until I found them in you. And that I want you closer, not farther away, while I sort out my life, and whatever effort it takes to be together, even long-distance or while we've both got a lot of other shit going on, you are worth every bit of it? *We* are worth it, okay?"

Warmth spreads through my chest, pricks at the back of my eyelids as she goes on. "And you don't even acknowledge how much you've done for me this summer. You not only helped me find my dad, but you've also shown me how to love myself as I am, apart from my family situation or one hurtful rejection or any other factor that doesn't have to define me. I knew it in theory before, but I feel it now because of you." Her hand presses to her heart and mine leaps in response.

"You are the calm to my storm and I like to think that, sometimes, I can bring a little storm to your calm, just to shake things up, while also letting you know you're safe and protected and cared for, and . . . I just . . . I love you, okay? I still do, even when you do goofy shit like try to flee the country to set me free or whatever. But I am not about to let us repeat history, go our separate ways without so much as a conversation, both miserable and alone and—"

I take a page out of Cammie's playbook, leaning forward and cutting off her words with my kiss. The world narrows to the place where my lips meet hers. Our breaths mingle, each of us pulling the other in like we're each other's cool glass of limonata after a long day of traipsing around in the Italian summer heat, refreshing and sweet and exactly what we need. I need this with her in an endless supply, always in arm's reach.

I don't know how I ever thought I could walk away from this feeling, from the rightness that is the two of us together. I knew, logically, that we've started something real and good, something I don't want to let go. But I've spent a long time convinced that space away from me is the best thing I can give to Cammie, when life gets tough, and I guess old habits die hard. I needed to hear it from her, needed to feel the truth in her words when she says that she wants me by her side, wants to be the best versions of our flawed selves together. I needed to feel the strength and certainty in the love she has for me, and she's made that happen.

"Okay," I say when we finally come up for air.

"Okay?" she echoes after only a moment's pause, voice tinged with disbelief. "I chase you down a gravel road, break my shoe, become a bird toilet, then pour my goddamn heart out to you, and you say 'okay'?"

"Give me a second to recover," I say defensively, but I can't hide the smile pulling at my lips. "What I mean is okay, let's go back to the villa and stay awhile. I don't know, maybe the rest of the summer? Then we'll go where we each need to after that. Never running away from each other again. Because I love you, too—I basically don't remember a time when I didn't love you, and I'd rather not find out what that's like. How does all that sound?"

She purses her lips like she needs to consider, before her expression breaks into the sweetest smile I've ever seen. "Okay," she answers.

"Do you know how to ask Luigi to turn this cab around?"

Cam smiles against my cheek while she presses a kiss there.

"Not at all," she answers cheerfully. "But we've solved bigger mysteries."

EPILOGUE

One Month Later

Cammie

"I REALIZE LUCA'S ONLY BEEN IN MY LIFE FOR, LIKE, TWO MINUTES," I TELL West as we watch the man in question order a drink at the bar, oblivious to his onlookers, "but he needs to remember he's a father now. And there are some things a daughter can't unsee."

West laughs into his club soda. "I don't know, I think he rocks the white jumpsuit."

I scoff, bumping my hip against his. I bet it almost looks like we're using this dance floor for its intended purpose, rather than standing here playing costume police. "You don't have to side with him in some effort to win his approval, so he'll give his blessings upon our courtship or whatever. Luca's still concerned with winning *my* approval."

As if he can hear us clear across the deck, Luca catches my judgy gaze, meeting it with a teasing lift of one sandy-brown brow. I hide my smile behind my limoncello spritzer—heavy on the spritz, as I take bambina steps into the world of adult beverages.

"Which he did pretty quickly," West teases as he bumps me back. "Not that you give him any sign of your good opinion."

I give a faux indifferent shrug. "Yeah, well. He missed my most angsty teen years. Making him work for it a little bit is probably healthy, for his . . . parental development."

"A very mature take. I can tell you're in your twenties now."

As of today, that's true—it's the very reason we're on this boat, cruising along through the Mediterranean waters under the glow of the late-August evening sun. Paolo was generous enough to offer the largest vessel in the Bianchi Voyages fleet for my big twentieth birthday bash, one they normally use for their "Sunset Booze Cruise." Tonight, it's been transformed into a nautical nightclub, complete with karaoke, a photo booth, a DJ, and a dance floor, all aligned with my chosen theme, "Bambina di Disco."

So in that way, I am personally responsible for every hideous outfit on board.

The good ones, too, like Ilaria's bell-bottom flares and scandalously sheer lace top, with matching orange platform heels. Or Mom's belted minidress in this swirly, psychedelic floral print with white go-go boots. Those two were together when I first saw them, as the whole group of partygoers—thirtysome of the people I've spent the most time with this summer, basically—met up at Villa Russo to shuttle over to the marina.

"It's rude to upstage the birthday girl," I told them.

"Bellissima Camilla, we could not if we tried," Ilaria insisted as she fawned over my own outfit and fluffed my hair. One of the girls on my hall helped me style it today, blowing it out into long, sleek, straight layers that still have volume, thanks to how much freaking hair is on my head.

"Come on, my little disco ball." Mom wrapped an arm around my waist, rustling the silver sequin fringe that covers the short sheath dress. "Let's try this party thing again, maybe without an almost-physical altercation or paternity bombshell? Not that those weren't their own boatload of fun . . ."

"Do you ever think it's pretty impressive that someone as unserious as you has kept another human alive for twenty years?" I mused as we headed toward the driveway, checking over my shoulder to ensure West was still following, talking to Dr. Danny a little behind us.

"Darling daughter, you have no idea."

Our most recent Villa Russo terrazzo–hosted party was the reason I immediately ruled that out as a location for ringing in my twentieth. But it was my mother who reached out to Paolo and got us here, on just about the dreamiest birthday party venue I could've imagined. And even without the extra "excitement" tonight, it's been the best birthday of my life.

"Okay, everyone, it's cake time! Birthday song and candles and cake and crying—but maybe the last one's just me—on the upper deck, if you'll all make your way there," Mom announces, projecting her Dr. Lovett voice enough to reach a boatful of pupils, a good number of whom have certainly been enjoying the open bar.

"May I escort the Birthday Bambina to the upper deck?" West asks, extending his hand my way. I smile as I turn to take him in again, head to toe, just to bask in my own luck and love and happiness. Not only because I have the kind of boyfriend who let me choose his entire costume and offered no complaints.

It's also because I have a boyfriend who—miraculously—looks damn good in faded jeans that are tight on top and flared at the bottom, a button-down with flowy sleeves that I left unbuttoned to his mid-chest ("showing *all* my cleavage," West had said, cheeks flaming red), and a fake Tom Selleck–style mustache.

"Naturally," I answer primly, sliding my hand into his and still feeling the little swoop of excitement in my stomach when we touch, even with a couple months to get used to it. "There's no other man I want to accompany me there, or to kiss me senseless despite the squirrel stuck to his upper lip."

I can barely see West's lips twist under the so-called squirrel. "I can't decide if that's more a reflection of my good looks, or your weird taste."

"How does one say 'por que no los dos' in Italian?"

"Maybe by the time we come back to Italy, we'll know."

We ascend the stairs hand in hand, amid all the strangers who became friends this summer, dressed in their wild combinations of patterns and colors, postcard-worthy views in every direction from this party boat, and I'm hit with both sorrow over leaving this remarkable place and happiness knowing that I *will* be coming back. Again and again, for the rest of my life.

Starting on my next school break, which serendipitously aligns with one of West's from his research program in Germany. It'll be our first reunion after we go long-distance in a couple weeks, happening right back here at the Villa Russo Research Residency, where we'll visit its new director—my mom. It'll double as a visit with the man I may or may not ever come to call Dad.

For now, he's just Luca. But getting to know Just Luca has been a gift in so many ways I didn't expect. He's nothing like the many iterations of a mystery dad I imagined, but even better for it. Because he's real, and quirky, and cares so deeply and tries so earnestly to learn everything he can about me and my life without smothering or scaring me off. He hasn't yet realized that I don't scare easily.

But he will, as we spend more time together on my future trips here, and his and Mom's visits to the States to see my grandparents and me. He'll also realize, at some point, that he's already won me over.

It took no more than a few minutes in his apartment on Via Camilla, our first meetup with Mom and me a few nights after we all learned the truth. Luca made us his nonna's Bolognese recipe, and walking into the open living area that was exactly as inviting and cozy as young Alex had described it, surrounded by the smells of tomatoes and garlic and spices marinating on the stove, I'd suddenly felt tears welling in my eyes. They spilled out before I could hide them or find an onion to blame, and I wasn't even sure of their real cause.

Mom had already beelined for the kitchen and lifted the lid of the sauce pot for a sneak peek, practically sticking her face down in it, and didn't immediately notice my meltdown. But Luca had barely looked away from me since we'd arrived, and instead of pretending he didn't see the waterworks or calling out in panic for the nearest available woman, he'd efficiently gathered up a box of tissues and a fresh glass of water—not even carbonated—and guided me gently to his couch. He hadn't said anything, but emotion shone in his eyes, too, when I chanced a look at his face. Our watery gazes locked, and one corner of his lips had turned up in the slightest smile while his head dipped in what could barely be called a nod. But I felt it—his unspoken *I understand* and maybe *I'm right there with you.*

It settled in my chest like a puzzle piece I hadn't even known was missing until I found it. Luca got me, in this innate, intangible way I wouldn't have believed if I hadn't experienced it myself. Finding him has felt like not only discovering a whole new side of who I was and where I came from, but also like coming back to a familiar home that'd always been there.

It wasn't hard to see why my mom fell for him twenty years ago—nor why they've more or less picked up where they left off, as much as two people can with all the time and struggles between them. What I haven't said out loud to anyone yet—though I know West can tell—is that watching Luca love my mom has made me love him. It's complicated, and an ongoing process, but I think this family of ours might just go the distance.

Just as I plan to with the guy beside me, who draws me forward to the cake table, right as the DJ starts "Dancing Queen." Every single person in the circle around us begins to sing along, and when Mom appears at the fringes and holds up her candles and lighter with a questioning look, I wave her forward.

It feels fitting as my birthday song this year. Celebrating twenty years since the redheaded wild woman walking my way brought me into the world on the dirty grounds of an ancient villa, surrounded by friends from around the world who know every word to the universal language of ABBA.

Behind Mom, Luca carries the cake carefully, like a life hangs in the balance rather than a combination of butter, sugar, and flour. When he delivers it oh so gently to the table in front of me, I see the design for the first time, and my head falls back on a belly laugh just as the chorus kicks in.

A picture of my newborn baby face, one that became synonymous with the Bambina di Bronzo story as it had its moment in global news, has been transposed onto a disco ball in a way that's both the best thing I've ever seen and completely horrifying. I adore it.

Almost as much as I adore singing and twirling through the rest of the song, lifting my arms in the air and clumsily shouting "TWENTY" with everyone else over each "seventeeeen" in the chorus. Adore not knowing what to wish for as I blow out my candles but sealing it with a kiss from West afterward.

Adore our long history of birthdays spent together and a future with many more to come.

"I adore you," I whisper against his lips, as effortlessly as breathing.

"I'm keeping you," West whispers back, a promise that never gets old.

I wrap my arms around him as the song fades out on the speakers but replays in my mind, on a loop for the rest of the night.

I am, in fact, having the time of my life.

ACKNOWLEDGMENTS

IT'S POSSIBLE THAT I'M FEELING THE MOST RELIEF THAT I EVER HAVE WHEN finishing a book, due to the many challenges this one presented over the course of writing and rewriting it. But the relief is paired with the most pride in the final product, and gratitude for the village of folks who got *Ancient History* and me to this point! That immense gratitude goes out to:

My editor, Hannah Hill. Thank you for believing in me so consistently throughout our four (!!) books together, even when my belief in myself has been put to the test. I feel very lucky to have had your patience and support while I figured out the story I wanted to tell, and your ever-brilliant editorial vision to make that story the best it could be. Bonus thanks to Baby Hill (still no relation) for entering the world at the perfect time to give me an extra few months to write this book!

My agent, Laura Crockett. Thank you for being the biggest champion of my work since the beginning, and for being such a solid ally through all the ups and downs of publishing. Your emails still soothe my brain at its most chaotic moments.

The rest of the amazing Delacorte Romance and Random House Children's Books team, who have done such amazing work for my books! In particular, thanks to Wendy Loggia,

Mallory Loehr, Makena Cioni, Tamar Schwarz, Tracy Heydweiller, Jamie Johnson, Cathy Bobak, Katrina Damkoehler, and Sarah Lawrenson. Thank you to Georgie Stewart for the absolutely stunning cover artwork!

The Papyri Gang, including Federica, Marzia, Claudio, Fabrizio, and all the other wonderful friends I've made because of some ancient scrolls. Grazie mille for making me fall in love with Napoli (and a little bit with all of you) and for the inspiration to set a book in your home. It's hard to capture its beauty in words, but I did my best!

Author friends, without whom I can't imagine navigating the wild world of publishing. Thank you to Samantha Markum, Ava Wilder, Rachel Runya Katz, and Betty Corrello, for endless laughs and commiseration in the RAV4 of Silence; Alicia Thompson, for not only writing some of my favorite books, but truly changing my writing life for the better by introducing me to your writing journal process; Julia Seales and Martha Waters, for letting me escape into your kooky historical worlds, and sometimes chat about our kooky modern one, too; K. L. Walther, Jenny L. Howe, and Kristy Boyce, my YA romance idols and favorite humans; and so many others who make me laugh, cry, and feel happy just to be here in Romancelandia, including Anita Kelly, Neely Tubati Alexander, Jen Comfort, Jo Segura, Kristina Forest, Rachel Lynn Solomon, Kelsey Rodkey, and Marisa Kanter.

The friends who have helped ground me in life outside of books and shown endless support for this weird job of mine. I'm more thankful than I can say for my people, including Katie Cambron, Aaron Cambron, Megan Wall, Elora Ditton, Nolan Meier, Lee Kiefer, Gerek Meinhardt, Sydney Norman, Daniel Cambron, Barton Lynch, Margaret Sumney, and Graham Marks.

All the incredible readers who have supported my books and me thus far and remind me all the time why I love telling stories. Thanks also to the booksellers, teachers, and librarians who have gotten my words into readers' hands, and who do such important work every day.

My family. Michelle, Brad, Ginny, Ron, Brianna, Cam, Julian, Grant, Reagan, Max, Julie, Michael, Laura, and the rest of the wonderful Hill-Tudor-Parsons web. I'm very lucky to have you all.

My perfect puppy, Jolene. This is the first book I've written with you in my lap, doing everything you can to prevent me from writing a book. You're still perfect.

And, as ever, my Stephen. I love our real-life miscommunication trope story, love even more that we got the third-act breakup out of the way ages ago, but love the *most* living the HEA with you. Thanks for all the best adventures—and book inspiration—of my life.

ABOUT THE AUTHOR

KAITLYN HILL is a writer who lives to tell love stories and make people laugh. While books make up most of her personality, Kaitlyn also enjoys messy reality TV, has never met a tea she didn't like, and thrives on overly ambitious home improvement projects. She resides in Kentucky with her real-life romance hero and their perfect dog, Jolene. Kaitlyn is the author of *Love from Scratch, Not Here to Stay Friends, Wild About You,* and *Ancient History Between Us.*

thekaitlynhill.com

@thekaitlynhill